Maryam
Thanks for the inspi...
this.

HEARTLESS CRUELTY

I hope you
life.
Best.

Michael Coffin

HEARTLESS CRUELTY

A MR. BACHMAN MYSTERY

by

Richard W. Goffman

99%BOOKS

New York City ◆ Sussex, NJ

HEARTLESS CRUELTY
A 99%BOOK / published by arrangement with the author
Copyright © 2012 by Richard W. Goffman

ISBN: 978-0615680545

PRINTED IN THE UNITED STATES OF AMERICA

HEARTLESS CRUELTY

Dedication

To Jayson, for his courage and tenacity.

To Sarah, for her creativity and clear vision.

To Linda, for having the aforementioned qualities in her so that our children could have them in themselves; and for her belief in me which has never wavered, not even when mine did; and for her love.

I must also acknowledge

All my students, past and present, for all they taught me.

The Inklings, Diana Watkins, Amy D'Annibale, William Higbie and Linda Watkins-Goffman, for all their encouragement, criticism and help in bringing Mr. Bachman to life.

The Masters Program in Writing at William Paterson University, and in particular Dr. John Parras, for his encouragement and expertise.

Father of the Year

At 10:15am on the last day of his life, Lemmy Fender awoke on his living room couch wondering where he was. Then he remembered: the little shitbox in Atlantis. He'd ducked the last few months rent up in Highlands, found this place only two months ago, and moved in along with his kid in September.

The kid. He vaguely remembered fighting with him last night. *Or was it yesterday morning?*

Annoying pest. I kept him, taken care of him since his mother ran out on us when he was just a baby—but do I get any credit? Do I get any thanks for that? Shit, he must be, what, at least 16 or 17 by now. When he was small, he was cute. Women loved him, and they thought I was a goddamn prince, father of the year. Him being cute was useful in other ways, too. He could do errands. But a teenager? Teenagers aren't worth shit. Either be a little kid, or be a man. In between was a big fucking waste of time.

Maybe the next time Lemmy ducked out, he'd leave the kid behind too. *Little fuck*, he thought. *He probably won't even miss me. After all I done.*

Lemmy hefted himself up off the couch, and stood himself up. Stuck to the jellied flesh of the back of his right upper leg were two quarters, a dime, and a bottle cap. Rolling Rock. He had a woman's pink fuzzy slippers on his feet – he thought they were funny. For such a large man, pushing three hundred pounds, he had small, you might even say dainty feet.

If a blow to the head with a tire iron some years back had not robbed him of his sense of smell, he'd have noticed that, for all the empty beer bottles around him, the place smelled surprisingly good, or at least not awful. Lemmy himself needed a shower. He'd get around to it.

He scratched himself through his underpants, the only thing he had on beside the slippers. He rubbed his swollen eyes, and then his enormous midsection. Hungry, Lemmy shambled toward the kitchen. The bottle cap fell off when his flesh puckered, but not the coins. The light in the refrigerator made him squint. Inside, on a paper towel, was a half a sandwich. He wasn't sure what kind of meat it was, but it had mustard and mayonnaise and ketchup on it, which was just how he liked it. He stuffed it into his mouth.

Back in the living room with the last remaining beer from the fridge, Lemmy dropped with a house-

ZWW.0615680542.A

delist unit# 16068664

XXXXX

shaking thud back into the sagging couch. He reached between the cushions and pulled out the remote control, with which he brought the TV set to life. Scanning up through the channels, he stopped at 11. "Tom and Jerry" had started. Lemmy got a kick out of the way those two fuckers beat the shit out of each other. It made him laugh out loud. He was only marginally aware that they were meant to be a cat and a mouse. The cat didn't really look like a cat, and the mouse was too big to be a mouse, and he didn't know which one was Tom and which Jerry. He just knew that they were always together, and they always beat the shit out of each other. Funny.

A commercial for gum came on – and then it went away. The TV was dark. In fact, everything had become dark. And quiet, too. Lemmy put his hand to his head, and then his chest. A lot of people had told him over the years that he would have a stroke if he didn't lose some weight and get some exercise. Had he just been struck blind and deaf?

He'd left the light on in the kitchen, but he could see that it wasn't on anymore. The fusebox was behind a framed picture of a sailboat on the wall by the bathroom. He got up again and walked the three steps. Moving the picture, he put his big hand over all eight of the fuses, feeling to see if one had burnt. Nothing. Very little illumination leaked into the house from the late October sun.

Lemmy knew he hadn't paid the electric bill lately, but he believed in his heart of hearts that Jersey Central Power and Light was required by law to let a customer slide for three months before turning off the juice. He hadn't even lived there for three months yet! *What the fuck?*

There was nothing to do but return to the couch. The remote was still there, and he clicked it in the general direction of the vacant space where Tom and Jerry had been cavorting. Nothing happened. He threw the remote at the TV screen.

In a few hours, Lemmy would be dead. In the meantime, he lay back again on the couch. He put both his hands between his legs and rolled on his side, his face against the corduroy upholstery on the back of the couch. He slept.

Part One

FINDING LEMMY

Chapter One

It was only like October 25 or something like that, not even Halloween yet, but Mikey Lusick had already been required to return to Mr. Bachman's classroom at 2:58 when school was over so many times, that it had just become a habit.

There were several advantages to this. For one thing, more often than not The Amazing Debbie Seleski was there, helping Mr. Bachman, organizing his files and his papers and crap like that. Another advantage was that, without discussing it, he and Mr. Bachman had both come to the conclusion that there was no longer any bite in the sentence, meted out so frequently in September, "Mikey, please come back here today at 2:58 so we can have a talk." This made Mikey feel like he had accomplished something; he would have been surprised to know that it made Mr. Bachman feel the same way. In any case, after about seven weeks of school, Mikey felt like he now "got" Mr. Bachman, and the English teacher got him.

Those weren't even the only reasons. There was no way Mikey would claim that hanging out in Bachman's room after school was cool or anything. No way would he even try to say that to Stang, or Paulie, or Burke, or anybody for that matter. But he had told them that Bachman was ok, he was cool. Not cool in the sense of style, or attractiveness to chicks or anything like that. He was "cool" in the way you meant cool when somebody sat down at your lunch table while you and your friends were discussing matters of a sensitive nature, and somebody might be tempted to tell the new guy to get gone, but one of the group might say, "It's ok, he's cool." And then the new guy would know he could sit down, that he was trusted not to spread anything around. That's kind of how Bachman was. You could talk to him, even about stuff that wasn't exactly kosher, and you had confidence that you wouldn't get into any trouble with your parents or the school. He even sometimes had an interesting take on stuff. For a grown-up. And a teacher.

Hell, even some of the black kids popped into Bachman's room for a while sometimes in the afternoon, and Mikey was pretty sure that whatever you wanted to say about blacks, many of them were cooler than he and his friends were. He didn't have anything against the black kids, he just didn't hang out with any of them. What Mikey thought was pretty interesting was that most of the black kids in the eleventh grade, at least the ones he knew from classes, they were pretty tough. If a teacher told one of these guys to come in after school, most of 'em wouldn't show. The only time they'd go to detention was when, the next day, the teacher who couldn't get them to come to his detention put a pink slip in Mrs. Carson's mailbox, and then the kid got real detention, or maybe in-school suspension. And some of the teachers, especially some of the white teachers, they wouldn't even follow up with the pink slips. Intimidated punks.

For a lot of the kids though, black and white ones, the usual rules didn't apply to Mr. Bachman. Stang said it was because most teachers didn't show them any respect, but Bachman sort of did. The Amazing Debbie Seleski said it was because he had a sense of humor, which Mikey said was a stupid thing to say because Bachman told nothing but the corniest jokes, and sometimes would say things that made him laugh and nobody else. Mikey thought it was because Bachman knew how to listen to people. Most teachers, when you told them something, even when you asked them a question, you could kind of see them check out behind their eyes, to go somewhere else in their head. When you asked Bachman a question or just told him something, you got the impression you were the only person in the world, for that moment, anyhow.

Dwayne (pronounced Doo-wayne, often shortened to "Doo" and sometimes doubled into "Doo-Doo" by his buddies) Franklin popped in and looked around. Mikey didn't care much for Dwayne, mostly because he thought he was such a comedian. He thought he was Eddie Murphy, the "Saturday Night Live" guy who was in Trading Places, which happened to be Mikey's new favorite movie. Doo could be amusing, but he wasn't nearly as funny as he thought he was.

Doo was showing off, doing a pretty killer impersonation of Mr. Bachman. It was true that Bachman was a lousy dresser, and Doo had hiked his pants up so his socks were showing, and was doing Bachman's distinctive, long-stride walk, stroking his chin, looking at the ceiling, and then suddenly calling on kids in the room. The real Bachman was out in the hall, missing this.

Doo strode toward Mikey who was sitting on one of the desks. He jerked him up to stand and addressed the other kids. "So here we see old Ethan Frome. He walks with a limp, 'cause he's a big, pussy-whipped crippled up white man." Mikey obliged with a funny walk.

"Now who is Ethan married to?" Doo-as-Bachman continued, gallivanting like a leering Groucho Marx around the room. He tried to get the weird quiet kid to join, but he turned and walked to the back of the room without so much as a word. Nobody wanted to be Zeena, Frome's dried-up witchy wife, because everybody hated that character, so Doo drafted Mr. Bachman's wooden coat tree. He tilted it toward Mikey and did a high-pitched, screechy voice. "Ethan! I may be a flat-chested old bitch, but I think you're messing around with my fine cousin Mattie!"

With that, he pulled The Amazing Debbie Seleski up and pushed her toward Mikey. She chose to portray Mattie Silver as a cheap floozy. "Oh Ethan, puleeze take me sledding. It'll be fun." She said it in a drawn-out southern accent, which was kind of dumb because the story took place in Massachusetts.

"So, what really happened to these messed up white people?" Doo narrated. "Did they really hit a tree with their sled? Did Zeena put a spell on 'em? Did the black cat rat them out? Did Ethan get some off of Mattie before they got all crippled up?"

"I don't think so."

Mr. Bachman stood in the classroom doorway, and despite themselves, everybody in the room froze for a second. Was Mr. Bachman pissed? He looked pissed.

"Nobody 'got some'," he said, indicating air quotes. "Zeena wasn't a real witch." He picked up the coat tree that had been Zeena Frome and replaced it in its spot. "That was – what? – a metaphor." He shook his head as if he were mightily disappointed. "Debra, Mattie Silver was not a hooker from Alabama. Ethan," he turned to Dwayne and Mikey, "was frustrated. He was thwarted. He was not p-- not whipped."

In mock despair he said, "Didn't anybody read the same book I did?"

* * *

When all the laughter had died down and the room had cleared out, William Bachman gathered his things to go, a task made infinitely easier because Debra Seleski had put each period's tests in separate folders, labeled them, and put them in Bachman's briefcase, an organizational feat that often eluded the teacher. He closed the briefcase, locked his desk and stood to leave, when he realized he was not alone.

Richard W. Goffman

It was that quiet kid who always dressed in black, still sitting, almost invisible, in the back of the room, his hair obscuring his face. Bachman surreptitiously glanced at his seating chart for Period 3, which Debra had taped to his desktop. (She *was* amazing.) Jason, that was his name. Jason Fender. Every year Bachman met the challenge of committing to memory by the end of September the names of his hundred twenty-five or so new students. But there was always one kid, sometimes a boy, sometimes a girl, whose name refused to stick in his head for weeks and weeks into the fall. He was never quite sure why, or what these students had in common.

"Mr. Fender," he said. "Did you need to talk about something?"

The boy lifted his head, revealing a little more, but still not much, of his face.

"To tell you the truth," the boy said softly, "Mr. Bachman, I don't get this Ethan Frome guy. I don't get him, and I don't get his wife."

Bachman's attention was now fully engaged. They had essentially left the book behind today, with the final essay test. He would begin the next unit, on Greek mythology, tomorrow. He would refer back to Ethan Frome off and on throughout the year, but most kids had begun the process of forgetting whatever they might have learned about the Edith Wharton novel. Now Jason, who never volunteered in class and had to be called on to get him to participate, was still wrestling with the raw human issues the book evoked. And now Jason had spoken the longest string of words Bachman had yet to hear from him.

"When you say you 'don't get' them, what do you mean?" Bachman said.

Jason visibly concentrated, struggling to get his thoughts into a coherent form for his English teacher. "Those two basically hate each other. I mean, they sure don't love each other. So why don't they just get divorced?"

"Well, that's a very good question Jason. It would seem like the logical way to go to us, but that's only because we're looking at it from our point of view, today, here. In 1983 divorce is common, and people have lots of options. In 1983, when a man and woman get divorced, the woman doesn't starve to death. At least we would hope not. But Ethan and Zeena lived in a very different time, in a very different place, and under very different circumstances than us."

Jason had a faraway, dissatisfied look while his teacher was talking, and his response, which almost sounded as if he had ignored Bachman's statement, caught Bachman by surprise. "I mean it's not like they even had any kids. Some people, they want to get divorced, but they don't want to fuck up—oh, I'm sorry Mr. Bachman."

"I think it's ok, Jason. There doesn't seem to be anyone around who will be too damaged by the word 'fuck.' Go on."

"Sometimes people stay married, don't get divorced, because they don't want to mess up their kids? Right? And then, like, sometimes they stay together and it works out ok, the things that made them want to get divorced don't seem, like, so important anymore. And then other times, stayin together messes the kids

13

up even worse, because of all the fightin and cussin and stuff."

Bachman was looking closely at Jason as he spoke. The boy was dressed all in black, and not fashionably. Black t-shirt, black jeans, black sneakers, sort of late Judas Priest. He didn't look at Bachman as he spoke. His words came out in a jerky torrent, and his awkward adolescent frame moved in fidgety, illogical ways. He was a skinny kid, and his clothes didn't exactly fit.

Then Bachman noticed something else, something he hadn't seen earlier. When his long, dirty black hair twitched away from his beautiful, immature, broken angel face, there were dark circles around the eyes. And weirdly, there was sort of a shadow of a circle around Jason's neck, too.

It wasn't stray wisps of whiskers, the teacher realized. Dirt? Bruises, maybe. Caused by what? How could he know? He couldn't even be sure they were bruises, or that they had been intentionally inflicted. Bachman looked elsewhere, but the picture was still in his head. If they were bruises, how did they get there? Rope? Two encircling hands, maybe. Whose?

"How are you getting home Jason?"

"Walkin."

"Where do you live?"

"Taylor."

"That's the way I've got to go," the teacher lied. "Can I give you a lift home?"

"No. No, thanks."

"Really, it's no trouble, let me take you. You can—You can help carry some stuff to my car. You'd be doing me a favor actually." He didn't want to push it too hard, but he really wanted to see where Jason lived.

"All right."

*   *   *

The real estate values of the residential streets in this part of Atlantis declined in presidential order. Washington Street was a main thoroughfare, three or four blocks from the beach; Adams and Jefferson Streets had some beautiful, old, three-story homes with wide, wraparound porches and leafy yards displaying the best of autumn's paintbrush. It was locally accepted that you wouldn't want to live on any street later than Jackson, and many people wouldn't even drive down Van Buren or anything west of there. Bachman lived nowhere near this section, and didn't have such a firm grip on the order of the early presidents. He never could remember the difference between John Tyler and Zachary Taylor, but he knew that both were long after Andrew Jackson.

From the moment he sat in the VW's passenger seat, whether or not Jason Fender realized that Mr. Bachman was heading in the opposite direction from his home, he returned to the taciturnity which he normally displayed in school. Bachman pulled into the Dippity Donuts at the corner of Monmouth and Polk.

"I'm getting coffee," said the teacher as he opened his door and stepped out. "Can I get you something?"

But Jason Fender was already getting out his side of the car, lighting a cigarette clumsily as he did so.

Through an exhalation of smoke he said, "No. No thanks. I gotta go. Thanks for the ride." He looked down as he said this, then turned on his heel and headed down Polk like he had a very important meeting.

After the comparative torrent of conversation they'd had in the classroom, Jason had said nothing more than monosyllables. In fact, he hadn't made eye contact with his teacher since then — maybe, come to think of it, not even then. Jason had taken off so quickly he'd neglected to shut the passenger side door, and it remained open, like an unanswered question. Bachman could only watch the dark figure grow smaller in the growing gloom, raincoat flapping like the wings of a bat.

Chapter Two

Sunrise over the northern Atlantic Ocean, as seen from the sands of the formerly fabulous Jersey shore, was a precious gift available to many but enjoyed by only a few. From the first eruption of liquid fire breaking the horizon, through the etching of a thousand tiny shadows cast by the wave-like ripples of windblown sand, the reawakening of the world was drawn in stark, contrasting colors, sounds and smells.

Bachman never went a week without riding his bike or walking down to the beach to watch the sun come up at least once; some weeks he found himself there almost every morning. Though the autumn cool was sharp and surprising, it didn't dissuade him. If anything, it made the scene more tempting, as the chilly mornings guaranteed that there would be few if any joggers or people just finishing their night's carousing. More and more now, it was all his.

Usually he brought his flashlight from his car's glove compartment, but that morning he'd found its

batteries dead, and rather than replace them he'd pro-
ceeded. It was more fun without it, in a way.

The wind was intermittent, but stiff. This was
not a function of the time of year; he couldn't remember a daybreak viewed through still air. Breezes were
always a part of it, as were the raucous cries of seagulls,
walking on the beach and on and under the boardwalk,
and the more distant calls of the gulls forever flying
north up the coast. He never bothered to find out why
this was, it just always was. Always north. Sometimes
he pictured a constant ring of gulls circling the globe,
flying from south to north along whatever meridian it
was that marked the east coast of the U.S. (When it
passed over the north pole the flying conga line would
go north to south in the eastern hemisphere.) He knew,
of course, that this was not the case. Somehow or other, they must fly north in the morning, and sneak back
during the day, probably while he was busy at work.

Maybe the most pungent and memorable thing
about this special solitary moment was the bracing air
itself: how it stretched his nostrils on the way in and
thrilled them on the way out. How it smelled like ocean
without once smelling like fish. How it tasted like the
very essence of the beginning of life on earth.

Bachman was unlike most, in that he never
took the daily reawakening of the world for granted.
That was why he went down to witness it so often.
Some voice toward the back of the crowd of souls calling for attention in the various circles of his consciousness, some crackpot voice of doom cast doubt on the
certainty of another new day. One day, there might not
be another day. One night, night might not give way to

the light of day. Or something else, neither night nor day, might come next.

He simply didn't trust day to come as an inevitability. Or he didn't trust that he'd still be there when the light returned.

* * *

That day, Thursday, was a particularly frustrating one at school. A fire drill during second period managed to disrupt the staging of plays that the class had written and were supposed to perform, based on Greek myths they had studied. The kids who had to go outside in the chill in their homemade togas were particularly incensed, and Bachman had never quite gotten them back and settled down enough to finish even one of their skits. Many of the kids were thrilled because this gave them until Monday to finish or polish their work, since Friday was always a writing day in Mr. Bachman's English classes.

His third period juniors also veered far from his planned lesson. Thanks to a couple of absences, four kids pulled out for an "emergency" band rehearsal and three others on a field trip to the beach with Ms. Tonnery's Environmental Sciences class, something to do with kelp, it didn't make any sense to start anything new that he'd just have to repeat for almost half the group.

It was downhill from there. He didn't even get to eat his lunch because he had to cover a history class for Mr. Davidson who had apparently gotten sick and had to leave school suddenly. Now, in the closing minutes of his eighth period class, as the students were getting a head start on their reading assignment home-work, he was attempting to pick up the tattered shreds of the "best laid plans" of his day. As he tried to reas-semble those shreds of Thursday's plans into new plans for Monday, something nagged at him, as if he'd left something undone, something other than the obvious. Had he forgotten something amid the confusion of the day? Entirely likely. But what? Maybe it would come to him if he stopped thinking about it.

The piercing bell sounded, eighth period and the official school day ended.

A smaller number than usual of afterschool visi-tors dropped in, but fortunately Debra Seleski was one of them. A pretty 17-year-old with straight light brown hair and a stunning figure that attracted every boy's attention, Debra had quickly attached herself to Mr. Bachman as a kind of secretary. She organized all his paperwork in a way that was a huge help to him; so much so, in fact, that he recognized that he would need to "fire" her soon. Her nearly obsessive helpfulness now had most of the earmarks of a crush. Before he had to handle one of those situations, particularly after school, he'd have to get Debra involved in an extracur-ricular activity the schedule of which would afford her less access to him. It didn't happen every year, but it had happened several times before. First they come in for extra help, then to hang out, then to help him out with errands. Next step was sharing their innermost thoughts, hopes and fears. Often they showed him their angsty, breathless poetry. Then, the bemoaning of the immaturity of every single boy in the school. The first couple of times he hadn't known what was coming, and one time he'd had to literally peel a very aggressive, love-struck teen off his neck and torso, disengaging each arm, each leg, and her mouth as delicately but decisively as he could. After that happened he never let things get to that point, and no child had had the opportunity to put herself in such a humiliating position. Bachman didn't flatter himself that it was the result of any particular animal charm so much as his sensitivities as a teacher.

It would be a shame to lose her assistance. Bachman loathed the paperwork that plagued teachers. Too bad a boy – a straight boy – never voluntarily took on that helpful role.

"You missed one, I think," said Debra, indicating his attendance book.

Bachman's ears perked up, since he was pretty sure he had overlooked something today, but wasn't sure what. "What'd I miss?"

"Jason Fender. You should have marked him absent." She held up the variously sized yellow slips of paper indicating which kids were excused during third period. "Jason wasn't in class, wasn't on the science trip, and he sure isn't in the marching band."

"Was he out of school, or MIA?" said Bachman. Debra consulted the absentee list published each afternoon by the attendance office. Fender, Jason was on it, but there had been no call from a parent letting them know the student was staying home, and the call to the home had apparently gone unanswered.

"Interesting," Debra said.

"What's that?" Bachman asked.

"This is his first absence all year, according to this," Debra said. "Now that I think of it, I guess that's true. He's so quiet…"

"…that sometimes we don't notice him," Bachman completed her thought.

This was definitely it, the thing that had bugged him, nibbling at the edge of his memory most of the day. In his mind's eye he saw the black, asymmetrical flapping, Jason hustling down Polk Street amid swirling leaves and the wings of his unbuttoned raincoat, trailing wisps of white smoke. He felt cold.

* * *

Funny how thirsty teaching made a person. He'd meant to stop at Ava's Grill & Bar for one quick beer, but when he got there he found his pal, Mr. Davidson. It turned out that Bobby D's sudden illness, the one that had required Bachman's last minute coverage of his class, was the result of a message Bobby D had gotten from his upstairs neighbor. Apparently Rosette, Bobby D's former girlfriend, had shown up and let herself into his apartment. Had he not gotten there when he did, she would have wreaked damage of untold proportions. Once he'd calmed Rosette and persuaded her to leave, it made no sense to go back for his last class of the day, so Bobby had simply gotten a head start on his afternoon drinking.

Absorbing this entire narrative in detail necessitated Bachman to stay for not one but three beers. This had little affect on his mental acuity, but it had somehow caused most of the daylight to disappear by the time he stepped back onto the sidewalk, surprised at how early evening was now coming. Three beers had not caused him to forget that there was still one thing on his agenda before heading home.

He hadn't stopped in the office to look up the Fenders' address on Taylor Street, but it was not that long a street, and he might get lucky. Besides, he wasn't sure he wanted to knock on the door and make an official house call. He just thought he'd see what he could see.

The homes he cruised slowly past might have been described as ramshackle had they been larger. These were just grim, and poorly if ever maintained. A few cheap plastic witches and Caspers were tied haphazardly to fences and storm doors, but as the street lights that weren't broken winked on and gloomy dusk settled on unraked leaves and windblown metal garbage cans, it became sadly apparent that creepiness did not need to be purchased from the Woolworth's. It was one of the things Taylor Street had in abundance.

He did get lucky. Attached by bits of wire to a swinging gate in a cyclone fence around a tiny yard was a black metal mailbox decorated with the word Fender in what looked like Wite-Out. Bachman parked the VW across the street and considered why he was there, and what, if anything, his next step might be.

The Fender home seemed neither poorer nor better than those on either side, and no sense of foreboding glued Bachman to his car seat. What harm could come from a simple *Hello, I wondered how Jason was doing*? A few furtive dogs but no people were to be seen on Taylor Street as he shut and locked the VW's door, and stepped through the open gate, down the cracked walk and up the stoop to the front door.

The front door gave him pause. The doorknob and lock looked like they'd been manhandled, and from the casual way in which it wobbled, it looked as though the door itself was not only unlocked, but also unlatched. It gaped slightly ajar and back. Through that crack no light emerged. Rather, darkness seemed to emanate from within to dim the weak illumination outside. As he thought about this it now occurred to Mr. Bachman that there was not a single light visible within, and the house had a kind of stillness that even hushed the breezes and the rattly dry leaves that crackled through the neighborhood. He wished now that he'd replaced the batteries in the flashlight in his glove compartment. As it was, the thing was currently useless.

Refusing to be daunted, Bachman knocked carefully on the hinge side of the door so as not to knock it open. Nothing. He knocked again, louder, and this time the door did swing inward several inches. Still no response from within. But then there was something. Or he thought he'd heard something. Soft. It was a gravelly kind of sound, a scratching maybe. Maybe it wasn't soft; maybe it was loud but came from farther away, or from a room and through some walls. Maybe it was from behind him on the front lawn, not from inside the house at all. Maybe it hadn't come at all.

Bachman looked behind him, and then back again through the opening in the door. The skin on his hands and fingers tingled in an unpleasant way. He didn't know what the sound was, but he didn't see how it could be anything good.

"Jason? Mr. Fender?" In a fifteen second conversation passing in the hall, Ellie Nelson, the guidance counselor, had let him know that Jason and his father lived alone together. Bachman couldn't leave, and he couldn't go forward. His hands were in the pouch of his pullover, and touching his keys he felt the little fob with the tiny LED light on it. The door was now open about a foot. No sound at all now emanated, but with the echoes of that maybe-sound in his ears, armed with a pin light that was meant to help you find the ignition lock in your car, he poked himself inside.

There was a light switch on the wall immediately to his left, but flipping it had no effect. Clearly the house was without power. Was there a general blackout in the neighborhood, or had the Fenders' bill gone unpaid long enough for Jersey Central Power & Light to pull their plug? Some lights were on around the neighborhood, and the streetlights worked, so the latter seemed more likely.

"Mr. Fender? Jason? Hello?" he now called loudly, not wanting to surprise anyone. The house feels empty, he thought, followed by *How the hell can a house feel empty?* "It's Mr. Bachman. From school."

It was no longer gloomy but rather pitch dark outside, and likewise within. With his pin light held before him like a magic charm in a haunted forest, he sidled carefully through the first room, apparently a living room, avoiding a couch, toward what was likely the kitchen. Some flatware on a counter reflected a streetlight, and Bachman moved toward it, continuing to call, although he was rapidly coming to the conclusion that sound he'd heard had been something else, and that the place was empty and he had no call to be there. That was the moment when he tripped over what felt like a large log and tumbled forward into the kitchen, his keys skittering across the linoleum, his pathetic little light blinking out, his elbows and knees cracking into the floor. He hurt. *This*, he thought, *is what I deserve for going into someone's home without being invited.*

His pants leg had gotten something sticky on it when he had fallen. Stretching, he grasped the keys. He squeezed the little light and sat up, turning to see what he'd tripped over, hoping he hadn't broken something.

He saw. He moved the light up and down the length of the obstruction until his right brain could confirm what his left brain had immediately recognized: a man. A large man lying on the floor. Dead.

Chapter Three

Rather than climb over it, or duck under it, the overweight man wearing a grey fedora tore the yellow plastic police tape with his fingers, and tied it together behind him before walking into the Fender residence. Like the hat and the sense of special entitlement, everything about Detective Dick Raumbaugh was a kind of throwback. As he passed through the living room on his way to the murder scene, he nodded briefly to Bachman, who was sitting on the couch with Tommy Gallagher, Jr., the acting Police Chief of Atlantis.

The lights were on in the Fender home now. This had been accomplished in short order after the first police officers arrived. Steve Ardente was the first cop on the scene, in response to Bachman's call from the phone booth outside the Dippity Donuts. Ardente had called headquarters, Tommy Jr. had called

JCP&L, and in fifteen minutes power had been restored, despite the account having gone unpaid for over three months.

That had been two hours ago.

Except for the summer of the riots, Atlantis had never had more than twelve homicides in a year. On the other hand, it rarely had a year without one. For seventeen years, Raumbaugh, a disheveled, dyspeptic fellow in his late forties, had investigated almost every one. A juicy, unlit couple of inches of cigar was in constant motion in his mouth. It looked as though it might be a good luck charm that had been with him that entire time.

Bachman and Tommy Jr. exchanged bemused looks when Raumbaugh had passed into the kitchen. Bachman was reacting to Raumbaugh's unchanging persona. He was a type, and he seemed to stubbornly cling to being one. Tommy Jr.'s reaction had more to do with his awareness that Raumbaugh had little respect for him and in fact resented his promotion to chief, which was likely to become permanent soon. He knew that many people thought that nepotism was involved in Tommy Jr. succeeding Tommy Sr. in the role on the latter's retirement. In any case, Raumbaugh did not hide his disgruntlement at reporting to a man more than twenty years younger than himself.

Tommy Jr.'s radio squawked, and he walked out into the front yard to answer it. Finding himself alone in the living room, Bachman got up and gingerly poked his head into the kitchen. Raumbaugh waved him over to where he stood, an invitation to watch him work. He was looking down at the body and making notes in a little notebook.

"What a mess," said Bachman.

"I've seen messier," said the detective. "Listen, just watch where you step." There were spots or clumps of blood around the body, and also in patches on other parts of the gray linoleum floor. "But yeah, a mess. Somebody did a job on this guy. Plenty of blood-shed, that's for sure. Look at him."

Bachman did as he was told. The body had not been touched or moved, nor was it covered with a sheet. That wouldn't happen until they prepared to get it up on the gurney and roll it out the door for its ride to the morgue. It was certainly not the first time he had seen a body of someone who had recently died or been killed. It was the largest one, though. And the bloodiest.

Lemmy Fender was naked except for a soiled pair of briefs and one fuzzy slipper. Probably messed himself as he died, Bachman thought. The other fuzzy slipper was on the kitchen counter, already labeled and sealed in a plastic bag. He would have to be called a great big bear of a man, because he was as hairy as he was huge. There was hardly an inch of him besides his scalp that was free of thick black hair.

More than size or hairiness, the most eye-catching thing about the corpse was the black, blood-filled concavity that was the entire center of the chest. It looked as though another bear had taken a bite out of the chest of this bear. It was truly a horrifying sight. Bachman could barely take his eyes off it.

When he did, he looked at the face. It too was mangled, as if it had been clubbed. No prior experience could prevent Bachman from being stunned by the damage that had been done to this man. Dick Raumbaugh's voice pulled him back into the moment.

"You okay there, Mr. Bachman?" said the older man. "You not gonna faint on me are ya?"

"No, don't worry, I'm fine," said Bachman. "What — what do you think —"

"It's pretty simple, Mr. Bachman. I've seen this kinda thing before. The attack happened pretty much right here, where you see this big dead bastard. The assailant – ok, I'm not saying it's the kid, but face it, that's what we're both thinking – busts him in the face with something -- a baseball bat, a frying pan, I dunno -- knocking him down. And out. Or at least stuns him, while also crushing his nose, which is why the eyes are blackened. Busted a few of his pearly whites, too. He leaps on the guy, who has landed hard, on his back. The coroner will find trauma to the back of the head, just watch.

"The killer straddles the victim" -- Dick demonstrated – "and proceeds to do Lemmy like Tony Perkins did Marty Balsam in Psycho." He made long arcing sweeps with his extended arm, reaching up above his head and plunging downward toward the gaping, ragged hole.

Bachman was impressed by how familiar Dick was with movie stars of the '50s and '60s, as indicated by the casual tossing off of first name diminutives.

Dick continued. "Once Daddy's – sorry, I mean Lemmy's heart is no longer fulfilling the role its maker had intended, the perpetrator gets up and goes" – he looked around for a minute and then pointed –

"he goes over here and sits down on this chair to catch his breath. See this mess here?" he indicated a red stain on the linoleum, and stared at it quietly for about a minute. "Dollars to donuts we'll pull a print of the perp's sneakers outta that."

Bachman nodded, set aside his doubts and allowed himself to envision the murder as Dick Raumbaugh described it.

"But what about me?" asked Bachman. "I came in here in the dark, stumbled and fell over the body. Maybe I, I don't know, accidentally contaminated the crime scene. You know, before I realized it was a crime scene."

"As I understand it, you came in here, into the living room, in the dark," said Raumbaugh. Bachman nodded. "The door wasn't locked or even closed. You call, you don't get any response. You cross the living room, come in here, take two, maybe three steps and – Whamo! – you trip over our friend here." The heavy older man was enthusiastically painting pictures in the air, a storyteller on a stage, confident in his tale, clear of vision. Bachman nodded.

"Here." The detective pulled out a pair of latex gloves and put them on. He grasped Bachman's arm and said, "Show me the bottom of your shoes. I'll bet you coffee they're smooth." Bachman did as he was told, lifting first one foot and then the other, leaning on the detective for support. Not only was the sole of each shoe smooth, they were both also free of blood. Raumbaugh squatted, grunting, his knees sounding like two packs of firecrackers, and got his face down close to the floor near the chair in which he had envisioned the murderer resting after his exertions. "I'll bet there's a patterned footprint here. Like a sneaker would make."

Raumbaugh was on all fours now, his face a couple of inches off the floor. After a moment he grunted with satisfaction.

"Here we go. And it ain't from your shoe." Bachman watched him intently, anxious to hear what he'd say next. Raumbaugh misinterpreted the look.

"Sorry, Professor. '*Isn't* from your shoe,'" he corrected.

"But is it from--"

Raumbaugh nodded solemnly, as he labored to his feet. "Sneaker."

* * *

"I have to get out of here," Bachman told Raumbaugh, placing three ones on the counter at Dippity Donuts to pay for their coffees. He was wearing a black T-shirt with APD in big yellow block capitals on the chest, and a pair of gray sweat pants. Tommy Jr. had given these clothes to him in exchange for the white shirt and black pants he'd been wearing all day. His own clothes were now in a plastic evidence bag in the acting chief's car. Unlike the shoes, they'd had blood on them. The Atlantis PD T-shirt didn't fit, and he wasn't convinced it was entirely clean.

"What's the rush?" Raumbaugh's breathing had only now returned to normal after his kneeling and stooping exertions at the crime scene.

"I have to be at school half an hour before my first class tomorrow to make some copies, so I'll be lucky to get" – he glanced at the big clock over the old fashioned cash register – "four hours beauty sleep at best."

"Besides," he continued, "any minute now one of those reporters is going to come here and find you and ply you with questions. And they'll see me here with you. And after what happened last time" – he gave Raumbaugh a meaningful look – "it will be much better if my name stays out of the paper. I'll come down tomorrow afternoon so you ruffians can grill me."

"Yeah? And when the local version of the fourth estate asks me who discovered the body?" said Raumbaugh.

"Tell them it was the butler. In the library. With the candlestick."

Chapter Four

Bachman was the first teacher in the building on Friday morning.

The Press was a morning paper, and they didn't publish on Saturday. So the good news was that maybe the majority of the town, the students and the faculty hadn't heard yet. The bad news was that everybody got the fat, messy Sunday edition, and this could only be a huge banner headline, probably with gruesome photos.

He wrote notes to Helen Carson, the principal, and Hilda Steinmetz, his department chair, sealed them both in envelopes. Hilda's he left on her desk in the department office, peeking out from under her desk blotter where he knew she would find it. He relocked the English Department door and headed back downstairs to the main office. He thought about printing Personal and Confidential on the principal's envelope, but then chose not to. If the note looked uninteresting, Sheri or Shari, her watchdogs, might not open it. Putting Personal and Confidential on the outside would be like waving raw meat in front of them. They'd figure out how to read it without it looking like the envelope had been molested.

If they did that, this is all they would have seen:

"Dr. Carson,

"Please page me as soon as you arrive. One of our students [here a word was crossed out] won't be in school today, is in some serious trouble. I will explain in person."

Wm. Bachman"

Ellie Nelson was the guidance counselor for the first third of the alphabet, and that included the F's. Bachman sat on the tiny couch in her cramped office to wait for her arrival. He didn't have to wait long.

She came in and put her briefcase beside him on the couch. He stood and she gently pushed on his shoulder to sit him back down as she squeezed around her desk to her chair.

Bachman opened his mouth to speak but stopped. Ellie's blue eyes were shiny, moist, and her lips were pressed so tight they were almost white.

He exhaled. "How do you know already?"

"The Early Birds told me." The Early Birds were three or four ninth grade girls who waited outside each morning until 7:27 am, the earliest minute students were allowed to enter the building. "So it's true."

Bachman guessed that the grim look on his face was confirmation enough.

"Do you know what happened?" she asked.

"As much as anyone other than the killer," he said.

"How come?"

"You won't say anything to anyone?"

"Not if you say I can't. Guidance counselors have to pass Secret-Keeping 101 in grad school."

"I was there," he stated softly.

Ellie's jaw literally fell open. Bachman continued quickly. "No, not when Mr. Fender was killed. But not very long after."

Ellie stared in amazement. "You…"

"…found him. Yes."

She tried to ask him a question, tried to grasp what had happened, but the questions kept interfering with each other so nothing intelligible could come out. Finally she said, "Jason…"

"Not there. As of one am, no sign of him."

"He might be – might be killed also?"

"I don't know. Nobody knows anything."

"What do they think?" She looked more closely at him. "What do you think?"

"The police think Jason killed his father and ran away. Apparently Mr. Fender was a petty criminal of some sort, and they suspect he beat Jason. They think they've got the print of a sneaker in the blood near the body. They searched the house and couldn't find a single shoe of Jason's to compare it to. I'm guessing he only had one pair, wore 'em all the time. There's an empty lot behind the house, used to be a gas station. They were trying to find traces of the prints there, and in front, but they weren't having any luck with the arc lights last night. They'll be back today in daylight, I'm sure."

Ellie Nelson, guidance counselor and child advocate, had recovered her voice. "So let me get this straight: One of our students was absent from school. A call to his house didn't turn up anyone at home. A visit to the house finds the boy's father violently murdered, and the boy missing, and all the police can think of is to *accuse him of the crime?* What if the actual criminal, after killing the father, has taken the boy? Jason might be held by the murderer right now. He might be..." She trailed off, unable to say what she was thinking. "They should be trying to rescue him, to save him, not arrest him."

"Ultimately it doesn't matter. Either—"

Ellie was appalled. Her voice leapt an octave. "Doesn't matter? How can it not matter?" She was almost beside herself.

"No," he said, trying to sound soothing. "What I mean is, whether they're looking for him to question him, or looking for him to save him, either way, they are highly motivated to find him."

"So, officially...?"

"Officially, Jason is a missing person, possible witness to a murder, an endangered 16-year-old."

"An orphan," Ellie pointed out.

"And unofficially, they may not be saying it, but they all think he did it."

* * *

October 28, 1983   Freewrite   debra l seleski

Richard W. Goffman

That kid Jason isn't in school, and there's all kinds of wierd rumors going around. One rumor is that he got KILLED last night. Another one is that he KILLED SOMEBODY and is running from the cops. Stang says that his brothers girlfriend lives not too far from Jasons street and he said that his brother said that there were like a million cops with lights on inside and outside his house all night and that his house is like this horrible dumpy place. Whats also weird is that jason stayed behind in Mr. Bachman's room Wendsday afternoon after I left, he was like the last person their and he wasn't in school yesterday either and so if he's like disappeared or killed or something then maybe mr. Bachman is the last person to see him!!! Now all the kids are talking about jason like they no him and stuff but really before today most of them didn't even know his name. I knew his name from Mr. Bachman's gradebook but I hardly ever heard him say two words or anything unless the teacher made him talk and he always sits by himself in lunch but thats probly because none of the boys will let him sit with them because they are so STUPID and hes not gonna go sit with the girls so what choice does he have I guess. I tried to ask Mr. Bachman if he had heard the rumors and stuff and he gave me this strange look and told me to do my work which didn't make any sense because I was already done with my work – duh! and its writing day anyway. I think Mr. Bachman is worried about Jason too because the other teachers act like they care but there mostly just like the kids most of them probly don't know Jasons name either but mr. Bachman is SENSITIVE.

* * *

"How do you make sense out of this?" asked Jason Fender's guidance counselor.

HEARTLESS CRUELTY

It was eleven hours later. Bachman had spent from 3:15 until 6:15 at the Atlantis police station, describing and redescribing everything that had happened the night before. Yes, he had had a couple of beers at Ava's. No, he didn't have a specific reason for stopping by the kid's house. No, he didn't usually go to kids' houses every time they were absent. He'd just had a funny feeling, call it a concern, because the kid was so shy and such a loner and he hadn't been absent before. Yes, that could describe lots of teenagers. Were they suggesting that he knew something he wasn't telling them? No, he wasn't holding anything back.

In fact, he had held back his impression of a necklace of bruises around the skinny kid's neck. He wasn't sure why, except maybe because, while the school district trained staff to notice things like that, they also trained them not to make accusations unless he had more than just a sneaking suspicion. Had Jason not disappeared that night, Bachman would have sent him to Miss Leibowitz, the school nurse, on some pretense, to see what she thought. In any case, the police already suspected, even assumed parental abuse. Not that that was the only possible answer to the question of those bruises.

Other than that, he had told them everything he could think of about Jason Fender. Really, if he had to pick a reason why he'd made the house call, it was something to do with the way Jason had hopped out of his car and stalked off down Polk Street without even closing the car door. The kid seemed distracted and disturbed about something. What, Bachman had no clue.

He'd given them a list of Jason's other teachers, and Ellie Nelson's name and phone extension too. Now he and Ellie sat across from each other in a booth at Alfonzo's. The booth was not much smaller than Ellie's office, and their conversation continued as if the hours of the day had not intervened. By this time Bachman desperately wished that there were anything else in the world to talk about.

"I mean, a different sense from the cops and everyone else?" said Ellie.

He took a deep breath before he tried to answer her. As he opened his mouth to speak the waitress arrived with their pizza and placed it on the table between them, the metal pan resting on a little pedestal. He hesitated and looked at Ellie across the steaming surface of the bubbling cheese. The waitress had a knowing kind of smile. She was a bit too old to be a former student. She might have been the mom of a student he'd had a few years back.

When the waitress withdrew – had she winked, or had he imagined that? – Bachman tried to answer Ellie's question.

"They all assume Jason did it. Why? Because they think he'd be justified in doing it. If it were them, they figure, they'd have done it."

"And your take?" Ellie asked. "Are you the devil's advocate?" She quickly regretted her choice of words and tried to rephrase, but he stopped her.

"No, I know what you mean. And don't mean. It's just that I'm just – I'm not satisfied with their assumptions," he said. "I don't know if I know this kid any better than anyone else does. But it doesn't seem true to me. Why now? Why would he have borne up under it all this time, and now murder him? And so brutally?" He took a deep breath. "I don't care about fights he's had in school. This is a gentle kid."

"Oh, Billy," Ellie said. "Did you ever think that maybe you just love these kids too much?"

Bachman began to protest, surprised by the suggestion.

"I don't know, Billy. I'm just asking."

Chapter Five

In the chill dark a window shattered. The shards fell roundabout on the metal floor with a tinkling sound that was not unpleasant, but lasted longer than it should have. Then black icy silence again. How long? *How long?* The window shattered again. This was truly unexpected, startling really. How can the same window shatter twice? It made him sit up in bed, jump up almost, and in so doing Bachman realized the darkness was his sleep, the cold was some kind of nameless fear that melted the moment he tried to identify it, the floor was carpeted and free of glass shards, and the shattering window was the ringing of his bedside phone.

He answered it despite the fact that today was, he was fairly certain, Saturday, and it made no sense that someone should be calling him at – what time was it? – at whatever time in the morning this happened to be.

"Hello?"

"I'm sorry to call so early. Did I wake you?"

"No. Yes." Let the caller figure out what he meant. Who was it? Something sounded like... like maybe he should know. He searched his head but came up empty. "Who is this please?"

"Oh, darn. I'm sorry Mr. Bachman. This *is* Mr. Bachman, right? Of course it is. I should have told you it was me right away. That's what I'm supposed to do and here I am messing it up from the beginning."

"And..... ?"

"Of course, sorry. It's Alice. Alice Kimsbrough. I'm sorry I woke you Mr. Bachman. Really sorry. I should call you back later, shouldn't I? Of course now I've already woken you up, so calling back later would be bothering you again, in a way, wouldn't it?"

He'd recognized her seconds before she identified herself, as much from the rushed cadence and rising inflections than the actual timbre of her voice. How, he wasn't sure. He'd had some 600-700 students since Alice Kimsbrough had graduated AHS – was it five years ago? She'd gone to Syracuse he seemed to recall. Must have graduated from there by now. Hadn't heard anything about or from her in a long time, a couple of letters from college, one asking for help on a paper. What was she doing now? Hadn't Hilda Steinmetz mentioned Alice just recently? Regardless, why the hell was she calling him early on what was now undoubtedly Saturday?

"Hello Alice. What's up? Is everything okay?

"Well, sure, yes, everything is okay. With me, anyway. I'm great, thanks for asking. I've got a great job and I've been meaning to call you or come by the school to see you because I wanted to tell you about it, and to thank you too, because I wouldn't have this job if it weren't for you. Only now I wish I had already called you because now I *have* to call you. I mean to ask you about... See... "

"You 'have to call' me, Alice? Alice. What is your job?"

"Oh. Well, I work for *The Atlantis Press*. Isn't that something, Mr. Bachman? I'm a writer for *The Press*."

He was going to offer to call her back after he'd had his coffee, but then he'd remembered that he was out of coffee, so he'd agreed to meet her at a diner for breakfast. ("My treat!" she'd fairly exclaimed.) They met at the Bayview in Belmar. He loved their pancakes, he told Alice. The truth was that they were far less likely to see anyone he knew there than at the Boulevard in Atlantis.

It was so unfair. Had any other reporter called him, particularly at such an hour, he'd have brushed them off, knowing full well what they wanted to talk about. He could hardly do that to one of his kids, no matter how uncomfortable it made him. This, he knew, was just another reason why he needed to not live in the town where he taught. He had a long list of them.

She was waiting for him when he got there. Alice Kimsbrough jumped from the booth when she saw him enter and gave him an awkward hug, all pretense of professional interviewer-interviewee objectivity momentarily set aside. She waved to the waitress to bring coffee, which she was already doing anyway. When they were settled across from each other behind their cups, Alice took a deep breath.

"It was you, wasn't it?"

This was more alarming a question than he had anticipated. What did she mean?

She lowered her voice to a conspiratorial whisper. "The 'Atlantis High School staff member.' You found the body, didn't you? Tommy Jr. won't let anyone say who it was, just that it was an AHS staff member who dropped by to check on a student. Everyone knows that Ziskin doesn't get out of his office and personally check on a kid who's been absent one day."

Bachman blinked dumbly. He hadn't said a word since he'd reached the diner. It was true that the AHS truant officer rarely left his chair, let alone his office. Besides, no truant officer would make a visit like Bachman had made. Why had he done it again? He couldn't remember. Something to do with a black raincoat.

"Well it is fairly obvious. Sure, they don't identify the kid but once they told us who the victim was and there was another person who lived at the address and that he was being sought and that he was a minor, well where else would you look him up but at school? Not in school Thursday, his first absence; out Friday. He's MIA. Plus, then, he's in the eleventh grade. Bachman's grade, if you'll pardon the expression. The other kids in the school don't know him. I asked my cousin Emily, she's a senior, she asked around. All the kids in school are talking about what happened, and talking about this kid Jason, but nobody knows the kid, really. So it had to be you. Loner kid, drug dealer dad. Classic Bachman."

"Nice to see you Alice," said Bachman.

"Oh, please don't be mad at me because—"

"I'm not mad, Alice." He drained his coffee cup, and the waitress materialized to refill it. Bachman expressed his gratitude and ordered eggs. Alice went for the bran muffin. With effort she stopped talking and waited for him to speak. She had the same long curly hair she had had back in high school, only it was longer and wilder. She sported hoop earrings with little blue feathers of some kind, and hoop bracelets on both arms, so that she jangled unless she sat perfectly still, which she was struggling to do. She looked exactly like a child waiting to be told if she got the lead in the school play.

"If someone found a dead body, that would make him or her a witness of some kind," Bachman said. "A 'witness after the fact,' I guess you would call it. And if the police had no other information about such an event, then this person would be, for the time being, the only witness. And therefore a fairly vital link to the crime. For the time being."

"For the time being."

"Listen, Alice. I don't know any more about this than you do. In fact, it sounds like you know a lot more than I do. I'm proud of you. You're making a living writing. But I don't see how I can help you with this."

"Why did you go there? Did you think something was up?"

"No, I didn't think—" He looked at her with exasperation, realizing she'd just tricked him into giving tacit acknowledgment that her theory was correct. "Alice, I would love to help you with this."

"If I write a substantial piece, or series, on this mess," Alice said, "they're going to make me a staff feature reporter. For the last year I've been getting coffee, writing obituaries, and reorganizing the files."

"I hate talking to reporters. No, not you. But, well, yes. I hate this, and if it weren't you I wouldn't be talking to you."

"Why?"

"I hate talking to reporters, because it never comes out right. Here's what I mean. On very rare occasions in my life, things that I have had some first hand knowledge about have for one reason or another been written about in the paper. Maybe three or four times. Five, maybe. Doesn't matter. The point is that every single time I have read an article in the paper – not just *The Press*, any paper – where I've known something about the facts, something in the article is always wrong. Wrong. Not necessarily something earthshaking, but sometimes." The waitress brought the eggs and the muffin, and Bachman took the opportunity to look at his plate instead of Alice's anxious face.

"It may not be the reporter's fault. Sometimes it is, and probably sometimes it isn't. I know how it works, and I know how many different people's hands the copy passes through before it gets set in type and printed. Getting it right isn't the editor's first priority. Getting it printed is." He looked at her. She hadn't touched her bran muffin yet.

"Give you an example. My second year teaching, the teachers' union went on strike. You wouldn't believe me if I told you what we were getting paid in '72, '73. But let's not get sidetracked. Reporters came to our meetings, covered our picket lines, interviewed the leadership, the administration, the Board, the parents. They took pictures. Lucky me, I got my picture in the paper. Page one."

"The first time," said Alice, in a more subdued voice than usual.

"Yeah," said Bachman. "Anyhow, the article about the strike got several key points wrong: the length of the contract, the fact that we were without a contract for two years. Not the end of the world certainly. But if the paper were your only source of information about the strike, you would definitely have the wrong impression, and it might affect your sympathies.

"Okay, but stuff happens, right? They wrote a few more articles during the strike, got some of that stuff right, some wrong, never acknowledged that they'd printed anything wrong, even though subsequent articles contradicted earlier ones. Okay, get over it.

"Remember when the apartment building on Madison Street burned down?"

Alice nodded.

"*The Press* described it as a twelve story building with fifty-two apartments. They said that a lady from the old folks' home two doors down broke her leg while being evacuated. A friend of mine lived in that building. It's nine stories, thirty-two apartments. And my friend broke her leg, and she really didn't appreciate being characterized as a senior citizen."

Alice cut her muffin in half but didn't pick it up. "But that's not me."

"I know it's not you Alice. But once you hand the copy in it goes through several editors, and often that's where mistakes slip in. Not that any of this is that important. It's just that it made me start thinking about every other article I read in the paper. Why would any of them wind up any more accurate? It hasn't made me stop reading the paper. It's just made me skeptical about the accuracy of everything."

"You're the one who always said, 'The more you write about something, the closer you get to the truth of it.'"

"I said that?"

"Of course you did. Over and over. You also said to 'use your writing to figure out what you're thinking.' If you don't remember that, I'll show it to you in one of my old notebooks."

"Okay, that sounds like something I would say," said Bachman. "But what's that got to do with..."

"Look, I guess you're right, there are lots of mistakes that seep through into print. But I think you're also right about the best way of getting to the bottom of something. To find out the truth. You got a lot of us addicted to using writing as the best way to understand what we were writing about."

Bachman looked at Alice as if for the first time since he'd sat down. Regardless of her frenetic way of talking, she was a grown-up, not the girl he'd had in her junior year. It always shocked him when a student quoted back to him something he'd said in class years before.

"You also always said that there was a big difference between facts and truth. Don't say you don't remember that."

He had nothing to say to respond to that. Ultimately, they agreed that he would speak completely off the record. She wouldn't quote anything he said, not even as "an unidentified source," wouldn't use his name or anything else that would identify him. He didn't want the cops to be mad at him or to make their jobs harder, and he needed to make absolutely sure that no attention was drawn to him at school with regard to the whole mess. That just could not happen.

Alice understood and swore to keep him totally out of everything she wrote. He thought of Woodward and Bernstein's Watergate source, nicknamed Deep Throat, but felt it inappropriate to make the reference.

She pushed the narrow notebook she'd been edging out of her purse back down into it. "First time I ever discouraged a student from taking notes," he said, and they both laughed. And then he told her whatever he could. When they were done talking and eating, he promised he would give her feedback on her article when he read it. She refrained from asking him why he hadn't ordered pancakes.

* * *

The New Jersey coastline is 125 miles of Atlantic Ocean beachfront. It stretches from Sandy Hook in the north, just below the mouth of Lower New York Bay, to Cape May in the south, a peninsula that divides the great ocean from the Delaware Bay. If you stand on the southernmost tip of Cape May Point you can actually see the difference in the water where the ocean becomes the bay. The bay is a different color, greener actually; it's also far less choppy. There's a distinct line, as if a cosmic geographer had painted in the boundary. If you stand on the spit of land beyond the Sandy Hook Lighthouse and scan the panorama to the north, you see the islands: left to right, Staten, Coney and Long.

New York Bay is a huge, hourglass-shaped inlet. The Narrows, the point that was narrow enough to be bridged in the 1950s, but even so only by the world's longest suspension span, is only a bit west of north from Sandy Hook, perhaps 12 nautical miles. On a clear day, which is a far more common occurrence than people who live far from the upper Jersey Shore assume, you can stand on the beach and stare right up the throat of New York Bay, between Staten Island and Brooklyn, and you can see Miss Liberty, the Lady of the Harbor. Walk a few hundred yards back and climb to the top of the oldest operating lighthouse in North America, and look north up the Hudson, west across the state to the Delaware Water Gap, east along the flat, jutting megasuburbopolis of Long Island and out to sea toward Europe and Africa. Look south, and behold the Jersey Shore.

Between Sandy Hook and Cape May lies what other places call beach or coast, but which here is called The Shore. When you're at The Shore you may go to the beach, or not, as you choose; but regardless of whether you are eating a pork roll sandwich on the boardwalk in Point Pleasant, fishing for marlin or tuna

51

miles out to sea from Beach Haven, all dressed up and getting fleeced for all you've got in one of Atlantic City's notorious casinos, or watching your child vomit from the deadly combination of greasy food and gut-wrenching rides at Seaside, you are Down The Shore.

Celebrated musically with tunes from coy lady singers on vaudeville stages crooning along with player pianos in the late 1800s and with arena shaking electronically amplified anthems in the last third of the 20th century, The Shore has always been a destination. For whom? That has varied somewhat across the years. In the 19th century, Presidents, Rockefellers and other Titans of Industry and Power built mansions up and down its length. In September of 1881, a special spur of track was built to carry the dying James Garfield to the front door of his friend's house in Elberon. It was hoped that the restorative qualities of the ocean air would aid in the President's recovery from the assassin's bullet wound he'd received three months earlier, and from the clumsy medical care he'd received from his 3 Stooges-like team of doctors since then. Alas, it didn't work, and he died there a couple of weeks later.

Far from dissuaded by this sad event, or perhaps spurred by it (spikes ripped up from the temporary length of track became valuable souvenirs), the rich and famous flocked south by rail from New York City and east by rail from Philadelphia to establish their massive "cottages," visions of a Newport for the richer, newer-moneyed set dancing in their heads. With their arrival grew entire towns whose economies were based on serving the wealthy residents. The classic symbiosis of the rich and their servants thrived for several decades. But it stopped like President Garfield's heart when, in the beginning of July 1916, a marauding great white shark terrorized 80 miles of the Shore for two weeks. Seven-and-a-half feet long, weighing 325 pounds, it ate most of three men and one boy. Like the fifth victim, "lucky" 12-year-old Joseph Dunn, the Jersey Shore tourist trade lived on, but in a permanently mutilated condition. Visitors who had arrived singing of packing up their troubles in their old kit bags and smile, smile, smiling packed up all right, but they weren't smiling and they didn't come back for a generation.

With the post-war baby boom the middle class colonized the region. Blue collar towns like Toms River, Brick and Atlantis were building modern schools and hospitals to accommodate the needs of bankers, lawyers, brokers and other businessmen who found the 90-minute commute to Manhattan a fair trade off for idyllic, salt air villages in which to raise their families. Housing developments sprouted everywhere, instant neighborhoods where farms and fields and woods had remained undisturbed for hundreds of years. Wherever a greased palm or a political favor could prevail, the oceanfront became a construction site. Like alien invaders of brick and steel, apartment buildings and oceanview condos rose twelve, fifteen and twenty stories high, and were tenanted immediately, even before they were complete. Sea walls were strengthened or at least appeared to be strengthened, as a bulwark against the late summer and early fall hurricanes that bashed against the beachfront towns, oblivious to real estate values, construction projects, and demographic shifts.

Richard W. Goffman

Amazingly, sixty years on, the great white shark returned. When Jaws, the very first "summer block-buster" movie, played at the Dolan Twin Theater across the street from Atlantis' most popular beach, tourists spent more time on the sand and less time in the waves. The posters for the movie said, "Don't go in the water", and many didn't, but the fictional man-eater proved a boon to business. After the first week, Arty Dolan put Jaws on both his screens, and ran it nonstop from noon to two a.m. throughout July, and on one screen again for the rest of the summer of 1975. Beachgoers who spent less time swimming spent more time spending, and everyone was happy.

While success built upon success, failures filtered through too. By the end of the seventies, for every five beachfront condos there was a half-completed framework of a building, left stranded by bankruptcy or mendacity in mid-completion. Like a massive stranded skeleton bleaching in the sun, rusting beams and twisted rebar were clear signs for those able to read them that the Shore's go-go days might continue for some time, but a new round of decay, a new cycle of depression was not far off. Salt water eventually corrodes everything.

The Nautilus is what Vaitikus Brothers Inc. would have called their twenty-story condo near the south end of Atlantis had it ever been completed. Construction was halted, however, when in the chill winter of 1979 funds stopped flowing to the subcontractors. On investigation, the companies that had drawn the blueprints, laid the foundation and framed out the building discovered that Aleksas, Mielasis, and Patsy

Vaitikus were no longer reachable at their offices, were possibly no longer in the United States, and were subject to a long list of federal fraud and corruption charges if they were ever apprehended in the United States. By 1983, all that was left of the Nautilus Condominium boondoggle was the aforementioned skeleton, unchanged except for the relentless progress of rust and corrosion, an impressively weed-filled lot, and a graffiti-covered billboard picturing a completed building beneath a happy sun which shone on bikini-clad mothers who sunbathed while overseeing their children frolicking in the Nautilus' Olympic-sized pool. The irony was completed by the image of an old-fashioned biplane pulling a banner above the building. The banner had once read "FUN IN THE SUN," but had long ago been amended in black Magic Marker to say "SUCK MY DICK."

Ownership of the building site and the work remained thoroughly entangled in years' worth of litigation and liens, involving local, state and federal agencies. As each new town council tried and failed to take possession of it in order to realize the millions in tax revenue that was going to waste, most residents had stopped noticing it, letting it blend into the background. Many of them would have been surprised, however, to learn that the shell of the Nautilus was not completely unoccupied. Its location, its darkness, and its semi-completeness had combined to make it a temporary haven for transients, dealers and buyers of hard drugs, and users of same.

The Atlantis Police were not blind to this activity at the abandoned building site. Periodically they would make a sweep of the place at night; sometimes they would even catch a few of the ones too wasted to jump down from their first or second floor girders, roll in the sand, and scatter like cockroaches. Most, sometimes all, would get away, and this, after all, was the point. The few they caught they busted. Those who got away stayed away, sometimes for a few weeks, sometimes permanently. After a few weeks the place would start to get used again, at first very surreptitiously, gradually more carelessly, and the cycle would repeat itself. No amount or configuration of fencing or plywood or wire kept the derelicts out.

It was on one of these nocturnal raids that Tommy Gallagher, Jr. cut his teeth, literally and figuratively, on his very first night as an Atlantis policeman. He'd accompanied his dad and five other cops. They'd parked five blocks north and walked with flashlights off up the beach and approached from the ocean side. Bill Jacszewicz, a thirty-four-year-old officer who was packing a bit more than the officially recommended weight limit for active duty policemen, stumbled in the dark and wound up in the shallow end of the pool, crying out as he splashed in the fetid rain water and other accumulated detritus. The surprise approach was spoiled, and alleged perpetrators took off running in every direction. Young Tommy Jr. picked one and gave chase. He would have caught his man and "lost his cherry" within hours of beginning his career had he been able to imitate the jump his quarry made off a concrete outcropping onto the beach. The fellow ran, leapt, landed, rolled over twice and came up running south; Tommy Jr. ran, leapt, landed and rolled over face first into some rocks sticking out of the sand. He lay stunned for a minute or two. He'd chipped his two front teeth but was otherwise unharmed.

* * *

Local man murdered; son missing
By ALICE KIMSBROUGH
ATLANTIS PRESS STAFF REPORTER

Sunday, October 30, 1983. ATLANTIS – The body of a 40-year-old white male was found on Thursday evening in the Taylor Street home he shared with his teenage son. Upon initial examination of the victim's remains, authorities have ruled the death a homicide. The body has been remanded to the office of the city medical examiner where an autopsy will be performed in the next two days.

The victim was identified as Sylvester A. Fender. Mr. Fender had resided in the one-bedroom frame house at 488 Taylor Street for approximately five months. Mr. Fender had been a resident of Atlantis and surrounding communities in Monmouth County for at least seven years.

Acting Police Chief Thomas Gallagher, Jr. told reporters on Friday morning that the crime was reported on Thursday night at approximately 8:00 pm, by a staff member of Atlantis High School. An ambulance was immediately called to the crime scene, however the nature of Mr. Fender's wounds and the condition of the body when it was found left little doubt that he was dead at the scene.

Traffic in the vicinity was disrupted by the initial phase of the investigation. A three-block section of

Taylor Street and a two-block section of Fillmore Street were cordoned off until 4:00 pm on Friday, while police and detectives searched for evidence in the vicinity. Traffic was rerouted around the section via a detour on Eighth Avenue, Polk Street, and Ninth Avenue. Residents of the cordoned off section were asked to either leave their homes on Friday morning, or remain on their property. The restrictions and the detour were removed on Friday afternoon.

Information about Mr. Fender's son, a juvenile, including his name, has been withheld. The teenager is described as a "person of interest" in the case who is being sought for questioning. At press time, the youth's whereabouts were unknown.

According to a source who preferred to remain unidentified, the body of Mr. Fender had been severely "mutilated." The source described a "gaping chest wound" that was apparently caused by multiple stabbings or slashings with a knife or axe. The Atlantis Police Department would not confirm the means or the method of the murder, nor the nature of the weapon or whether or not it was in police custody. However several sources report that the search for a weapon and other clues conducted in the vicinity of the Fender home has so far been inconclusive. Acting Police Chief Gallagher would only say that the case would undoubtedly require "an in-depth investigation," and that "all necessary resources" were being brought to bear on all leads.

Mr. Fender, a one-time bouncer at various beachfront nightclubs, was unemployed at the time of his death. He had an arrest record dating back to 1970, including convictions for misdemeanor drug possession, procurement, disturbing the peace and resisting arrest.

This is the second homicide in Atlantis in 1983, equaling the number that took place in 1982.

Anyone with any information about this crime, or about anything which may be of assistance to the police in completing their investigation, are requested to call 201-555-5454. All calls will remain anonymous.

* * *

When it came time to disappear, he knew where to go.

He'd been here, alone, so many times before that he felt comfortable. What a difference from the first time. Of course, he'd only been ten years old that time. It had been cold that night, much colder than this. But it was the aloneness, the fear and the dark and the echoing echoing harsh cries and laughter that came from no direction and every direction that made the first time such a nightmare. Yes, all that, the aloneness, the fear, the dark, the sounds, the confusion... and the not knowing.

Daddy had walked him past during the day, first along the cracked Ocean Boulevard sidewalk, then back the other way along the beach. He'd pointed to the spot where he needed to stand when he came there in the dark, told him what to call out, who to ask for, what to say, what to give, what to get. There was nothing to worry about, Daddy had said, nothing to be afraid of.

"You got the advantage of being you," Daddy told him. "I ain't got that no more. I can't just show up

59

places anymore. You can, though. Nobody's gonna bother you. Just do it like I told you. It'll be perfect." Jason didn't know, at least not then, exactly what Daddy meant. He went over the words again and again, but he knew better than to ask questions. Did Daddy mean that he wasn't able to be himself anymore? Did he mean that he had a secret identity, like Batman, and his secret got found out?

It didn't matter though. There would be no questions, not spoken aloud. Daddy had dropped him off a few blocks away. He carried the package against his skin, inside his coat. It was wrapped in plastic and aluminum foil. He walked away from Daddy without looking back at him. "Go where I showed you," Daddy had said. "Do what I said and come back to the diner with the envelope." And with that, the car door had closed and he'd driven away.

Jason had walked to the spot he'd been shown. He'd called out the name that had made no sense. The sound of his own voice didn't sound like himself. It felt like cotton blowing away in the night wind. But it must have been heard, because he'd heard a response: noises from above, ahead, behind. A skittering sound like something metal kicked across the cement. And then the face that lit itself up from its center with a glowing ash. This was Crabface. It had to be, although he didn't look like a crab, he looked more like a dog, a rangy poodle that had no home and had never been clean. When Crabface drew on his cigarette, the circle revealed most of his face, which was a wilderness of shadows and tangles and scratches, an unreal moonscape wrapped around a tiny bonfire. When Crabface exhaled, the glow subsided, the smoke obscured him, and there was a foul smell, worse than cigarette, that reached all the way down to Jason's nose, despite the night wind that should have blown it away.

"So this is Lemmy's partner," Crabface said to someone behind him whom Jason couldn't see.

"Lemmy. What a fuckin asshole," the voice behind Crabface said from the darkness. Another voice broke in from the pitch black above them. It didn't speak, it cackled. It reminded Jason of the witch from The Wizard of Oz.

Jason couldn't remember much else from that first night, other than walking back along Ocean Boulevard past the traffic light to the diner. The plastic and foil wrapped package was gone, and there was a thick envelope under his coat, and he smelled bad from having pissed himself. Daddy didn't say anything about that, once he saw the envelope. Daddy must have been glad, because he gave Jason the rest of his soup.

So he knew where to go, where he wouldn't be found, or even noticed. A couple of local losers were sparking up pipes when he approached the place, but they didn't see him. Often people didn't see him in broad daylight. In the dark, at night, he was as invisible as he wanted to be.

He went to the opposite corner from where they huddled. Without even having to see them, his hand found the rusty, unused rungs that went up the inside of the vertical beam on the street side of the building. Without hesitation, he went up. And up. He stopped when he was 200 feet above Atlantis, and the Atlantic.

Richard W. Goffman

It wasn't the first time he'd come here. No one, he knew, ever came above the second floor. They didn't even think of it. He thought of it though. Most people just never look up.

Chapter Six

Arthur Scanlon wouldn't have wanted it widely publicized among the Atlantis electorate, but he spent as little time in the city as his job as mayor permitted. He had a huge house in Lincroft, fifteen miles west and a world away from Atlantis. He maintained a condo on the beach, of course. Dorothy, Mrs. Scanlon, liked to use it when she visited the beach club. Arthur stayed there several nights a week, as business required. Although luxurious, there was only one bedroom, the second bedroom having been taken over by a pool table. This would have proved a problem had their son, Joseph, not become used to spending most of his time at a private preparatory school in Connecticut. A senior at Tollivers, he'd applied early admissions to Princeton, and would likely go from prep school to summer vacation abroad to the Ivy League without once needing a bed in Atlantis. Anyhow, the election laws required it, so the Scanlons' official residence was also the one they stayed in the least.

The Scanlons banked in Morristown (and sometimes overseas), invested in New York, dined at the finest restaurants in New Jersey's posh "horse country," shopped at The Mall at Short Hills, and socialized in circles that did not have much in common with Atlantis or include many Atlanteans.

For these and other reasons it was not unusual for Mayor Scanlon to settle his substantial bulk into the specially designed chair behind his massive desk and spend most of a Monday morning reading The Atlantis Press, getting caught up on what, if anything, had happened over the weekend. He was an impressive man in size, shape and manner. His six-foot two-inch frame carried nearly 275 pounds, very few of which consisted of fat. He wore expensive clothes and sported an expensive haircut. He was particularly proud of his hair, which, while almost entirely gray, was fulsome, wavy, and always perfectly arranged atop his great square head. The same could be said for his eyebrows, with which he was capable of expressing himself as clearly as with his stentorian voice. His mustache was carefully attended; if his hair and eyebrows were the fairway, the mayor's mustache was the green. His eyes brimmed with confidence and more than a hint of disdain. His jaw was a brick.

Mayor Scanlon wore hats. The hat of choice for winter weather, which seemed to be making a peremptory appearance, was a pearl white fur felt homburg custom made for him by a London haberdasher.

It was this treasure he was taking care to stow safely on the top shelf of his closet when a witch walked into his office.

The witch carried the Sunday paper, his coffee carafe, and a list of notes and messages. She wore the traditional broad brimmed high black hat and long black crepe dress, and featured a poorly conceived false nose in the center of her face. She was in all other ways recognizable as Marcia, his secretary. The mayor's reaction was beyond disapproval, and the rearrangement of his facial features spoke volumes. Marcia, however, was nonplussed.

"Halloween, Mr. Mayor. It happens every year. Doesn't Mrs. Scanlon stock up on candy for the all the little spooks who'll be trick or treating today?"

Scanlon spent little time around children and their holidays, Mrs. Scanlon, to his knowledge, had never "stocked up" on anything in her entire life, and the less said about spooks the better. But it did now come back to him that many city hall employees wore childish costumes to work on the last day of October in recent years.

Marcia placed the items just so on her boss' desk and was almost at the door when he called her back.

"Why don't I know about this?" he demanded. He was pointing an angry, wavering finger at the article on page one of *The Press*, the one that had been written by Alice Kimsbrough. He looked down at it again, not sure if he were angrier at Marcia for not letting him know about this sooner, or at this Kimsbrough person for writing about it in the newspaper where everyone would see it. He craned his neck to look closer at the offending newspaper – he had been stopped in mid-sit by the bad news – and noticed the dateline of the piece.

"This happened on Thursday!" He looked at Marcia for any sort of explanation. "And take off that fucking nose!"

Marcia, who was one of the few who did not quail in the face of the Mayor's temper, did remove the nose. She realized that the rubber band holding it on would not go over the hat, so she took that off too, placed the nose inside the hat, and held both behind her, feeling just a bit more vulnerable without them.

"This happened late Thursday night. You weren't here on Friday. Tommy Gallagher tried to call you, and so did I, but we couldn't reach you."

"That's why I have an answering machine," the mayor said.

Marcia was not yet totally comfortable talking to answering machines, though she realized that she'd need to get used to it soon, as it now seemed almost as many phones were being answered by them as by people. "I did leave you a message."

"Yeah. Your message said, 'It's Marcia, please call the office.'"

"Yes, well, it doesn't seem right to leave a message about somebody getting murdered on a tape recorder."

Naturally enough, he had ignored her meaningless message.

If Mayor Scanlon hated one thing more than any other, it was murder. He was against it. He despised murderers. He didn't exactly love murder victims either, because you couldn't have a murder without both a perpetrator and a victim. Many times you could have murders with victims but never have a murderer. If, like Mayor Scanlon, you particularly loathed murders occurring in your town, having one sprayed across the cover of your morning paper was simply offensive. The Mayor was duly offended. He sat.

"Get Tom Gallagher in here," said the mayor to Marcia.

"You mean Tommy Jr., Mr. Mayor?" She regretted having to use the diminutive, but that was how people usually distinguished between the father, who had recently retired from his long held position as Chief of Police, and the son. Arthur Scanlon's eyebrows flew up, and then plummeted, as he recognized the distinction and recalled that his current chief of police was little more than a kid.

"Yes, get Junior in here. Please."

* * *

"Here to confess?" Dick Raumbaugh's greeting to Bachman, while surely sardonic, nevertheless felt as if it contained just a hint of menace, and the teacher's face must have shown it. "Relax, Professor," Raumbaugh said, indicating his office guest chair with his now-lit cigar. "Only the guilty have reason to fear the long arm of the law."

Raumbaugh's small, crowded office was an extension of the man himself. His fedora sat atop a pile of papers on top of a dented gray filing cabinet, three of whose four drawers were incapable of closing properly.

Bachman looked at the thing as if it were about to top-ple forward and kill someone. There were a window too grimy to see through, a typewriter buried under some folders, and, on the desk and on a shelf, mustard-stained wax paper that could not all have been from today's lunch. He now noticed for the first time that Raumbaugh had an acute case of dandruff; here in his enclosed den, the stuff seemed to have settled like vol-canic ash – or maybe cigar ash – on every surface. Bachman lifted some newspapers and phone books off the chair and sat down.

"It's a joke, Mr. Bachman," said Raumbaugh. He paused but went on before Bachman could reply. "And it's funny, because it could be true. See?"

"I'm not quite ready to confess, no," said Bachman. "I really just want to know if you have any lead yet on Jason Fender. Have you found him, or have any idea where he is?"

Raumbaugh looked closely at Bachman, and took a contemplative pull on his smoke. He opened a drawer and removed a flask and what appeared to be a clean glass, holding the latter out toward Bachman who thought about it a moment before declining politely.

Raumbaugh shrugged, put the booze away, then visibly considered his guest's question. Exhaling, he said, "The short answer is 'No.' Come to think of it, and just between us, that's the long answer, too. I got nothing on this kid yet. Oh, I found faint bloody foot-prints leading out the back door. But once he hit that crappy excuse for a backyard, I got nothing. I don't know if he went back through the old gas station behind the house, or around front. All I know is that he ain't still there."

Raumbaugh warmed to the subject of how much he did and didn't know about Thursday night's events. "I suspect, but don't know, that he took his father's car. He doesn't have a license but that don't mean shit. Red Bank cops found a '69 Volvo station wagon that was once registered to Mr. Sylvester Fender behind the Carleton Theater last night, and though he hadn't renewed the reg in two years, chances are he still had the vehicle. Did the kid use it to leave the scene? County and state cops and all the municipalities have Jason's picture, everybody's got their eye out for him. Nobody's seen nothing. The car wouldn't start. The battery was gone. Not dead, gone. But even with a jump they couldn't start it. It's in their impound lot, and they're supposedly keeping it secure" – at this, Raumbaugh rolled his eyes dramatically, indicating his skepticism about the maintenance of this important piece of evidence. "So I'm going up there this afternoon to check it out."

"But at this point, there's still nothing," said Raumbaugh. "I got no assurance that the kid ever touched the car, let alone used it for his getaway. For all we know, that junker was left behind the theater by Lemmy, or by somebody else who had come into possession of the old Volvo by hook or by crook. Maybe Lemmy parked it there, between the dumpster and the wall, took his own battery and sold it, or traded it for some good shit."

Bachman recalled a simple tenet voiced by Hercule Poirot: Until you know exactly what sort of person the victim was, you cannot begin to see the circumstances of a crime clearly. "Have you ever reflected," the pusillanimous but effective little Belgian once asked, "that the reason for murder is always to be found by a study of the person murdered?" Bachman realized with dismay that he knew almost nothing about the dead man, Jason's father. Until Raumbaugh had referred to him as Sylvester, Bachman hadn't even known the man's real name. He had suspicions and fears, the ones which had brought him to the house that night in the first place. But what sort of person was he? Sure, people would make plenty of assumptions, based mostly on the condition of the house. But what did anyone know?

Raumbaugh must have read Bachman's mind – or his face. "See, Lemmy Fender is not a stranger in local law enforcement circles."

"He's not?"

"Nope. He's got quite a long paper trail in the justice system. He is your typical small time small town criminal. He's a thief when it's easy, drug dealer, occasional enforcer for hire, bagman. If it doesn't take a lot of brains or effort, Lemmy is up for it. Or, I should say, was up for it, as he's obviously not going to be getting up to anything anymore. Don't get me wrong. Lemmy had a few useful talents. He was quite good at beating up anyone smaller than him, which is 90% of people. He was very good at breaking people's knees so that they're hard to put back together. His favorite tools for this were either a police baton or a sawed off baseball bat."

"But if you know all this…"

"'...then why hasn't he been put away'? Well unfortunately, Professor, we are unable to lock people up based on what we know. For that, it's gotta be what we can prove. And don't get me wrong, Lemmy has been inside plenty, but mainly a couple of months here and a couple of months there. That's one of the reasons he and the kid have moved so much, to try to relocate to places where his face is less well known, especially to local cops. Of course the down side of that is that eventually everybody gets to know him. Also, he had a funny habit of hardly ever paying his rent."

"Or his electric bill, apparently," Bachman said, recalling the tangible darkness of the house he had entered without invitation only four days ago. "And when he was in jail for months at a time..." Bachman looked to Raumbaugh to complete this sentence as he had done his last, but was met with a blank gaze. The detective didn't anticipate the teacher's primary concern. "When he was in jail, who looked after his son?" Bachman said.

"Right. Well, social services generally takes a minor and places him in a foster home when the sole parent is arrested or convicted. Sometimes, I think, Lemmy had a girl living with him and the kid remained with her."

"A girl?"

"Sorry. Woman. Probably a whore he was pimping."

"No mother?"

"Well, I guess you could say everybody has a mother. Or had one." Raumbaugh shuffled through some of the chaos on his desk, located the folder he was looking for, and flipped through its contents until he found what he wanted. "Oh yeah. Here you go. Lemmy was married to the former Roberta Johansen of Oneonta, New York. She bore him the fruit of his loins in '67. That would be your student." He flipped a few more pages. "As far as I can tell, Mom must have split a couple of years after the kid was born. Not sure, but I don't think she's been in the picture since the kid was a toddler."

"So he may have been in foster care for all the time that Lemmy was in and out of jail," Bachman said. "Or in an institution. Or in the care of a hooker." The two men looked at each other. In different recent decades, both had been boys just as vulnerable as every teenager tried desperately to pretend not to be. In each other's eyes they saw an unspoken truth.

Or he may have been alone.

Bachman thanked Raumbaugh and got up to leave. He couldn't wait to breathe fresh air after the fetid stuff in the detective's office. Despite this, he had a good feeling about Raumbaugh. He liked him. Despite how open and shut the cops thought the case was, he felt that this man wanted the truth, even if it wasn't the easiest or most convenient truth. He wouldn't railroad Jason. Assuming they found him. Assuming he was alive.

There was an expression on Raumbaugh's face now which Bachman couldn't read. Apparently the detective was trying to decide whether or not to say something, and then, apparently, he decided. He motioned Bachman to sit back down. He shuffled around his desktop some more, and he came up with a thick manila envelope, from which he pulled some papers stapled in one corner.

"Coroner's report on Fender, Sylvester A. Got it this morning. You ain't supposed to know what's in it. Nobody is, except us." A slight gesture of Raumbaugh's cigar indicated that "us" meant people employed in this building. Police. Bachman recognized that Raumbaugh was going to tell him something that he wasn't supposed to share, which meant that he trusted him.

"Does it say anything special? That you didn't expect?" said Bachman.

"Well, yes and no. I mean, no, Lemmy died from massive trauma caused by a sharp object, a big knife, or more likely a machete or an axe. Whatever it was that the killer used to dig into him. Hell, he might have stood on his chest and dug a hole in him with a coalscuttle. And that's what everyone expected. What else could there be?"

Raumbaugh took a deep breath. Bachman remained silent, as there was obviously more. Raumbaugh flipped the first couple of pages and studied the coroner's report again. Bachman waited.

"But, well, yeah, there is something unexpected. At least, *I* didn't expect it." Raumbaugh found a specific notation on the report, read it over to himself silently, for what could not have been the first or second time. "According to the coroner, Lemmy had no heart."

Chapter Seven

"You don't mean…" This non-sentence was all Bachman could get out, and this was after struggling for some half-minute or so. He was blinking his eyes and working his jaw, but words were not coming.

"No, Professor. I don't mean he was mean. I mean literally. Dr. Patel don't use metaphors in his autopsy reports," said Raumbaugh. The cigar was in the ashtray now, and it had gone out. Raumbaugh's face compressed into a tight, unpleasant grin. He squinted at Bachman.

The image of the bear-like corpse looking as though its chest had been dug into by the teeth and claws of a pack of hungry scavenging wolves was before Bachman's eyes now as if he were back in that dark, cramped kitchen. Bachman had never witnessed an autopsy and, if he had his preference, never would. But he had respect for doctors who understood the relationship between humanity and the stuff humans were made of. He knew that Lemmy's nude corpse had been laid out on a stainless steel table under bright lights. It would already have been photographed, examined, and described in minute detail, with a notation of every external blemish, bump, bruise, scar, tattoo and irregularity the large man had accumulated on his skin throughout his life on the rough edge of civilization. The doctor would have described the bloody cave in Lemmy's chest prior to touching it, telling only what he could see, and perhaps smell, of that viscous horror. Now Dr. Patel would have opened it up, first with a curving swath from his left armpit to his right one, dipping downward with the big serrated knife toward the gaping wound. The killer had begun the coroner's work for him in the act of killing. From the lowest point of the cross cut, or from the bottom of the wound, Dr. Patel would have cut vertically downward, stopping in the midst of Lemmy's pubic hair. Now, what had been Lemmy was burst open to the world like an overripe plum.

Did Dr. Patel, with his training and experience, see the irregularity before he began the next phase of the job, which was to reach inside the great opening he had made and examine and then remove the organs? Did he know before he reached for it what would not be there? Or was there an array of human mechanisms lined up in a bin: liver, kidney, stomach, another kidney, pancreas, gall bladder, lungs... *hey, where the hell is this guy's ticker?* When Bachman had peeked into that hole he had seen only chaotic gore. Once the chaos that was Lemmy had been reorganized, the lack of that central organ would have screamed out its blatant wrongness. There would have been a careful search of the gurney and the ambulance, and a re-scouring of the crime scene. But this was not something that a careless cop dropped or a sleepy paramedic misplaced. There was no use looking around, as if for a lost ring of keys or a wallet gone astray. Lemmy Fender had no heart. And no one knew where it was.

"I can only think of a couple of reasons why somebody might do that," said Detective Raumbaugh. "First, some sort of cult thing. You know, like Satan worshipping shit or something. Voodoo."

"And second?" said Bachman.

"I lied. I got no second idea. I'm not saying there ain't no other reason, but I sure as shit can't think of it, and I've been trying to since this morning when I read this thing."

"Did you ever hear of anyone doing that before?" said Bachman.

"Me? No. Ears, yes. Cocks are popular keepsakes." Raumbaugh was now tripping down memory lane, in his comfort zone of gruesome murder stories told over whiskeys in bars and beers at barbecues, to impress rookies, civilians, women. "Fingers, tongues... a nose one time. Oh, they decapitated Johnny Twat down in AC and took the head with them, but they didn't keep it. They FedExed it to his wife."

"Thoughtful," said Bachman.

"'When it absolutely, positively has to get there overnight,'" said Raumbaugh.

* * *

Tommy Jr. had been called into the mayor's office a few times since taking over from his dad, and it had never been for a pat on the back and a hearty "Well done." Marcia had clued him in to Mayor Scanlon's reaction to the news of the murder – not that it was unexpected – so he had with him the case file. It was amazing, he thought as he strode the two blocks to city hall and bounded up the long staircase, how thick a case file could be without it really containing anything of substance about a solution to the crime.

At Marcia's desk the young acting chief of police communicated with the secretary, more via eye darts and rolls and quick jerks of the head than with words. Marcia wore her witch's hat again, but had opted to leave the nose in her drawer. It had been making her cross-eyed, and she was glad to be rid of it. She got up, removed the hat, knocked briskly on the mayor's office door, opened it and poked her head in. Mayor Scanlon was on the phone. She waved her hand and opened the door a bit wider to show Tommy Jr. standing behind her. Scanlon continued his serious conversation, in growling tones, without looking up, leaving his secretary and the man he had summoned in limbo. Marcia began to close the door and back out when the mayor, still without looking up, waved Tommy Jr. in. Marcia and Tommy Jr. looked at each other. The former ducked out and the latter entered.

Mayor Scanlon pointed to one of his visitors' chairs and Tommy Jr. took it. Scanlon had still not looked up. He was still grumping into the phone, punctuated with occasional slaps of the big front page article from Sunday's paper. He hasn't actually seen me, Tommy Jr. thought. What if he looks up and I'm not who he thought he invited in?

Mayor Scanlon stopped talking. He squinted, drew the corners of his mouth down and elevated the eyebrows, and froze like that for about a minute. Then he returned the phone to its cradle with a surprisingly gentle touch.

"So," he said. And then, finally, he lifted his face to meet Tommy Jr.'s. The mayor's face did not register surprise, so the acting chief of police knew that the mayor knew that it was he sitting across the big desk. Tommy Jr. wasn't sure if this made him feel better or worse. In either case, he didn't know if "So" required a response from him, or if it was the beginning of a longer sentence, perhaps a question. When the wait became just about as uncomfortable as possible, the mayor spoke again.

"So." What, again? "So do you or do you not understand the policy of keeping me in the loop?" said Scanlon. The big man's height was imposing even sitting down. And the desktop, Tommy Jr. now noticed, had to be higher than standard. The mayor's chair had perhaps been adjusted to further accentuate his towering presence, or maybe just to make it possible to work at such a high desk. In either case, Tommy Jr. felt like a little kid who had been invited to sit at the grown-ups' table at Thanksgiving and one of the grownups was telling him to mind his manners.

Before an answer to the question could be formulated, let alone produced, the mayor spoke again. "Do you think I'm not in charge when I'm not here in my office?" He lifted one big paw to stifle the protest that Tommy Jr. hadn't even offered. "Or do you have your own private city you're running here?" The powerful man's face was leaning forward. Big as he was, the mayor couldn't reach him across the desk, but regardless of that fact, the darkening all over the silver-haired, neatly trimmed, still-tanned face made an impression that felt like a backhand across the mouth.

"No, sir. No such thing, Mr. Mayor. I tried several times to reach you, and your sec---"

"Look, kid. Stop telling me what you tried and failed to do. It isn't going to impress me. Knowhutimean?"

It took an effort of will not to simply reply "Yes, sir." Instead, he placed the case file on the edge of the mayor's desk in front of him, and opened it. "I understand, Mr. Mayor. Next time, if need be, I'll send a uniform to your house to let you know when something like this happens."

"I'll make it easier than that," said Scanlon. "Call my machine and say 'Code twelve.'" Gallagher's face showed confusion, so the mayor asked, "What, is something else already a 'code twelve'? Wanna make it 'code one-twelve'? No? Okay then. So from now on 'code twelve' on my answering machine means there was a murder or an earthquake or a goddamn flood or some other major fucking happening that I wanna know about. You say 'code twelve,' I'll call you back, okay?"

"Okay," said Tommy Jr.

"Good. I'm comfortable that we understand each other now," said the mayor, in an entirely different, almost soothing tone of voice. Then, indicating the open file on the far edge of his desk, he said, "Now what do we have here?" Just two guys trying to solve a problem together.

Tommy Gallagher Jr. was shocked by how quickly the mayor's face changed back to a normal hue from the blackish purple it had been heading toward a moment before. Which was the real man? The bully, or the hale-fellow-well-met?

"This is everything we've got, and everything we've done so far. The body was discovered on Thursday evening, around eight p.m., by…"

As the young man spoke to him, the mayor noticed a brown envelope labeled CRIME SCENE PHOTOS. He reached out and flicked it toward himself, barely listening to the droning voice. It was obvious his police force had nothing, or this kid would have said so immediately rather than launching into a goddamn recitation. I got a wet behind the ears kid for a police chief, a witch for a secretary, a goddam moron for a lieutenant. No wonder I gotta do everything myself, he thought.

Two dozen color pictures, some 8x10s, some snapshot size, spilled onto his desk, face down. He picked one up. He couldn't tell what he was looking at; it was just a purple mess that filled the whole print. It looked like some of that abstract art crap, and Scanlon could make nothing of it. The next picture he turned over was of the same thing, only from several feet further back: a shot of the murder victim from about the crotch up. In an instant, the mayor knew that the previous picture had been a close-up of the wound which, here, in context, was a thing of true horror. Despite himself, his head jerked back.

To cover his involuntary reaction, the mayor whistled and shook his head. "Good goddamn," he said.

"You said it, sir," Tommy Jr. said, interrupting his verbal report.

The mayor picked up another face down picture at random, and then another, like a game of concentration. One stopped him: a close up of the victim's face. He wasn't sure, but he thought he recognized the fellow, though of course it was hard to tell with the bloody, broken nose, the blackened eyes, the distended mouth. He looked at the back of the picture, but it was only identified by a number and a date. He looked at the case file that the younger man was now halfway through describing. He interrupted him.

"Excuse me," said the mayor. "What is the victim's name again?"

"Fender, Sylvester A. A real piece of work, dozens of priors. Drugs, pimping, B&Es---"

"You're saying his name is Sylvester Fender? Sounds like a cartoon character. Or a --- Excuse the stupid question, Gallagher, but this guy is white, right?"

"Yep. Sylvester Fender, aka Lemmy Fender, male Caucasian, six foot-five, 330--"

"What did you say about aka?"

81

"Lemmy Fender, sir."

"Lenny?"

"No sir, *Lemmy*, Ms, not Ns. Class A lowlife. And we're pretty sure he was knocking his kid around."

"Kid?"

"Jason Fender, 16, eleventh grader at Atlantis High School."

"Kid white too?"

"Sir? Yeah, Jason Fender is white. He's been missing since the murder, absent from school Friday and today. There's an APB out, but so far nobody's spotted him anywhere."

"And you think…?

Tommy Jr. hesitated. "Strictly unofficially, Mr. Mayor, all signs point toward the kid having taken it and taken it and then finally stopped taking it."

"And the Sherlock Holmes of the Jersey Shore?"

"Yes sir. Raumbaugh thinks it was probably the kid, too, but he's checking everything out. We don't have anything yet that ices it."

"And you still haven't picked up the kid."

"He couldn't be too far, sir. His picture's out up and down the whole eastern seaboard. We'll find him soon."

"You'd better," the mayor said. A bit of the earlier menace had seeped back into his voice. He controlled it. "Tom, do you know how I feel about murder? How I react to murder in my city?"

"Yes, sir," said Tommy Jr.

"Your dad understood my feelings about it, I know that."

"Yes, sir, he did, and so do I."

"Do you, young man? Do you? Tell me how I feel about murder in Atlantis."

Damn, every time you started to feel a little comfortable this bastard kept you off balance, Tommy Jr. thought. Blood rushed so quickly to his face that his ears felt like they were on fire and the back of his head felt like it was filled with helium. He couldn't answer without sounding stupid or making the mayor sound stupid. It was impossible, yet he heard himself say, "Murder is a terrible crime." He scraped the toe of his right shoe against the heel of his left, and gripped the arms of the chair.

"Murder is a terrible crime *when it's committed in Atlantis*, Tom. Murder has no place in Atlantis. I truly hate it. I couldn't give two shits if every nigger in Asbury Park stabbed every spic in Neptune. In fact, I'm fine with that. Makes Atlantis look better. But when a body turns up here, it hurts everyone. It hurts real estate prices. It fucks up the tax base. It scares the voters. It blows our statistics right out of the water. Do you understand me, Tom?"

"I do, sir," said Tommy Jr. "Perfectly." I also understand how badly in need of a psychiatrist you are.

"And if somebody gets shot in the head in the middle of Franklin Ave., I'd be very pleased if he fell north, not south. Knowhutimean?" Tommy Jr. knew precisely what he meant. Franklin Avenue formed the southern border of the city with the township of Monmouth Beach. A murder that could be shifted into someone else's jurisdiction was one that the mayor didn't give a fat rat's ass about. He'd known that

Scanlon was fanatical on this matter, to the point, probably, of looking the other way at someone tampering with evidence, like actually dumping an Atlantis vic in another town. But he had never thought the man would come right out and say it, as he had pretty much just done.

"But there's no doubt where this victim got done in, and there's nothing we can do about that now, four days later. Is there?" The mayor took a deep breath. He relit his cigar, neglecting to offer one to his guest. "Okay, I'm calm now." He blew blue smoke upward and contemplated it as it flattened out and dispersed at the ceiling. Remembering his manners, he pushed the cigar box toward Tommy Jr., who knew that it would not do to decline. The mayor slid his Zippo across the glossy desktop.

"The last two – no, three murders in Atlantis, the perps have all been black, right? There was that stupid thieving scumbag TJ Swenker who killed the clerk at the bakery...."

"Yes, Ray Sanchez, the baker actually, who came in for the night shift," said Tommy Jr., immediately wondering why he was correcting Scanlon.

"Right. Mexican baker. Found him face down in dough. Before that it was three black punks who killed another little bastard. Beat him dead, didn't they?"

"That's what we thought, sir. The victim had a gun, but---"

"Who was before that?"

"Selucci."

"Who?" asked the mayor.

"David Selucci. College kid. Brought his girl-friend home for Christmas vacation, found her talking to another kid and threw her off a balcony at the Ramada."

"Oh, right. Poor kid landed on Rita Manahan's brand new Seville. Forgot about that one." The mayor took a deep breath. "Tom, I got a reputation in this city. Some people love me, some hate me. Some people call me a racist. Why? Because I throw the book at criminals. Is it my fault that most of the crimes are committed by the blacks? Fuck, I would say that's *their* fault, wouldn't you?"

Tommy Jr. could have sat there all day without coming up with a good answer to that question, so he said nothing. Scanlon didn't notice.

"But this kid" – he looked down at his newspa-per – "this Fender kid is white. And I am going to throw the book at this kid harder than ever. Getting slapped around by your father is no excuse for murder, mister. Remember that. Hell, who didn't get slapped around a little when they were a kid? This white kid is going to get his ass handed to him, but good. He's just another nigger to me."

Tommy Jr. wanted to protest, or at least lend a little sanity to the "conversation," but they were so far off the sanity map that he had no idea where to begin. And he wasn't about to interrupt the mayor, who was now on a roll. So he kept his face as stoic as he could and feigned rapt attention until Scanlon asked him an-other question.

"Is there anybody who doesn't think it was this missing kid who did it?"

Richard W. Goffman

A picture of his old English teacher appeared in Tommy Jr.'s head as if a TV show had been switched on by Scanlon's question. How to explain…

"Well?"

"Well, Raumbaugh, like I said, thinks it's *proba-bly* the kid, but he's still looking at everything. You know, all the possibilities, the angles," said Tommy Jr. "It's not like it's a total slam dunk."

"But you said…" The mayor let the half a statement hang there like the threat that it implied. Now Tommy Jr.'s neck was stuck out based on capturing and convicting the sixteen-year-old, based on having gotten the mayor's hopes up.

"I know. It's probably him." He paused, and the pause was like a window into his doubt through which Scanlon poked his head.

"There's a 'but' coming, isn't there? Ok, out with it," said Mayor Scanlon.

"Look, Mr. Mayor," Tommy Jr. began. He liked his job, sure, but he wasn't going to be bullied into a corner by this maniac. At least, not so quickly. "We'll pick up the kid one way or the other, and if there's good evidence, we'll book him. And if there's not, we'll figure out who else could have done it."

"I'm sure you'll see that justice prevails. That'll be just peachy. Tell me: Is there anybody else? Any other suspect I mean?"

"Not yet, but this Lemmy Fender, like I said, was a real first class asshole. Probably a bunch of people pissed off at him."

"I'll ask you again: Is there anybody who thinks it is not the kid?" said Scanlon. He watched Tommy

Jr.'s face carefully, and seemed to see something there. "Out with it, boy."

"Mr. Bachman – he found the body – he isn't sure at all…"

"Who the fuck-- Is this the 'high school staff member' referred to so mysteriously in the paper? Who the fuck is he? And how did he happen to discover the body? What's a high school teacher doing in the kid's house at night?" The mayor leaned closer, and his eyes got wider. "This isn't some kinda fag thing, is it?"

"No. No, no no. Nothing like that. Mr. Bachman went to check on Jason, who hadn't been in school that day. I guess he suspected something bad was going on at home and decided to drop by."

"Is that what teachers do? I don't remember teachers ever doing that when I was in school. None of Joey's teachers— Did any of your teachers ever pop over for a visit when you were absent from school?"

"Well, actually, one of 'em did one time," said Tommy Jr., squaring the edges of the papers in the already reclosed case file, not looking at the man across the desk. "Same one, actually."

Scanlon's nose wrinkled, though no new aroma had wafted through the room, nor would one have been perceptible amid the smoke from the now forgotten cigars. He leaned in and looked even closer at the young police chief in front of him. "Are you telling me… Are you telling me that the closest thing you have to a witness is the kid's teacher, who was once *your* teacher? And that this guy has some opinion on who did or didn't chop up the dead guy?" With each question the mayor seemed to put together another piece of a little jigsaw puzzle, and as the puzzle picture got clearer he liked what he was seeing less and less. "And that, because he was your teacher, his educated opinion carries some kind of special weight around my police department? Tell me that's not what you're tellin' me, please."

"No sir," said Tommy Jr. "Not at all. No." There was another longish pause during which the mayor merely scrutinized him, and he looked back. Finally, he sat up a little taller and said what he had to say. "No sir, it's not that Mr. Bachman's opinion gets any special attention paid to it by me or Raumbaugh or anybody else." Tommy Jr. inhaled in order to project the next few sentences into the room. "But he is a really smart guy, regardless of being an English teacher. He's got a clear way of thinking and seeing things. You can ask..." He had been about to say, "ask my Dad." He did not. "You can ask around. He just sees things clearer than other people do sometimes. Fewer distractions, I think, or something like that. I dunno.

"But if it wasn't for him, that Selucci case might never have been solved."

The mayor appeared to be fascinated by this outpouring. The eyebrows were way up, and the eyes were open very wide, for the first time during the entire meeting. His cigar was relit, and his head was nodding ever so slightly. "I see," he said. "Anything else? Anything else I should know about this crime fighting schoolteacher with the twenty-twenty vision? Bachman? Mister Bachman?"

"It's not like that, Mr. Mayor. Look, I do think Jason Fender killed Lem—killed his father.

Raumbaugh found a sneaker print in the blood that most likely belonged to Jason. It led from the body and out the back door of the house. That's where we're focusing our energy, and I know we'll have him in custody in the next few days. Other than discovering the body and calling it in, Mr. Bachman is not relevant. I shouldn't have mentioned him."

The mayor's face managed to unclench without becoming any less watchful. "Pick up the kid. A teenager in bloody sneakers on the run from a butcher job on his old man should not be too hard to find, should he?" The mayor pushed a button on his desk phone, then looked back at Tommy Jr. "You're still here, Mr. Acting Chief of Police. How about you start acting?"

The door opened and Marcia came in with a notebook and a pen, responding to her boss' summons. The mayor was giving her instructions before Tommy Jr. realized he'd been dismissed. He snatched his case file from the edge of Arthur Scanlon's big desk and beat it out of there before the door could swing closed.

*   *   *

Climbing back up to his high perch in the dark, he checked around. The couple of boards stretched diagonally across the corner where the floor was supposed to be were in place, a spot for him to stretch his sore legs. The coffee can with the tight lid was still in the corner where he'd hidden it and its secret. It was untouched.

He pulled the plastic Cumberland Farms bag out of his shirt. He removed the creamy Skippy, the

Doritos, the Wonder Bread and the quart of milk he'd bought. He only now noticed that it was skim milk, and he wasn't sure what that meant. Then he realized he had nothing to spread the peanut butter with. Oh sure, he had a knife, but he couldn't use *that* knife. Besides, it wouldn't fit in the mouth of the jar.

The bread was too soft to scoop out the peanut butter. The Doritos broke when he tried to use them. Finally he'd have to use his fingers, and clean himself after with his shirt.

The traffic was quieting below him. The wind whistled, but only a little. It was a clear, crisp night. He liked being closer to the stars than anybody else in town and they did look closer and bigger from here, though he knew that was probably in his head. Still, the night was clear and moonless, and he found himself dazzled as he looked out over the sea.

He wasn't worried about money. He'd always known all of Daddy's cash hiding places, and now he had enough to keep him safe for a while, if he was careful. He wasn't worried about being found, and he wasn't too hungry.

The cold was going to be trouble soon though.

Chapter Eight

"Aaargh! Not the liver again! Can't you bite me anyplace else?" screamed the immortal Titan Prometheus, in mortal agony.

"Forget it, Prometheus!" Zeus' eagle was having none of it, gleefully ripping away at the helpless god's midsection with her cardboard beak. "This is what you get for defying the will of Almighty Zeus! I bet you'll think twice before stealing fire or anything else from Mount Olympus again, you idiot! Besides, you're supposed to have foresight. Didn't you see this coming? Don't you know any better?"

At this point, Prometheus (aka eleventh grader David Weymouth) unchained himself from the rock where Hephaestus (Zak Stempel) had restrained him for disobeying Zeus (Rosie Lyman, in an excellent example of race- and gender-blind casting) by bringing the spark of fire and wisdom to the pathetic race of humans. He joined the rest of the cast in a slapdash kick line. Linked arm in arm with Zeus' eagle (Sandy Holcomb), they and three other juniors caterwauled their big closing number.

> "Zeus sees you when you're sleeping,
> Zeus knows when you're awake,
> Zeus knows if you've been bad or good
> And he'll stick you with a thunderbolt
> for   badness' sake!!!"

As they took their bows to the not quite thunderous applause of their classmates, their teacher shook his head in awe. "It is truly amazing," Mr. Bachman said, clapping his hands slowly, "how you have taken some of the greatest ideas of the golden age of ancient Greece, an intellectual, artistic and spiritual renaissance unequalled in the 2300 years since, and reduced it to a Santa Claus fairy tale Hallmark card sentiment." Despite the sarcasm, Mr. Bachman's smile, and his laughter throughout the performance, were dead giveaways. He'd enjoyed the skit thoroughly.

With some difficulty, the teacher extricated himself from the student desk in the last row, stood and gathered his papers and grade book. He strode toward the front of the room with his characteristic long-stepping gait which had been compared at different times over the years to that of a camel, a giraffe, and a praying mantis. His friends attributed his odd walk to bicycling; his kids attributed it to the fact that he was a teacher and, as such, had to be weird in at least some way. Bachman was completely unaware of walking in any recognizable or unique manner at all, but he had been told often enough that he could be recognized from a great distance simply from his stride that he accepted it as fact. Being a few inches over six feet tall emphasized it. Beside his desk was a small framed certificate given to him by the class of '81 attesting to his Chairmanship of the New Jersey Division of the Ministry of Silly Walks. It had a picture of John Cleese strutting like a crazed stork, with Bachman's face glued in place of the original.

The gods who had just finished performing gathered their lyres, their flagons of nectar, their wreaths of olive branches, their sandals and their caducei and returned to their seats, mortals once more. Bachman took a yellow piece of chalk and began to write with it on the little side blackboard where he posted homework assignments. The students who noticed him with the yellow chalk began to groan pathetically even before he wrote the first word. Not only were they trained in an almost Pavlovian manner to know that the yellow chalk meant homework tonight; the groaning complaint was their automatic response. Mr. Bachman had long ago stopped responding to it; it was possible that he didn't even hear it anymore.

On the assignment board he wrote, Select one of today's or yesterday's performances and write a publishable in-depth review. Returning the chalk to its shelf and wiping his hands against each other, he asked, loudly, "And what is a review *not*? Mike?"

"It's not just, 'It sucked!'" Mikey Lusick said.

"Right, thank you. Constructive criticism please, everybody."

Richard W. Goffman

"Yo, but what if it *did* suck?" Doo-wayne Franklin asked.

"Nothing is all bad, Dwayne. At least none of our performances completely sucked," their teacher said. A few of the kids giggled to hear Bachman use vulgar slang. "In fact, I'd say they were all pretty good in one way or another. And if you ever find yourself reviewing something that is completely awful in every way, then you had better be able to describe exactly where it went wrong. 'It sucks' doesn't give us any information. Give me news I can use, please."

The bell rang ending period 8 and the school day. An hour later Bachman walked to the parking lot. He was deep in thought: what role would Jason Fender have played had he still been around? Which clique would have welcomed the loner, the stranger into their midst? One of the pillars of ancient Greek culture was hospitality: you always welcome the unknown traveler into your home, give him the best bed and the largest portion of the evening meal, and you send him on his way with valuable gifts. It was the right thing to do; besides, one never knew when the ragged, hungry stranger at your gate was actually Zeus himself, moving about his domain incognito.

The image of Jason as an emaciated, bedraggled traveler in an antique land distracted him until he was quite near his car. That was when he noticed that several kids were standing around it. He hoped they weren't looking for rides home, because his only desire at the moment was to be alone. He put a smile back onto his lips, but before he could say anything the four guys stepped back and Bachman could see what they'd been looking at: his left rear tire, which was so flat that the wheel's hub was touching the blacktop.

"Dag, Mr. Bachman. You got you a flat," a boy whose name Bachman didn't know told him. "Want us to change it for you?"

"Yeah, I see that," said Mr. Bachman, blowing a loud breath out. "And thanks, but I'm sure I can handle it. Changing a tire on a VW is a snap."

"I know, but we want to," said Wesley Alston. A junior who was older than some of the seniors, Wesley was getting Cs and Ds in Bachman's first period class. In auto shop he got straight As. His red hair looked to Bachman as though it had never had benefit of comb, but this did not seem to be a problem for the girls in AHS, who found something the teacher could not see beneath the unibrow canopy sheltering Wesley's deep-set blue eyes.

Bachman looked around the nearly empty parking lot to see if any other teachers were around. It was a simple matter to jack up a Volkswagen and switch the spare for the flat, but it was one of his least favorite chores. Still, it wasn't a good idea to let students do it for him, despite the fact that they could probably do it better and faster than he could. And despite the compelling fact that "they wanted to." The way my luck is going these days, he thought, one of them would get hurt, and his father would be a big litigator.

"I can handle it, guys," he repeated, "but thanks." He unlocked the trunk in the front of the Beetle, but as he did, Wesley and two of his friends were proving that he didn't even need a jack by lifting the lightweight convertible off the ground by its rear end. This was getting out of hand.

"Guys. I got it." He watched them as they lowered the back of the car gently to the ground. Meanwhile the first boy had reached in for the jack, which was in a vinyl sack along with the handle which doubled as the lug wrench. Anthony, that was the new student's name.

Anthony slid the apparatus out of the sack and began to hand it to Bachman when he noticed something. "Hey Mr. Bachman," Anthony said. "What's this? Instructions?" Wesley chuckled at the idea of needing to read instructions for such an easy job. But there was a folded piece of paper stuck between the arms of the scissor jack. Bachman could not think of any reason why it should be there. He suddenly noted a chill in the air that hadn't been present when he walked out of the building on the unseasonably warm early November afternoon.

Anthony pulled the piece of paper out of the slot in the jack where it had been inserted and handed it to the teacher. Mr. Bachman opened it. He read it. He folded it up to put it in his pocket and looked at the four boys who were all watching him. He unfolded it and looked at it again, confirmed to himself that it hadn't changed, refolded it and stuffed it in his back pocket.

"Instructions," said Mr. Bachman, shaking his head as the boys laughed.

Ten minutes later he was putting the jack back into the car. The spare was on the wheel, the lugs were retightened, the flat was in the trunk, and Bachman was thanking the boys who, in the end, had had to be happy watching the teacher, handing him tools, giving advice and commenting on his work. He gave them a wave and a "thanks!" as he swung around and out of the lot.

When he was a little over a mile away from school he pulled the car into the empty lot of Our Lady of Paradise by the Sea Roman Catholic Church, a huge, radish-red wooden edifice on Ocean Avenue across from the beach. He turned off the engine and just sat still for a moment, looking at nothing. Then he undid his seatbelt, swiveled his body a bit, and fished in his back pocket for the folded note which had been stuck to his jack which had been inside his locked trunk. Before he opened it to reread it, he pictured the flat he'd removed. The hole in the tire had been quite visible. It was in the tire's outward-facing wall, not hidden between the treads. It looked like it had been drilled through with a center punch and a hammer.

He spread the paper across the steering wheel. He looked at the note, hand-printed in capital letters on unlined paper.

LET THE POLICE DO THEIR JOB. KEEP YOUR THERIES TO YOURSELF. TEACH YOUR STUDENTS. <u>DON'T INTERFEAR</u>.

Thinking about it once more, it was the painstakingly neat, emphatic double underlining under the ironically misspelled last word – surely not an intentional irony? – that was the most chilling thing about the note.

He refolded it once more, stuffed it in the glove box, started the engine and turned the car back in the direction he had been coming from. He drove past the school parking lot which was now completely empty, made a left on Montclair, cruised by the college, and turned right on Allendale. Four miles later he parked across the street from Ava's. A beer and a shot might be helpful in sorting this through. Going home and reading and being by himself, which he had been looking forward to all day, no longer seemed to be the prudent thing to do.

* * *

R2, the bartender at Ava's, was alone and therefore glad to see Bachman. Someone probably knew the squat, tattooed, full white-bearded, bullet-headed tap jockey's real name, but not Bachman. He'd been tagged with the robot's moniker since the summer of Star Wars six years earlier, and no one's memory seemed to go back past that.

"Ho there, Teach," R2 called out to him as Bachman walked into the bar. "Kids a bigger pain in the balls than usual today?" The powerfully built barman, good at his job, knew that Bachman, as well as Bobby Davidson and the other teachers who sometimes popped in for an afternoon taste, were more likely to show up at 4:30 on a Tuesday afternoon if their students or some other aspect of their day were particularly annoying. Troublesome students and their disciplinary issues were, however, far down the list of things weighing on the English teacher's mind at this particular moment.

He shook R2's meaty fist which enfolded his own hand like an old catcher's mitt. He requested his shot of Pura Sangre accompanied by a very cold Corona. R2 complied briskly, adding the traditional slices of lime on a cocktail napkin, and the salt shaker. Bachman eschewed the salt and the ritualistic licking of the back of the hand; he knocked back the shot, kissed a bit of juice from the lime wedge, squeezed the fruit over his beer and dropped the rinds into the mug. They made a little splash. The chill of the beer offset the golden glow brought on by the two ounces of Tequila, and the lime juice seemed to give it all a little green outline. Abbreviated as it was, something about the entire procedure, as much as the chemical reactions, began to have the desired soothing effects on Bachman's nerves.

"Dude," R2 said. That was it. Just, "Dude." He shook his head with an all-purpose weariness that made a generic editorial comment on life itself. Bachman felt silly about it, but he finished the glass of beer, replaced it on the cardboard coaster, and, nodding and then shaking his head, agreed with R2. He let R2 refill his beer but declined a second shot of tequila; his aim was merely to soothe some shattered nerves, not numb them entirely.

Bachman pulled all five of Ava's darts out of the thoroughly pitted and perforated target hanging alongside the ladies' room door, an arrangement which was clearly a fatal accident waiting to happen. Sure, the regulars all knew how to predict when a girl would be coming out of the bathroom and not drill her, but newcomers were a cause for concern.

Bachman aimed the feathered missiles at the bullseye, coming close more often than not. He had not figured out what to make of the note that had been delivered to him in such a bizarre manner. Couldn't whoever they were have just tucked it under his windshield wiper like a normal mysterious messenger? Did they have to ruin a nearly new tire just to send him to the jack to then find the note? And let him know that they could get into his locked trunk, and then relock it and leave? And what "theries" did he have that they were referring to? It must have to do with the Lemmy Fender case, but what did that have to do with him, really? All he had done was discover the body. By mistake. He had known before he'd hit the floor of the Fenders' kitchen that this tumble was going to lead him to regret ever having entered that house. The truth of this had been reproven half a dozen times already, and clearly, would be again.

"Let the police do their job," it had said. *Ungrammatically*, he thought. *Shouldn't it be "jobs" if it were "theirs"? 'Course, the police (plural) could work together on a single "job,"* he supposed. *Why am I parsing these sentences? What's wrong with me?* A better question to ask himself was: *What should I do about this note?* Part of him wanted to call Raumbaugh and show it to him. No, all of him wanted to do that. Yes, that would be his first step. And yet... what if this had nothing to do with the murder? Then again, what else could it be about? But he didn't have any theories, and he sure wasn't preventing the police from doing "their job." He wouldn't know how to even if he wanted to.

Walking back to the bar for another sip of the second cold draft lager, he took a few of his coins off the polished surface and, beer in hand, sat down in the phone booth near the front door. As he dialed the Atlantis Police, he thought for a moment about showing the note to intrepid *Atlantis Press* reporter Alice Kimsbrough. The desk sergeant answered and at Bachman's request transferred the call to Raumbaugh's extension. As it rang, he clearly saw exactly how the note would look reprinted in the Wednesday afternoon edition. There was a tiny spasm in his stomach, and for just a second he tasted vomit in the back of his throat. He washed it away with the rest of the beer.

Bachman hung up the phone when he realized that it had already rung uninterrupted at least fifteen times. Maybe it was just as well. What could Raumbaugh do?

He went back to hurling darts at the target. He had his own style. Instead of pushing the darts forward from the chest, he took each one and held it flat against his palm with his thumb, point pressed lightly into the center of his palm. Then he bent the arm back over his shoulder, paused dramatically, and whipped his hand forward, releasing the projectile at precisely the right moment. The dart would zip at the target at about twice the speed of ones delivered by the more standard method, striking the cork with a satisfying *thwock*. Often his darts were hard to remove from the board, because they'd gone through into the wood of the wall behind it. He told opponents and drinking buddies that it was a secret Asian style that had been taught him by a Vietnamese guy in an after hours basement bar during a high stakes darts tournament in New York City's Chinatown, but that was pure bullshit. It was all just part of an effort to psych out his opponents, and it sometimes worked.

Bachman realized that R2's initial question still hung unanswered. "Nah, the kids are fine. No worse than usual. Better this year, surprisingly."

But the bartender still stared at him, apparently aware that something was going unspoken. R2 poured Bachman another beer. He rapped his knuckles lightly on the bartop to indicate that number three was on the house, and put both hands flat on the bar. Bachman paused in mid dart-flick, looked at him for a second, and then flicked the dart directly into the bullseye. He walked the five paces to the board to view his handiwork up close, pulled all five darts out again, went back to the throwing line after a short detour to pick up his full cold mug, and began to let fly with his next set of throws. And as he did, he told R2 what little he knew about Jason, Lemmy, and the murder. In the process he was struck by how little he knew.

He kept it mostly in general terms, leaving out a couple of details, but he gave him the big picture. He didn't mention Lemmy's heartless condition, or the note he'd just received. R2 listened thoughtfully. When he was done, they were both quiet for quite a while, the only sound a steady *thwock! thwock! thwock! thwock! thwock!*

"Bill, do you read mysteries?" R2 asked. "You know, detective stories?"

Bachman paused a second between throws, giving R2 a sidelong glance. "No," he said, refocusing on the dartboard.

"How come? I'd think they'd be right up your alley."

"No interest," Bachman insisted. "They're too formulaic—" this was a tricky word to pronounce behind a shot and two-and-a-half beers "-- and the characters tend to be two-dimensional."

"Whatever, man."

"Why do you ask?"

"Well," R2 said, and his voice took on a low, conspiratorial tone, though they were still the only living souls in the place. "I took a crack at writing one once."

This broke Bachman's rhythm. He stopped throwing and looked at the man. He tried to picture the thoroughly inked arms, and the fists with LOVE and HATE permanently etched, one letter to a knuckle, hovering purposefully over a Smith-Corona. "Really, I didn't know…"

"You repeat this to anyone, you'll be that coroner's next project," R2 said. "Anyhow, you're kinda right in a way. There're a few general rules in a murder mystery story. One's that, usually but not always, the victim is sympathetic. Another's that the murderer is powerful. And evil."

"So?"

"In your version of this story, the villain is the victim. The only sympathetic character is AWOL. And, to make matters worse, if we follow your version of events, that character's got nothing to do with the murder."

"Well I don't know…" Bachman said.

"But that's what you think, right?" said R2.

"Yeah. Well, not exactly. See, I don't think you understand my story."

"Really?"

"Yes," Bachman said. "The story I'm telling is not a murder mystery. My story is about child abuse." *Where is this coming from?* wondered Bachman, listening intently to himself. "Jason is the victim, and Lemmy, his father, is the powerful, evil villain."

"Okay. I hear that," R2 said. "But still, there is a murder that's gotta be, you know, solved."

"That's-- That's not my story," Bachman said.

"Then what do you do about the big hole in the front of that large carcass downtown on the slab?"

"I haven't figured it all the way through."

The two men looked at each other carefully, trying to find the answers to their questions in each other's eyes. R2's glittering blue eyes probed the teacher's weary brown ones. Three customers came into the dusky bar and sat on stools near the other end. The bartender did not immediately move to serve them.

"Because now, not only is your victim nowhere to be found, your villain is the victim," R2 said. "So who the hell is the hero?"

There was a long silent pause that was finally broken by throat clearing from the thirsty guys at the far end of the bar. R2 stood and moved toward them without taking his eyes off Bachman.

"Hero?" Bachman said.

"Hope your story has one," R2 said.

"I don't—"

"Because without a hero, not only is your story not really a story," R2 said as he worked, drawing three beers from the taps without breaking eye contact with Bachman. "Irregardless of whether it's about murder

104

or child abuse, it don't matter. But more important, without a hero, you got no happy ending."

"But who… There is no hero," Bachman said.

"Then it don't matter who's right," R2 said, "or what kinda story it is. 'Cause whether that kid is the victim, the villain, or both, either way he's totally screwed."

Chapter Nine

Most of what had happened in school was a blur now. He hadn't been there for more than a week, and already school felt like another person's life. In fact, he couldn't remember much of it. He could remember Miss Chasen, his biology teacher. She was an older lady, probably 40 or something, but still had a great figure. He heard the other boys talk about her large breasts. Whenever she came and checked on his progress with an experiment or a dissection in the bio lab, she always smelled like a perfume that he had a feeling his mother probably wore. Most of the other teachers all blurred together. In fact, the teachers at Atlantis High School had become blurred in Jason's mind not only with each other, but also with their counterparts at the last couple of high schools he had attended. Except Mr. Bachman.

HEARTLESS CRUELTY

He wasn't sure what it was about Mr. Bachman. Maybe it was how he never seemed to get mad, even when a normal person would. Or maybe it was how you always felt like you figured stuff out on your own in his class. Mr. Bachman had a way of making you feel smart. Even when you were dumb.

Like that *Ethan Frome* book. Nobody could figure out why Mr. Bachman made them read this crazy book about some messed up people trapped in a frozen old town in a Massachusetts winter. It didn't make sense. English books usually didn't. Ethan Frome was a tough guy, strong, but he couldn't stand up to his wife. Zeena, the wife, was a dried up old woman. She was like a witch, right down to the black cat. It didn't make much sense that his wife could make him do what she wanted, especially when there was this other, younger, prettier lady living right there in the same house.

Despite how grim and frozen over everything and everyone was in that book, for no reason he knew the fact that two women lived in that house had riveted Jason's attention, and so he had read the entire book, which wasn't all that long. Mattie, Zeena, and Ethan. It couldn't be *that* cold...

When Jason pictured Ethan, the man wore Mr. Bachman's face. He even walked funny, as did the English teacher. The female characters had only generic faces in Jason's mind – Zeena's witchy, Mattie's dark and pretty, neither anyone he recognized. And he could imagine Mr. Bachman making the choice Ethan makes in the book, to refuse to live in an impossible situation.

Richard W. Goffman

Ethan Frome was always cold. When he stayed up at night to figure out his problems, he didn't want to use up any of their precious fuel in the stove, so he just took in the cold. Jason was cold too. He had taken in so much cold in the last – was it a week, or was it much longer? Even before he'd climbed up here to his perch, a real frosty cold had entered him. He wasn't sure how it was affecting him, though, other than that his teeth chattered sometimes.

He remembered now that he was hungry. For a while he'd been too cold to be hungry. The hunger in his stomach was frozen, and thus it had been silent. But it was awake now. It was awake, and it was calling him, calling for his attention so that he heard it even over the sound of the wind. The wind had a voice up here. It was louder than he'd ever heard it anywhere else, and it spoke and sang and whistled. This had freaked him out a little at first, but he'd quickly realized that this was because many of the steel beams were secured with guy wires. The wind blowing across these wires at different speeds and different angles gave it a voice, just like vocal chords gave people a voice. Loose rusty metal plates badly secured to the beams rattled, too, and these gave the voice a gravelly quality.

The voice knew some words. Sometimes it sang without words. Sometimes it spoke.

He couldn't stop the voice, but he could do something about the hunger. He still had peanut butter. It was in a plastic bag hanging from a rusty steel shaft bent up at one end and shaped into a circle, like a huge screw eye. The peanut butter, Skippy Creamy, would not be at all creamy any more. It was easier to scrape out of the jar with his fingers now that it was so cold. He could just reach in and make little lumps of it.

Jason scuttled across one of the boards of his triangular wooden perch above what would have been the twentieth floor of the Nautilus condominium. He'd developed a crabwise way of moving around up there that didn't involve his hands or feet too much, more his forearms and his butt. He noticed now as he reached for the plastic bag that his right hand was quite stiff. In fact, it looked a little like a crab claw because of the shape it was in. His hands were pretty dirty too, he knew. Next time he went down he'd wash up in the public bathroom by the beach pavilion. Then he would have to get those wipe things, the ones with the soap and water already in them. He knew where to find them: with the baby stuff. He had seen mothers changing their babies and cleaning them with those things.

He hooked his hand through the loop and brought the bag to his lap. He saw now that his left hand was as dirty and as stiff and clawlike as his right. Fortunately this was a good shape for unscrewing the blue plastic cap from the Skippy jar. With both hands he reached into the bag and brought out the jar. He held it with his right and applied his left like an open-jawed plier to the lid.

"Righty-tighty, lefty-loosey," Jason said. He twisted his hands in opposite directions. The jar slipped from his hands. It fell into his lap, rolled out of his lap, landed on the nearer of his boards, rolled toward the edge of it, and disappeared. Jason crawled to the edge and looked down. He watched the Skippy jar becoming smaller and smaller as it got farther and farther away, accelerating as it fell at a rate of thirty-two feet per second per second. *How do I know that?* he wondered, as he continued to watch.

The jar was a bullet now shooting toward the earth or, in this case, the building's unfinished cement lobby floor. The blue plastic cap was still visible, but was now just a shrinking turquoise dot in the early evening gloom. Light blue was for creamy, dark blue for chunky.

It fell, and it fell. Twenty stories, Jason said to himself, was a long drop. Was it a football field? People always compared distances to football fields, but Jason didn't remember how long a football field was anyhow, so it would have been pointless.

The voice of the wind through the rusty skeleton in the sky made a harsh laughing sound, a kind of "har-har" in a deep bass. This sound, this wind laugh, covered any sound that the jar made, if it made one, when it hit. To Jason, it appeared to have disappeared. He knew to keep listening after he couldn't see it anymore, because the light would reach his eyes before the sound would reach his ears, because sound travels slower. He didn't know how much slower, so he waited for a full minute, but he heard no sound from below, just the barking guffaw of the wind. Either the laughter covered the sound, or there was no sound, or else maybe the jar just kept on falling and falling and would never hit the ground.

The wind's laughter sounded derisive now. It had been laughing with him before, but now it was laughing at him. It had not done that before. He was quite familiar with the sound of derisive laughter. It had accompanied him through the halls of three high schools, two middle schools, and two elementary schools. In his most recent high school, Atlantis, he had finally gotten good at being invisible and so had escaped most of the mockery of classmates. He'd learned that important lesson: if you were out of it, you got teased. But if you were far enough out of it, you could be invisible.

Jason listened to the laughter for a good long time, until he realized that he had to go. Climbing down was not going to be easy now that his hands had become claws. He could just see himself slipping from the rusty rungs and falling, like a peanut butter jar, accelerating, and yet somehow never quite hitting bottom.

He'd have to get ready. This gave him something to do, and having to do something made his mind clearer. The first thing would be his hands. He tried to put them in his armpits to warm them, but he found that the position was too uncomfortable. His back and shoulders had become very inflexible so that he could just barely reach his armpits with the opposite hands, and it was painful to keep them there. Instead he put both his hands in his crotch and squeezed his legs together. This was better. Not only was it a comfortable position, but the crotch was probably a better, warmer place, being in the middle of the body so to speak.

He sat like that for what seemed like a long time. When his hands got a little warmer he could feel his balls, and that was a good distraction. He had an erection. Now he could rub himself through his pants, stroke himself with his right hand. He thought about

111

opening his pants, but knew it would be difficult, and he didn't really feel like masturbating. The thought of the wind on his penis, the cold and the laughter, there was just no way.

And besides, it was time to go. It was dark now, so at least an hour or two must have passed since the peanut butter jar had fallen, attracting absolutely no attention from anyone, making absolutely no one look up and say, "What the…?" He may even have fallen asleep for a bit, hands in his crotch, face resting on his kneecaps. His black raincoat covered him like a thin cloak. He was truly invisible now, he knew. Someone could be standing ten feet away on the beam and they wouldn't notice this black shape in the corner.

Jason emerged from his black raincoat hiding place. His hands, still stiff and now more painful, were no longer crab claws. He still had the now empty Cumberland Farms bag. Slowly and with much difficulty Jason managed to stand and face the juncture of the huge beams. Stepping on the first of the topmost set of rungs, Jason reached up into the notch in the beam where he had stored the coffee can.

He brought it down slowly. He knew he'd dropped the peanut butter because his hands had been in such bad shape, and they weren't anymore, but still he wasn't taking any chances with the coffee can. He placed the coffee can in the Cumberland Farms bag. He put the bag inside his shirt, against his skin. He pushed the tails of his shirt into the top of his pants all around. That wasn't easy, but it was easier than buttoning the raincoat. That degree of manual dexterity turned out to be impossible.

And now he was climbing down. The rusty rungs were almost 3 feet apart. He couldn't grasp them, he couldn't tighten his hands around them, but he could climb with them so long as he didn't lean away from the building. The rungs were flaky, though they never felt like they would break. *Flaky, not breaky*, he thought. After every two or three rungs he checked the bag. It wasn't going anywhere, but he kept checking it nonetheless. At each floor level he could stop and rest.

When he was nearly halfway down his left hand began to throb. At first he thought he had grabbed a nail or something sharp sticking out of the rung, but there was nothing there, and he knew it must just be a cramp. A minute later his right hand felt the same way, right in the center of his palm. There was something to be said for numbness, he said to himself.

He checked the bag again and took another rung downward. Right foot, right hand, left hand, left foot. It didn't sound right, but it worked. That was how he'd gotten this far, so he was sticking with this method. When he was midway down the fourth story his right foot slid off the rung below him, and his left foot followed. Somehow he held on with his hands, even though they were just sort of hooked around the rungs above. He hadn't realized it, but his feet were numb too. He'd thought that his sneakers were stiff, but he dangled now and realized that it was his feet that had become inflexible. Monkeys had prehensile feet as well as hands. Why had the feet of humans evolved the way they had -- just so they could fit into shoes? That didn't make sense, he knew, but he pictured how much easier it would be to climb down a ladder or a building with hands and feet that all had opposable thumbs.

Jason pressed into the building and just breathed. He placed his numb feet on the rung below, and he rested his chin between his hands on the rung in front of him. This gave him a fifth point of contact. When his breathing was back to normal, he checked the bag again and climbed the rest of the way down.

On the cement floor he felt strangely disoriented, like a sailor on land who feels as though the whole world is a ship that's still rocking, so he stood still until that feeling went away. When he had his "land legs" back, he took the bag out of his shirt and walked toward the beach. He was still very hungry, hungrier than ever. Thirsty too. But there was something he now knew he had to take care of first, so he walked onto the beach.

All along this part of the Jersey Shore, huge stone jetties reached out into the sea. They were spaced about an eighth of a mile apart, were composed of enormous irregularly shaped boulders bound together with cement and topped with massive flat black shalestones so you could walk on them. On the jetty nearest to the Nautilus Jason stood as far out as he could go, and guessed that he was about a football field from the beach. The ocean was on three sides of him. Sometimes waves seemed to hit it from two sides at once, and the spray was so thick around him that it felt like the air there was partly saltwater.

He took the bag out of his shirt. He reached inside and removed the coffee can. He removed the tape that held the plastic lid on tight, and he tossed the lid aside. He reached inside and removed the object within, leaving the can on the jetty, forgotten.

It was wrapped in aluminum foil, and it was inside a Ziploc bag, just as he had taken care to do. He bent over it. It still felt heavy, much heavier than he would have imagined. It still felt soft. He'd thought it would be hard by now, but it wasn't.

A dull light glinted off the foil through the clear plastic. Jason blinked, but the foil was still shining. Standing, he looked toward the horizon. The first pink of the sun was there.

Jason put the Ziploc bag in the Cumberland Farms shopping bag. He flexed his fingers as best he could. With two fingers and his thumb he held the loops of the bag and swung it around his head. He extended his arm and he opened his fingers. The bag flew up. It flew over the nearest waves. Without a splash or a sound, it dove into the sea.

Chapter Ten

Something, he was pretty sure he knew what, must have thrown Bachman's very regular system askew. Not only did he sleep through his alarm on Friday morning, leaving him no time to walk or pedal to the beach, he was almost late for school. Once, last year, he had been late—about fifteen minutes. Fifteen minutes was a lifetime in the world of high school, ruled as it was by simultaneous, coordinated, cacophonous bells of warning and deadline. To his surprised pleasure, his first period class had remained relatively calm and quiet. Most importantly, they hadn't called attention to the fact that they were teacherless in room 323. They'd even taken attendance and sent it down to the office as a way of covering for him, had even stood up and droned the pledge of allegiance along with Richie Calabrese, the senior class president who "led" the school in the recitation each morning over the PA system, before butchering the morning announcements.

That had been gratifying, and he'd paid them back by—he couldn't remember what now, but they did something fun the rest of the period, instead of the lesson he'd had planned. Fair was fair, after all.

He wasn't late on Friday – he just made it -- but he was nearly the last teacher to arrive, necessitating parking at the farthest edge of the parking lot. He got to his class a full 20 seconds before the "late bell." A dozen juniors crammed in after him, but before that final bell tolled. He dropped his shoulder-slung briefcase on his desk with a heavy thud, withdrew the attendance book from his top drawer, and smiled absentmindedly at his students as they and he settled in.

Before he could begin, he spotted a textbook, a math book, lying open on the floor behind his desk. Someone will be missing this, he thought, as he bent and retrieved it. Flipping to its inside front cover, he saw, unsurprised, that it belonged to Dwayne Franklin. He would be coming in next period, so Bachman tossed it on his desk where he would remember to give it to the forgetful Mr. Franklin. Before he moved to the board to craft the morning's first assignment, Bachman took note of the picture Dwayne had used to cover his math book. It was a two-page spread; it looked like it came from the center of Sports Illustrated. In their dramatic photojournalistic style it depicted the complete arc of a basketball shot. The young chucker must have let fly from deeper than half court. Looking closer, Bachman found the caption. Apparently this was the final shot of the decisive game of the NCAA Tournament, the winning shot that gave North Carolina the exciting win over Georgetown. In the picture you could see the scoreboard clock, which registered 00:00. You could also see in detail hundreds of faces of fans, each glued to the arc of the ball, each reflecting some version of hope, excitement, amazement, or dread. The headline of the page was folded over upside down, taped down inside the math book's front cover. Four words: Freshman Hero – Michael Jordan.

Bachman didn't know the name, but he knew from experience that there were no heroes outside of buzzer shots, extra inning home runs, and comic books. "In literature as in life" it used to say at the beginning of essay prompts on the SATs. As in, "In literature as in life, fear of death is often a great motivator…" In life if not in literature, he knew, heroism was a myth. People did things for one of two kinds of reasons: either they had to or they wanted to. If they had to then no choice had been made, so where was the heroism? And if they wanted to, then they received something, something – money, satisfaction, ego gratification, physical or emotional pleasure – in return for what they did.

There were protagonists, not heroes. And there was no way in hell he was going to let himself become the central character in the Jason Fender tragedy.

On the other hand, he couldn't walk away and let Jason face it all alone. The kid seemed so vulnerable. He was like one large open wound walking around in a spiky, jagged world.

HEARTLESS CRUELTY

No, he wouldn't let Jason face what was coming alone, if Jason was still alive. He wasn't sure what his motivation was, and he didn't care. He had to do something.

But what?

* * *

Friday. Writing day. It was a pattern Bachman had gotten used to for the last few school years, and his students very quickly got used to it each year as well. The idea was to get them to associate writing with the pleasure of the end of the week and the approach of the weekend. Inevitably some kids tended to see this as a way of coasting into the weekend. Bachman's job was to get them to take their writing seriously while also considering it fun. Sometimes the line between creative fun and slippery goofing off was extra fine.

Bachman kept his students mainly on the right side of that line by walking around. Many times it had been suggested that Bachman didn't need his big wooden desk and wheeled, high-backed chair, because he hardly ever sat down in class. In reality, he used them extensively, but mostly when the students weren't there. When they were there, he was among them: walking around with that crazy, storky stride of his, poking his nose in, offering suggestions, prodding, coaxing, goading, teasing, stirring the complacent, calming the hyperactive, lighting fires here, putting them out there. There were always kids who needed to be encouraged to let loose, and those who needed to learn how to rein themselves in, and he usually knew which were which.

Richard W. Goffman

Today they were writing poems in the style of "Jabberwocky," the so-called nonsense verse classic by Lewis Carroll. One of the many small pleasures of his job was watching as students glanced at the poem, with its "slithy toves," its "frumious Bandersnatch," and its "beamish boy," rejecting it as the work of a lunatic or an untranslated piece of non-English idiocy. It brought him pleasure because the trip from utter confusion to "Aha!" was an easy, pleasant one for almost every kid, and within five minutes of that first reaction, right after Bachman delivered his dramatic recitation of the piece, they were conjugating the verb "to gyre," "burbling" and "galumphing" grotesquely around the classroom, and developing noun and adverb forms out of the purest twaddle and thin air.

"Mr. Bachman. Mr. Bachman!!" Thörsten Mjelde liked to write fast and hand his paper in first, no matter what kind of paper it was. The first goal Bachman had for his first-ever Norwegian immigrant student was to get him to revise, to edit, to at least look his work over. He took the blond boy's paper without protest, however, and began reading it without missing a stride or slowing his herky-jerky promenade up and down the rows of desks and students. He only stopped when he rounded the last row near the windows. He placed his foot on the windowsill and his forearm across his raised thigh, and he read the first verse of Thörsten's poem.

> In the trick of treaty trumbles
> Freaky Franny flubbed the flee
> Tiny trumpets tooty-totaled
> Underneath the Funyun tree.

Bachman chortled. Thörsten got it, sort of, opening with a seemingly bucolic scene setting with a hint of something just a little… off. Sometimes the kids went too silly with this exercise, but this was fine. It didn't bother him that "Funyun" was the name of a foul-smelling snack food many of the kids loved to gorge on. If anything, this boy's poem reminded him of John Lennon more than it did the creator of Alice and her looking glass. Lennon's assassination, still a painful memory, was only two years in the past, and Bachman had taken it way too personally.

With this melancholy thought in mind he gazed over the top of the paper, between the slats of the Venetian blinds, and out across the school parking lot which spread out below his second story window. Since the "friendly note" had been left inside his trunk, he'd gotten into the habit of checking the car from time to time with a glance from up here.

The day was all bluster and bite, with winter now scouting turf, staking its claim in no uncertain terms. The special bite of salt in your windblown seaside late autumns made the air sharper and the need for scarf and gloves come earlier than it did elsewhere. Huge piles of brown and yellow leaves laid in drifts in the parking lot's corners, particularly on the side that bordered the woods along Benson Creek, where cigarettes and pot were smoked by students when the leaves were green and provided cover from disapproving eyes. This blowzy morning animated the leaves from their drifts, swirling them around the filled parking lot like its own weather system. The leafstorm obscured details, making everything look like it was in motion.

Bachman's yellow VW was in the most distant file of parked cars, probably an eighth of a mile from the window. Far as it was, and screened as it was by the dancing debris racing through the air, he couldn't tell if, as he'd suspected, he'd have to scrape frost off his windshield in the afternoon, as he'd had to do that morning. No sun broke the clouds to prevent the moisture and temperature from glazing the cars with ice. He peered out, but he couldn't see it well enough.

"Thörsten," Bachman said.

The eager boy was up out of his seat, beside his teacher at the window.

"This is good. Nice job." The tall blond boy was, indeed, beamish. Without turning from the window, Bachman changed the subject. "Would you do me a favor? Go to Miss Tonnery's room and ask to borrow her binoculars."

It didn't take sixty seconds for the student to return from the science teacher's classroom next door and press the pair of binoculars she kept for her birdwatching club into Mr. Bachman's hand. Everyone else in the room was busy, except for two girls in the back who, pleased with themselves, were whispering, sharing some of their made-up words with suggestive, illicit glee.

Bachman focused the binoculars. It took a moment to find the car now through them. Something had caught his eye, some movement, and it seemed to have nothing to do with the chaos of the leaves. Finally he located the dull yellow of his car and, with this closer image, shaky though it was at this distance, and buffeted though it was by the blowing stuff, he saw it. It was something, something that didn't belong. Something was on the rust-pocked hood of his car, laying across it. Some blown garbage? A branch of a tree maybe?

Bachman's stomach made a lurching movement, and he thought for a moment that he might throw up, though in fact he hadn't eaten anything so far today.

The binoculars couldn't get him close enough. "I'll be right back," he said to the class. They looked at him with wide-eyed surprise. This was unprecedented. Where was he going?

"Stay here. Please just… Look, don't leave the room, finish your poems, I'll be back in a second. Just sit tight. It's nothing, I'll be right back." With that, forcing himself to appear casual, he stepped out of the room. When he got to the stairwell at the near end of the corridor he took the stairs three at a time, until he got to the bottom, and smacking the crashbar with both hands thrust forward, burst through the double doors.

It was cold, but he didn't feel the cold. Not the cold of the air, anyhow. He fast-walked, then jogged; then, as he got closer to his car, he ran. He was confident that his class would at least obey insofar as not leaving the room, but he knew that by now they were, to a kid, glued to the windows, observing his dash through the faculty parking lot. Despite this, he didn't slow. And the closer he got, the more specific his fear, his dread, and his certainty at what he was going to find.

Then he was there.

Jason Fender lay motionless across the hood of Mr. Bachman's car. His feet were on the pavement, his shins were up against the front bumper, and the rest of him lay still on the hood, arms akimbo. Each of his ungloved fingers, Bachman immediately noticed, was curled. His hatless head was matted, a twist of long, greasy hair, leaves, and sand. His face was turned to the left, away from Bachman.

Bachman stepped carefully to the boy. He touched him lightly on the back, hoping to reach up to his neck, to feel his carotid artery, to reassure himself that Jason was merely sleeping. But that light, almost negligible touch somehow dislodged the still form from the round VW's surface. Before Bachman could react, Jason slid to the cold cement at his feet.

Bachman's jaw fell open as the boy fell sideways. Recovering, he fairly leapt on the boy, now lying on his back, eyes closed, mouth open, fingers still curved into ten purple claws. It was not a shade of purple he'd seen on fingers before. The thin black unlined raincoat was open, and Bachman laid his own face on the boy's chest. With his ear he listened and he felt. Bachman's eyes closed. Then they opened, and in them was a thing like hope. *"...the thing with feathers,"* he thought.

Since the intrusive day of the punctured tire and the warning note, Bachman had begun locking his car each day in the lot, something he'd formerly done only sporadically. Now he cursed the locked vehicle, because the keys were back in his classroom, in his coat pocket, on the coat tree. Bachman got to his knees, swiveling his head back and forth. Not a soul was moving anywhere in his sight. He did some rapid calculations, and then he acted.

Scooping his right arm under Jason's knees and his left under his shoulder blades, Bachman stood. He was appalled by how easy this was to do. The boy felt nearly weightless. His head hung limply, mouth gaping, Adam's apple pointing at the clouds. Bachman took a deep breath, and he began to run with his burden back toward the double doors.

This vision – teacher racing toward school with unconscious person in his arms – had the expected catalytic effect on his students. As if they were a flock of birds they turned in unison from the windows where they'd been watching, but had been unable to see what was going on until Mr. Bachman had risen with Jason from the far side of the car. As one voice, they began shouting, and as one body they darted, faster than Bachman had, out of the room, down the stairs, and out the doors toward the rapidly approaching teacher.

Through their shouting they couldn't hear what he was shouting. As they neared him they flocked around him, quickly realizing who it was he had in his arms, but in the chaos they failed to recognize that Mr. Bachman was still shouting. He was shouting one word, repeating it, but they didn't hear it. How could they? No one had ever seen anything like this before in school. Their minds were effectively blown.

Bachman kept moving through them toward and then through the doors. By this time several teachers and a security guard were there, and Hector, the security guard, heeded Bachman's cry. "Ambulance. Ambulance. Ambulance."

Bachman kicked open the door to a first floor classroom that was not in use. He turned in the doorway, still carrying Jason, and picked Ellie Nelson out of the rapidly growing crowd. "Please get my kids back up to my room." This snapped the other teachers out of their torpor, and they turned and did their best to restore order.

Bachman turned back to the empty classroom. He walked to the teacher's desk at the front of the room. With a wordless look he compelled his pal, Bobby Davidson, who'd just walked out of the faculty men's room and happened upon this unusual form of chaos, to sweep the desk clear with one motion of his arm. Bachman laid the boy on the cleared surface of the desk, and collapsed into the empty teacher's chair. Mr. Davidson put his hand on Jason's neck, held it there for a moment. As Bachman watched, Bobby took off his brown corduroy sports jacket and wrapped the boy's torso with it.

Hector dashed into the room and, with quick gestures, conveyed that an ambulance was on its way. With that, Bachman drew an enormous breath, as though he hadn't inhaled for the duration of his cross-parking lot run.

Ellie Nelson had apparently gotten someone to cover Bachman's class upstairs, because she came in now, carrying his coat. Behind her rushed three paramedics. Two of them were all over Jason, checking his pulse, blood pressure, airways, pulling his eyelids open and covering him with an insulating blanket. The third paramedic shone a light in Bachman's eyes. Bachman weakly waved him off and donned his coat. In less than a minute he was jogging alongside a gurney, climbing awkwardly into the back of the ambulance with the still, shallow-breathing boy who was, even then, still being sought up and down the east coast of the United States.

Part Two

FOR ELISE

Chapter One

"Nobody's forcing you."

If Louise Brantley had recited those words to her daughter, Elise, once, she'd said them one hundred times. Maybe two hundred. She wasn't the only person who expressed this concept to Elise, of course. But she was the only one who, in Elise's way of seeing things, had the right to say it and was allowed to get away with it. Her Moms had, after all, worked two jobs to help Elise pay for law school. Likewise her father had taken every single hour of overtime he could get. Unlike Moms, Daddy never made a single comment to her about her choice of job.

Without her parents Elise would not have earned her law degree. With their financial and emotional help she had, three years ago, become the first black woman to graduate magna cum laude from Yale

Law School. How the offers had poured in, from prestigious firms, including ones she hadn't even heard of! Moms could still tell you the name of every single one. Washington. New York. San Francisco. London. *London!* She'd put it down, at the time, to the pressure law firms felt to "diversify" themselves. In some of those firms she would have been the first woman *and* the first African-American. But she knew that was only part of it. Both her parents and her Yale mentor, Professor Izak Metts, told her a simple truth: the top graduates from Yale Law were among the hottest commodities in the profession.

But they wouldn't remain so unless they acted on it. Heat had a way of dissipating in direct relation to the passage of time and the appearance of newer, younger, and even more accomplished rising stars.

Oh, she'd gone on several interviews. Even some second interviews. But in the end, Elise Brantley had sought out and taken a job with a firm that hadn't recruited her. In fact, when she had contacted Sostyoprak Wepner and Froelich L. P. of Atlantis, NJ, they were skeptical. But every law firm in New Jersey had to fulfill its pro bono obligations. Any New Jersey law firm would have been thrilled to have such a highly qualified young attorney whose wish was to specialize in those cases. As Elise's talent and work ethic soon showed that her law school transcript was neither a fluke, nor an outgrowth of affirmative action run amok, Fehme Sostyoprak had had to insist that Elise make herself available for some of their paying clientele. With all the other attorneys on staff, it took pressure to get them to take the indigent ones.

"I know," Elise said to her Moms about the frustrating behavior of her most troublesome current client. "I know. It's just, well, you'd think he'd have at least as much interest in getting these charges dismissed as I do. Now wouldn't you?"

"Well, you know, Elise," said Mrs. Brantley. "You can not go by what I would think. I would think that that young man would be down on his knees to the Lord giving thanks for the gift of such a wonderful lawyer defending his sorry self." She sipped tea from a china cup rimmed in red, transferred what had spilled into the saucer back into the cup, and then placed the saucer atop the cup, trapping the remaining heat inside. "I would think that the young lady in question would hardly have accused Mr. Santorino of the awful things she says he did out of the clear blue sky. And so, yes, I suppose that I would think that, considering all that, and considering his previous encounters with the legal system, your Mr. Santorino would move heaven and earth to follow your every single piece of advice." Removing the saucer and replacing it on her kitchen table, she took the last sip of her tea. "But you can't go by what I think."

Elise's only acknowledgment of her mother's response was a full-bodied, all-purpose sigh. Gathering the papers that represented the 29-and-a-half hours of work she'd already done on behalf of Elpidio Santorino, accused rapist and thief, Elise swept them into a folder, which she placed into her leather briefcase. She kissed her mother's head. How she loved that head. How surprised her Moms would be if she knew just how influential her comments were to Elise. That thought lived in Elise's consciousness all the way from their Red Bank house to her Atlantis office.

* * *

When the sounds coming from her stomach startled her, Elise realized that once again she had forgotten to eat lunch. Pushing back from her desk she peered over the half wall of her cubicle, blinking. It was the first time she'd taken her eyes out of her work all day.

Santorino had skipped, it now seemed clear. She would have to appear before Judge Eichler one more time on his behalf. Then she'd be able to close that file – not permanently, of course. They often came back, sun-tanned but wide-eyed, humble, filled with regret and good intentions. No, Santorino went in the cool drawer, not the cold drawer.

Meanwhile the hot drawer was wide open. One alleged seller of 500 doses of Ketamine, a large animal tranquilizer. His alleged customers at Vincente Morelli Middle School in Atlantis were too young to be board certified large animal veterinarians. One alleged prostitute and corruptor of minors. One multiple-incident alleged indecent exposer. Three alleged serial breakers and enterers. It did not help that the three, Peter, Simon and Mark Farrell, a set of triplet brothers, continually referred to themselves as "The Farrell Gang," while simultaneously, though not as enthusiastically, proclaiming their innocence. Elise had never met a triplet before, let alone a whole set. As it turned out, they were not much different from twins or – what were the rest of us? Singletons? Except each of them had a couple of clones who laughed at his jokes before he finished saying them. Real hoots, the Farrell Gang.

4:00 in the afternoon, looking for lunch in the office vending machine. Was there anything sadder? Was this the crusade she'd imagined? Izak never talked about this. Izak never mentioned the relative nutritional values of a Nutter-Butter vs. a Toast-Chee. In fact, Elise was pretty certain that Izak Metts, her patrician, septuagenarian mentor, had never eaten anything that had ever been wrapped in cellophane.

Scooping her cookie from the tray at the bottom of the machine, Elise stood, giggling at the image of Izak examining a Nutter-Butter. He'd know what to call the rest of us non-multiple birth children. And he would provide it in the same gentle, non-judgmental voice in which he offered hints and guides to the whereabouts and histories of the most appropriate precedents to every case Elise and the other students in his seminars had studied.

"What's so funny?" Jeromy Clifford, a recent hire, wanted to know.

"My life," said Elise.

"Why?" said Jeromy.

"Because I am knocking myself out to help a bunch of degenerates who don't seem to care whether or not I help them," said Elise. "Because I'm eating a Nutter-Butter. For lunch. At four in the afternoon. Because—" She began to form the words "because I'm a single, 29-year-old lawyer and I haven't had a date in eight months," but decided that she had no desire to give Jeromy the wrong idea, or, for that matter, any other idea about her personal life.

"Because Elpidio Santorino is exactly as big an asshole as everybody thinks he is," she said instead.

"Big shock," said Jeromy, sounding more sarcastic than he had probably intended. Elise knew that the kid looked up to her with something approaching reverence, and that he probably also harbored an unrequited little crush on her too. She let it slide.

Elise turned back toward her desk. "Maybe this one will be different," Jeromy said, and this turned her attention back toward him. He was holding out a new case file.

"For me?" she asked. Elise knew that SosWep-Fro's indigent clients were unofficially code-named Lisey's Losers, though never within her earshot. She snagged it from Jeromy with an air of "no rest for the weary," but the truth was she was glad for the new case. A new case was, initially, like a wrapped gift. Shake it; does it rattle? Heft it; does it have any weight? Hold it out at arm's length; does it give off an aura of importance, or have the shape of destiny?

Or was it just another p.o.s.? Elise had a letter recently from one of her buddies from New Haven, Jed Steubenfeld. Jed was working for the public defender's office for Kings County, City of New York, State of New York. He had a windowless sub-basement office in a massive stone edifice across from the even more massive Brooklyn Criminal Court Building on Schermerhorn Street, where he toiled in obscurity under a daily load of what he and his colleagues, according to the letter he'd written her, mostly called p.o.s. Pieces of shit. Not the defendants necessarily, but the cases. The seemingly endless, apparently hopeless, grindingly depressing cases of poor people who needed defending against The People who accused them of doing depressing, repetitive bad deeds to other poor people. As in, "Here's a new p.o.s. for you to sink your teeth into, Steubenfeld." Would she soon be as cynical as Jed seemed on the verge of becoming?

Too tired to walk back to her cubicle, Elise flopped onto the cracked leather couch and opened the new case file.

And it was, at least, something new. For her. It was a homicide. Her first.

She dug in. It smelled funny, but it was, she pretty quickly determined, not a piece of shit. For one thing, the defendant, a white sixteen-year-old Atlantis resident, was in custody, and seemed unlikely to make bail. She flipped a few pages over, then started poring through it in detail. No mother. No father? No— oh, see there? No father, because the father was the victim.

Oh, yes. This was the one that had been in the paper every day for about a week. She hadn't read the articles, but she'd seen the headlines. The mayor, that pompous empty suit, had been quite enthusiastically quoted about it. His nose was out of joint, it had seemed, about this one. The father found on the kitchen floor, hacked up pretty good. Found by... somebody, not clear who... Oh yeah. This was the one, the dead guy with no heart. The missing kid. Guess the kid wasn't missing anymore.

Elise wasn't tired anymore.

Chapter Two

Andrew Jackson Daggett had long legs. When he stretched them out they seemed to go on forever. At the moment his long legs were extended onto a small table which had once been a spool for Jersey Central Power & Light electrical cable. Though the spool table was three feet from the couch on which he sat, his knees were bent. In the V made by his jean-clad thighs and his bare chest was a shiny, white album cover – "The Wall," by Pink Floyd, which, not by coincidence, was playing at considerable volume through a pair of coffin-sized wooden speaker cabinets. The rest of Daggett hunched forward over the open album cover. He was carefully crumbling a marijuana bud the size of a golf ball over the creased cardboard jacket. The overall impression he gave, or would have given had anyone been observing him, was of a busy, recumbent question mark.

Daggett was rolling joints and speaking on the phone, unimpeded by the ocean of bombastic sound around him. The phone was on his right shoulder, and his head was cocked slightly off center, holding it in place. Mostly he was listening to the person on the phone, and nodding. Occasionally he nodded and commented. Sometimes he lip synced to the lyrics blasting through the room. In a circular amber glass ashtray next to him on the couch were about a half dozen already rolled joints. They were nearly uniform in their size and shape. There was also one behind his left ear, nearly hidden by his stringy brown shoulder length hair. Daggett's lips silently made the shapes of the words:

> *When I was a child I caught a fleeting glimpse*
> *Out of the corner of my eye*
> *I turned to look but it was gone*
> *I cannot put my finger on it now*
> *The child is grown, the dream is gone*
> *I have become comfortably numb*·

Crumble, pinch, sprinkle, lick, twist – another joint was finished, and it went behind his right ear.

"I know what you're sayin', Roon," Daggett now said aloud, into the phone. In addition to the music blasting, Daggett's television, which sat atop the left speaker, was on, although the sound was not. Of all the activities and stimuli competing for Daggett's attention at that moment, the images of a cartoon on the televi-

---

· Comfortably Numb, lyrics by Roger Waters and David Jon Gilmour, ©1979 Warner Chappell Music.

sion seemed to command the majority of it. The conversation appeared to require the least. "I mean, right, I know, dude. Right, I know, I know, no names," Daggett said. "Don't worry. It's mellow. It's all mellow."

Suddenly, his features tightened. In a lower but more definite tone he said into the phone: "Dude, I gotta go. Call ya later."

His hands had frozen in midair, and his eyes had shifted to the line of light at the bottom of the door which led to his apartment's parking lot. The phone fell silently from his shoulder into the cushions of the couch. Carefully and silently he lifted "The Wall" jacket and, without spilling so much as a seed, slid it under the couch. The ashtray full of joints quickly followed. With surprising agility for someone who had lain in one awkward position for half an hour, he hopped silently off the couch, crossed the room, and pressed his back against the faux pine paneling alongside the doorway. In his right hand had magically appeared an eighteen-inch long two-inch diameter wooden cylinder. He held the scuffed, burgundy club − it was, in fact, an official issue New Jersey State Police billy club − cocked above his head as he concentrated all of his silent attention on the doorknob.

It jiggled.

Now, despite the volume of the music, he heard the quiet clicking of a key finding its way into the opening of the newly installed $110 Deluxe Yale dead bolt door lock. His wiry arm coiled a bit tighter, the club drew back another inch, his attention focused preternaturally upon the just barely animated doorknob.

The next song had begun.

HEARTLESS CRUELTY

Hey you! Out there in the cold
Getting lonely, getting old, can you feel me?[·]

With a soft but solid click, the key slipped home. With a loud *clack!* the bolt slid open.

The door swung in, and through the doorway came a petite, brown-haired woman in her thirties. She carried a large shoulder-slung bag, the strap of which could not be seen where it disappeared amid the fake fur collar of her jacket. Disregarding hair height she could not have been more than five feet tall. She stepped into the room, relocking the door behind her, unaware of Daggett's presence.

"Well, look who the fucking cat dragged in," Daggett said. As magically as it had appeared, the billy club was gone. Daggett managed to appear as though he were entering the living room from the general direction of the bathroom and hadn't even looked up until he'd almost bumped into her. By the time he finished pronouncing this sentence he was settling back into his horizontal question mark position on the couch, rolling joints on the Pink Floyd album cover.

"Shut up," the woman replied, not unpleasantly. "We don't have a cat. Unless you're talking about all the pussy that's been here while I been away." She cut the stereo volume in half.

"Janice, I swear to Christ. Don't accuse me, I been keeping it in my pants. Like totally." He hit the turntable button lifting the tone arm, interrupting side

---

· Hey You, lyrics by Roger Waters, ©1979 Warner Chappell Music.

3 of "The Wall." If it wasn't loud, it didn't make any sense.

"Well then, I guess you're glad to see me."

"Of course I am," Daggett said. "And I guess it's safe, now that they have the killer in jail."

"That's what I figured. That's why I came back."

"How's Davey?"

"Oh he's fine," Janice said, emphasizing the word so that it was fraught with whatever meaning one wanted to find there. "If you call casually trying to fuck his brother's girlfriend almost every night 'fine.'"

"I'll kill him. I swear to Christ. What did he—"

"Relax. He was very polite about it. It's not like he jumped my bones or anything. He just made various suggestions. Created, you know, little opportunities."

"But you—"

"Stupid. *Think.* Would I have brought it up if I had done him?"

"So what happened? I mean, with Lemmy?"

"Well," Janice said. She hesitated before going on. "Well, now, that's a good question."

"Sure is. I thought you were just gonna scare him, threaten the big stupid ox and get back what he owes you."

"Yeah." She clapped her hands together and pointed at Daggett with both forefingers. "Well, that was the plan."

"And instead you hacked him up with a fuckin meat cleaver or something? How the hell did you manage it?" Daggett said, lowering his voice to a whisper. "Musta been a big job."

"You're a real idiot, you know that, AJ?" Janice spun around and stepped into the kitchen now, which did not put her out of range for conversation. The whole apartment was strangely silent, but when she opened and closed the refrigerator door there was not so much as a clinking sound from the empty unit. She stuck her head back into the room just as Daggett finished rolling the last joint from the little pile on the double album jacket. "As it turns out, I didn't hafta do a thing to him. He gave me some bucks and we called it square and goodbye. 'sides, haven't you heard? Lemmy was killed by his son," Janice said. "It's in all the papers. The goddamn mayor says it. And that's good enough for me."

"You sound all broke up about it."

She looked at him to determine if he were being jealous, sarcastic, or just stupid. "Not. At. All."

"Okay by me. I'm just glad now you didn't let me come with you."

"Like I said that night, there was nothing for you to do. It was just between me and him."

"When did you decide to make him into hamburger?" Daggett said.

Janice walked to the couch and looked down on him. With her coat off she was a diminutive yet still quite formidable presence. When she leaned down toward him, he could imagine her accomplishing almost any physical task, even kicking the ass of a man who outweighed her three-to-one.

"Listen, asshole," said Janice in no uncertain terms. "I didn't do nothing to nobody, okay, and I sure didn't chop anybody up. We had a nice conversation, we came to a civilized understanding, and I left."

"And?"

"And he was in one fucking piece when I left him, okay?"

"Fine by me," Daggett said. Janice wheeled and went into the bedroom. To the empty space she left behind, Daggett repeated, quietly, "I'm *still* glad you didn't let me go with you."

Chapter Three

Lou Rooney guided his new crystal blue and black BMW down the ramp into the dark of the underground parking facility beneath the Crescent condominium complex. When he got out and slammed the driver's door, it made a sound: *Thunk*. The *thunk* echoed in a very satisfying manner in the subterranean garage. It was a solid kind of sound, and it gave Lou Rooney a good feeling. He remembered distinctly the sounds that other car doors had made, doors of cars he'd driven in the past. When the Beamer's door closed there were no rattles from the window mechanism, no tinny vibrations. This car closed with authority, solidity. Every single time he closed that door Lou Rooney felt like he was closing a door on his past and stepping solidly into his present.

The elevator took him to the eighth floor – the top of the Crescent. This was Scanlon's floor. The Scanlons shared the top floor with Mr. and Mrs. Alphonse de la Croix, owner of Scarborough Funeral Homes, a chain of four establishments spread across the waistline of New Jersey from Atlantis to Hightstown. From the Scanlons' terrace you could see, if your vision were acute enough, sixty miles out into the Atlantic Ocean. From the coffin-maker's place you could see a blue haze which was Pennsylvania.

He had his own key to the mayor's apartment. Of course he never went there on his own, even though it was unoccupied most of the time. He'd been tempted to do it. He'd been particularly tempted when he was with a woman other than Patricia, his wife. It would be so much more convenient than the Atlantis Ramada or the little place up in Keansburg, the Peach Tree Inn. Not to mention cheaper. The boss stayed in the condo mostly on Mondays and Tuesdays, sometimes not even then. Mrs. Scanlon was there even less, especially once the summer was over. But he never asked to use it, and it just wasn't worth the risk of going there without permission, even though it would have been a cinch to get away with it. Maybe he could have asked, as a favor, just between "us guys" kind of thing, but he didn't want to chance it. You had to be careful what favors you asked for, and what favors you accepted. The BMW was a favor. Unless it was offered, he'd stay away from the boss's condo.

With a clatter he dropped the keys into the silver tray on the little table in the front foyer, walked through the living room to the sliding glass doors of the terrace and looked out. What a perch! Without stepping outside – it had gotten pretty fucking nippy, not terrace weather anymore – he could see big tankers out in the shipping lanes. Closer in there were at least six or seven commercial fisherman in sight and, closer still, even a couple of late season party boats. Who the hell rented out a Jersey shore party boat on the Wednesday before Thanksgiving? Rooney wondered.

He pulled his forehead back from the glass door, wiped the glass with his sleeve, and then turned to go about his business. His business was in the closet of the billiard room, so he went there. The balls were racked neatly, and the cues perched in a row on the wall. Rooney wondered when the expensive table had last been used. "Not my problem," he said aloud.

Kneeling in the walk-in closet of what had been the second bedroom, Rooney slid a cardboard box full of encyclopedias to the side and lifted a piece of carpeting which, had one not been in the know, would not have appeared to be cut separately from the rest of the pale blue wall-to-wall in the room.

With the carpet flipped back he was able to reach down into the opening where the mayor's safe hid. Rooney pulled a little flashlight from his inside jacket pocket, turned it on, and stuck it in his mouth. He knew he looked like a burglar, or would if there were anybody looking at him, which, of course, there wasn't. The safe's combination was committed to memory; he'd opened this safe so many times, his hands remembered how to do it, he didn't need to remember the five numbers. In less than ten seconds he'd flipped open the safe door, removed exactly four fat bundles of hundreds -- as he'd been instructed – placed them in the zippered bank bag he'd brought with him, and clanged the door closed again.

He spun the dial just to be safe, but just as he was about to replace the carpet piece and the box of books, something disturbed him. *What was it?* He looked down at the safe in the floor. It was closed perfectly. *What was it?* he asked himself again. It was a sound. In his ear's memory, a moment earlier, there had been an unaccountable sound. Or had there? Like a "shhhh." Like the sound the box of heavy books would have made had he slid it back into place, only he hadn't done that yet.

Still on his knees, Rooney looked at the back wall of the closet. What was on the other side? He thought about it and determined that this closet probably backed onto the closet in the master bedroom. He felt a sudden itch on his back. Like a cigar clenched too long in the teeth, a little drool slid down the length of the flashlight he still had in his mouth, and in that same moment something hit him in the ass really hard, driving him forward. His face hit the floor and scraped on the carpet, and the top of his head hit the wall with a crunch. Had he not opened his mouth in surprise when he did, he might have deep-throated his flashlight. As it was the thing busted open, cutting his lip. He had to spit out a battery. Triple A.

Lou Rooney did not lose consciousness. Once, when he'd had to have all four wisdom teeth out at once, the goddamn dentist had not been able to knock him out, and had finally done the job on a woozy but still awake Lou Rooney. But, taken by surprise, he was completely at a loss, his weight leaning on his hurting face. He rolled to one side, into a ball, trying to get into the farthest corner of the closet, at least long enough to figure out who was attacking him and if he was about to be killed.

Now on his side, he could look behind him. What he saw was the open end of the barrel of a .45 caliber pistol. From his point of view it looked like the entrance to the Holland Tunnel. Only, unlike the Holland Tunnel, the handgun was shaking. And behind it was a half-naked woman.

He was confused and in pain, and therefore unsure of what he was seeing. Taking a breath, he realized that the pain was not only in the top of his head, his neck, his mouth and the side of his face that had slid a foot along the carpet, but also in his balls and his ass, where the well-aimed kick had made contact. Hot tears oozed helplessly from the corners of both eyes, and their salt stung in a hundred tiny abrasions. He took a deep breath while trying not to move. In this way, he figured, he was slightly less likely to get kicked again, or get shot. The breath calmed him a little, and it helped clear his vision.

Just beyond the gun was Dorothy Scanlon, his boss's wife. Dorothy had the gun in both hands. Her right forefinger had the trigger partially depressed. Her left hand supported her right. Clearly she hadn't recognized him yet, so Rooney put both his hands up into an open, don't-shoot-me-please position.

Mrs. Scanlon had kicked him with the square toe of one of her brown leather calf-high brass-featured boots. She had on beige Levis which were tucked into the boots. The Levis clung to Mrs. Scanlon's form like Lycra tights, from where they emerged from the boots, up the length of her long legs, to where they ended at her waist. They were cinched around her waist with a gold chain.

That was all she had on. With both hands on the gun she was only partially concealing her breasts with the upper parts of her arms. Her black hair was too short to be of any help there – this wasn't no Lady Godiva. It tucked around her face in what Rooney thought might be called a pixie kind of style. Blazing from beneath the black pixie bangs, her eyes were wild. They were diamond points of fury.

Rooney knew he was in several different flavors of incredibly deep shit. In the next fraction of a second he could be dead. If not, he could be screwed for letting Scanlon's wife find out about the safe – if she wasn't in on it, he didn't really know. He could be fucked for going there at the wrong time: Scanlon had mentioned that he should pick the money up in the morning, but Rooney had put it off because he'd had business all morning over in Freehold, and he didn't need to meet Scanlon with the cash until that night. And he could be castrated with a rusty bread knife for being in the same room with Dorothy and her naked tits.

He was leery about saying it aloud, but Lou Rooney identified himself to Mrs. Scanlon. "Mrs. Scanlon!" he called her, shifting his weight onto his butt, scooting back to the closet wall, still keeping his hands in front of him in a cross between supplication and prayer. "Dorothy! It's Louis Rooney, Mrs. Scanlon. I'm here for the Mayor, I'm just picking something up for him. Please put the gun down Mrs. Scanlon?" Somewhere along the line someone had told Rooney that it was important to repeatedly use a person's name if you wanted to calm them, and, after a terrifying few seconds, it seemed to be working.

He saw recognition finally dawn in the eyes of the bare breasted Dorothy Scanlon. He saw her body start to relax, abandoning the wide, flat-footed shooter's stance. Although she didn't stop aiming the gun at him, she straightened up to her full height. The .45 was still pointed at him, but no longer at his face. Now that the gun was in Mrs. Scanlon's right hand, she managed to use her left arm to cover her left breast, while her left hand covered her right breast.

"It's me, Mrs. Scanlon. Lou Rooney. Don't, please don't shoot me. It's just me."

Dorothy Scanlon was lowering the gun. Slowly, although she now knew that it wasn't an unknown prowler, the adrenaline that still pumped through her veins made her cling to her fierce defense.

"What in the blue fuck are you doing here?" the Mayor's wife asked him. Clearly she should have known that her husband's right hand man would have access to the place up on top of the Crescent. Something must have made her forget that key fact.

Dorothy Scanlon, he now realized for what must have been the first time, was a fine piece of ass. It had never seemed prudent to give Mrs. Scanlon a lot of thought, nor did Rooney have the time or the inclination to think too much about her. That way only madness lay. Now he realized that his boss's wife was seriously, dangerously hot. He'd assumed she was forty-five years old, like Scanlon. Now, on closer inspection—hell, on very close, intimate inspection -- Dorothy, if she wasn't a decade younger than her husband, had kept herself in good enough shape that it really didn't matter.

She cocked her head to one side and took a scary step closer to him, still holding her breasts, but with the gun now pointed down and pressed against that chain around her waist. She repeated her question. This time she sounded more incredulous than threatening. "What are you fucking doing here, Louis Goddamn Rooney?"

When she said his name, including the new added middle name, he knew that in all likelihood she wasn't going to kill him. And he realized that, along with a badly abraded cheek and eye socket and still throbbing testicles, he had a newly raging hard-on.

He sat up now, touching his hands to his face, gingerly assessing the damage there. "The Mayor sent me here, Mrs. Scanlon. I had no idea you were here. I'm sure he didn't think you were either. I'm sorry. I'm—"

Mrs. Scanlon put the gun on the pool table and squatted down in front of him. Forgetting somehow to cover herself, she reached out and examined the scratches and abrasions on Rooney's face with both her hands. Her face was very close to his. Her eyes were remarkably large and, now that they were no longer ablaze with anger and fear, had a mysterious sense of humor in them. It wasn't easy to keep his eyes locked onto hers, but it was the only safe place for him to look. He saw now that they were green, but that one, the left one, had a brown flaw, a tiny brown island in a glowing green ocean. She was very close. He could smell her perfume, some kind of exotic flowers. "I forgot you had a key, Lou. I don't think Arthur knew I'd be here this afternoon. In fact, I'm pretty sure he didn't. I came on the spur of the moment. There was something I had to get."

She licked her lips. Rooney's head jerked back in an involuntary reaction.

"Are you going to be all right?" she asked him. She straightened his hair with her fingers. "I'm sorry I kicked you so hard. Did I get—"

"Yeah, you did. Not your fault."

"Will they be ok?"

Holy mother of god, she was expressing specific concern for his balls. With her tits out.

"Can you get up?" she asked, stepping back and standing. Rooney got to his knees, and with difficulty pulled himself up by the closet door frame. His breath was normal again, and when he regained his feet she finally, mercifully, turned and left the room. She must have taken the .45 with her, because it was no longer on the pool table. Had it even been loaded? He took the opportunity to quickly replace the carpet and the box, and close the closet door. Then, with the zippered bag in his jacket pocket, he walked into the living room.

Dorothy rejoined him there, buttoning a man's white dress shirt as she came into the room, more or less concealing, finally, some of the intimate details of her beauty that would be stuck in her husband's chief-of-staff's head long after his bruises had healed.

153

Richard W. Goffman

"You must need a drink, Louis. After the or-
deal I put you through." She smiled warmly at him. "I
know I do. You really freaked me out."

He thanked her, and she poured Chivas from a
bottle that was already out -- and open – on the bar
opposite the glass doors to the terrace. She gave him
another smile. Somehow she looked down into her
glass and, without lifting her head, looked up at him
with those big eyes. The effect was instantaneous – it
drew him into a little circle with her, an intimate little
conspiratorial circle of knowing.

"Are you going to tell Arthur what happened?"
she asked in a voice that was softer than the one she'd
been using.

What had happened? "I don't—I'd hate for
him to—" Rooney stammered. He didn't know what
he should or shouldn't tell Scanlon. Furthermore, he
didn't know what he should or shouldn't tell Mrs.
Scanlon about what he was doing, or why he was there.
The more he thought about it, whatever he said, he
was probably fucked. "I guess you'll tell him. You're
probably pissed that he didn't let you know..."

"I think maybe I *won't* tell him," she said. "Why
upset him?" She took her first sip of the Scotch.
Rooney watched her do it. She drank slowly, sipping,
savoring. He admired the muscles of her throat as they
worked the liquid downward.

Showing him her eyes again, she repeated herself. "I'm not gonna tell him. It would only upset him,"
she said. She looked down. "You didn't do anything
wrong—we didn't do anything wrong. Nothing happened. I mean, you got hurt. That could have hap-

pened some other way—right?" She gave herself a little hug. "Are you mad at me?"

"Of course not," Rooney said. "You thought a burglar was in the place. If youda shot me, it woulda been understandable."

"I'm glad I didn't," she said.

"Not as glad as I am," he said. He swirled his drink. It tinkled.

She gave him the conspiratorial smile again.

Rooney finished his drink and sucked a piece of ice into his mouth in the hope that it might help with the pain. He thanked her, apologized a couple more times, and let himself out. On the way down in the elevator, which was paneled with mirrors, he finally saw the damage to his face. Had he been flirting with her with this face, he wondered? A huge angry red scrape ran from the corner of his right eye back to his ear. He had a fat lip, and there were speckles of blood on his collar and his tie.

When the elevator stopped at the parking level Rooney almost jumped. I gotta get a grip, he thought. Maybe another Scotch. As he thought about the drink he'd just had, he wondered -- how had ice had appeared in the glass? There was no ice bucket on the bar, and Dorothy had not gone into the kitchen. He pictured her lifting her glass. It too had tinkled with ice. More interestingly, there'd been lipstick on it, he was sure, before she took that first sip.

"Shhhh." That's what the little almost-sound had sounded like. No, neither of them would mention their little tete-à-tête to the Mayor.

Rooney took a closer look at his facial damage in the Beamer's rearview mirror. He sighed. He backed out of the space, and then drove forward at an angle, crushing the front driver's side fender, creasing the bumper and obliterating the headlight on that side. Then he backed out, turned and, with a squeal of tires and a spray of shards, sped up the ramp and headed toward city hall.

Chapter Four

VICTIM'S SON, SLAY SUSPECT, HELD
Ambulance carries teen from ICU to Cell
By ALICE KIMSBROUGH
ATLANTIS PRESS STAFF REPORTER

ATLANTIS, December 2– Nearly three weeks after he was brought, unconscious, into Monmouth Regional Medical Center's emergency room suffering from frostbite, pneumonia and other serious medical conditions, Jason Fender was transferred Wednesday to the county jail in Freehold. Fender, 17, a junior at Atlantis High School, has been arrested by Atlantis Police who are accusing him of the murder of Sylvester Fender, his father, in October.

Acting Police Chief Thomas Gallagher, Jr. told reporters on Friday morning that the young man had been formally accused of the stabbing death of his father. Fender is expected to appear before the Grand Jury in Freehold next month. If indicted, trial proceedings would begin in March next year.

Fender appeared with counsel before Judge Denise P. Atherton Friday afternoon. A court appointed defense attorney, Elise R. Brantley, of the Atlantis firm Sostyoprak Wepner and Froelich L. P., entered a plea of not guilty on behalf of her client, who sat silently in a wheelchair. Fender did not speak during the five-minute-long proceeding. Judge Atherton denied Brantley's request for bail. Citing the young man's medical condition and lack of family or other support system, Atherton told the accused and his attorney that jail was the best possible option for him at this time. She did promise, however, to reconsider setting bail at a later date.

Fender was brought to Monmouth Regional Medical Center November 11 by ambulance from Atlantis High School and placed in the intensive care unit. He was listed at that time as being in critical but stable condition. A hospital spokesman declined to answer reporters' questions about what, if anything, Fender might have said to them at any time during his hospital stay.

Though he was on school grounds when he was located, Atlantis High School attendance records show that Fender was absent from school on that day. In fact, Fender had not been in school for the previous two weeks, and his whereabouts had been unknown since the night, October 27, that the brutally stabbed body of his father, 40, was found. A manhunt had police departments up and down the east coast as well as the Federal Bureau of Investigation searching for the missing boy who, it now appears, had never left Atlantis. He was found, unconscious, in the high school's parking lot by Mr. William Bachman, an English teacher at the school. Fender has been enrolled in the eleventh grade at Atlantis High School since September of this year, and is a student of Mr. Bachman.

Bachman, a veteran teacher with eleven years at Atlantis High School, is highly regarded by the administration, faculty, and student body. He was voted Teacher of the Year in 1981. Bachman could not be reached for comment for this article.

November 30, 1983 12:30am WRB

I don't get it. Maybe, maybe I can pick it apart.

From what I can gather, Jason hasn't uttered a single word since he's come back. I wish I could see him. Wait, that's not entirely true. I think he said something to me in the ambulance. He didn't really open his eyes, but they fluttered a little. I couldn't catch what he said. Maybe it wasn't anything. Probably he hadn't spoken a word out loud since that night. Hell, he hardly ever spoke on a good day. Maybe it was just groaning, just a noise. But that's not what it sounded like. Wish I could rewind and listen to it a couple of times, maybe I could figure out what he was trying to say. Like trying to catch the lyrics of a new Dylan song.

Anyhow, now they say he'll live. I wasn't sure at first. His pulse sounded so weak, and he felt like he weighed nothing. I can't believe this kid has nobody, not a relative or family friend who... who am I kidding, I can believe it. That house did not look like a place where a family lived. So, other than cops and lawyers and authorities, I'm the only one who has even tried to look in on him. (Guess I'm an "authority" of sorts, eh? Ha.)

The emergency room was a real trip. They kept asking me my "relation" to him. There was no category to check called "Teacher," and "None" sounded so... pathetic and lonely, I guess, not to put too fine a point on it. I care about Jason, and I'm worried about him, but I gotta be careful to make sure I don't become his "family."

He does have a mother. (Everybody has one at some point, right?) Raumbaugh told me.... What? I don't remember, just that she was there, but she left. Still alive? Possibly. Wonder where she is, when Jason heard from her last – never? And what about Lemmy? Doesn't seem likely, but he must have had some kind of relatives.

Speaking of Raumbaugh, his was one of two phone messages in my mailbox when I swung by the main office this afternoon. I've got to call him, as well as a Ms. Elise Brantley, Esq. who is apparently Jason's lawyer. Everybody seems to think I know more than I do. I hate having to disappoint them.

The bulk of the reporters had stopped hanging around the station, with a few exceptions, one of which was Alice Kimsbrough. Alice had been a freshman when he'd graduated AHS, but Tommy did remember her. She was the girl with the long crazy curls, the tallest girl in the freshman class. One of his buddies, Carmine Solamini, said she was a lesbo, but Tommy was pretty sure that was just because she'd shot him down when he'd asked her to go to the Red Bank game. She looked pretty much the same now as she had all those years before, except she had even more curly hair. A strange girl, but there was something about her.

Anyhow, Tommy Jr. had gotten into the habit of coming in through the back parking lot entrance, mainly to avoid having to talk to reporters. Secretly he hadn't minded so much – at first, that is. But having to find new ways to say "I don't know," got old pretty quick.

The receptionist's voice cut through to him before he got to his desk. "Senior on two!" Celeste had worked for Tommy Jr.'s dad since Tommy Jr. was a child. It was natural, he supposed, that she openly referred to them as "Senior" and "Junior."

He punched line two. "Hey, Dad. What's up?"

"Nothing," his father told him. "I'm taking the boat out today. You can't get away, can you?"

"Take Mom."

His father laughed. "I think you're missing the point. Of fishing, I mean."

"No, Dad. I know the point of fishing ain't the fish," Tommy Jr. said. "But I can't believe you're forgetting—"

"I haven't forgotten," Tommy Sr. said. No one knew the pressures of the job better than the man who had held it previously for so many years. "I know what you're going through. Just thought I'd ask, is all. Sometimes it helps to clear your head."

"Yeah, I know. I just can't afford to right now is all."

"Has the kid said anything?"

"Not a word," Tommy Jr. told his father. He couldn't hide the exasperation; fortunately, with his dad, he didn't have to try.

"You mean not a word to you, right? Has he talked to anybody else?"

"Not that I know of," said Tommy Jr. "You mean, like his lawyer? If I'm not mistaken, she's as frustrated as I am. Raumbaugh too. Doctors and nurses at the hospital all say he never spoke. And I'm sorry to say he still hasn't."

"Can't?" Tommy Sr. asked. "Or won't?"

"Tough to say. Raumbaugh says that he thinks the kid hears us, but he can't even be sure of that. Dr. Kingson says he's in shock. High Hat" – this was their private nickname for Mayor Scanlon – "is sure the kid's carefully laying out his groundwork for an insanity defense. He'd like to come down here and beat a confession out of him. I'm sure he thinks I'm a girl because I haven't done it already."

The Acting Chief said this last to the former Chief with just a touch of sardonic laughter. As he did so, lines one and three on his phone started to blink simultaneously. "Dad—"

"I know, I understand," the father commiserated with the son. "Hey, Tommy..."

"What Dad?"

"What does Mr. Bachman think?"

This was a question the younger Gallagher had been asking himself, too. It wasn't clear which of the two men on the call had a higher regard for the English teacher's wisdom when it came to reading what took place inside the heads of young people.

"I don't know, Dad. He hasn't talked to Mr. Bachman, either. And I... I don't want to ask him what he thinks just yet."

"Why the hell not?"

Three officers knocked on the open door and walked into the Chief's office. "Dad, I gotta go. Go catch some fish. Talk to you later."

December 11, 1983

Dear Jed,

Thanks for your very funny letter, sorry it has taken me so long to get back to you. Of course, I don't have to tell you about how busy I am, because I know you're just as buried as me. In fact this will have to be short. Maybe we can get together over the holidays to really catch up?

Yes, I have had more than my share of Pieces of Shit. When we both have more time, make sure you ask me about the Farrell Gang. You'll laugh.

Finally though, it looks like – MAYBE -- I may have my first non-P.O.S. A 17-year-old accused of hacking his father to death. I know what you're thinking, sounds like more of the same only bloodier. But I think this will be different. For one thing, the mayor of Atlantis has weighed in heavily, law and order, blah blah, in favor of putting the kid away, why bother with a trial, etc. Why is the mayor even talking about it? Maybe because the kid is white, the father was white, and the mayor (also white) has an opportunity here to show how non-racist he is. (Is

163

there such a word?) Maybe he's got a thing about patricide. I don't know.

With the mayor shooting off at the hip and all the related publicity – which is no help, of course – the whole town is very freaked. My client was found near death in the parking lot of his high school, having been MIA two weeks, since the night of the murder. I've met with him twice now, for a total of about an hour, and – guess what? He's got nothing to say. No, I don't mean he doesn't want to talk about it, I mean he's got NOTHING to say. The kid hasn't spoken – to me or anybody else – since he's been brought in. And I don't think he's being tight-lipped. He's got this weird, faraway look on his face, his eyes are not completely focused. Hell, I don't know if he's hearing what I'm telling him. I've got to figure he saw the murder, was traumatized, is in shock... like that, right? Except I'm not completely sure that's what's going on. It may be my best defense, but I don't know enough yet. In fact, I only just now got the coroner's report, just as I took a few seconds to write you, so I've got to pore through that now and see what there is to find.

Anyhow, my name's been in the paper, although it's just a local Jersey Shore rag. Still, I guess I'm more famous than you so far, right?

Fight the good fight, and call me sometime, will you?
Lise

Mr. Bachman turned right off of Ocean Ave. onto his street. Bradley Avenue formed the southern boundary of Atlantis. The next street over was Asbury Ave., in the village of Sea Haven.

He drove the block and a half west to where the white curbstones changed to grey; this was where he lived. Pulling up his steep driveway, he stopped at the top and set the parking brake. He turned to get his bag out of the back seat. The phone message from the lawyer lay beside his bag on the seat. He tried to convince himself that he didn't need to return the call immediately, that he could go in, pour himself a little something, relax. Call her back later. Tomorrow, maybe.

Cutting across his lawn, Bachman was surprised to see someone standing on his porch. Dark-skinned and well dressed, the stranger had turned and watched him approach, one foot on his porch, the other on the top step. Who...? He looked at the leather briefcase she held, and her upright stance that made her appear taller than she was. He wasn't going to have to call Elise Brantley, Esq. back at all, he now saw. As he walked up his own steps, he could not for the life of him remember: had he left yesterday's clothes on the living room couch this morning?

Chapter Five

"I've done my homework, Mr. Bachman."

Bachman couldn't suppress a small chuckle, but before he could comment his guest picked up on the irony.

"I guess you hear that a lot," Elise Brantley said. "In my case, it's true." She didn't smile when she said it. He could tell that this young woman took her homework seriously. In fact, she looked like she took everything very seriously.

The lawyer sat with her ankles crossed on one of Bachman's three unmatched porch chairs; the pitcher of ice water he'd brought from the kitchen and placed on the small, round, glass table remained untouched. By agreeing to talk on the glass-enclosed part of the porch she'd relieved him of the embarrassment of having to expose his poor housekeeping skills.

Whether she had done this for his benefit or her own didn't matter to Bachman. Although he had not, in fact, picked up his clothes in the living room last night, or washed his breakfast dishes that morning, he had remembered to leave kindling and sticks in the little cast iron stove that now warmed the otherwise unheated room. A single match had soon made the seating area habitable.

He observed her from the vantage of his favorite chair. With its bamboo frame and soft cushions, he thought of it as his drinking chair, because he could easily rest a glass on the wooden porch deck and retrieve it without a strain, while watching the gentle pace of life in the south end of town pass by.

From this position he looked up at his guest. She was young, but maybe not so young as she looked, he thought. Her manner, her outfit, her vocabulary... everything about her spoke of formality. The briefcase bore her initials, etched into the brass closure.

He noted belatedly that she was beautiful. He hadn't seen it right off, partly because he'd been intimidated by her lawyerliness, and partly because her arrival had made him think about Jason, sitting silent and alone in the county lockup. But once he saw it, he found it harder to concentrate on what she was saying. Instead his attention was drawn to her high, round cheekbones, and percolating just above them the depth and inquisitiveness of those big almond eyes. Her skin was dark and rich. Despite her subtle gray pinstripes she shone like mahogany. Although she was all business, he knew what those eyes would look like if they smiled. He could see it.

"By homework I mean research," she said. "I've read all the police and court files on the decedent, Sylvester Fender. I've looked at my client's school records, and not just from your school. This kid has been to eleven different schools in six different school districts in his short life."

"Wow," Bachman responded.

"Yes. And, of course, I've read everything in the file on this case. I've talked with Detective Raumbaugh, the cops on the scene, Chief Gallagher, Dr. Patel, the coroner." As the attorney ticked off each contact she'd made, she thumbed over a notebook page, barely looking at it, each corresponding to an interview she'd done.

"Those are the officials, the folks who have come to know Jason Fender or his father since the incident," she said. "Now I need to get to know Jason more personally. And, as you know, Jason himself has not been forthcoming."

"He hasn't spoken to you, either?" Bachman asked.

"To my knowledge, Jason hasn't spoken since he has been in custody. Maybe he hasn't spoken since this horrific event happened." She paused, as if something had just occurred to her.

"Has he said anything at all to you?" she asked him.

He said "No," but his brief hesitation was apparent to both of them. She pressed the question with a lift of both neat eyebrows.

"I wish he had. When I— In the ambulance, after I—"

"I understand that you found Jason in the school parking lot and carried him into the school, then accompanied him to the hospital. Please go on."

"In the ambulance he opened his eyes and tried to speak," Bachman said. "I don't even know if he knew where he was or who I was at that point. Nothing much came out. He might have been moaning in pain. He was in terrible shape."

She looked at him in attentive silence, as if he were still not finished with his thought. Was he finished with his thought? The expectation in her face made him question himself: What am I holding back? Nothing, he told himself. Then, to her, he said, "I was terrified. I had thought he was dead when I got to him, and then I thought he was dying right in front of me."

Ms. Brantley looked down, and this seemed to release him from her grasp. Then she was back.

"Do you mind if I ask you a few questions?"

"Not at all," Bachman said. "That's what we're doing, right?"

"You're Jason's English teacher. You've had him in your class since September. His attendance has been pretty regular since school began, until the day after the incident.

"You don't have Jason for study hall," she went on, "or homeroom, or any other classes during the day. No extracurricular clubs or teams or anything."

Bachman smiled. "I'm still waiting for the question," he said.

Elise Brantley smiled then also. It was just for a second, but it was memorable. Then she was completely serious again.

"Why you, Mr. Bachman? I guess that's the first question I'm driving at."

"It's a pretty good one, Ms. Brantley. But it's one I don't really have an answer for. Why did I go with him to the hospital? Because I'm the one who saw him in the lot, and he was lying, unconscious, across the hood of my car when I spotted him. Why did he go to my car? Did he even know it was my car? I'd have to say he did know. He would have known because I had given him a ride home – or to his neighborhood, any-way – the afternoon before the— his father's—" The word "murder" would just not take shape in his mouth.

"That night," the lawyer offered helpfully.

"Right," Bachman said. "And, to answer the next question, which has to be 'Did Jason say or do anything that seemed unusual to you?', the answer has to be 'No.' I mean, he was a really quiet kid before this. He would speak to me on occasion, about school stuff, but usually only one-on-one, rarely in class in front of the other kids."

"Are you aware that there is nothing in the po-lice record about your drive from school to his home?"

"I am."

"Making you the—"

"—the last person known to have seen Jason before the night of the murder."

They were quiet for a bit. She could wait for an explanation of the apparent lapse, although none was forthcoming. Finally Mr. Bachman broke the widening silence. "I'm not surprised. The fact that I gave Jason a lift is not significant. However, the police do know about it, just as they know the specifics of how I accidentally discovered the body the next evening. I'm grateful that my name is not any more prominent in the public record than it has to be."

"Why?" she said.

"'Why?'" he repeated, as if it were a self-answering question. "It's bad enough to be involved at all, if, by 'involved' we mean being the person who discovered the body. Being a teacher in Atlantis brings with it a certain amount of scrutiny of one's actions beyond the classroom. And if you are as curious and thorough as I'm beginning to understand that you are then you will find out that this will not be the first time I have had peripheral involvement with a criminal case in this town." Bachman exhaled mightily after saying this, making it sound like more of a confession than he'd meant it to be. "And I emphasize the word 'peripheral.' Nevertheless, that involvement has not endeared me to my department head, or my building principal."

Elise Brantley was a good listener, Bachman now saw, and he added this to the inventory of surprising characteristics he was noticing about this young woman. For the first time during their conversation, she made a small note with a ballpoint in a little notebook. She folded the page before closing the notebook. Then she stood.

With far less grace Bachman climbed out of his low perch. Ms. Brantley shook his hand.

"Mr. Bachman, I find that the longer I talk to you, the more questions I have. And please understand that that's not a bad thing, nor does it imply anything that could possibly irritate the powers that be at Atlantis High School. But if you do not mind, I would like to make an appointment for us to talk at greater length."

Bachman did not reply right away, and she was prompted to reassure him. "Really, I won't take up an inordinate amount of your time. It's just that I believe you may have more insight into Jason and his situation than anyone else I've spoken with. Maybe more than you realize. I won't drag you into anything, Mr. Bachman."

"Okay," he said.

"Would Friday afternoon be okay for you? Say, four o'clock?"

"Okay," he said.

"Could we meet somewhere else to talk?" she asked.

He almost said "Okay" again, but then he recognized that he was sounding like a robot. He indicated his porch and his little wood stove. "Not impressed, hm?"

"Actually, I am impressed, Mr. Bachman." And then she smiled. For more than a second.

"Really, this is lovely. I'd just like to sit and talk someplace where the chairs are the same height. Perhaps you could come to my office?" She hadn't stopped observing him acutely, and perhaps for that reason she added an alternative. "Or we could have coffee somewhere else?"

Indeed, Bachman hadn't relished the prospect of possibly being spotted going into the office of Sostyoprak Wepner and Froelich L.P., across from the municipal building, the courthouse and the police station. They agreed to meet at the Bayview Diner, then

172

she had her coat on and they were outside on his porch, where he'd first seen her. Ms. Brantley thanked Bachman warmly, descended the wooden stairs and walked toward her car, which was parked just up the street. Before she left his front yard she turned back to him.

"You seemed surprised," she said, "when I told you how many schools Jason had been enrolled in in the last several years."

Again, not a question, but he answered the implicit one. "Yes. I mean, I wasn't surprised exactly, but it is pretty shocking. Because no, I hadn't known that. I almost never read a student's file. I can, but I don't. I like to wait, to form my own impressions, before I find out what people before me have said about a kid, or what his past has been like. Then, once I have formed my own impressions, I generally forget to get around to looking at the files, at the history. The few times I have, it's never done me, or the student, much good."

Elise Brantley digested this last bit of Bachmanalia, gave him a little wave, turned and left. For his part, Bachman remained coatless in the chilly breeze on the porch for several minutes after she was gone.

Chapter Six

Bachman knew why Raumbaugh wanted to see him: the note. He'd mailed it to the detective, with a note of his own describing the punctured tire, the note's placement inside the locked trunk of his car, and begging him to keep it to himself. He'd actually felt an irrational sense of relief to get it out of his house and out of his possession; the thing had creeped him out that much.

Would the note, the physical thing itself, provide Raumbaugh with any clues to the true identity of Lemmy's killer? The paper it was written on? The ink? Was he kidding himself, picturing the dingy old gumshoe getting a chemical analysis of the note? Was he watching too much TV? On the other hand, *give Raumbaugh some credit*, he thought. He'd earned a level of respect over the years that belied his crappy office and shabby appearance. He'd caught some bad guys.

If not physical clues, what about the note's content? Persons unknown wanted Bachman not to "interfear," to keep his "theries" to himself. What theories would the note's author assume he had? Would it be assumed – correctly, he supposed – that Bachman didn't buy Jason as the murderer? It was true, he didn't. At least, he didn't buy it automatically, as everyone else seemed to have done. And the fact that somebody had threatened him with harm to induce him to "let the police do their job," as ridiculous as it sounded, did lend credence to the likelihood that there *was* more to Lemmy's murder than an angry son striking back at an abusive father. So, it could be said to have the opposite effect from its intended one. Okay, maybe persons unknown were none too bright. And why threaten Bachman? It didn't make sense. Nobody gave a crap what he thought, did they? Or, if they did care what he thought, why did they care? He didn't have any influence with the police.

It didn't make sense to him, and for that reason he was actually looking forward to talking with Dick Raumbaugh. Maybe the detective would be able to put his mind at ease, about the note if nothing else.

Pulling into the parking lot at Atlantis Police headquarters, Bachman cruised the lanes looking for a spot that was both empty and not adorned with a proprietary identifier stenciled in white paint. Finding one at the end of the third row, he wondered if his frequent invited visits would soon merit him a spot with his initials painted on.

Richard W. Goffman

Sergeant Calabrese at the desk greeted him by name, reinforcing Bachman's reluctant realization that he was rapidly becoming known around the police station, and buzzed him through the outer door. Bachman nodded to him. To be fair, the sergeant knew Bachman from school more than the cop shop. His son, Richie, a pleasant goofball of a student, had had a remarkable hook shot and an equally impressive jumper. Bachman had filled in as assistant basketball coach for a couple of games two years ago when Bill Thompson had broken his foot, and he'd gotten to know Richie and his dad pretty well back then.

Bachman found the door he was looking for wide open. He knocked on the doorframe, walked in, and shook hands with Detective Raumbaugh.

"Leave the door open," Raumbaugh said as he sat back down and indicated the chair before his desk for Bachman. Bachman preferred it open, relieved to have less claustrophobia in that cramped space than last time. Looking around, he noticed a few other changes. Had someone cleaned up in here? Not much, but it did appear less crowded than it had before, and just possibly the piles, though still everywhere, were sort of squared up and neater. Wonders never ceased.

Even the man himself looked a little tidier, the tie a little straighter, the shave a day or two more recent. Maybe he was up for a promotion? Maybe he had a new lady friend. Bachman decided to stop thinking about it.

Raumbaugh opened his mouth to speak but Bachman cut him off. "Listen, I know you're probably pissed off at me. About the note. I mean, about holding on to it for a week before sending it to you. I'm sorry about that. I was pretty frazzled by it, so I put it out of my mind. I put it so far out of my mind, I guess, that I forgot about it for a few—"

"Fuhgeddaboudit," Raumbaugh told him in no uncertain terms. "Not a problem."

"I know," Bachman said, "but—"

"I said forget it, and so forget it," said Raumbaugh. "It don't matter anyhow."

"Really?" Bachman was astonished. He knew Raumbaugh to be, despite all outward appearances, a very thorough guy. How could that note not matter at all, he wondered?

"Yeah," Raumbaugh said. "Really and truly. I got no idea how you got that note, but it ain't important."

"How do you know it isn't important?"

"Lookit. Number one, we don't know who sent it. Number two, you got no idea if it even was meant for you."

This confused Bachman, and Raumbaugh responded to the confused look on his face. "You found the note in your car?"

"Yes," Bachman began, but then corrected himself. "Well, no, actually a student found it – they – some kids wanted to help me fix a flat tire. One of them took out the jack and it was stuck in there. But—"

"So. The note ain't addressed to you. Or anybody. It ain't signed. A wise-ass kid messing around with your car says it was in the trunk. The kid mighta written it and given it to you for a joke. Or it mighta been meant for somebody else's car. Or, or, or. You get any more mysterious notes lately?"

"No, but—"

"Okay. So forget the friggin' note, okay? I mean, I know you thought you were doing good by sending it in, and that's fine and all. But it's over."

"'Over'?" Bachman repeated, now a little more confused.

"Yeah, over. This thing with the big dumb dead guy. Lemmy Fender is dead. He was killed by his kid. And you know what else? If I was that kid, I'd a killed that cocksucker too."

Bachman hadn't expected that. The surprise and disorientation made him a little nauseous. He'd thought Raumbaugh would have some ideas that differed from the party line. Had the detective discovered something that reinforced the idea of Jason's guilt? Or had Raumbaugh simply gotten tired of swimming against the tide?

As if he'd read Bachman's mind, Raumbaugh spoke. "And you, professor. Holding off sending me that note, that wasn't the only thing you held back, was it?"

Now Bachman remembered how he'd felt nervous and guilty the last time he'd walked into this office, and Raumbaugh had teased him. He didn't seem to be teasing now, however.

"Come on, professor. There was something you held back, something you didn't tell me about Jason Fender, wasn't there?" Raumbaugh didn't give Bachman enough time to figure out what he meant. He placed a smarmy smile on his face and pushed on.

"That's right. Something important. And you didn't tell me. The kid told me."

"Jason spoke to you? When? What—what did he say?"

"Naah, he didn't say a word. But he showed me something. Well, that ain't exactly true either. He showed it to the ER docs. Or they saw it. And like you, professor, my fine friend, they chose to be discreet about it." Raumbaugh scanned his desk until he found the ashtray. From it he removed his cold cigar. He leaned back in his big chair and pointed the cigar at Bachman. That odd smile was still there. It was a "gotcha" smile. "They didn't let the reporters know. But unlike you, they told me."

Raumbaugh turned and opened a drawer in the file cabinet behind him. He removed a folder, closed the drawer, and turned back to his desk. From the folder he pulled a large envelope, and from the envelope he slid several photographs. Flipping through them quickly, he found the one he sought, put the rest back, and looked at it, the sardonic smile intensifying. He looked up at Bachman, who waited, baffled. He passed him the eight by ten photo.

At first Bachman couldn't tell what it was a picture of. He wasn't even sure which way to hold it, which was the top of the picture. Then, recognizing that it was an extreme close-up of a person's neck, Bachman focused. Realization began to dawn. A necklace of bruises, a shadow that circled a skinny neck. Was this what Raumbaugh was talking about? Brutal, of course. Vicious. Would it still have been there more than a week later when Jason emerged from wherever he'd been hiding? Perhaps. Sometimes bruises get darker before they fade away. But even so, it didn't prove anything. Although, he realized, it may have proved to Raumbaugh that he, Mr. Bachman, was more interested in protecting his student than in getting to the truth, no matter how unpleasant that truth might be. Bachman had nothing to say. He visualized the flask in the top right hand desk drawer, but this time it was not proffered. Too bad.

"Don't worry, Mr. Bachman," Raumbaugh said. "I understand. I don't always tell everybody everything I know either." He took a match from his middle drawer, struck it a few times until it blazed, and then held it to the end of his stubby, wet cigar. Bachman wondered if it would even light, if the saliva hadn't soaked all the way down to the end. He watched the process silently, knowing that, having been caught in a lie, albeit one of omission, it was not yet his turn to talk. After much sucking and maneuvering, and the striking of another match, the cigar finally blazed. Raumbaugh exhaled, and smoke completely obscured his head. If this were a magic show, Bachman thought, the magician might be about to disappear. He didn't disappear. But when Raumbaugh emerged from the cloud of blue smoke, the gotcha smile was nowhere to be seen.

"It was kinda interesting," Raumbaugh said. He spoke slowly and his voice had a cold undertone. "I mean, what with the kid being at the Medical Center, and his daddy around the corner on the slab, it was almost too easy to match it all up – you know, Lemmy's grip with the marks that were still on the kid's neck. And sure, Lemmy coulda been strangling his kid on the fateful night – or afternoon, as we now know – in question, and that's when the kid snapped, got the meat cleaver, and hacked the bastard up. But I had this hunch that the kid didn't do it in the heat of the moment as they say. What do they call revenge, Mr. English Teacher? A cold dish?"

"'A dish best served cold,'" Bachman automatically quoted Edgar Allan Poe.

"Yeah," said Raumbaugh. "Right, like I said. I had a hunch that you saw those marks when you drove Jason home. You're too smart to miss a thing like that. After all, you care about these kids. Maybe too much."

Bachman had nothing to say. He felt as though he had betrayed a trust which, in fact, is exactly what he had done. Still... "Look. I'm sorry I didn't mention that. You're right. But surely you don't convict based on —"

Raumbaugh cut him off again. "I don't convict. I investigate. I analyze. I arrest. I charge. The D.A., the court, *they* convict." The correction, though academic, made Bachman see the process for what it was. He sank down a little further inside himself as he pictured Jason sliding further into the machinery of justice. "Professor," Raumbaugh continued, "under the circumstances, you are gonna hafta understand when I tell you that I got reasons – *more* reasons – to say that I know what I know." He still spoke deliberately, as if he were selecting each word with care. "And what I know is that however you may feel about it, so far as I and the Atlantis P.D. are concerned, this case is closed pending trial, and the perpetrator is in custody."

Bachman stood to leave. Under the circumstances he felt as though his tail were between his legs. Raumbaugh stood also, which surprised Bachman, who had never known the older man to display ceremonious manners of any sort. His face softened, relenting a bit. "Don't feel too bad, Mr. Bachman. Shit happens," said Raumbaugh as they stood together in the narrow corridor outside his office. "You figured what you were doing was for the best interest of the kid. You made a mistake, an error of judgment; you didn't rob the poor box. Don't beat yourself up too much."

Bachman was so embarrassed that he simply conceded the rightness of the detective's remarks, grateful to be leaving the humiliating scene. As he did, Raumbaugh left him with a comparison to ponder. "Reminds me of Bogart in The Maltese Falcon. I mean, I ain't calling you Ida Lupino, 'cause Ida Lupino lied to him again and again. But Sam Spade forgave her. Oh sure, he turned her in, but he still loved her. That Bogey. What a romantic."

Chapter Seven

Being invisible was a tricky business. Jason knew that he no longer was invisible; nevertheless, he retained the habit, the policy of remaining as still as possible. If you don't call attention to yourself, sometimes people forget that you're there. If he could, he'd prefer that as few people as possible paid attention to him. Now that he thought about it, he'd always felt that way.

He knew where he was. He had been here before. He had been here before to visit Daddy. This was one of the places they'd taken him to visit Daddy when Daddy'd "gone away." And now he, Jason, was on the other side of the bars.

And Daddy, he knew, would not be visiting him.

Richard W. Goffman

Other people came and went. There was a pretty black lady who said she was his lawyer. There was another lady, an older white lady with a fake smile. The white lady asked him lots of questions. He knew what that was all about: she was a doctor, and she was trying to find out if he was crazy. The other lady didn't care if he was crazy or not. For some reason that he didn't understand, she wanted to be his lawyer regardless of whether or not he was crazy.

Other people came too. More came before, while he was still back in the hospital, than now. Since he'd come here, to the jail, nobody was allowed to ask him any questions unless Miss Brantley, the lawyer lady, was there, too. Except the doctor. Her name he couldn't remember. But he knew she was a psychiatrist.

He knew, too, that he wasn't crazy. He didn't care one way or another if people thought he was or wasn't crazy. He had discovered something very interesting: If you don't answer people's questions, after a while they begin to answer them for you. He had discovered this accidentally. When he first was in the hospital he was unconscious a lot of the time. He'd sleep and wake up, but it wasn't like regular sleep. He had completely lost track of time. The only reason he eventually came to know how long he had been there was from listening to the adults around him talking. And one time, the man doing the news on the radio was talking about him. That was weird.

At first it was too difficult, too painful to talk. Later, when the pain was not such a big problem, he found that it was still difficult to talk because he just didn't know what to say. Everybody had questions, and he didn't know how to answer them. So simply not talking at all was the easiest thing to do.

Before the lawyer came, back in the hospital room, a guy had asked him a bunch of questions. Jason could tell he was a cop, although he didn't wear a cop uniform. He'd ask a question, and Jason didn't answer, he just stared at the ceiling. Then he'd ask another question. After a while, instead of asking questions like "What was it like at home?" and "Was your father mean to you?" he began to ask questions with built-in answers, like "Lemmy beat you, didn't he?" He asked, "You just couldn't take it anymore, could you?" Jason gave the same answer – no answer – to these questions too. Without knowing exactly why, Jason felt certain that it would be best for him if he just let everybody think whatever they wanted to think. And this cop already knew what he wanted to think.

Once he'd let this young cop guy ask his questions and answer them himself, it didn't seem fair to start talking to other people. Another cop without a uniform, an older guy who wore a suit that looked like it was as old as he was, asked him questions, too. This one wanted to know more detailed kind of stuff. It seemed like this older cop was testing Jason, to see if he really knew what had happened to Daddy. At that point he was glad he had adopted his no-talk policy, because he couldn't have answered all the older cop's questions even if he had wanted to.

* * *

Brenda, the coat check girl at Casa Como in Jersey City, was absolute sex on wheels. The clingy little pink and black dress she wore would work just as well as lingerie. Her breasts were pushed up and out as if they were treats being offered for sale on a tray; her little round ass stuck out like a black chick's. She stood on tiptoe to help Arthur Scanlon off with his coat. Though it weighed almost as much as she did, she carried the big camel hair in both her arms and hung it carefully, lifting her pointy heels to reach up to the coatrack. When she returned for the white homburg, Scanlon clung to it. As he seemed reluctant to part with it, Brenda looked up at him. They stood there like that for a couple of seconds, linked by their hands through the hat, eyes locked on each other's eyes. With a hungry leer, he relinquished his grip and she smiled mockingly at him, as if he were a bad little boy. Scanlon evaluated the space inside of the coatroom and envisioned entering, shutting the top half of the split door, and taking this little bit of stuff in his arms. Instead he removed his wallet from inside his suit jacket and, making sure she saw him do it, placed a twenty-dollar bill in the highball glass on the shelf on the bottom half of the coatroom door. Then he turned and went in toward the maître d'.

Honoré, the maître d', welcomed Mayor Scanlon warmly. When Scanlon told him whom he was there to have dinner with, Honoré made an even more obsequious little half-bow and led him away from the large main dining room in which only two tables were occupied by well-to-do patrons enjoying inch-and-a-half thick steaks, brandies, and cigars. Honoré brought him instead through the dark bar, through a door, into a private dining room.

HEARTLESS CRUELTY

Only one table was in this room. Two men sat there. Scanlon and Honoré hesitated at a polite distance as one of the men at the table stood and bid goodbye to the other, shaking a proffered hand with both of his own, and left. Scanlon avoided eye contact with the departing man as he passed. Then the man who had remained seated turned toward Scanlon and smiled broadly at him as though they were old friends. Although he was curious as to the identity of the fellow who had just departed, the Mayor of Atlantis was focused now entirely upon the gentleman who held court here in Casa Como's back room.

Arturo Montalvo appeared to be about sixty-five years old. His suit was pearl grey, pinstriped and expensive. His pale pink tie was secured with a fine gold chain. Silver wings swept back from his temples. With one manicured hand he gestured magnanimously to the seat which had just been vacated; with the thumb of the other hand he needlessly neatened his perfectly straight grey mustache. Both hands sported rings of exquisite diamonds. The left ring finger lacked its final digit.

Honoré placed an etched lead glass half full of clear liquid beside Scanlon, communicated silently with his boss, and disappeared.

"I can not thank you enough for coming all the way to Jersey City to sit with me," Montalvo said. "I am well aware of how busy you are."

"It is a pleasure—an honor, to meet you, Mr. Montalvo," Scanlon said.

Montalvo held up both his hands in protest. The subdued light of the nearby chandelier glinted off the older man's rings. "Please. The pleasure and the honor are both mine, and you will kindly call me by my first name. After all, we are only a couple of Arturs here. Isn't that right?" Montalvo raised his glass, and Scanlon did the same. When they clinked together, Montalvo said "Arturo è Arturo."

Scanlon sipped his drink – it was grappa – and manfully swallowed without coughing or otherwise losing his cool. He knew he was batting in a league a couple of levels above his usual one, despite the "just a couple of Arthurs" crap. He was determined not to make any mistakes, if he could help it. So far he was doing ok. Just to have gotten this far – to be having this private sit down with Arturo Montalvo in the much-fabled back room at Casa Como -- placed him on a fast track that few New Jersey Republican politicians ever saw. If he did well here, if he did well tonight, there was no telling where he might wind up.

But there *was* telling what the next step could be. No mistake: tonight was Scanlon's audition for the United States Senate. New Jersey had two Democratic Senators, neither of whose seats was due to be contested in the November 1984 elections. That's what the public knew. What the public didn't know was that the junior Senator from the Garden State was in serious legal hot water. Thanks to a messy divorce and several careless errors, the house of cards which he had assembled to finance his election campaign in '82 was about to fall apart. If the Senator was lucky, in the next two weeks he would merely lose his Senate seat and be forced to return to mixing sand in the cement of the buildings his company put up all over the state. If he wasn't that lucky he could be doing three to five years in Rahway State Prison. If this were to take place the irony would be complete, as the new prisoners' wing was one that his company had built. He would have one more reason to have difficulty sleeping there than any of his fellow inmates.

The good news, if you were Arthur Scanlon, was that the electorate had just a few weeks ago seen fit to send a Republican to occupy Drumthwacket, the governor's mansion in Princeton. The new Republican governor would take the oath of office in January of 1984. If the timing could be worked out properly, and it seemed quite likely that it would, the new Republican governor would be forced to appoint a replacement for the unused portion of the disgraced Senator's term.

Scanlon politely listened to Arturo Montalvo's explanation of the situation, despite the fact that he already knew exactly the nature of the stakes. What it came down to was this: the Mayor of Atlantis was one of three finalists secretly competing for that Senate appointment. Each secret candidate in this "beauty contest" had come up with the required non-refundable entrance fee. The entrance fee consisted of 2,000 hundred-dollar bills neatly inserted inside the Sunday issue of the *Newark Star Ledger*, itself placed inside a new, brown Hugo Boss leather briefcase with the candidate's monogram engraved on the brass clasp.

Arthur Scanlon appreciated the significance of the beauty contest entrance fee. Any contestant unable to pony up at that level didn't belong in New Jersey politics above the alderman level. And any beauty contestant without the balls to take the risk that two of the three would be helping foot the bill for the third one's re-election campaign in 1988 would be better off staying home.

Scanlon paid rapt attention to Montalvo's description of the coming events, his face a study in respect and fascination. It required less effort, however, to maintain this mask of studious absorption when Montalvo went on, speaking to Scanlon in a way that he could not have spoken to the other two contestants.

"The truth, Arthur, is that you are my first choice in these proceedings," Montalvo said, prompting a humble head tilt from his listener. "No, no. I am not blowing smoke up your ass, my friend. There are several reasons why I say this. One, I think anybody who can successfully run a city of more than 20,000 people in this state is an outstanding administrator. I've always felt that mayor is one of the toughest jobs there is, like a cross between a schoolmaster and a prizefighter. You have done this.

"Second, anybody who can do this successfully, in this state, in this day and age, without kowtowing to the coloreds, this is a strong leader. You have done this, too.

"Third, you have managed to do all of this while maintaining a strong record of law enforcement in your city. Your reputation in this regard does you proud, Arthur."

Montalvo paused. He offered Scanlon a Cuban cigar. Honoré appeared from nowhere to light both their cigars, and just as quickly disappeared again. Scanlon drew deep on his smoke, and wondered how the fuck a mobbed up joint like Casa Como featured a gay blade French maître d' as its frontman. *Focus, Arthur*, he told himself. He focused.

"I have been reading about this recent murder in Atlantis," Montalvo said, exhaling a blue cloud. "The boy who killed his father. This is a, what... a Greek tragedy, is it not? The newspapers have sold many extra copies because of the gruesome nature of this crime. After all, thanks to the efforts of your administration, murder is a rare crime in Atlantis."

Scanlon couldn't resist the softball. "We have, since I came to office, the lowest number of homicides per capita of any city in New Jersey."

"And you have every reason to be proud," Montalvo said. "Plus, this case presents you with a bit of an opportunity." He paused, letting Scanlon guess what came next. "Sometimes having your criminal be a white kid, and your victim another non-colored, is to your benefit. No one will ever call you racist for throwing the book at this fucking kid, this father-killer. Will they?"

"How could they?" Mayor Scanlon agreed.

Montalvo took another puff of the cigar. He looked up, at something on the ceiling that Scanlon could not see. He exhaled more thick blue smoke. Scanlon waited. It was not yet his turn to speak again. Montalvo removed the elaborately folded silk handkerchief from the breast pocket of his suit coat, wadded it, and coughed discreetly into it. He placed his cigar in the ashtray to his right, then meticulously removed and examined a couple of tobacco flakes from his tongue. As he had done earlier, he drew the back of one thumbnail across his left and then his right upper lip, grooming the pencil-thin mustache. Then he pressed his palms together, placing the fingertips against the tip of his nose, and his thumbs below his sagging under-jaw. His eyes were closed. He appeared to be in prayer, or in deep, silent contemplation. The silence was sacrosanct, unbreakable, until Montalvo himself broke it.

"I ask you this, Mr. Mayor," Arturo Montalvo said, opening his eyes and leaning in closely to Arthur Scanlon. "Will the conviction of this father-killing teen-ager be a simple matter?"

Scanlon was duly impressed with his host's ready grasp of the subtleties, if they could be called such, of Atlantean culture. "Mr. Montalvo. Arturo. I can comfortably give you my personal guarantee that this sad business will be resolved in January." Montalvo's eyes widened at this. "The finalization of these things, I'm sure you know, will take several months. However the conclusion will be certain long before then."

"Mr. Mayor," said Montalvo, smiling and leaning back in his chair. "I expected no less." He stood, and Scanlon did also, remembering that Montalvo had not stood when the previous visitor had been dismissed. Montalvo placed both his hands on Scanlon's shoulders in a fatherly sort of gesture which filled the mayor with great confidence about his future.

When Montalvo spoke again, however, Scanlon's confidence shook.

"I thought that you understood the procedure for this evening's meeting," Montalvo said.

Scanlon's face was a total blank. Montalvo looked down at the new brown Hugo Boss briefcase beside Scanlon's right foot. "You did not check your bag."

He had fucked up. He should have checked the cash-filled case along with his coat and hat; then, on leaving, he should have claimed just the garments, "forgetting" the leather case. After everything, would he blow his whole political future because a sexy girl had distracted him? He'd been thinking with his dick, picturing the little piece of ass slipping out of that pink dress instead of following instructions to the T. What an asshole he was!

Montalvo's face crinkled in a warm smile. "It is a chilly night. I assume you checked your coat with the girl at the front?" Montalvo said.

"Yes, I did. I should have also – I meant to check the bag," Scanlon said, stammering.

"Do not worry about it," said Montalvo. Scanlon dared to breathe.

"I'll check it now," Scanlon said.

"That's fine," Montalvo said.

"Pretty girl," Scanlon admitted.

"My granddaughter," Montalvo said with a patriarch's pride.

Scanlon bid his host farewell amid many thanks, followed the fag out of the private room, traded the briefcase for his hat and coat without any further potentially life-threatening faux-pas, and headed out into the frigid Jersey City night.

Chapter Eight

The headlamp mounted on his handlebars did little to illuminate the boardwalk ahead of him. If anyone was in his path, however, they'd be able to see the fuzzy white blur glowing and growing as it zoomed toward them at nearly thirty miles an hour. Unless they were deaf, they would already know something was coming at a damn good clip as Bachman's skinny black tires glissandoed across the boards like a manic xylophonist. At 5:35 on this December morning, it was highly unlikely that anyone lurked in the gloom ahead as he powered southbound out of Atlantis through cotton candy towns which had long depopulated in winter's tourist-free zone. Bachman would do a solid twelve miles before making his U-turn just north of the Seaside Light and retracing his way home.

Normally he'd try to shave a half a minute off his southbound time on the return trip, but this morning his concentration was not on his speedometer or his watch. Nor was it on the salty subzero air he was pumping through his lungs. Though the cold raised the pitch of the boards by half an octave, the energy he expended kept him toasty. This morning's trip was more mental-emotional workout than cardio-vascular, although it also had a reliably therapeutic hangover-removal effect.

Bachman wasn't proud of the fact that it had taken three scotches last night to throw the switch in his brain that finally let him get to sleep after midnight. It was just a fact: there was too much going on. Stalwart pal Bobby Davidson had come through, bringing not only the club soda and the new Springsteen, but by providing the company. Not having the first drink alone, at least, helped Bachman cling to the mythology of social drinking. Bobby D, a committed weeknight drinker, needed no such self-delusion.

Even thus anesthetized, Bachman's sleep had been restless enough, and his jaw muscles twitched their telltale signal. First, it was work. Distractions upon distractions this fall had left him face to face with looming Christmas break two or even three weeks shy of where he liked his curriculum to be. He'd have to compromise something if he was going to get caught up.

Next, of course, was doom, doubt, danger, death, and Jason Fender. Friends like Bobby D and Ellie Nelson knew the toll this was taking on Bachman before he did. Sure, sad but true, he'd seen dead bodies before. But it was safe to say he'd never literally tripped over a corpse prior to Lemmy Fender's. No, that was certainly a first. And he'd become entangled in the surprisingly complex subterranean lives of teenagers and their families before this, too – more often than he, Principal Carson, or Hilda, his department chair, cared to recall. And this particular entanglement smacked way too much of ambiguity and enigma. The more he considered the facts about Jason Fender, the more he found himself in the confusing realm of feelings. What right did he have to be so defensive of this kid? Maybe Raumbaugh had been right on the money. Who better than William Bachman knew the depths of depravity to which a defensive, semi-formed, hormone-addled teenager could plummet? (Answer: *No one.*)

And if these marvelously perplexing brain-teasers were not already enough to keep a divorced, celibate, semi-compulsive, thirty-three-year-old high school English teacher twisting his sheets of a deep, dark December night, what exactly had happened Monday afternoon? What in point of fact was the story with Elise Brantley, Esquire?

Gripping the front and rear brake levers simultaneously and so abruptly that his hands surprised the rest of his body, Bachman skidded to a sideways stop and put both feet down. He laid the bike on its side and stepped away from it, toward the rail on the ocean side of the boardwalk. With his elbows on his knees he bent forward, catching his breath and stretching the long muscles at the backs of his gangly legs. Then, so they wouldn't cramp, he stood and walked a few slow circles, puffing white clouds of condensation into the predawn gloom. His time on the return twelve miles would not be measurable now; nor did he care. Reflexively he put two fingers to his right carotid artery and counted pulsebeats for twelve seconds.

He leaned his arms on the railing and stared out to the spot where he knew the sun would, in a matter of 14 or 15 minutes, break the horizon. Something within his chest felt like the horizon, like a world-encircling dividing line that might be on the verge of rupture. His head swam. He had to shake it off before he could get back on track. With an effort of will he pulled the scope of his vision back into local mode, turned, and walked back to his bike. With both hands he lifted it over his head and stretched up toward the invisible starless sky. Then he turned north, the direction of home.

* * *

Bobby D was in a three-handed game of hearts with Patty Tonnery and Don Leeds. Leeds was a fifty-nine-year-old math teacher who felt that, as such, it was incumbent upon him to win games by dint of his superior skills at counting cards and judging probabilities. The fact that historically he won no more frequently than anyone else made no impression on him or his continued expectations of eventual victory. Tonnery was a smoker who, now that the teachers' room, once the last sanctuary of the pedagogical nicotine addict, was no longer a haven, had to have something to do with her hands. Bobby D looked up from his cards and waved to Bachman who sidled into the room, elbowing the door open, toting a cardboard box filled with student binders.

"Notebook check," Bachman said to the room, struggling with his load, making it clear he had no time to be the card players' fourth; besides, he had no tolerance for Leeds' brand of kibitzing. He established himself at the other end of the teachers' room's long table, where Lydia Chasen was grading lab reports. Bachman placed the box on the floor by his feet, brought the first few notebooks onto the table, and began to peruse.

Bachman's students were required to have loose-leaf binders, and though they were less than four months into the year, many of them were already heavily filled and some were badly misshapen. The only thing binding Mikey Lusick's "binder" was a thick blue rubber band. The original front and back covers of the notebook still sandwiched its chaotic contents, but the spine with the three locking rings was no longer part of the equation. If Mikey thought this would discourage Mr. Bachman from trying to make sense of the mess within, he was at least partly right. It just wasn't worth the effort, and they both knew it.

Debbie Seleski's binder was, of course, the epitome of organization. The cover featured an artistic collage of dancing pop stars: Cyndi Lauper, Michael Jackson, Tom Cruise in his underwear, Boy George in his androgyny. From each blossomed a comic strip word balloon or thought balloon: "English!" shouted Cyndi Lauper. "Mr. Bachman!" sang Michael Jackson. "Class of '85 Rules!" asserted Tom Cruise, sliding sideways in sweatsocks. Her quizzes, her tests, her returned homework assignments, her vocabulary list and her notes were all chronologically arranged in their clearly labeled (and color coded!) sections. In the section for journaling almost every page of lined paper was unfolded. Mr. Bachman's students were encouraged to journal freely and unselfconsciously. If they preferred to keep their self-expression private, they had only to fold the page in half. Debbie's innermost thoughts were almost disconcertingly open to her English teacher's perusal. Just as he assiduously avoided reading those pages which his kids asked him not to read, he felt obliged to read or at least skim those which they did not declare off limits.

Like many girls her age, Debbie Seleski poured entire gallons of pastel colored ink onto reams of narrow-ruled paper to create overwrought confessional poetry about the pain and pressure of adolescence. Every single letter of every line was lower case, notably including the first person singular nominative pronoun, a choice Bachman took to indicate either genteel humility or an abject sense of personal worthlessness, depending on the child's mood. Every lower case i was dotted with a tiny circle rather than an actual dot. Undoubtedly this represented an evolution from the little daisies that must have been used in sixth and seventh grade.

Bachman was surprised to find more prose than usual among Debbie's entries. Reading it reminded him that it was now urgent that he find a way to get this kid involved in something that would channel all that emotional and sexual energy more appropriately and productively. Ellie Nelson had just started a girls' peer counseling group; he'd give Ellie a note about recruiting this child.

Several of Debbie's prose entries and a couple of her poems alluded to Jason Fender. One poem was entitled "The Lost Boy;" another, "The Boy in Black." The prose entries extolled Mr. Bachman as Jason's savior, as the only teacher who truly cares about kids. In one she wondered aloud about Jason's mother. Even The Lost Boy had to have a mother, she pointed out.

Hadn't Raumbaugh mentioned something about Jason's mother during one of their first conversations? Was she still alive? It seemed to Bachman that the detective had indicated that Jason's mother had been a prostitute. He couldn't remember if she was supposed to be alive or dead.

He looked up from his work and dwelled on this fact, this lack of knowledge. Debbie Seleski may not be a real poet yet, but she had good instincts. He closed her big, orderly, decorative binder and marveled at how frequently he felt as though he learned more from his students than they learned from him.

Chapter Nine

Elise Brantley had to take Bachman to dinner. It was only right, she explained, having kept him waiting at the diner for over an hour. He'd been waiting for her in the parking lot when she pulled in, flustered, relieved to find him. Instead of going back inside, where he'd been drinking coffee after coffee, she asked him where he liked to eat.

Now it was almost seven as they arrived at Alfonzo's in their two-beetle parade, Bachman's yellow convertible leading the lawyer's red hardtop. The place was packed, and they had to park almost a block away. As they walked back up the street toward the loud, neon-lit restaurant, she apologized for at least the fifth time. Bachman noticed that she kept pace with him, despite the large disparity in their strides. Normally he had to slow himself down to walk and talk with almost anyone.

To her further mortification, Ms. Brantley read the sign in the lobby:

NO SHIRT? NO SHOES? NO SERVICE.
NO CHECKS. NO CREDIT CARDS.
NO PROBLEMS.

When they sat, she had to explain to Bachman that the only way that the law firm of Sostyoprak Wepner and Froelich L. P. was accustomed to paying for meals and other forms of entertainment was via her corporate American Express Card. She, personally, was at that moment almost entirely devoid of cash. Bachman did his best to put her at ease.

"We'll be in and out of here for under forty bucks," he said. "Please relax. I've got it."

"This is so unprofessional of me," she said. "First to keep you waiting. Now—"

"I'm begging you to forget it," he said. "I sat in my car and graded papers. Notebooks, actually. I used the time well."

"But you must let me reimburse you for dinner."

"No."

"Why not?" she asked.

"I'm trying to protect you," Bachman said.

"What are you talking about?"

"I don't want you to have a real ethical dilemma. How can you buy me dinner? Aren't I – I don't know, a potential something or other? I mean, on some level aren't you wondering where I fit into this whole Lemmy Fender mess?"

"Mr. Bachman, if there were any way I thought you could be a suspect in this case, then you're right, buying you dinner would carry the appearance of impropriety, and I wouldn't do it."

"And you're pretty sure I'm not?"

"Well, when I first began reading the case notes," she said, "I did wonder. But having spoken with everyone from the police chief on down, your reputation is just..." She spread her hands like an open book.

"Is what?" Bachman wanted to know.

"Mr. Bachman, from what I can tell, I am the only person in Atlantis who hasn't studied with you, or is related to someone who did, or who knows you in some way. Serves me right for going to parochial school."

"And what do they know about me that you don't? Or didn't?"

"They seem to know you are someone who would confront an abusive father, nail an abusive father, would testify against an abusive father. But not possibly kill him."

"And you're convinced?"

"I am. Mr. Bachman, you should run for mayor."

Bachman shuddered. "No thanks. But thanks for the endorsement. Under the circumstances, do you think you could call me Bill?"

She looked surprised. "Well, we're still having an official interview here. Let's keep it professional. For now."

And they did. After splitting Alfonzo's famous big antipasto, Elise Brantley had the pasta primavera and a glass of white wine. Bill Bachman had chili, piz-za, and two beers. And for two hours, they talked. They talked about Jason Fender. Bachman learned about the messy, confused record of child abuse accusations against the boy's father, made difficult by their frequent address changes. He also learned that he knew more than he realized he knew. Brantley dug from his memory things that he didn't realize were there. Details about the crime scene, impressions of Jason Fender from the first day of school, even specific things Jason said and did the day that Bachman gave him a ride home.

Brantley took notes so quickly that Bachman never had to slow or repeat anything. She appeared to have her own shorthand system, and by the time they finished dinner she'd nearly filled an entire notepad with facts, opinions, and new questions and ideas for follow up that would take her investigation in several directions.

She closed her notebook and excused herself to the ladies' room. Bachman seized the opportunity to pay the check while she was away, so as not to open that whole can of worms again. When she came back to the table he was standing, holding her coat.

* * *

Outside, the night was cold, the sky was clear, the air was still and the streets of Bradley Beach were quiet. Alfonzo's was still enveloped in its trademark cloud of garlic, but customers emerging from dinner never noticed it as they did upon arrival. Without hesitating or consulting each other they walked right past their cars. Alfonzo's was a short block-and-a-half from the boardwalk, and their talk wrapped about them like an extra long scarf as they headed in that direction as if they had planned it.

At some point between the restaurant and the boardwalk, the talk had shifted from what they each knew about the Fenders and the murder to matters of each other, and Ms. Brantley and Mr. Bachman had evolved into Elise and Bill. Now Bachman learned about undergraduate life at Yale for a black prodigy on a scholarship, and the crushing workload at Yale Law. Now Elise learned about Bachman's passion for writing, his belief in its power to help struggling kids. She learned about his disastrous first marriage and his bicycle. He learned about her family and her black belt in karate.

Entirely by coincidence they stopped walking and leaned on the railing to consider the pounding ocean flashing in the darkness at the exact spot Bachman had done the same thing during his ride, seventeen hours earlier. Standing side by side, Bachman felt the need to change and lighten the subject. He asked her to name her favorite movie.

Elise turned and looked up at him. "Have we reached the 'What's your favorite movie stage?' already?" she said. It was at once a joke, a flirtation, and an irony meant to distract from the fact that neither of them was sure just what this now was. It was clearly not part of their meeting.

"I'm not sure," Bachman said, "but I thought I might risk it."

"Very bold," she said.

205

"I'm noted for my boldness," he said, batting it back to her. "I've been known to boldly go."

"And to be an English teacher who splits an infinitive," she said. "Tsk."

"If it's good enough for Captain Kirk's log..." he countered.

"Almost anything directed by Michael Curtiz," she said. Bachman looked blank. "I mean, sure, Casablanca first and foremost, I suppose anyone would say that. But I'd hate to leave out Angels with Dirty Faces. Or Mildred Pierce. How amazing is Joan Crawford?"

"Nothing in color?" Bachman said.

"Don't be dumb," Elise said.

"I'm trying," he said.

"And yours?" she said.

"My—"

"Favorite movies, silly."

"No offense to Joan Crawford or Michael..."

"Curtiz," Elise said helpfully.

"Right," said Bachman. "Used to be Bonnie and Clyde. Then it was 2001: A Space Odyssey. Then it was Day for Night."

"Nice, love Truffaut," Elise approved.

"But now I think it's 2001 again," he said. "And Psycho."

"I thought you were anti black and white," she teased.

Bachman held his head high. "I prefer to judge films by the content of their characters," he said. "Not the colors – or lack of colors – of their skins."

"Oh, please," said Elise. She rolled her eyes and swatted his arm. He caught the playful blow in his own hand. He gripped her hand, and she gripped his back. Then, somehow, they were kissing. When it was over they searched each other's eyes.

Elise turned. Bachman watched the back of her head where it poked above the hood of her parka, the down parka he'd helped her into a few minutes earlier. He watched her walk slowly away from him, hands in her pockets. When she was about twenty feet away, she stopped and turned. He didn't know what was happening. Had he overstepped? He couldn't make out the expression on her face because, though she was standing closer to one of the boardwalk's high light stanchions, she was under it and her face was in shadow. They remained like that, twenty feet of gray, cold boardwalk and clean, chilly night air separating them.

Elise tilted her head a bit to the left, enough for him to see her face. Bachman revised his earlier appraisal: it was an exquisite face, not merely a beautiful one. The wind had picked up, a fact that he realized only because her black, chin-length wavy hair had become animated like a living thing. He felt as though he were deep in the ocean, in the original Atlantis, face to face with an undersea princess.

Now that she could see that he could see her, she said *Come here* with her eyes. He could hear clearly, although she remained silent, and her face otherwise conveyed no additional clues or information. Must be how undersea denizens communicated, he thought.

He went there.

Where Elise stood, the boardwalk railing ended at the top of a flight of wooden stairs that led down to the beach itself. Elise stepped down onto the first step and, with a crook of her finger commanded Bachman to do the same. When he had complied, she stepped back up to the boardwalk. He turned to see that now they were at eye level with each other. Another breath of ocean breeze whipped her hair back and forth; they were close enough that a strand of it tickled his brow. She didn't move a hand to restrain it, nor did she even for a moment break eye contact with him. He thought he could see his own face reflected in those eyes, and, implausibly, her face in his. He thought he might fall into them.

She put her hands on his shoulders and said, "Again, please." Then they kissed for a long time.

Bachman was very worried about being out of practice, but Elise seemed to be responding positively. He couldn't figure out how it was that she tasted like almonds rather than pasta primavera. And he was pretty sure that she was humming. He hoped that was a good sign. No one had ever hummed into his mouth before. Maybe it meant she was bored? She didn't seem bored.

He hugged her to him. He squeezed her tighter, and leaned back, lifting her momentarily off her feet.

"Mm," Elise said.

Bachman agreed.

"Beach?" she said.

Bachman agreed. She took his hand and they walked down the stairs to the sand. They kissed there again, as if to celebrate the arrival, and when they pulled their faces a little away from each other to see what they could see, they both saw pleasure in the face before them.

Standing on the beach, Elise had given back the height advantage, yet she felt somehow taller than she had been when she woke up that morning. She took Bill Bachman's hand and they walked toward the waterline. It was thirty yards ahead of them, and they could hear it better than they could see it. The soft sand didn't agree with the heels of her boots, and it was too cold to kick off their shoes as if they were Annette Funicello and Frankie Avalon in a Beach Party movie. Bachman unzipped his jacket and enfolded her in it with him, holding it closed around them both as they walked.

They stopped and looked up at the stars. There were hundreds visible. To the north, their left, was the blue glow that was New York and its electric environs. Bachman spoke first.

"I didn't expect—I mean, I didn't plan to kiss you tonight."

"Neither did I," she said. "This wasn't a date. I mean, it was supposed to be an hour in my office, me taking notes, you giving an account. Me picking your brain, you helping your student."

"We did that too, didn't we?" he said.

"Oh yes," she said. "I think it was very valuable. You gave me—I think I got a lot of insights that I couldn't have gotten from anybody else."

"And then, when we left Alfonzo's..."

"Then the meeting part ended." She said this last into the space between the second and third button of his shirt.

"I like this part," he said. And he kissed her once more.

They turned and looked out over the ocean from the vantage of the crest of the beach. He stood behind her, held her in front of him, his arms around her, keeping her warm. His arms crossed over her chest and she crossed her arms over his, squeezing him to her. He kissed the rising and falling waves of her hair.

After a while – neither of them could have said if it was one minute or ten – they turned and, as before, walked with one destination as if they had consulted, although they had not. They climbed the beach, climbed the stairs, walked down the boardwalk and up Saltaire Ave. to where the two Volkswagens were parked. Bachman double checked that his was locked. They got in Elise's car and drove to Bachman's house.

Chapter Ten

Elise Brantley, Esq. woke up in Mr. Bachman's bed on Saturday morning, but for the moment she kept her eyes closed. She knew exactly where she was. She was a little worried about this, about having slept with Bill Bachman. He had joked the night before, at dinner, about the appearance of some sort of conflict; of course, he'd been wrong about that. But this... she wondered if perhaps she had done something stupid.

It seemed awfully right last night, that was sure. Elise had always selected lovers carefully in the past; this time seemed to her both impulsive and, well, overly romantic. She wasn't sure precisely what it was about this high school teacher that compelled her into his arms on the boardwalk and into his bed right after. He seemed somehow familiar to her. Who did he remind her of? It wasn't her father. (Ew, why had that even occurred to her?) And yet.

He wasn't handsome, that hadn't been it. Of course, that had never been a top criterion for her. Not that he was ugly. He was an odd-looking man, tall in a disproportionate way. He was muscular, with long, knotty calves and arms, apparently from compulsive bicycling, but he had a pot belly. And no ass. He had large hands and feet, and his face was a strange mix of large features, too. His eyebrows were thick and black, arching over deep black eyes and a big nose. His mouth was big too, and his lips were lush—for a white guy. His hair was left over from the seventies.

He was a good kisser. No, he was an excellent kisser. Of course, she hadn't known that until she'd kissed him, had she? Oh what difference did it make? Who cared why? She *had* kissed him, and they had made love and spent the night together, and she was a little nervous about it, but she was glad. He tasted good, too. She'd noticed that at their first kiss. How was it that he didn't taste like chili or pepperoni? He actually tasted a little like popcorn. Could be worse.

* * *

Bachman knew the exact moment Elise woke up, because he was watching and waiting. He had not slept all night. After making love he'd not wanted to let go of her. She wanted something to sleep in, so he'd given her one of his T-shirts; it came down to her knees. When he got back under the covers she buried her face into his side, threw a leg over him, and, in a minute, began to emit a high-pitched snoring that he found adorable. When, around dawn, she'd rolled over and hugged the other pillow, he slipped out of bed, sat in his chair, lifted the shade to let some light in and grabbed a book. But, though he occasionally turned a page, he kept looking up to take in the sleeping figure in his bed.

Yes, he thought, he *had* turned a page. Early the morning before he'd wondered about this woman. Now, this. It had been long enough since his divorce that Bachman had begun to question, at thirty-three, if the disaster of his first marriage hadn't turned him off to love permanently. Love? He turned another page in the book, realized that he hadn't read a word, checked to see what book was in his hand, put it down on the dresser and leaned back, scratching his hair with both hands. Calm down, Billy.

Now she sat up; Bachman held his breath. For a terrible moment he imagined she might remember where she was, realize she'd made an awful mistake, and begin screaming. Instead she opened one eye and smiled at him. He walked back over to the bed; she watched him approach. Standing by the bed, in his loft above the living room, he reached down to touch her face with his hand. Now she had both eyes open, and both her eyes watched him, while he held her chin. He seemed to be studying her, checking to make sure that she was real.

When she reached up and pulled his face down to hers, her reality was proven beyond question. She pulled his T-shirt over her head as they kissed, entangling him in it with her, exposing her breasts to him, enfolding him in her arms. He freed them both from the shirt because he wanted to see her. He noticed the rainbow of shades of brown, from the lightness of her round breasts, to the near-blackness of her nipples, the deep chocolate of her belly, the freckles that danced across her shoulders.

He said, "I'm torn."

She gulped air in when they stopped kissing. "Why?" she said. "What are you torn between?"

"When I'm kissing you, I can't see you," he said. "And when I'm looking at you, I'm not kissing you."

"I have no appointments today," she said. "I'm not in a rush. Are you?"

"No," he said.

"All right," she said. She threw the T-shirt out of the bed, onto the floor, and she pushed the covers back. She stretched her nakedness diagonally across his queen-size bed, crooked her arm, resting the side of her face in her hand, posing for him. "Let's take our time."

And they did. He walked around the bed, and then back again. When he'd committed everything he could see to memory he took her right foot in his hand and put two toes in his mouth. From there he kissed his way all the way up, and then all the way down the other leg, missing nothing along the way. Then she couldn't stand it anymore, and she pulled him to her, onto her, into her.

* * *

Elise watched Bachman work in his kitchen. The kitchen was small; indeed, the whole house was small, but it was well-organized. She was amazed to see him grind coffee beans by hand, twirling a little iron crank atop an antique grinder, noisily filling a little wooden drawer with grounds.

"You're very handy," she said.

"I can cook any meal you want, as long as it's breakfast," he said. "How do you like your eggs?"

Over breakfast he told her that he hadn't been to bed with a woman since his divorce, more than a year now. She didn't volunteer any similar information, but she took his hand, and she squeezed it. She said, "Well, you haven't forgotten what you're doing."

She was sorry as soon as she said it. Had she sounded insincere, as if she were trying to buck up his confidence? He wondered if he appeared to be asking for encouragement. Had he shared too much too soon? They experienced their first uncomfortable silence. Elise blushed. Bachman grimaced.

He scraped their plates into the garbage can.

"So, I interviewed the detective," she said.

"Raumbaugh?" he said. "What did you think of him?"

"An interesting character," she said. "A real throwback. Reminded me of Broderick Crawford, pre-Highway Patrol."

"Was he much help to you?"

"Not as much as I had hoped," she said. "He seemed to be not too into the case anymore. If he ever was. Like he was moving onto other things. I didn't get it. It's not like he has so many murders to investigate. Right?"

"True," Bachman said.

"He mentioned you though," she said.

"Really?" he said. "Why?"

"Yes. I told him that I had gotten some strange hang-ups on my phone at home, and also at the office. That it made me a little nervous, and it started the day after I took Jason's case. I told him that if I didn't know better I'd feel a little threatened. He told me, 'Well I got somebody you should get to know. You two would really get along.' He told me you got a threatening note?"

"Yes," Bachman said, and he told her about it. Then he asked her, "Did Raumbaugh seem odd to you?"

"Compared to what?" she said. "I only met him this one time, so I have no basis of comparison."

"Well, I've met him several times since the murder, and a couple of times a few years ago. And I have to say, the last time I talked to him, he seemed weird. It was extremely uncomfortable. You're right: he is a throwback. He can fool you with that old fashioned look and that funny way he has of talking, the beat up hat and the Peter Falk raincoat. But he's perceptive. I've seen him work once before. Don't ask me now how come. I've seen him work. He's good. He knows how to analyze a situation. He knows how to break it down. But when I spoke with him on Tuesday, he seemed to have given up on the case, seemed to have given up on Jason, or anybody other than Jason as a possible perpetrator. And when he said it, somehow he didn't sound like he believed himself."

"Maybe he is onto something more interesting," Elise said.

"Maybe," Bachman said. There was another long pause. Then Bachman spoke up again. "And to make matters worse, he called me Ida Lupino."

"Ida Lupino? Why'd he call you Ida Lupino?"

Bachman explained how he had neglected to tell Raumbaugh that he had noticed marks on Jason's neck the day of the murder. Bachman said that Raumbaugh took it very personally that he had held information back. "He said, 'Don't feel too bad. It's not like you're like Ida Lupino in The Maltese Falcon. She lied to Bogart over and over again.' I think he likes to see himself as Humphrey Bogart."

He looked up to see that she was looking at him with her head cocked to one side and a funny look on her face. "What?" he asked her.

"I still don't get why he said Ida Lupino."

"Because I lied to him, I guess. Apparently she was this big liar in The Maltese Falcon."

"Ida Lupino wasn't in The Maltese Falcon. That was Mary Astor."

"But—"

"Ida Lupino co-starred with Bogart in High Sierra. She was actually a bigger star than he was at that point. Mary Astor played Brigid O'Shaughnessy, the woman who kept lying to Sam Spade," Elise said. "The woman Spade turns in, but promises he'll wait for her, until she gets out of jail for murdering his partner."

"How old are you?" Bachman asked her.

"Twenty-six," she said. "I like old movies, ok? I took every class I could in school. Someday I might go to Hollywood and get a job as a cutthroat entertainment attorney."

"Sure," said Bachman.

"Anyhow, I guess he just got mixed up," Elise said. "Raumbaugh. About the actress, I mean."

"Yeah, maybe," Bachman said. "Although, that wouldn't really be like him. He's a big movie nut, like you. People make mistakes, but that's not the kind of mistake he'd make."

"Yes, I know," Elise said. "He told me a little."

They were both quiet for a minute. Then Elise shook her head and said, "But he did. Make a mistake."

Bachman was quiet.

"Right?" Elise said.

Bachman was still quiet. He was replaying his recent discussion with Raumbaugh over in his mind.

"What?" she asked.

"So, he uses an analogy, compares me to this actress, but he names the 'wrong' actress. And he'd talked to you earlier in the day. He knew I didn't know Ida Lupino from Mary..."

"Astor," she said.

"He knew I didn't know these actresses. Hell, I'm not sure I ever actually saw The Maltese Falcon. But he also knew that you were probably going to be talking to me some more."

"He definitely knew that, because I mentioned it," she said. "So, if I hear what you're saying, it sounds like you're saying that he said something wrong that you wouldn't know was wrong, but he suspected you'd repeat it to me, and I would know it was wrong..."

"...and realizing this, you would realize..."

"...or we would realize that.... what?"

"That the other things he was saying weren't right either?" Bachman said, sounding unsure to himself. "This is crazy."

"You did say that he didn't seem like himself," she said.

"Why would he be so cryptic?" Bachman asked.

"Only one possible reason," Elise said, picking up the thread with both hands. "He thought someone else was listening."

"Someone eavesdropping on him, bugging his office?" Bachman said. "It looked neater than it had before, I remember that."

"Maybe you aren't the only one who has been threatened to keep your theories about the case to yourself."

Elise and Bachman both shook their heads. Elise got up and left the kitchen. When she came back a couple of minutes later she had her own clothes on, and the business card of Detective Dick Raumbaugh in her hand. It had his office number printed on it, and his home number handwritten beneath. Elise took Bachman's wall phone and called. She got no answer at either number. They looked at each other again.

Bachman took the phone from her hand and dialed the desk sergeant, the main number of the Atlantis Police Department. He didn't have to look it up. A familiar voice answered.

Bachman said, "Is Detective Raumbaugh around?"

"Who wants to know?" It was Ron Calabrese.

"It's Bill Bachman. Is he around?"

"Oh, Mr. Bachman. No. Raumbaugh's not around," Sergeant Calabrese answered him. There was a noise on the other end of the line. Bachman held the phone away from his ear for a moment.

"What's going on Sarge?" Bachman asked.

"It's Raumbaugh," Calabrese said. "He was in an accident last night. He's over at Monmouth Regional. It don't look good."

Chapter Eleven

When Mikey Lusick got to room 323 on Monday afternoon, Doo-wayne Franklin was going over a paper with Mr. Bachman at the teacher's desk; a boy and two girls, neither one of whom was The Amazing Debbie Seleski, all sophomores, were changing the bulletin board in the back of Mr. Bachman's classroom to a Shakespeare theme; three or four other kids were hanging out, doing homework, shooting the breeze, or just avoiding going home. Mikey was all, like, hurry up, you wanted to talk to me and now I'm here, but he decided not to interrupt. Doo was probably embarrassed to be seen getting "extra help." On the other hand, Mikey had recently learned that Doo-Wayne Franklin had like straight A's or something. Somebody had said at lunch the other day, in a hushed voice, that Doo-Wayne could wind up being the Class of '85's valedictorian. Mikey wasn't sure what a valedictorian was, but the person who was talking, some Honor Society dweeb, made it sound like it would help him get into a good college. Mikey figured valedictorian was probably one of those special programs for black kids to help them get over not having civil rights back in the old days, but he didn't ask, because he didn't want to look dumb.

When Doo-Wayne and Mr. Bachman were finished, Doo-Wayne got his stuff, nodded to Mikey, thanked Mr. Bachman, and left. Mr. Bachman checked on the work that the kids were finishing on the bulletin board before finally calling Mikey up to his desk.

"I've got a present for you, Mikey," the teacher said.

Mikey was wary. Nobody else was listening, but he still didn't want to be the punch line of a teacher's joke. "What?" he said.

Mr. Bachman reached under his desk and brought out a large, red, three-ring binder. The binder was empty, but it wasn't new. It had a girl's name, Jo-anne, written on it in Magic Marker.

"What's this?"

"It's a binder," Mr. Bachman said.

"I got a binder."

Mr. Bachman reached under his desk again. This time he brought out a brown paper grocery bag from Pathmark. "No. You have this."

He placed the bag on his desk. Mikey opened it. It was, of course, filled with the contents of Mikey's own "binder," including its broken covers, and a riot of disordered loose-leaf pages, handouts, journal entries, and unrecognizable detritus.

"Now, this—" Mr. Bachman pushed the used red binder in Mikey's direction – "is your new binder. You can replace it with another one if you want to, but you're going to sit here this afternoon until you've transferred this mess into some semblance of order in that binder. You can leave as soon as you've taken care of it."

Mikey grumbled, but he took the stuff and got to work. Mr. Bachman turned his attention to papers he was grading. A minute later, however, Mikey interrupted him with an aggrieved protest.

"Not all this junk is mine, Mr. Bachman," he said. "This is no fair."

Mikey was right. Bachman was surprised to see that there were papers mixed in with Mikey Lusick's that belonged to other students. On closer examination he saw that they weren't even English papers. They were biology lab reports. He realized that he must have accidentally picked up some of Lydia Chasen's work when they sat near each other in the teacher's room. He helped Mikey sort through the pile, then told him he could leave and take it all in the bag, but to come to class tomorrow with his English binder in decent shape. Mikey was glad to get the hell out of there, but first he handed his English teacher a couple more pages.

"Here's one more lab report, Mr. Bachman," he said. "Look, it's the weird kid's."

Bachman looked up in surprise. Mikey, misinterpreting the look for disapproval, said, "I mean, sorry. You know. Fender's."

When Mikey and the other kids were gone and Bachman had finished straightening his desk, Jason

Fender's lab report was the last thing left out. The other lab reports he'd put in a big envelope with a note to Mrs. Chasen, which he would leave in her box on the way out. He picked up the one with Jason's name on the top and looked at it for the third time. In the upper left hand corner was the standard heading:

> *Jason Fender*
> *Oct. 24, 1983*
> *Bio - Mrs. Chasen*

Below that, Jason had painstakingly followed Mrs. Chasen's strict lab report template.

> *NAME: Dissection of a fetal pig – Part Two*
> *OBJECTIVE: Identify the major features of the cardio-vascular system.*

Bachman skipped down a few lines, to

> *PROCEDURE: 1. Using the big tweezers and the scalpel, separate the bones of the rib cage from the breastbone.*
> *2. Incise the aorta and the vena cava.*
> *3. Remove the pig's heart.*
> *4. Weigh the heart and measure its circumference.*
> *5. Place it carefully in a small jar, saving it for the next lab.*

Mr. Bachman put Jason Fender's last known written work in his briefcase, turned out the lights in room 323, and closed the door.

"Didn't you read the message?" Elise Brantley asked her visitor.

Bachman was confused. He had indeed read the phone message which Shari had placed in his mailbox in the main office. It discreetly listed only Elise's office number, not her name, and the words "Please call."

Bachman had recognized the number as hers and mistakenly assumed that, since he had to drive across town, passing near the office of Sostyoprak Wepner and Froelich L.P., that he'd be best off stopping in at her office on the way home. He drove there with the remembered image of Elise, naked, floating before his eyes. Now, her reception cooled him down.

"I really did want you to call, not come here," Elise said.

"Because... ?" he wanted to know.

"Because," she said, "I don't think it's that great an idea for us to be seen together." Elise took Bachman from the reception area and brought him not to her cubicle, but to the smaller of SosWepFro's two conference rooms. Inside, she closed the door. Bachman was about to ask her if she was serious, but she spoke first.

"Raumbaugh slipped into a coma this afternoon," she said. This stopped Bachman.

They'd tried to visit Raumbaugh in the hospital, together on Saturday and separately on Sunday, but they were rebuffed each time. Only immediate family members could gain access to the intensive care unit; Raumbaugh had no immediate family. It was like

Catch-22. Not only were the Monmouth Medical Center staff unusually vigilant regarding visiting rules in this particular instance; Atlantis cops were on hand, backing it up. One of their own was down, and they weren't taking any chances.

Bachman had repeatedly tried calling Tommy Jr., both at the police station and at his home, without any success. This afternoon his plan was to give the old chief, Tommy Gallagher Sr., a call.

Elise had gotten an update on Raumbaugh's status by asking her boss to call the hospital. "But that's not all," she told Bachman.

"What else? There's more?"

"I heard from Detective Raumbaugh about two hours ago," she said. She looked at him with an expression he had not yet seen. It was a look that bore into him, almost daring him to question her. He had to question her.

"I thought you said...?"

"I did," she said. "He went into a coma about one o'clock. And then today's mail comes, and I've got a package. No return address. I open it." Bachman could see beads of perspiration on Elise Brantley's brow; he felt gooseflesh pucker his arms. Elise looked to the door of the conference room. It was just as closed as it had been a moment before. She lowered her voice, which had already been barely audible. "No note inside, no letter. Just a notebook."

"A notebook?" Bachman repeated.

"Raumbaugh's notes. About the case. Hand-written."

"His case notes?"

"No. And yes. I think our detective kept two sets of notes. I think his official notes are in the case file in his office. And I think his own personal ideas, theories, guesses... I think he kept those in this little separate notebook."

"Where is it?" said Bachman.

Elise's eyes flashed. She leaned closer to him. "Locked up," was all she would say.

"You are probably the only person who knows it exists," said Bachman. "You haven't told anyone else, right?"

"Not even Fehme," she said, referring to her boss, the senior partner.

"Have you read it?" Bachman asked, his voice now a whisper to match hers.

"Just enough to recognize what it is. And you know what it is? Or what it might be? It might be the only thing between Jason Fender and twenty years in Rahway."

"You know what else it might be?" said Bachman. "It might be what got Raumbaugh—what caused his accident."

"I know," said Elise.

"So if anybody finds out you have it..."

"I know," said Elise.

* * *

They agreed that Elise would make a pretense of putting something else in the safe, and remove what she had put there earlier, placing it all inside an innocuous-looking brown envelope with a label from one of her other cases. She frequently brought work home with her.

They took other precautions. They exchanged car keys. Sitting low in the driver's seat, he drove her car out of SosWepFro's garage into the late December afternoon twilight. He took the long way home, through Allenhurst, doing a figure eight around the upper and lower parts of Casino Lake, constantly checking the rearview. He didn't pull up his steep driveway until he was sure there was not a single car in sight ahead or behind him on his street. He parked her car in the back of his yard where a couple of old spruces blocked the view from the street.

Elise retrieved the material as planned, then sat and waited with it in her office. She couldn't concentrate on any other work, and she did not want to even open the envelope there. After a while she walked outside, crossed the street to Bachman's VW, got in and took off. She drove straight to Bachman's place. Though she left half an hour after he did, he'd driven so circuitously that he'd only been there long enough to order delivery from Alfonzo's when she pulled in. He'd been glued to the front window; it was strange to see his own car pull up the drive, but not as strange as the wave of relief he felt when Elise got out of the car.

She hurried up his porch steps with her bulging briefcase. Bachman held the door open for her. She relinquished the case to him. After locking the door behind her, he brought her and the case back into his living room. He placed it under his television. Then he turned back to her and took her in his arms. They held each other and kissed each other for minutes. He felt a strange combination of affection, lust, protectiveness and fear. When the Alfonzo's delivery guy rang the bell they both jumped, and then laughed.

Over pizza they dissected the notes. Bachman's initial reaction was disappointment. Some of it was barely legible, and what was legible didn't seem to offer any new ideas that might shed light on any theory other than the accepted one: Jason was abused by his father one time too many, and the boy turned on him, somehow overpowering him, and then hacking him to pieces. In fact, from the notes they learned that a big serrated knife had been found in a garbage can behind a house at Lincoln and Atlantic; it seemed likely that this was the implement used to take Lemmy apart. Although there were no clear prints on it because the handle was smeared with blood, mud, dirt and other debris, there was one partial of a palm print which had at least a 50% chance of matching with those taken from Jason.

On his own, Raumbaugh had brainstormed. He was a brainstormer and a listmaker. He'd made a list of every name he could find who had been in contact with Lemmy in the 48 hours before the discovery of the body, and everyone outside of school who had been in contact with Jason. Bachman's name was on both lists. He'd made a list of items found in the house, in the backyard, and in the recovered automobile, even though the latter had turned out to have been out of Lemmy's possession for a year.

And he made a list of questions.

Why now?

Where's mom?

What had L been up to?

L's enemies?

L's friends?

How did he do it?

And again,

WHY NOW?

Raumbaugh had tried to answer his own questions on the pages that followed, in small, meticulous printing. In pencil. It was close to ten pm when they finished.

"I can see why he kept this secret," Bachman said. "He's brainstorming. If anybody were to look at these notes they'd see that he was desperately trying to find some explanation other than the accepted one."

Elise agreed. "And there's not much here that offers any hope. I wonder why he kept trying. The last entry was written only" — she looked again — "only three days before his accident."

"But he sent it to you," Bachman said.

"You almost said, 'Bequeathed it,'" Elise said.

"Yeah. So he must have thought something would help you."

"And he must have known he was in trouble," she said. "Do you think he knew how much trouble?"

"You really think someone tried to kill him?" Bachman said.

"Or tried to scare him, like they tried to scare you, and did too good a job."

"Now I feel like I have to – to do something," Bachman said. "For Raumbaugh's sake as well as Jason's."

"Okay," Bachman said. He stood up. "You have a ton of work to do in preparation for the hearing with whatever you have, right?"

"Definitely," she said. "Even if it's red tape, slowing things down, looking for delays, putting together Jason's history, figuring out a way to get Jason to talk to me…"

"When do you have to be ready?"

"The grand jury is scheduled for January 22nd. A Monday. And that means… that means that in about a month I have to do two months worth of legal preparation and research."

"Is any of it stuff that I can help you with?" he asked.

She shook her head, sadly. "Not really."

"I mean, you know, I could maybe take something that's in legalese and try to make into a, you know, more emotional kind of story?" What had started out inflected as a suggestion turned into a question to which he surely knew the answer.

"I'm sure you could do that, and beautifully, Bill. And then I would have to translate it back. That's why they call it legalese."

They were quiet for a moment. He removed a page with a Raumbaugh list on it that he'd slipped into his shirt pocket.

"Christmas vacation starts on the 21st. I'm going to spend a few days with Ernie and Elaine."

"The folks," Elise guessed. She couldn't imagine referring to her parents by their first names, even in private. But even without meeting them, she could see how he could.

Bachman dashed into his kitchen, yanked his calendar with pictures of bicycle parts and new bikes on it off the wall, and dashed back out.

"Yeah. Then..." He made a few marks on it. "Then I'm gonna come back here, onnnnn..."

"On the day after Christmas so I can take you to dinner to pay you back for the dinner you bought me the other night?"

"Exactly!" he said. "On the 26th we'll go out to dinner, and...."

"...and I can pick the place this time?" she said.

He looked at her. "Did you hate Alfonzo's?" he asked, in the same tone he might have said, "Do you hate this puppy?"

"No, no, I loved it. I was just thinking about going somewhere that doesn't even have to remind its male customers to wear shirts." She smiled, and he did too. He couldn't remember the last time he had eaten in a "nice" restaurant.

"And then, the next day, I'm taking a trip."

She looked at him. "I'm going to..." He scanned down the page he had removed from his pocket, and found what he needed. "I'm going to Saratoga Springs. Upstate New York. Apparently that's the last known whereabouts of Roberta Johansen Fender."

"The mom? How old is the last contact?"

"Can't tell," said Bachman. "Maybe four years ago, it's hard to tell from this. I mean, it may not help to find her—"

"--But maybe it could."

"And it's a long shot that I'll be able to find her. But I have the time, and Jason is sitting there with absolutely no one…"

"And…" she said, drawing the word out. "And, an ex-wife of a murder victim is always a good person to talk to, even if he's got plenty of even more recent enemies."

"I'll take the shot," he said. "I'll go and I'll see what I can see. If anything."

* * *

And that's what they did. Elise threw herself into her work, spending ten hours a day at the office and doing more at home at night. The waning days of school before Christmas break saw Bachman trying his best to catch up with his curriculum, even as holiday assemblies, concerts, a big football game, Christmas shopping, parties and everyone's anticipation of a dozen days off in a row diverted attention to everything other than what was going on in classes. They went for a walk on the last Sunday before Christmas, but even then they spent no more than an hour together, because they were both drawn by things they needed to get done. They did speak on the phone at least once a day, and that became their pattern.

And then the days were gone. Bachman wished his kids a great vacation and gave them all little gifts: a chocolate, a pen, and a vacation reading assignment, which many thought was a dirty trick, and then he took off for the house he had grown up in, in Fort Lee, NJ. Elise's brothers and sisters, all older than she, began arriving in Red Bank with spouses and significant others and children.

She did take him out to a fancy dinner the night after Christmas, and they did their best to talk about things other than Jason the Silent as she had taken to calling him and the impending hearing, now only three weeks away. When the entrees were cleared, Elise remembered she had something to show him. It was a small yellow slip of paper with a "while you were out" phone message.

"It was folded inside another piece of paper. It literally fell in my lap," she said.

"You mean, from Raumbaugh's papers?"

She nodded.

"It's three weeks old," he said, examining it. "410 area code."

"Baltimore," she said. "Almost definitely unrelated, but, what the hell. I'll answer it for him. Never can tell."

"Why not?" he said. "We're grasping at straws anyway."

She drove him home. He had to rise early the next morning for his long travel day, so she did not plan to spend the night. She kept the motor running when she stopped on his driveway.

"You don't want to just come in for a little while?" he asked.

"You know it wouldn't be 'just a little while.'"

He grinned.

"We could neck right here for a few minutes like teenagers," she suggested. She showed him what she meant, but they quit even as the windows began to steam up.

"I guess those teenagers you were talking about don't drive foreign cars," he said. They agreed that what with the bucket seats and the stickshift, the VW was not a romantic vehicle.

"You'll call me? From there?"

"If I find her? Of course. Who else would I call?"

"No. Will you call me each day, and let me know you haven't been in a mysterious car accident?" She looked down. When she looked at him again, he saw actual fear in her eyes. "I'm serious."

"Yes, of course I will," he said. He held her face in both his hands. "This will probably be a waste of my time, but it seems like time is about the only thing I have to contribute right now." She shook her head and opened her mouth. He thought she was going to try to talk him out of going, so he kissed her again. "It will be fine," he said. "I'll be careful."

Bachman got out of the car and walked around to Elise on the driver's side. She had already rolled her window down despite the freezing night air. He leaned in for one final kiss.

"I promise," he said. She watched every step he took until he got inside. She watched the light come on in the living room, and she heard the door lock click in the silent night. Finally, she backed out of the driveway and drove home.

"How come Detective Raumbaugh didn't call me back himself?" The voice on the other end of Elise's phone on Tuesday morning was simultaneously serious and humorous. "Hell, I'd'a thought he'd'a been right on the phone to me. I left him the message 'most three weeks ago." No, maybe he was just serious, she decided. And miffed.

"I apologize," she said. Then, figuring a modicum of truth was the best way to lie, explained. "He's in the hospital. He was in a car accident."

The voice on the phone, that of Sheriff Andrew Sandister of Worcester County, Maryland, shifted again. "Well, hell. I'm sure sorry to hear that. He hurt bad?"

"To be honest with you, Sheriff, it's kind of touch and go right now. Anyhow, he asked me to follow up on some of the things that have piled up on his desk, so..."

"Well, hell. You tell Raumbaugh I'm thinking about him, okay? Him and me met at one of those law enforcement confabs up in Philly one time. 'Boondoggle,' Raumbaugh called it. Funny guy. 'Boondoggle.'"

"Sheriff, is there anything we can do for you?" Elise prompted, hoping to get this man back on track, if there was a track. She was already looking around her desk, setting up the rest of her day. "Anything you want me to tell Detective Raumbaugh?"

"I guess so. Okay, here it all is. You folks were looking for a boy a while back," Sheriff Sandister began. Elise put her Day-Runner down. She took the phone from the crook of her shoulder and held it steady with her left hand. "And then you found him, 'bout a week or two later, right in your own backyard." Sandister chuckled. "Always winds up that way, don't it?"

"Yes," Elise said. "Frequently."

"So we took that notice down off the board, outta the call sheets, outta the books we give the guys. But I remembered it, because of having met your Raumbaugh that time. And then I read about it in the paper, the Annapolis paper. I guess they thought it was big news, on account of the son-father thing. And the chopped up body thing. And the missing heart thing." Elise now felt like a violin string that was being bowed mercilessly by a tuneless player. Maybe the Sheriff could sense this, maybe he'd elicited this reaction from people before, because he apologized. "Sorry, Miss. What did you say your name was again?"

"Brantley. Elise Brantley."

"Anyhow Miss Brantley, I will get to the point, if you'll bear with me just a few more seconds. See, last week some fellas outta Ocean City are doing some late season shark fishing. Hard to believe, but they bring in this huge bull, fifteen feet long. Never heard of anybody getting a bull shark in late November, but there you go.

"So they get done taking their pictures, celebrating and getting drunk and all, and they send it in to get processed. The bull, not the pictures. First thing the processor does, he opens 'er up. These big ones always got lots of stuff in their guts, just like in that movie, Jaws, remember? This one's no exception, got pieces of metal shopping carts, tin cans, the whole nine yards.

These sharks, you might say they commute along the coast, from Canada down to South America, you know, for the winter. Back north again when the weather comes warm again. Anyhow, they find this bag. Plastic shopping bag. With a package inside. Wrapped real neat. Looks like it's from a deli or a butcher shop, you know, meat, special order. So they open the package up. Guess what?"

He paused. Was he literally waiting for her to guess?

"Well, it's a special order all right. It's a heart.

"Guy processing the shark figures it's from a cow or a calf or something. Long story short, somebody says no, looks like it could be human. Finally they call my office. I send my M.E. over there. It's only a few blocks from here. Medical examiner takes one look and establishes it as definitely a human heart. Big though, so you can see why the guy thought it came from a cow.

"Funny thing, right? Human heart, wrapped in foil, inside a Zip-Loc Bag, inside a shopping bag. Inside a shark. Can't tell where the shopping bag is from, shark's digestive juices have pretty much destroyed it. But naturally I remember this homicide you got up there, with the heart cut out of the body. I figure may- be this is it? All wrapped up, neat-like.

"You still there, Miss Brantley?"

Elise realized she'd been holding her breath. "Yes, Sheriff, I'm still here," Elise said. "Where is the heart now?"

"Well, it's here. I mean, it's in the fridge. Dr. Bloustein's fridge. But it won't be for long. Agent –"

she heard him shuffling papers on his desk – "Agent E. K. Stimson from Annapolis FBI is on her way over here this afternoon to pick it up."

"What-- Why is the FBI involved?" Elise said.

"Well, hell, all my talkin' and I still haven't told you the most interesting part," Sheriff Sandister said. "Dr. Bloustein, our M.E., he takes it upon himself to do a little mini-autopsy I guess you might say of the heart. And what does he find in there? A twenty-two short. What do you think about that?"

What was he talking about? A shirt size? He must have heard Elise's confusion over the line. "A *bullet*, miss. A little twenty-two caliber short bullet. They usually use 'em for targets and what-all. Lady's gun, usually. But even a little old twenty-two short can make a nasty hole at close range."

When Elise finally got off the phone with the long-winded Maryland cop, she immediately dialed Bachman. She wanted to tell him that Jason didn't kill his father.

Part Three

KILLED TWICE

Chapter One

"Talk." Lester Rooney didn't always answer the phone like that – "Talk." – but he liked how it sounded. It had an impatient, aggressive sound, as if to say "Why the fuck are you interrupting me, whoever you happen to be?" As if to say, "Now what?" Sometimes he'd just pick up and let the caller speak if he wanted to. He never said hello. Why would he?

"It's me," the caller said.

"So what?"

"So nothing. I just..."

"Hang up." Lester Rooney shook his head and sighed with exaggerated impatience. This was how most of his phone conversations went. His business calls, anyhow. There was little doubt in his mind that anything and everything he said on the phone was of interest to someone in authority somewhere. Phone lines could be bugged. *Were* bugged. So, if anybody's phone was bugged, surely his. In the last year his business dealings had escalated to the point that there must be several different parties who wanted to know exactly what he was up to. And these different parties, some on the supposedly clean side of the law, some on the dirty, all had the capabilities. Hell, *he* had the capability.

So, not for nothing, he had worked out a system. You need to talk to Rooney, you call Rooney. You don't say anything important when you call, just enough for Rooney to recognize your voice, and Rooney calls you back. That was the beauty part. Rooney had another phone. Not an extension – obviously – but another line. But this second line didn't have a number, because it wasn't installed by the phone company. It was installed by... Rooney himself. He had gained access to the switching box on the pole on his street through the attic of the building on the corner. Rooney had got in good with the Polack who had the grocery on the first floor. All he'd had to do to accomplish that was to break the arm of one of the kids who had shoplifted cigarettes from the Polack. Now that kid's friend, the other punk shoplifter, shoveled the Polack's walk for free whenever it snowed, and nobody had ever shoplifted nothing from the Polack again.

Being in good with the Polack meant that Rooney could use him for favors, like bringing him messy wads of singles, fives and tens and walking out with fifties and hundreds, neatly folded. Like using the back of his store for occasional meetings. Like getting rolls of plastic bags for various kinds of merchandise.

Like using his phone booth. Sometimes the Polack used to take messages for him when a call came in to the old-fashioned phone booth in the store, with its windowed wooden accordion door and its dial phone. But it was better, smarter, when Rooney realized he could, by way of the little window in the Polack's attic, reach the switching box on the pole, jimmy it open, install his own line, close the box back up, and run the line in through a seam in the window frame, sealing the crack with putty. He ran the line across the Polack's attic, out a knothole on the other side, across the alley by way of and hidden by a convenient tree branch, over the roof of the three-family next door, across the next alley to his own two-family by way of and hidden by the phone company's own fucking line at the front of the houses, right over the sidewalk, and down into his place, to his safe phone.

On this phone he would call back whoever had called him each time. The cute part: this phone was red. The smart part: the line wasn't tapped. The best part: everybody thought he was a short, muscle-bound moron, while in fact, Rooney was a fucking genius.

He'd call back whoever it was, assuming he recognized the voice. And if he didn't recognize the voice after a couple of words, then, fuck 'em, he didn't need to talk to them. Not on the phone, anyhow. And even though the line was safe, nobody used his name when talking to Rooney on the phone. Not even his brother, Louis.

The call hadn't been his big, important, big brother. It had been Daggett. He called Daggett right back. (That was another thing: he'd discovered he had an apparently limitless capacity for memorizing phone numbers. Realizing this, he'd burned his phone book. Nothing was in writing. Smart.) After he'd dialed the last of the digits but before the first ring, Rooney picked up a shot glass off the floor. As if he were drinking, he brought it to his lips and carefully tongued out one Black Beauty, leaving four or five others in the glass, and scraped the amphetamine capsule down with a moisture-free swallow.

Daggett answered midway through the first ring. Rooney was surprised that the sleepy-eyed pot-head's reflexes worked that well.

"Hello?"

"What?" Rooney said.

"Hey," Daggett said. Rooney sighed. Daggett knew better than to call just to chat. "Need to see you," Daggett said.

"What for?"

"Can you come to the bar?"

"What for?"

"Just come, willya?" Daggett persisted, whee-dling. "Need to see you. Gotta talk."

Rooney put the red receiver in the red cradle without another word. He didn't slam it. He placed it so quietly that Daggett would probably still be talking for another minute before he realized the line was dead.

He was pretty sure he knew what Daggett wanted, and why. It was getting so hard to get good help these days. Daggett was gonna tell Rooney that he had done his last job too well. Rooney would counter that Daggett had fucked it up. Then Daggett would say that he'd done what Rooney had asked, exactly what he was told, and now, instead of just having to paint the Impala he'd had to get rid of it entirely. That it wasn't his, Daggett's, fault that the other car had turned over when the Impala, coming at the other car from its blind side, had nudged it off the road. It wasn't his, Daggett's, fault that the other car had caught fire. He'd done it right where Rooney had said.

Rooney remained seated on the weight bench that was the closest thing to a piece of furniture in the room he called his gym. He finished two more sets, on each side, of preacher curls, dropped the 40-lb. dumbbells into their niches on the rack beside the bench, peeled off his wife-beater, tossing it toward the wicker basket he used for laundry. He missed.

He went into the bathroom and without undressing further washed his torso, armpits, neck and shoulders with spray from a hand shower. Toweling off before the mirror, he flexed his bi's, then his abs, then his pecs. He glowered at his image as he did this, then he smiled, without showing his teeth. His teeth, he knew, were not attractive. He had a beard and a mustache that were wiry and long, but you couldn't always hide your teeth. When he had to muscle somebody, his crooked teeth were an asset, as was his reassembled nose and his bald head. He knew exactly how to use what he had. When he was trying to impress a woman, he was generally tight-lipped until she was already taken in by his other charms before he relaxed about his teeth. It didn't usually take too long.

Rooney, now in a clean wife-beater and a cloud of Arrid Exxtra-Dry Spray, pulled on his jacket. He transferred the contents of the shot glass to the zippered inside pocket of the jacket. There was no question in his mind where Daggett wanted to meet him and, though it was not what he wanted to do, he would go meet him there. Daggett, he expected, wanted to renegotiate after the fact, after the job. This was not a strong negotiating position, and Rooney was confident that he could bitch-slap Daggett verbally and, if necessary, intimidate him physically. On the other hand, Rooney was a businessman. A smart one. On the way over to Ava's Grill and Bar he would decide whether or not keeping Daggett happy was worth any additional investment on his part, and if so, how much. And how he would recoup.

There were three locks on the inside of Rooney's front door – a double dead bolt opened and closed by a key, a second standard dead bolt, and the basic door knob lock. He'd just undone all three when the phone rang again. Daggett was now pushing his luck, he thought.

"What!" he snarled into the phone.

"Douche bag," said the quiet voice on the other end.

Rooney hung up the black phone, picked up the red one, and called out. His brother answered before it rang. He was sitting, Rooney knew, in the booth at the back of the Oceanfront Diner on Ocean Boulevard. He could picture him stirring coffee in a brown mug, stirring incessantly. Louis drank his coffee black, no sugar; he just liked to stir.

"What," Rooney said.

"You killed him," said Lou Rooney. "Who told you to do that?"

Rooney started to answer, but stopped. He knew the call couldn't be overheard; that wasn't what caused his hesitation. All of a sudden, he was in Daggett's shoes, and big brother was in Rooney's, and the irony was not lost on him. Now he would be making the same protestations that he'd anticipated would be coming from Daggett. Rooney had always heard that shit flowed downstream. It was one of the tenets of his business. Of all business. Well, if shit flowed downstream, why was he feeling squeezed in the middle? Why the hell was he getting it from both ends?

* * *

Scare him. That was the instruction Lou Rooney had given to his brother. Scare him with a sideswipe. He'd be rounding the far end of the lake, Nessin Pond, behind the big red Catholic church on Ocean, around 5:30. All he had to do was have somebody -- not himself, somebody – parked under the old unused underpass at the far end of the lake. Pull out of there fast and loud, with no lights, and give the old cop's car a little surprise nudge, and centrifugal force would do the rest.

Knowing how and when and where should have made it simple, piece of cake. Knowing where to have the accident take place was easy, since he was able to have the cop's boss send him just when he wanted him sent. That took just one call. The poor, dumb bastard on the other end didn't like having the mayor's right hand man give him a "tip" and then insist that it had to be followed, by exactly who he said, exactly when. He wasn't so dumb that he couldn't smell a set-up. But neither was he so dumb that he was going to defy the mayor's office. Especially not if he ever wanted to have the "acting" epithet removed from the front of his chief's title.

Chapter Two

When Elise got off the phone with the long-winded Maryland cop, she called Bachman, but there was no answer. Then she remembered: He was on his way up to Saratoga Springs to look for Jason's mother. She wanted to tell him that Jason didn't kill his father. She'd have to wait until he called her.

She hoped he would call soon. The fact that Lemmy may have been killed by a bullet and not by a knife which might have Jason's fingerprints on it was the good news. The bad news: the grand jury date had been moved up three weeks, from January 22nd to January 2nd. It was insane. This bombshell had been dropped on her shortly after she'd gotten off the phone with Sheriff Sandister. She'd gone into Fehme's office to tell him the latest − she kept her boss apprised of everything, and she trusted him, because he clearly put so much trust in her. Now she had only six – make that five-and-a-half days to prepare for it. Five-and-a-half days, including New Year's Eve and New Year's Day, to compile enough facts to call into question what the district attorney was calling a slam-dunk. If she could persuade the grand jury that the evidence linking Jason to Lemmy's death was circumstantial at best, she might be able to prevent an indictment – or at least delay it. Arrayed against her were the mayor's office, the prosecutor's office, lurid headlines in the *Atlantis Press*, an impossible new deadline, and, truth be told, a few silent doubts of her own. On her side? The accused who wouldn't speak to her, her instincts... and Bachman. And she couldn't reach him.

* * *

His train pulled into Saratoga Station a few minutes past noon. The station was not in the center of town, and Bachman didn't have his bike. He hadn't brought it with him on the train for the same reason he had taken the train instead of driving his car: snow. Bachman wasn't crazy about snow. The bustling Adirondack Mountain college town had snow on the ground or in the air from October to May every year. This fact made him appreciate his hometown of Atlantis even more, with its warming ocean currents that deflected the winter white stuff more often than not. He hadn't gotten ten strides from the train station on the way into town before he plunged his left foot and ankle into a half melted mound of snow. With one cold wet foot he sloshed the rest of the way into downtown Saratoga Springs.

He was there on the slimmest of hopes: *if* Jason's mother were alive, *if* she were here, *if* she had any connection to or info about the murder... The more he thought about it, the more he questioned his and Elise's decision to have him run down this lead. Okay, *his* decision. Wasn't it a waste of time? After all, the grand jury was convening in four weeks. That seemed like a lot of time, but now that he thought about it, time was running out. Only a few more days of Christmas break remained. Once his vacation was over, Bachman would have little or no time to play amateur gumshoe. The first weeks in January were invariably busy ones in school.

If all went well, there was an 8:30 pm train back to New York. He could conceivably be home by midnight if he got what he came for, or, alternatively, discovered there was nothing to be found here. If it got more complicated, he might have to spend the night. He'd figure out where if he had to.

I'm here, he thought. *Can't change that. Now, is Sonia here?* They had found the name Sonia Tejiste in Raumbaugh's cryptic notes. He didn't know if this was an alias that Roberta Johansen Fender used, or if it was someone who knew her in some way. Raumbaugh's notes often consisted of disconnected words and phrases, names, lists, abbreviations, diagrams, and lots of question marks. All Bachman was going on was a page that said

Richard W. Goffman

Mom – Roberta Johansen
b. 4.17.48, m. LF 4.4.67, JF b. 11.4.67
last seen NJ, 70, 71???

The only other thing on that page had been

Saratoga Raceway, Saratoga Spgs.
Dongan stable. hot walker?
Sonia Tejiste summer 79

Raumbaugh's double underline of the name had seemed so emphatic to Bachman. It almost forced the name Sonia Tejiste to life, drove it up the relevance ladder, invested it with portent. It could mean nothing at all. It probably was a dead end. But he couldn't help envisioning Raumbaugh drawing those two lines under the name after he'd written it, and it was this image of Raumbaugh carefully, neatly, and decidedly underlining it, twice, in dark pencil, that had propelled Bachman 200 miles on this frozen journey. In his mind's eye, Raumbaugh had taken a puff of his cigar after writing and underlining Sonia Tejiste, had looked at the page, had shaken his head and then put the cigar back down in the filthy ashtray before closing the notebook for the night. *Stop telling stories*, Bachman told himself. *This is real.*

In the train station he had picked up a tourist map, a colorful foldout brochure for racing fans and other visitors. On it he saw that there were clusters of stables and horse boarding establishments large and small south and east of the famous old Saratoga Raceway. There was no Dongan Stables, nor could he find the name "Dongan" anywhere on the map or in the phone book.

Now, outside Shakey's Espresso, he entered a phone booth. He picked up the phone, dropped in a quarter, and dialed the first few digits of Elise's office, but then he stopped, hung up, and got his quarter back. It would make him feel better to call Elise, sure. But it wouldn't do her much good. He had nothing to add. Yet. He would call later, when he learned something. Even if what he discovered was that there was nothing up here to learn, and that he was coming right back.

The thought of Elise had a distinct physical effect on him. Among other things, he was no longer cold, though he was still outdoors on a frozen street. His foot was no longer damp. He stood straighter. An unaccustomed smile had crept, unbidden, across his face. Elise.

He went inside the coffee shop. Over a cup of Shakey's double espresso, he scanned the map one more time, as if it had a secret to tell. He read every word on both sides. Folded closed, it was a self-mailer, he saw. It was titled "1983 Guide to Fun in Saratoga Springs." One panel listed the schedule for the Saratoga Performing Arts Center, events at Skidmore College, downtown arts festivals, performances and master classes by the New York City Ballet which had its summer headquarters in town. At the bottom of that panel he read that the map had been designed and printed at Adirondack Media Group.

Great, he thought. Now I'm reading the copyright information. Maybe I should just admit that this was a nice long train ride for nothing. This thought was too discouraging, so he scoured the map one last time. In what looked like a residential neighborhood only a few blocks from where he sat, he saw that Adirondack Media Group had helpfully illustrated its own location. With a very slim hope of making the long train ride less than a waste of time, Bachman finished his coffee and walked there.

In ten minutes – it was only a few blocks, but these blocks were long – he found the place. Like much of the town, this was a neighborhood of huge, hundred-plus-year-old Victorian houses. One of these Victorians, on a corner lot, was right where Adirondack Media Group should have been. It had a big wraparound porch with kids' toys all over it and spilling down the wide front stairs onto the snowy front lawn. He approached the front stairs and then decided to look around the side. There, behind the house, where at one time a three-car garage or maybe even a barn had been, stood a workshop of sorts. Above its front door swung a neatly calligraphed wooden plaque, with a big "Adirondack" above the smaller words "Media Group". He knocked and entered.

He was surprised how noisy it was inside, because he hadn't heard anything outside. Somewhere beyond this front area with a couple of mismatched desks, unimaginable machines were pounding out copies of something or other. The drumbeat of the presses almost but not quite matched the country music honking loudly in this room, and several people were laughing hysterically, somewhere, about something. On the floor at his feet lay a discarded yellow Big Wheel trike that looked like it had migrated from the house's porch.

A big man with a bushy beard came into the front room. He looked at Bachman, picked up the bike, opened the door and tossed it toward the house.

"How ya doing?" he asked. "Can I help you?"

"I don't know," Bachman began. "Probably not."

"Okay then," Big Bushy Beard guy said, and turned to leave.

Bachman said, "Hey."

The fellow with the beard turned back. "Only kidding," he said. "What do you need?"

Bachman held out the map. "You printed this, right?"

"Sure did."

"Do you print a new one every year?"

"Sure do. Started doing 'em five, six years ago. I got a guy sells ads to local businesses, banks, restaurants, inns, bars, stuff like that. You buy an ad, we make your place stand out on the map. It's a money-maker, believe it or not."

"I do believe it," Bachman said. "Do you happen to keep back copies?"

"Of course we do."

"Would it be possible for me to see the one from 1979?"

The big man frowned. "You only asked if we *kept* back copies. You didn't ask if I could *find* them." After what he must have thought was the exact right pause, he cracked up, tee-heeing. When it wound up taking him several minutes to find one, the hilarity of his joke was undermined, but he eventually located one and handed it over. He left Bachman sitting on a white plastic lawn chair in the front room and went back toward the noisy machines.

There it was: Dongan Stable. He looked up for Bushy Beard to thank him, but he was alone in the room. Rather than take the archived copy of the '79 map, he located the spot on the current map, and circled it with a Magic Marker from the desk beside him. He found a scrap of paper, wrote "Thanks!" on it, placed it on top of the refolded '79 map, left both on the desk, hoisted his pack and headed out the door.

Where once Dongan Stable had existed, now something called Schmidt's Smith stood. It took Bachman forty-five minutes to walk there; by the time he found the place it was midafternoon. He still held out hope of returning home today, but if this led to another connection and then another, that possibility would be unlikely. Only five more days of vacation, he realized. Less than a month until the grand jury.

The day had warmed and so had he. He'd taken his jacket off and tied its sleeves through the straps of his daypack. If he knew that he looked odd, striding through the town two days after Christmas with what looked like a black cape flapping behind him, he showed no sign of it. His feet were getting a little sore, but he felt good otherwise. And why wouldn't he feel good? He was following a story from setting to setting, from character to character. Unless he reached a dead end, it was like reading a book. He just hoped the book wouldn't end abruptly. Or tragically.

Schmidt's Smith presented itself to the world behind a pair of nine-foot-high, ornate wrought iron gates. Their size and craft and shape like giant moth-wings would have been enough to remark on, but the fact that they were not attached to any wall or fence, but merely stood at the sidewalk before the less impressive one-story wood frame workshop, made them a sight to behold. As Bachman marveled at the imposing free-standing structure, he noticed that some of the filigreed ironwork formed letters. Stepping back he was able to read it: the left gate said Schmidt; the right gate said Happens. They were locked closed with a large, ancient padlock. Bachman took this to be an irony in iron; he walked around the securely locked gates and up a slate path to the shop's front door.

Schmidt, it turned out, was Esther Schmidt, blacksmith, farrier, and craftswoman. She had bought the Dongan Stable property after a devastating fire which not only destroyed the building but had killed one horse and caused severe enough injuries to two others that they'd had to be put down. She wasn't sure she remembered Sonia Tejiste or any Roberta, but once she listened to Bachman's story, over tea she served in massive purple pottery mugs, she made a couple of phone calls.

Schmidt happens indeed, Bachman thought, as he left, after thanking Esther repeatedly. She'd even recommended a motel not too many blocks away which, thanks to it being the bottom of the low season, would give him a clean room for the night for $44.95. The second person Esther called had said that she would speak to Sonia and call back. The burly yet decidedly attractive craftswoman went back to her work, which involved hammering on iron in a variety of musical tones in the next room. He watched her work for a bit. With nothing else to do, and not wanting to take up any more of Esther's work time, Bachman sat on what appeared to be a seat from a Ford pickup and paged randomly through a local newspaper. Despite the tuneless ringing of Esther Schmidt's hammering, he soon dropped off to sleep.

He was awakened by Esther with instructions. Bachman should go to a bar called The Pipes around ten o'clock tomorrow night, and sit at the end of the bar near the TV; if Sonia could and wanted to speak with him, she would show up some time thereafter. No, Sonia Tejiste wasn't unlisted. She had no phone to list. And no, he wasn't getting any more information unless it was from Sonia herself, tomorrow night, at the far end of the bar at The Pipes.

Was it worth it? he wondered. He wouldn't be able to reverse the charges, so he offered Esther a few bucks to allow him to call New Jersey.

"Forget it," she said with a dismissive wave. "Call. No biggy."

"No, please," he insisted. "The tea, the information, your help. Your time is valuable, and you've been very helpful to me."

She shrugged and went back to her work. *Now I've insulted her?* he thought. He just couldn't seem to get his bearings with people around here. He picked up the phone and dialed first Elise's office and her home, but was unsuccessful in both attempts. He left "please tell her I called" messages with Mrs. Brantley and with the receptionist at SosWepFro. He scooted out without saying goodbye, rather than get into another discussion about the five dollar bill he left on the table.

Maybe it didn't matter that he couldn't reach Elise. He was pretty certain he could hear in his mind's ear exactly what she would say: "You've already travelled all the way up there," she'd say. "Finish what you started."

He pointed his feet in the direction Ballston Avenue, where Esther had told him he could find the affordable Oval Motel.

*   *   *

Armed with a faxed copy of the Worcester County (MD) Medical Examiner's report, Elise Brantley paid a visit to Dr. Ravi Patel, the coroner for Monmouth County, New Jersey, in his office in the basement of the Monmouth Medical Center.

"Of course, you don't have any idea whose heart this is," Dr. Patel said, after Elise had told him her amazing tale of the itinerant shark bearing its well-wrapped gift. He cheerfully pronounced her story to be "of mythic proportion." His workspace was so neat it appeared as if he had just moved in and the desk had just been delivered and set up. He made a tiny adjustment to one of four small, framed photos. More seriously, he tried to make himself clear to her. "I can not speculate in these matters. I only report what I personally see, what I can verify to be true."

"I completely understand," Elise answered him. She had thought it through. "Can you tell me though, based on your dissection of Mr. Fender, how big his heart would be, if it were to be weighed now? I mean, how big would you expect it to be?"

"Of course, that's impossible to say, young lady," Dr. Patel persisted in his Bengali lilt. "First of all, you are asking me to guess the size of a man's heart from the size of his body. This is an impossible thing to do with any accuracy or certainty."

"And even if I could make such a speculation, you will then want to ask me to project how much deterioration would take place in the time between its removal from Mr.-- from the victim's body, assuming that is the body it came from -- which we believe took place on an afternoon in October and the time when it was recovered from -- *from the belly of a shark?* Do you see how utterly preposterous this is? Was this organ preserved? How was it preserved? What took place inside that animal's gut? And how did it get there? How long between the time it was removed from the body, until it was wrapped, and how long between then and when the shark came into possession of it? A day? A month? Two months? Frankly, I can not believe we are even having this discussion." He paused. "And why do you even assume that this great fish swam from New Jersey to Maryland to deliver this package?"

"That's the way they travel, sir," Elise told him, humbled by the absurdities that he enumerated. "They migrate. And there was other junk—there was other evidence taken from the shark's stomach that indicated a voyage down the east coast.

"The heart was wrapped, tightly, in at least three layers of aluminum foil," she continued, grateful that he had not yet thrown her out of his office for wasting his time. "This package was placed inside a plastic Ziploc bag which was, in turn, inside a plastic supermarket shopping bag. According to all the witnesses, including policemen, the shopping bag was in shreds, apparently from the stomach acids, not from tearing. And the Ziploc bag was intact. It was still sealed. The report describes the outer layer of foil as dry and free of any contamination."

Without mentioning the bullet, but she made a last appeal to his sympathies. "Sir, I have a duty to defend my client. He is an abused boy who is entirely alone in the world – no friends, no family, no one -- and he is in a near-catatonic state as we speak. The evidence against him is entirely circumstantial. If I could use the discovery of enough controverting circumstantial evidence of my own to raise questions that would show the weakness' of the district attorney's charges, a reasonable judge would have to be reluctant to charge. At least until much more were known.

The coroner rubbed his face with both his hands. He rocked his chair back at a disturbing angle, then brought its legs back to the floor. "There are certain tests." Elise's face reflected a crack in the cloud of doom. "There are tests that can be done." He spoke carefully. "An effort can be made to compare the genetic material, which might indicate a likelihood, a possibility of a match," he said. Even as he said it, he was shaking his head. "But you must understand that these tests are rarely conclusive. And furthermore, they are expensive."

Elise felt her own heart rise and then fall as Dr. Patel raised a hope and then dashed it. She pictured herself sitting across from Fehme, trying to convince him to spend who knew how much money it would cost to test this found heart to prove its rightful owner. In a pro bono case. And, once proved, would this really mean that Jason hadn't murdered Lemmy? Or merely that he had shot him before chopping him up? For the first time since she'd gotten the call from Maryland, she was glad she hadn't been able to reach Bachman. Maybe she'd be raising his hopes unreliably. On the other hand, she needed him back here. He still didn't know about the new grand jury date.

"Where is this peripatetic organ now, at this precise moment?" Dr. Patel asked her.

"It is in FBI custody in Annapolis, Maryland," Elise said. "Refrigerated."

"May I see it?"

"We have subpoenaed it," Elise said. "That's why I'm here: To try to persuade you to take a look at it."

"This is completely irregular," Dr. Patel said. "The key to my work is the security of the material I work with, the chain of possession from the moment a body is recovered until the moment I finish examining it. However" – and here Elise's heart, despite her caution, rose again – "as the possibility exists that this may be the missing body part, and if it is, and if it indeed contains a bullet, then I presume you would make a case for at least the possibility that the victim was not killed in the way we have stated, not necessarily at the time we have stated, perhaps not even in the same location… At that point I would have to withdraw my existing autopsy report and begin again." He trailed off, his eyes moving around the room as these different possibilities arrayed themselves in his consciousness, disturbing the orderliness of his previous assumptions.

"Miss Brantley," he said to her, and she could see that he had arrived at a conclusion that was both unpleasant and unavoidable. "I will examine this specimen in the context of the investigation. I may be able to make certain determinations."

Elise stood, trying her best not to look triumphant.

"I said, 'I will try,'" the medical examiner cautioned her. "So far as any benefit for your client is concerned, at the end of the day I strongly suspect that you are wasting your time."

* * *

He read for a couple of hours in his spartan little room at The Oval Motel, then he ate vegetable soup and a hamburger at The Spa Town Diner. Traveling north on the train alone had been interesting – it had brought out the explorer in him. Trekking alone around Saratoga and tracking down Sonia Tejiste had been very interesting – he'd gotten to play detective or, as he thought of it, scavenger hunt. But staying alone in the cheap motel, and particularly crumbling saltines into soup by himself at that diner had reinforced his aloneness. At the same time, it reminded him that, though he was here alone, there was someone important in his life. There was someone to whom he was becoming important. There was someone who, when he was far away and alone, he could, and in fact needed to call.

He had put off calling because he wanted to call her when he had something substantial to say. The point turned out to be moot. She was gone from her office by the time he tried her there. He left a message with the answering service, including the number of the phone at the front desk of the motel. Phones were not among the amenities afforded guests of the Oval, so he made sure the message included the fact that she would in all likelihood not be home tomorrow night either, but rather the next afternoon. He hoped that she would not read any positive sign in that. Her phone at home went unanswered, which was preferable to having to explain that to Mrs. Brantley. Although it was a comfort to know that there was someone for him to call, the result of making the calls was that he was lonelier than before he'd made them.

Chapter Three

Wednesday was a normal working day in Saratoga. It was a normal working day everywhere, for everybody except William Bachman. He awoke with a backache from a mattress that felt like plywood. He went to the Oval's office where he found two things that disturbed him mightily. First was the worst cup of coffee he had ever tasted. Second was a message from Elise. He had left very clear instructions with the night clerk that he should be awakened if any calls came for him. Today's clerk, possibly a different sallow-faced mumble-mouthed kid than the one he had spoken with earlier, seemed unconcerned. Why, he wondered, was Bachman giving him someone else's crap? *He* hadn't worked the nightshift. *He* hadn't taken the call. *He* hadn't heard Bachman's earlier request. In fact, he hadn't ever laid eyes on Bachman before, and would have preferred not to be doing so now. Apparently, if Bachman didn't *want* the ripped corner of a magazine page with Elise's first name and office number scrawled on it that he had been good enough to give him, today's desk clerk would be happy to toss it in the trash for him and go back to watching the nice lady on "Good Morning, America" teach him how to make gourmet popcorn. Bachman left the full cup of coffee with the helpful young man and left the office without another word.

He calculated that it was too far and he felt too lousy to walk all the way to Shakey's Espresso, but he was able to locate the Spa Town Diner just a few blocks away. The coffee there was a bare improvement over that at the Oval. What was it with this town? It had it's own natural spring for which it was named! Why couldn't they make a decent cup of coffee? He saw other people drinking it without spitting, so he ate some oatmeal and tried to calm himself. He'd just had a bad night.

He now faced a day without much of an agenda, at least until 10 tonight. It was snowing lightly when he left the diner. The very helpful woman at the cash register told him how to find the town's library.

The library was a pleasant surprise: large, airy, quiet, with an intelligent, helpful librarian and a huge collection. He spent the next six hours there. He read through every directory of every kind that he could find, searching for the names Johansen, Fender, Tejiste. He read all about the Dongan Stable tragedy, and learned in the *Racing Gazette* that it led to a political scandal which cost several people their jobs when it was discovered how much chicanery was taking place with the fire inspector and some of the owners of stables and other track-related businesses.

Then he read several weeks worth of news items for the period leading up to the murder in Atlantis. He learned from this way more than he wanted to about nothing he cared at all about.

When he realized that there was nothing he could ever locate in this library that would be of any benefit at all to Jason Fender, he found a copy of Kafka's *The Trial* and read it from cover to cover.

At three he walked back to the motel. Much to his surprise, his nemesis from the morning came out of the office to greet him as he passed by. Elise had called again. Buddy, as it turned out this young fellow was named, had knocked several times on the door of Bachman's room. Getting no response, and seeing no Do Not Disturb hangtag on the doorknob, he'd let himself in, briefly, just to make certain "that everything was okay."

Bachman thanked him graciously, though his frustration was apparent. When Buddy asked if there was anything else he needed, Bachman mentioned the bad night sleep he'd had. Buddy helped Bachman move his things from Room 4 to Room 12, which had the newest mattress in the place. "We're upgrading a few rooms at a time," Buddy explained. "Steven should have put you in here in the first place."

Bachman gave Buddy a five which he pretended for a few seconds to refuse but finally accepted. Room 12 smelled better – no smoke – looked cleaner, and had a newer TV, though still no phone. The bed,

as it turned out, was extremely comfortable. In the previous 48 hours Bachman had slept in fits, first on a rat-
tling, bumping train, then in a displaced car seat in a
working blacksmith shop, and finally on the torture
rack in Room 4. He immediately dropped into a coma-
like, dreamless sleep.

When he awoke, everything was pitch dark and
he hadn't a clue where he was. For a second it seemed
possible that he was in Lemmy Fender's powerless
house on Taylor Street. This time he would simply
back out, get in his car, and split. But a red glow
proved to be a digital alarm clock. It was past nine
o'clock.

Shit! He jumped out of bed. The light switches
mercifully produced light, which helped him confirm
where he truly was. He didn't have time to shower. He
changed his shirt, zipped up his coat, and stepped outside. It was really snowing now. He began jogging.

He got to The Pipes, an Irish-themed saloon,
around 9:30. It was one of those places that looked in-
consequential, nearly unnoticeable, from the outside,
but expanded once you went inside. The front room,
which apparently was the main bar room, was bigger
than he expected, and was growing more crowded by
the minute. Many people passed through this room
toward the back, through a door which apparently led
to a performance space. He could hear a band with
horns and at least one electric guitar and several singers
of both sexes playing loud music not all of which was
traditional Irish stuff. Much of it involved the audience
in singing along, and every time the door to that room
opened, especially if it happened to be at the end of a

tune, the unbridled roaring of the audience sounded as if it came from several hundred well-oiled throats.

There was another door leading, according to a sign, to a game room, and there was a kitchen door that never stopped swinging as waiters and waitresses raced in and out, bringing huge trays of hot food out and hustling back with clattering empty plates. But the door that Bachman kept his eye on as he sipped his red beers was the one the one he'd entered through. He didn't have a clue what the mysterious Sonia would look like, nor could she know him except by his assigned position at the bar, but he still examined each person as she or he appeared. If an entering woman looked in his general direction, he looked closer at her face. If a couple came through the door, he figured she couldn't be Sonia. When a gaggle of laughing young girls piled in, she could not be one of them. He had absolutely no information about her other than the fact that she didn't have phone service, but he couldn't help composing a picture of her in his head – an expectation. Her name sounded Hispanic, so he pictured black hair, brown skin. She'd worked at a stable, so he imagined a sturdy, strong person, maybe a big woman. Definitely not a kid. On the other hand, if she were a horsewoman, she might be petite.

At the same time, he wondered what connection Raumbaugh had made between this Sonia Tejiste and Roberta Johansen. Maybe Sonia *is* Roberta. After all, maybe it was an alias. Roberta had fled Lemmy and New Jersey; perhaps she'd changed her name and started a new life entirely.

Richard W. Goffman

As the bartender brought him his third Killi-
an's, he thought about Monmouth Park in Oceanport,
the racing mecca of the shore. A number of his students
got summer jobs there each year. He'd only been there
once, himself. Bobby D tried to get him to go once in a
while, but the track never appealed to him much. He
wondered about the people who bet, the people who
worked at the track, the people, like Esther Schmidt,
who worked in businesses associated with racing and
horses, businesses which grew around these famous old
racetracks all around the country. And not only the
Esther Schmidts, but also the others, the less legitimate
ones. Every entity that included gambling, albeit state
sanctioned, sponsored, and taxed, had its seamy side.
Wherever there was gambling there was lots of money
going this way and that. There was booze, and drugs,
and people who moved them around. There were
touts, and pickpockets, and wise guys. Where there
were gamblers, there were a few winners, and plenty of
losers. So there were loan sharks. And people who collected for them. Where there were guys throwing money around, there were hookers and there were pimps. It
was, he figured, a little subculture, a little world. Maybe
not so little.

Probably some people moved from track to
track, as one's season ended and another's began. "Hot
walker" it had said in Raumbaugh's notes. (See? One
didn't have to be an English teacher to appreciate the
value of writing in complete sentences, did one?) Maybe Roberta had worked at or around Monmouth Park,
and when it came time for her to split, Saratoga was

one logical destination, not too far, but far enough. Someplace she'd blend right in. Maybe...

Bachman hadn't had a conversation with anyone in the bar since he'd sat down a couple of beers ago, but now the guy on the next stool was poking him in the shoulder. When he had Bachman's attention, he pointed to the door. When had Bachman stopped looking at the door and checking all the entering faces? A woman was there, half in and half out. She was gesturing for him to come over.

He hopped down clumsily and wove through the crowd to her. This had to be Sonia. She looked to be in her forties, thick-waisted, but it was hard to tell with her parka and hood. She was holding the door open with one shoulder, dividing her attention between the room and something outside.

When he reached her he said, "Sonia Tejiste?"

She gave him half a nod and said, "Give me a hand." Her voice was like gravel. She stepped outside.

Bachman caught the door before it closed and followed her. Outside the door, engulfed in a similar parka, was a child or a small adult in a wheelchair.

There were two steps up to the front door of The Pipes. Bachman hadn't noticed them going in. In a flash he saw the steps, and all steps, from an entirely different perspective. Without another word Sonia leaned on the upper part of the wheelchair to tilt it slightly backward. Bachman grasped the small wheels at the front. They lifted together. He was shocked at how light the burden was. Now Sonia had to get the door open again, which she managed to do with a foot, swinging it wide and catching it with a practiced motion of one hip. In this manner, they carried the wheelchair with its still invisible passenger inside the bar and placed it on the floor.

The noisy crowd of drinkers accommodated them, parting to let them through with the wheelchair and reclosing behind them as Sonia moved it forward. It was impossible to hear each other speak. Bachman was relieved when Sonia pointed toward the game room door. As soon as they got through it the noise level dropped. On their left were two pool tables surrounded by players and watchers; to the right was yet another room. They went in there, which required lifting the wheelchair again and going down one step.

Now they were in a small dining room. There was no bar in here, no jukebox, and they could barely hear the band or the drinkers in the barroom. Half the tables were occupied. Sonia zipped open her parka and threw it into one of the empty booths. She moved a chair away from the outer edge of the table, and came back to Bachman and took the wheelchair. She positioned it at the table, then helped its occupant remove her parka.

Bachman could now see the face of a woman in the wheelchair. It was distorted – scarred, he guessed. Her right eye was open only part way. Both eyes looked at him. She had curly brown hair. She smiled a crooked, tight-lipped smile which was higher on the left than the right. He noticed a dimple on her left cheek.

"Are you a cop?"

He turned back to Sonia Tejiste, who was now seated comfortably in the booth. Nobody had ever asked him this before. Not sure whether to be flattered or insulted, he settled on neither.

"No, I'm a teacher," he said.

"What do you teach?" she asked.

"High school English."

"Are you here to correct my grammar?"

"I try not to do that," Bachman said. "People hate that."

The waitress came, and Sonia, after communicating with a look at her companion, ordered two shots of Bushmill's. The waitress looked at Bachman who held up three fingers indicating he'd join in.

"Would either of you like something to eat?" he asked them.

"We ate," Sonia said, without consulting her friend.

When the waitress left, Bachman plunged in. "My name is Bachman. Bill. I'm not here to—" He lost his train of thought. Maybe it was the beers. Maybe it was the way they both looked at him, or maybe it was something else, but he found himself struggling to explain why he was here. "I'm trying to figure something out," he said. It sounded stupid, to him, as soon as he said it.

"Well, I'm Sonia. And this is my friend, Roberta. You were asking about us, I hear. Whaddya want?"

When the first round arrived, heavy shot glasses brimming with whiskey, Roberta lifted hers an inch off the table with her left hand. At first he thought she was unable to get the glass to her lips, but then Bachman realized she was proposing a toast, so he gestured with his glass, and Sonia did too. Her voice was low and full of air, and though he watched her crooked lips carefully, he couldn't make out what she was toasting. He was prepared to agree with it anyhow. Sonia understood her friend and repeated the toast: "Here's to 'figuring something out.'" They clicked their glasses, and they drank.

Bachman wasn't sure how to begin, or where, but he recognized that he couldn't just start probing. "I teach down the shore. That is, at the Jersey shore. I'm trying to help somebody out. It's this whole puzzle kind of thing. And we found something with your name, Sonia. So I was hoping..."

Sonia didn't try to make it any easier. "What's it about? Where was my name?"

"It was in this detective's notebook," he said.

"He a cop?"

"Well—yes, he is."

"Why'n't he come look for me?"

"Well. He's sort of out of commission for a while. For now."

"And you're filling in for him."

"Well, no," Bachman said. "Not officially. But, in a way, I guess you could say that. Though I'm not doing a very good job. But now that I'm here, I'm starting to think it doesn't matter."

"I don't get you," Sonia said. "What the-- what's it all about?"

"It's hard to explain. A kid—a student—got himself into some trouble, and I'm trying to help out."

This – trying to talk without being specific -- was awkward, almost painful. But the ice was broken.

Sonia, at least, seemed to let down her guard a little. The whiskeys helped. When Roberta had something to add Sonia would lean her ear close to her mouth, and then sometimes, but not always, would repeat it to Bachman. They drank two Bushmill's each, and Bachman insisted on getting a pitcher of ale and a small mountain of onion rings, the favorite snack of the house. It came with three different dipping sauces. Bachman noticed that Roberta hooked her onion rings each time with the same hand, her left, the one that she used to lift her glass. The right hand remained so still on the arm of the wheelchair that it occurred to him that it might somehow be fastened there.

"Me and Roberta, we've lived together, since a little while − a few months before the fire," Sonia said. It turned out that their place was not too far from where they were now sitting, which is why Sonia had chosen this place to meet, since they had no car, and getting Roberta in and out of one was a tricky business.

"We don't get out a helluva lot these days, so even coming down the street here was a big deal."

Roberta, it seemed, had been badly injured in the Dongan Stable fire. Sonia had been out picking up supplies that day. The papers had talked mainly about the horse that was killed, and the other ones that had to be destroyed. Roberta had been burned, and she'd also been stepped on by a horse in the panic. They never talked to any reporters about it, and eventually the newspaper people stopped bothering them.

At several points in the conversation, Roberta appeared to fall asleep. It was during one of these moments that Bachman took the opportunity to explain exactly why he had come. Sonia did not act surprised. After all, she was aware that Roberta had left a little boy behind when she ran from "that shithead" at the Jersey shore. When Bachman had said where he taught, she must have anticipated the general direction this was going.

"Has she... Has Roberta had any contact with her old life? With Jason?" Bachman asked.

"No," Sonia said. "We have no phone, no car, and we don't get no mail, 'less you count bills. I know it wasn't easy for her to leave that kid. At the time, she figured he was better off without her."

She leaned a little closer to him and lowered her voice. "She tried to kill herself a couple of times, back in the day. Roberta's had herself one fucked up life." Sonia was looking at her friend as she said this last, and as he watched and listened, Bachman could not recall ever hearing the words "fucked up" spoken with such utter tenderness.

"She always dreamed of the day when she would get it together, and then go back and get her boy. These days she don't kid herself about nothing no more. And neither do I."

Roberta turned her head at this moment, pushed a brown curl of hair away from her eye, and looked at Bachman. He wondered what she had and had not heard, and if she had been sleeping at all. She crooked her finger at him, drawing him close to her face. It occurred to him that this was the closest he'd been to a woman's face other than Elise's in several years. He felt a sudden, distinct prickling sensation in both his thumbs.

He could hardly see her face, distracted as he was by the details of it. The patterns of scars, the outlines of skin grafts, the asymmetry. He was close enough to see his own reflection in her left eye, the one that was wide open. He thought he could smell straw, and manure. And smoke.

Now he could hear her when she spoke. Her voice was soft, but clear.

"You're Jason's teacher." It was a statement.

"Yes. I'm Jason's English teacher," Bachman said. "He's... he is a very nice young man."

Her eyes seemed to look into him as if she could see into his memories and get a glimpse of the young man her little boy had grown to be. Bachman kept very still. He tried to hold a positive, healthy image of Jason in his consciousness, not the image of the silent, damaged kid he'd ridden with in the ambulance. He realized he had no healthy, robust images of Jason in the cells of his memory. The best he could come up with was nervous Jason, sitting in Bachman's VW, saying "Thanks for the lift," and leaving without closing the car door.

After a brief eternity she whispered, "Thank you," and released him. They both sat back, she in her chair, he in the booth. She returned to the state she had been in before, which, even if it weren't sleep, did appear to knit up the raveled sleeve of care. Bachman's peripheral vision and hearing returned to him. He hadn't realized his senses had narrowed, but he felt that, in retrospect, he and Roberta Johansen had been communicating with each other from either end of a tunnel.

He and Sonia talked for a while more. Clearly the question he'd come all this way to have answered – Was there any way that Jason's mother, Lemmy Fender's estranged wife, could have had anything to do with, or shed any light on, the murder of the man who had caused so much of her grief? – clearly this question no longer needed to be asked.

She had a question for him.

"Why are you here?"

This confused him, as he thought this had been established.

"No," she said. "I mean, why are *you* here?"

Oh. It was clear to him why he was there, why *he* was there, but he couldn't think of how to begin to explain it to someone else. He started a couple of sentences but got nowhere.

Sonia tried to help draw it out of him. "I mean, you're a teacher. You're Jason's teacher…"

Bachman looked at her and came out with the only words he could, though he didn't think they did the job at all. "I'm not *just* a teacher."

The former Roberta Fender's head lolled to the right, and she was snoring quietly when Bachman and Sonia carried her through the bar and out to the street. It was close to one in the morning. The snow had stopped and a bright moon lit up the drifts on the ground. He wanted to walk them to their home.

"I can handle it," Sonia demurred. "It's only a few blocks. We got ramps and shit at home. We're handicapped-accessible."

Not easy words to pronounce while tipsy, Bachman thought, but all he said was, "Goodnight. Thanks for coming out."

"Thanks for the drinks," Sonia said, as she began wheeling her sleeping friend, her longtime companion, along the cracked sidewalk. "And the rings. I had forgot how good those onion rings were."

In truth, Bachman's bed lay in the opposite direction, and he had a train to catch in a few hours. So he waved goodbye, hunched down into his coat, and pulled his wool hat as far down over his ears as he could. He lengthened his strides in the direction of the Oval Motel, and watched his breath freeze in the air before his face. He pictured Sonia and Roberta, and Jason too, and his heart tightened as he considered the hard compulsions of the poor.

Chapter Four

Bachman rode most of the way from Saratoga Springs to New York City sitting in a backward facing seat. It was December 29, he realized. He had awakened at the Oval Motel barely in time to make the train. The young man at the front desk, a new one, had called him a cab, an extravagance that was necessitated by his lateness and a whanging hangover that precluded the notion of jogging to the station.

He'd hoped to sleep some more on the trip, but sleep wouldn't come. A trip to the concession car made his stomach churn. Clutching a cup of weak coffee and a box of Tums he returned to his seat. Back in the station he'd tried Elise's office, but got the service. It was too early. I'll call her when I change trains at Penn Station, he thought, as he'd boarded the 7:30 Amtrak for New York City.

HEARTLESS CRUELTY

Day after tomorrow would be New Year's Eve. It was an event Bachman typically spent alone, or else in the company of other unmarried buddies. What would this New Year's Eve bring? Elise, he assumed. *Assume nothing.* Elise, he hoped. Was she, he wondered, thinking the same thing? They had made love. They had worked together. They had eaten several meals together, and they had made love again. This meant... what? Did Bachman have a new girlfriend? Was he somebody's boyfriend? And wasn't there an adult euphemism for "boyfriend" and "girlfriend" that didn't make one sound like a child when using it?

The train banged and rattled south, and still sleep wouldn't come. He stared out the window at the slate gray world racing past. At times they passed within arm's length of the icy Hudson, and at other times he could watch it and the snow clad mountains from a comfortable remove. The semi-frozen river passed under impressive highway bridges and between daunting cliffs and palisades, occasionally disappearing from view entirely.

Had Elise ever taken this trip? Certainly she'd traveled between the Shore and New Haven plenty of times, but where else? He felt his head swim, but it wasn't the hangover, which had begun to abate. How very much he didn't know about her. Unbidden, his parents' faces appeared in his consciousness. To the inevitable question from his mother last week when he was home, he had indicated that, yes, he was dating, but no more. He imagined a dinner table conversation. His father would point out the obvious differences between Elise and Bachman. His mother would point out the less obvious things: the similarities. Their faces disappeared again. For better or worse, mom and dad had never gotten a vote in his love life. And if they had, they'd probably cancel one another out anyhow.

* * *

Mayor Scanlon paused in the act of stowing the white homburg in its spot on the top shelf of his closet in his office. It was dirty, he noticed. He'd known when he'd ordered it that a white hat was an indulgence that would require extra care and frequent maintenance, so he didn't allow himself a fit of pique. Back at his desk, he pulled a small folder of business cards from his desk drawer and began flipping through it. When he found the one he was looking for he removed it.

Marcia, his secretary, came in. She set the coffee carafe and cup carefully on the desk, followed by the morning mail, each piece opened, the contents stapled to its envelope, and stacked in order of priority. Last, the *Atlantis Press*. She accepted the business card with the haberdasher's number, trading it for a sheaf of telephone messages.

He pointed at the hat on the top shelf of the open closet. "Send it in for cleaning. And blocking," Scanlon said. He looked up at her then, for the first time since she'd entered for their morning ritual which started each business day. He looked back down and shuffled through the pink phone message slips. When he became aware that she hadn't left immediately, as she normally did, he looked back up at her again.

Marcia was biting her lower lip. It was an unaccustomed gesture. Scanlon knew her simply as his secretary. He respected the fact that she didn't fear him as much as most of his other staff members did. This made her more useful than the typical kiss-asses and yes-men and yes-women who surrounded him. If she was still standing there, she must have something else for him. If she was biting her damn lip, she must be having a problem saying it.

Marcia was the exact same age as her boss; a lifetime of service to men like him had taught her a lot. She knew how to give them what they needed as well as what they wanted, and she was adept at letting them think that they were responsible for the little, important things which she, in fact, accomplished on their behalf. She made them more effective than they would be without her, regardless of whether they knew or acknowledged it. This was her job, she felt, and she was good at it.

Through it all, she maintained a level of dignity that she carried with her, like a wallet card denoting membership in an honor society. She was a woman of regularity – regular appearance, regular attendance, regular habits. She went to church every single Sunday, and cooked with the women's group for two different homeless shelters, facts which would be of no interest to her boss. She didn't lose things, she didn't forget things, she knew where everything was, and she never called in sick. Her reliability made her an asset to the bosses she had worked for. Now she stood, hesitant, troubled, in front of Mayor Scanlon's desk.

"What?" asked Scanlon, realizing that there was something, not knowing how else to get it. He looked back down at the notes she'd given him, and then back up at her.

"There was another message," Marcia said.

The mayor looked at the message slips yet again. "Besides these?" he asked, confused.

"Yes."

"And...?"

"And—" she began. "It was from—"

He'd never seen her stutter or falter, or have any difficulty telling him anything before. His patience, never deep, evaporated.

"Marcia. Who called? What did they say? Please just spit it out."

"A man called. It was early this morning. He didn't—he wouldn't leave his name, but he said he was calling for a Mr. Montalvo."

Now she had one hundred percent of Mayor Scanlon's attention. He leaned forward as far as he could without getting out of his desk chair. Marcia, trembling slightly, stood her ground. With a slow "keep going" gesture of his hand he coaxed from her the message which she'd been unable to write down.

"He said that Mr. Montalvo wanted—wanted you to know something." Marcia took a deep breath. She understood that there was no way around this other than straight through it. She hadn't had to write down what the man had said. She'd had no trouble remembering it, but now saw she'd have to actually repeat it.

She didn't keep eye contact with him. She took a breath and said, "He said, 'Mr. Montalvo wants to remind you that whether you like it or not, that fucking retard you got down there in your jail is your running mate.' I-- I didn't know what he meant, but he didn't say anything else."

When Marcia looked back up, she saw that the mayor's expression had not changed, exactly, as much as it had stopped moving around on his face. After a couple of seconds he exhaled, and leaned back in his chair. In a much softer voice than she expected, he said "Thank you, Marcia." And then, "Get Lou Rooney in here. Now. Please."

* * *

When Elise Brantley called her office she learned from Mary Casey, the office manager/receptionist, that she had three more messages, all from Mr. Bachman. The first one said that he was on the 7:30am train from Saratoga Springs, and expected to get to New York City around 10:15. The second one, at around noon, said that snow and ice on the track had made his train late, and he'd just arrived in Penn Station. The third one, half an hour after the second, said that he wouldn't be getting to Atlantis Station until 4:30 at best.

"Did he say anything else?" Elise asked, and immediately regretted it. Had she expected him to tell Mary, "Also, please tell Ms. Brantley that I miss her, that I can't wait to see her"? Silly, she told herself.

"No, that's it," Mary said.

She knew he'd ridden his bike to the station. She hoped she might be able to go down there and pick him up. It was snowing pretty hard now, and she hated the thought of him pedaling home in this mess. On the other hand, she didn't know how they could take the bike in her car, and she was pretty sure he wouldn't want to leave it locked there another day. On the *other* other hand, if the weather kept up, he might not have a choice. Regardless, she thought, there are bigger fish to fry. He still doesn't know that the grand jury is not at the end of January – It's next week.

Today would be Elise's last opportunity to talk with – or to – Jason before the hearing. Although he had not said a single word to her, she believed, perhaps because she wanted to believe, that he heard her when she spoke to him, as she had done on three previous occasions, each time for an hour. An hour was a long time for a monologue. In a way, it reminded her of her orals at Yale. She tried so hard to communicate with him, as she had done with those professors, but she just couldn't read a reaction.

Now she was trying once more. The guard brought Jason, handcuffed, to the tiny consultation room. As he had before, he seemed even younger than his seventeen years, lost in the oversized orange prison jumpsuit. The guard reminded her, unnecessarily, that she had an hour, that she couldn't give the prisoner anything or touch the prisoner (what the hell did he think?) and that, if she wanted to leave before the hour was up, she just had to knock on the door, which would be locked from the outside.

The room held two old wooden armchairs, nothing else. There was no window other than the one in the door. The wall opposite the door had a large mirror, which Elise assumed enabled viewing of the room from a chamber next door. She assumed that their conversations were being monitored. Monologues, she corrected herself. Thus far, only monologues.

As he had done during each of her prior visits, Jason entered meekly. Despite his long legs, he managed to twist his body, drawing up his knees and sitting nearly sideways in the chair. He looked at her with an expression lacking in curiosity or concern. Then he assumed his position, and stared in the general direction of his knees.

"I have something new, Jason," she said.

No reaction.

Speaking to two audiences, as it were, one present and one hidden, Elise chose her words purposefully. If they were listening, they'd get an earful now. Unless Dr. Patel had already clued them in.

"We have reason to believe that Lemmy—that your father's death was not caused by a knife." She watched carefully now, hoping for a sign. Anything. "I think I can prove that your father was shot at close range with a small caliber gun."

Jason reached down and brushed an invisible something from the leg of his jumpsuit. He folded his hands in his lap and looked up at her. His face was as free of expression as it had been during every previous conversation.

"As you know, as I told you before, the heart— in his examination of the body the coroner discovered that the heart was missing from the body. Well, I think we've found it. This will change everything, in terms of the prosecution's case against you, if it can be confirmed. And I'm pretty sure it will be confirmed."

Jason appeared to be looking at her, but she wasn't certain. He may have been looking just a bit to her left.

"I can't promise you anything, of course."

The boy's utter lack of engagement was now weighing on her. His complacent features seemed flaccid. His whole personality seemed flaccid, and it was starting to make her angry. He could hear her, and understand her. She was sure of it. She remembered the guard's prohibition against touching the prisoner as she pictured herself taking him by his skinny arms and shaking him, and shouting into his face: "Care! This is your life, not mine. Why don't you care?"

Of course, she didn't do that.

Instead, she regained her composure by breathing deeply, something she'd learned how to do in the martial arts class she took last summer. This lowered her heart rate. She also relaxed the muscles in her jaw, because she knew she was clenching her teeth. Then she forced herself to smile.

Elise gathered the few sheets of paper she had taken out of her case, and pointedly snapped it shut. "Okay, okay. I get it. You don't care what happens. Forget all the work I'm doing. Forget your Mr. Bachman, dragging his butt all the way upstate New York to try to find your mother. Forget—" She caught herself. Jason was now looking at her. Not through her or past her. Not now. His eyes had, for the first time in her experience, come to life.

Had the guilt trip been the key to opening him up? Hell, she could have tried the guilt trip approach long before now if she had known... No, it wasn't that, but whatever it was, Jason was now fully alert. Elise stood, moving slowly to her right, in a manner she hoped would appear casual to anyone who might be observing. He followed her with his now intense gaze. As if by instinct, Elise kept moving to her right, to Jason's left, until she was standing between his chair and the see-through mirror. Maybe they weren't paying close attention, she thought. She hoped.

She lowered her voice. "Jason, what is it? Are you with me now?"

"Where did Mr. Bachman go?" Jason whispered.

"Saratoga Springs, New York," Elise said.

"Who— why— Why did he go there?"

"We thought your mother might be there."

"Was— did he...?"

Elise swallowed hard. "I don't know, Jason. Maybe. I haven't been able to talk to him since he left. Maybe not. I'll know tonight."

When his eyes had come to life, something like a spring had tightened every muscle in his body. Despite the ill-fitting jumpsuit, Jason appeared to be coiled and ready to—what? Spring at her? Jump up from his seat? She prayed that no one could see what she was seeing. An interruption now would ruin everything. And whatever she might learn from him now she hoped to be able to keep to herself.

Jason's hands gripped the arms of the wooden chair. The skin around his fingernails was even whiter than the rest of his pallid complexion. His eyes squinted, and his mouth was now taut. He trembled a little.

"We had to try, Jason," Elise said. "You weren't helping us. The detective-- he let us know that maybe, maybe, she..."

"She wasn't there," Jason said, as if he were answering a hostile question. His voice, unused for a month, sounded like steam and rust.

"Your mother?" Elise asked. "Wasn't where?"

"I've never seen my mother," Jason said. "She didn't do anything."

So now he was talking, but he wasn't making sense. Certainly he knew that he had seen his mother when he was very young, even if he didn't actually remember what she looked like. And no one had suggested that she had "done anything."

"Leave her alone," Jason said. It may not have made sense to Elise, but it was unambiguous.

* * *

At ten minutes to five, the train carrying Bill Bachman and several hundred Manhattan commuters who were getting a bit of an early start on their New Year's holiday finally pulled into Atlantis Station. He'd been watching the snow falling, and accumulating, for the hour since they'd emerged from the tunnel into north Jersey, but he no longer cared. He'd be so glad to be home, so relieved to be on his own turf after the wretched day he'd had, that he'd gladly walk the three miles to his house through the blowing snow, carrying his bicycle on his back if need be. As he waited for the doors to open, he reviewed one last time the indignities of the trip: He'd left his book on the bedside table at the Oval Motel; the Amtrak had sat still, above Peekskill, for more than an hour, with no enlightenment from the crew as to what was going on; they'd had to change trains in blinding slush when they'd finally made Peekskill; he'd missed an earlier connection for the Shore by less than sixty seconds, requiring an additional hour-and-a-half sitting in Penn Station's unfriendly confines; and he'd missed Elise each and every time he'd tried to call her. He was five hours late, and he was exhausted. But at least he was home.

The rack where he'd left his bike locked was around the far side of the station building. Five o'clock was nearly pitch dark this time of year and, if there had ever been a light on this side of the building, it was out. So he couldn't see his bicycle until he was nearly upon the rack. It was still there. But there wasn't much left of it.

"What the fuck?" He said it aloud, to the snow and the dark. Both wheels were bent, the handlebar was creased and the seat was gone. Had somebody gotten frustrated in an effort to steal it, and simply gone ballistic on it? This day could not be ending this way.

He was right. It ended *this* way: As Bachman bent closer to see what was salvageable of his beloved ride, the darkness went from deep to total. He couldn't breathe. As he realized that some kind of sack had been pulled over his head, he was jerked backward onto the ground. Then something contacted the back of his head, and the lights really went out.

Chapter Five

By the time Elise realized that she was overdue to hear from Bachman it was already well past five. It was dark outside, and she was, so far as she could tell, the only person still in the office. She dialed his house, and hung up after six rings. Maybe six rings wasn't enough? She called again and let it ring fifteen times. No Bachman.

Would he have gone somewhere else? They had not spoken now in almost three days. Had they said anything about getting together immediately on his return? Was she being stupid about Bachman? Was she thinking with her heart, or some other part, and not her brain?

No, of course not. Something had to be up. He had called three times, and left messages, each time updating her on his new estimated time of arrival.

So where was he?

She jumped just a little when the phone on her desk rang in the unusually quiet office. Despite herself, a big grin broke across her face. She calmed herself before she picked it up.

"Hello?"

Nothing.

"Hello!"

Nothing. No breathing, no background static, no room noise. Silence.

Her hands shook so that she missed the cradle when she hung up the phone. Elise looked all around her. Now she had to take action. And she could not stay here, alone, in this office, one more second.

Her footsteps echoed in the garage beneath SosWepFro's office. Besides her Beetle, the only other cars remaining were company Cadillacs that would be unused for the rest of the holiday weekend. The tiny spaces between the ringing of each of her footsteps sounded uncannily, to Elise, like the silence on the other end of the call she'd just received. The walk to her car seemed longer than it had on previous nights. She walked with her hand in her purse, fingering her keys. Her eyes scanned the space around her as best they could as she kept her neck rigid, her head not swiveling one degree. She would breathe in a minute, after she was safely in the car.

When she finally pulled out of the garage, seat-belted and doors locked, she remembered to breathe again. Elise scolded herself. "Things are bad enough, dumbass," she said out loud. "Don't make them worse by getting paranoid." And then, "And to top things off, I'm talking to myself." So she stopped.

The windshield wipers had their work cut out for them, lifting and pushing the heavy wet slush that accumulated quickly on the VW's flat windshield as she drove down Bath Avenue through Atlantis' Courthouse District. The low beams of cars approaching on the opposite side of the street left contrails of smeary light streaked across her field of vision. Involuntarily she leaned forward and gripped the steering wheel tighter.

In a matter of minutes she was at the train station. Now it was past six. Three or four commuters were dancing from foot to foot under the protective eave of the building, impatiently waiting for their pickups. Most people had worked short hours today. Without getting out Elise could see that Bachman wasn't one of them, nor was he in the brightly lit lobby inside.

She couldn't see around the side of the building from the car, so she pulled into a spot, parked, and jumped out. She damned herself for no umbrella, and instead sheltered under that morning's *Atlantis Press*.

Puddle jumping from the car to the walkway, she looped around the side. There, under a broken light, was the bike rack. There were no bikes. Bachman, clearly, had been and gone.

But where? After all the updates of when he'd be back, could he have gotten on his bike and headed – somewhere other than home? Or to the nearest phone to try her again? Was Elise assuming too much about Bachman? It made no sense.

She turned and ran back to the car. The keys slipped out of her hand as she tried to unlock it and sank to the bottom of a two-inch-deep puddle. Groping in the dark, pushing aside miniature ice floes, scraping her knuckles on the cold parking lot macadam, she finally recovered them. Her now icy wet fingers dropped them again trying to unlock the door, but this time caught them before they dove below the surface again. On the third try she got into her car. The sleeves of her coat were soaked, her hands were filthy, her knuckles were skinned and her teeth chattered. Where the hell was he?!

Shivering, she drove away from the station, without, at first, a destination. The heat was blasting, but she had to switch it to defrost and cool it down or she'd be completely blind. She alternated her hands, one holding the steering wheel while the other shook off the wet. There was nothing in the car to dry herself with other than tissues, and they proved worse than useless.

Did he go for a drink? Did he go to his pal Bobby's house? He hadn't gone to her office, and he didn't know where her house was. She didn't want to, but she would have to go to his house.

Her thoughts grew darker the closer she got there. What the hell am I doing? Am I about to humiliate myself, as well as lose precious time I could be working on this case? Maybe I've really screwed up.

Nothing seemed to be moving anywhere on Bradley Avenue. Anybody with any sense was safe and warm and inside somewhere. It wasn't a night for being outside, and the snow and the slush made driving treacherous. She noticed a Chevy Explorer across the street, vapor wafting from its tailpipe, but everything otherwise was lifeless.

Bill Bachman's house looked like Elise Brantley felt: cold, gloomy, and abandoned. She drove up his driveway. The glow from the streetlight allowed her to see clear through his porch. This was where they had first talked. There were the silhouettes of his low-slung chair and his little wood-burning stove. His bicycle, which normally hung from a big hook in the porch ceiling, was nowhere to be seen. Going further up the drive alongside the house let her see that there was not a single light on anywhere inside. It could have had its electric power turned off.

Her heart leaped up, for a moment, when she beheld his yellow Volkswagen with its black convertible top in the back by the trees, but it quickly sank again. With most people, the car in the drive means you're home. Not so, of course, with Bachman.

Elise shifted into reverse and backed slowly toward the street. A last look at the front porch showed her the front doorbell button glowing pink through the gloom. Apparently the owner was out, but the power wasn't.

The inside of her car lit up, and Elise wondered for a second if she'd accidentally turned on the dome light when she realized it was lit up from outside. Bright lights – the high beams of a car or a truck, just a few feet behind her -- were blazing through her rear window. She slammed on her brake. Her rearview mirror was useless, and she was nearly blinded when she turned to look back. Dazzled, for an instant she saw in her mind's eye Raumbaugh's car rolling over, bursting into flames and sliding down the embankment of Nessin's Pond.

There was nowhere to go forward. She couldn't go backward. She pulled the door handle and burst from the car. Maybe the porch wasn't locked. She scrambled toward it. It wouldn't be much protection, but she had no other plan, and sitting still was not an option.

"Hold on!"

A gruff male voice grabbed at her with authority. Now that she was out of the line of the vehicle's high beams she could see a shape. A man in a raincoat stood beside the car. In one hand he held an umbrella over his head; with the other, he pointed a flashlight at her.

He spoke again, his voice cutting through the freezing rain and the blood pounding in her ears. "Stop, there." She was looking down on him from the second step of the porch. He was twenty feet away. What good were her karate skills at this range?

Elise summoned, instead, her own voice. "Who's that? Who's there?" she called.

"I was about to ask you that," was the reply, in a voice that sounded like two packs a day times several decades. "Where is Mr. Bachman?"

He moved his flashlight beam from her body to her face. She flinched, and he turned it off. From the glow of the streetlight she saw that his car was the van that had been idling across the street.

"Who the hell are you?" Elise growled back, giving no ground. She planted her feet, slitted her eyes, clenched her fists, and extended her arms a few inches from her body.

The man took several steps toward her. Despite her outward show of strength, she slipped and fell back into a sitting position on Bachman's top porch step. She didn't unclench her fists.

The man now stood before her at the foot of the steps. He shined the light on himself, revealing his own lined face.

"I'm Tom Gallagher," he said.

She couldn't have been more surprised. "The police chief?" she asked.

"The ex," he said. "Retired."

"But— "

"The police chief's father."

He reached forward with the umbrella, offering her shelter. She didn't go for it.

"What do you want?" she asked him. "Why the hell are you blocking me in?"

"I'm looking for Mr. Bachman. I need to speak to him. Now, you can answer my question. Who are you, and why are you here?"

She became aware that her ass was getting wet. "I'll answer your questions... in a minute. First, move your car. And park it."

He turned to do as she told him.

"Wait," she said.

He stopped.

"Give me your umbrella," she said. Then she added, "Please."

They sat in the retired cop's Explorer with the engine running, the heat blowing, and the dome light on. Gallagher was behind the steering wheel, Elise sat facing him, her back to the passenger side door. Her fists had unclenched and the echoing of her pulse had abated, but she remained wary. She could see from the crags of his face that this man was pushing seventy, but nothing in his body language spoke of frailty.

"My name is Elise Brantley," she said.

He repeated her name. His eyes narrowed. "Wait a minute. Are you a lawyer?"

She was in no mood for comments about her chosen profession. "Yes. I'm—"

His eyes widened again. A few of the lines in Gallagher's forehead smoothed as his memory successfully retrieved the needed connections. Elise could see the wheels turning, and the light bulb come on. "You're defending the kid," he said, pointing a finger at her.

"So?" Elise said.

"So, nothing," Gallagher said. "I get it now. You're the defense attorney for the kid... What'sisname..."

"Jason Fender," she helped out. "That's right."

"Right, Fender," Gallagher repeated. "You're defending the kid, and Mr. Bachman is the kid's teacher." When he said the teacher's name, he pointed his finger at the front door of the house, as if it were Bachman himself. Then he looked at the dark, quiet house, and then he looked back at Elise. "And, unless I'm mistaken, Mr. Bachman doesn't buy the 'official version' of how the murder happened."

"And why are you here, Chief?" she asked him. "Why are you waiting in the dark with your engine running, outside this house?"

"If the engine's not running, I'm gonna get pretty cold," he said.

"Why here," she persisted. "Not why is the engine running."

"Okay," he said. "It's just − 'In the dark, with your engine running...' --you make it out to be so sinister."

She waited for him to go ahead. She saw the wheels behind that face turning again, and she saw him decide to tell her.

"I'm here, maybe for the same reason you are." This surprised her, and a question formed on her lips, but he jumped in ahead of it. "What I mean is, it appears that we both came to see Mr. Bachman tonight because we both need his help. Not about your case." He stopped for a second and seemed to consider what he'd just said.

"At least I think not."

Elise hadn't a clue what he was talking about. What help would a retired cop want from this ever-more-popular English teacher? She doubted that he came here on a snowy night to look for someone to help him paint his bass fishing boat or diagram sentences. She recalled something that Izak, her mentor at Yale, had told her more than once about interviewing witnesses. Sometimes the most effective question is the one you refrain from asking, he would say. Sometimes that's the one they answer.

Elise kept still.

Gallagher looked at her looking at him. "I don't know how well you know Mr. Bachman," he began. "But if you'll give me attorney-client privilege, I'll tell you a story that not too many people know."

"You are not my client, Chief Gallagher," she said. "How about a simple promise not to repeat what you tell me?"

"That'll do," he said. He drew in a deep breath and began. "My kid, Tommy, he was in Mr. Bachman's class. This is maybe ten years ago, something like that. Tommy's a typical, smartass teenager. He's got the long hair. He's drinkin' beer, stayin' out too late, the whole nine yards. Plus, I find out, he's skippin' school. And when he's in school, he's gettin' in fights all the time.

"It's not like today. Today, from what I hear, the school calls the kid's parents the first time he gets in trouble. Back then it was different. The school kept givin' him detention, he kept skippin' detention, and they kept assignin' him more detention. It was goin' nowhere.

"When the principal finally called my wife, things were already pretty bad. My wife said that she thought the principal was afraid to call me, me being the police chief, so he kept putting it off, hopin' it would get better on its own. Which, of course, it didn't.

"So we go in for a meeting. They set up this meeting for us, not just with the principal, but with all of Tommy's teachers. We're sitting in a classroom, I squeeze myself into one of those old student desks. The desks are in a circle, so we can all see each other. The principal introduces the teachers, and the guidance counselor. And the teachers take turns, they all take a turn talkin' about Tommy. 'He's a very nice boy, but he needs to apply himself.' 'He seems to be distracted.' 'He's not living up to his potential.'

"One after another with this bullshit, if you'll pardon my expression. Finally it's the English teacher's turn. By this time I'm rollin' my eyes, and to make matters worse, you shoulda seen Mr. Bachman back then. He looked like a kid himself. Mighta been his first year teaching, his first or second. Hell, he had longer hair than Tommy did! I figured, what can this freak tell me?

"And he didn't say much. He said Tommy had a C average in English, and he was a real good writer. A writer? I thought. Maybe he's thinking of the wrong kid.

"When the meeting was over, and my wife and I had promised to drive Tommy to and from school to make sure he got there, and to stand over him and make sure he did his homework, we leave. My wife's embarrassed. I think she wanted to clobber him worse than I did, but she's crying a little, too. I put her in the car, and I walk around to my side, but before I get in, guess who comes jogging up to me? Right, the longhair hippie teacher.

"He wants to know can he talk to me alone. We walk away from the car, and he says to me, 'Tommy's one of the smartest kids in my class.' Now people have said lots of things to me about this kid over the years, but smart isn't what they usually call him. But I'm listening.

"He says, 'Can I tell you what I think? And if I do, can you promise to wait a minute before you react?' Now I got no idea what's coming next, so I say 'Sure.'

"He says, 'Off the record?'

"And I say, 'Fine.'

"And he says, 'Tommy's coming to school high.'"

Tom Gallagher, the father, takes a deep breath. Clearly the memory still holds great resonance for him.

"I tell my wife to drive home, I'll catch up with her later. And I go back into the school, back into the classroom with the desks in a circle − Mr. Bachman's classroom, of course. And him and me, we sit there and talk for another hour.

"See, now I'm embarrassed, being a cop and not pickin' up on this -- my own kid. Mr. Bachman says he can't prove it but he's pretty sure, cause of how Tommy reacts some days, not others. His guess, Tommy's smokin' pot. Maybe takin' some kindsa pills, too. He even thinks he's smelled it on him. Pot, I mean. I don't ask him how he knows what it smells like.

"Then he tells me not to say anything to him about it! I thought I was hearin' wrong. He says that his guess is, bein' the police chief's kid wasn't easy, and Tommy was 'acting out.' Like he had to show the other kids he could be as bad or badder than anybody else. Then he asks me for my permission to talk to Tommy about it. Says he'll talk to him straight, off the record, not as a teacher, won't get the school involved. Says he'll talk to him as a grown up, but a young grown up who knew what he was talking about. Not a dumb old fart like me, he means, but I let it pass. Don't forget, he was only about six years older than Tommy.

"I guess I'll never know what he said to him. He started keepin' Tommy after school, makin' him do extra projects, writing things. I don't know what he wrote, or if anybody ever read it. But I kept up my end, I didn't break the kid's balls about smoking pot.

"Don't know what he said or did, but I know what happened. My kid stopped being a fuck-up. At the end of the school year the principal called me, told me how great Tommy was doing, like he had something to do with it. It was Mr. Bachman. But I couldn't tell him that. I kept my end."

The snow had stopped falling. It was quiet in the car. Gallagher wasn't looking at Elise, he was looking ahead, through the windshield, at the night. Finally, Elise spoke.

"Why did you tell me this story, Mr. Gallagher?"

Tom Gallagher seemed to come back to the car, to the present, as if from a distance. He turned to her again and said, "You asked me why I was here. I think my son may be in trouble. The only person who was able to help him the last time he was in trouble is the guy who lives in that house. I think I need his help again."

Now that each of them had some understanding of the motivation of the other, and each had seen the other's vulnerability, there seemed to be no point, to either Elise Brantley or Tom Gallagher, Sr., not to trust each other. Nor did it make much sense for each to be looking for Bachman separately. Elise wouldn't have admitted it – not then, anyway – but having someone to collaborate with in this quest made her feel a little less at a loss. She had no idea where to look next, no idea what to do next.

Gallagher did. Elise told him what she knew about Bachman's itinerary, and his last phone message from New York. She avoided the whole issue of why he'd gone to Saratoga in the first place, and the old cop didn't press her on it.

"He leave his bike at the station?" Gallagher asked her.

"Yes, but— how did you know...?"

"Everybody knows Mr. Bachman, they know he rides his bicycle everywhere he can," Gallagher explained. "Guess you don't know him that well. You from around here?"

Elise ignored the question. "I checked the bike rack at the train station," she said. "I know he took it there, but it's gone now."

"So he musta got back and gone somewhere," Gallagher said. "Any clue where?"

"None," Elise said. "I've been racking my brain but coming up empty." She felt the strangest desire to say something else to this man. For some reason she wanted to say, specifically to him, "It's not just about Jason Fender that I'm here. It's also because I am in love with our Mr. Bachman, and I have to know where he is, because I don't think I have ever felt this way about a man before, and I am scared to death." She didn't say any of that, though.

"Okay. Let's start at the station. Maybe somebody saw him."

Elise hopped out of the Explorer, walked to her car — the rain and sleet had stopped, for now, thank

God – and locked it. She was more than glad to let Gallagher drive. When she climbed back up into the big van he was placing a Styrofoam cup into a holder on the dash. He indicated his silver Thermos. She could have kissed him.

"It's black," he said.

"Me too," Elise said. "I mean, that's how I drink it, too."

"Funny," he said.

"Old joke," she said.

"Best kind," he agreed.

It was after seven, and if anyone had seen William Bachman detrain, he or she was no longer around. The place was deserted – no riders, no employees, nobody. Gallagher checked the posted schedule. Three more trains would stop here between now and 10:30, but there was no point in waiting for one of those. If the bike was gone, then Bachman had been there and gone.

Elise showed him where the empty bike rack was. Gallagher looked around. He looked up.

"There's a light up there," he said, pointing at the corner of the roof of the station building. "Shouldn't be dark. Guess it's broken." The non-functioning flood light seemed to trouble him in a way that Elise found curious.

He produced a large flashlight from inside his coat, the one he had used on her, and shone it up at the useless fixture. They could see the broken bulb. He shone it down, around the base of the building. He squatted, and came up with curved shards of glass. He tossed them aside. A deeper darkness clouded his face.

Now, with his light, he was searching in earnest. Elise looked too, but she could see the difference between looking, as she was doing, and searching for something specific, as Gallagher seemed to be doing. The remaining slush was an amorphous mess. She was sure it offered nothing in the way of footprints. There was nothing that could be called a bicycle tire track. Still, he bent and searched. He swung the light in short strokes, back and forth, all around, and he kept doing it as he walked from the bike rack back to the parking lot. When he got there, he turned and walked back to the bike rack, this time swinging the light in a wider arc. Halfway back to the rack, he squatted again. Elise saw something red glint in the slush when the light hit it.

Gallagher picked up the little piece of plastic. He examined it briefly, put it in his pocket, turned off his flashlight, and turned back toward his car. His body seemed a little more stooped now, and his step slowed a bit.

"What did you find?"

Gallagher seemed to only then remember that Elise was with him. He stopped and reached in his pocket. He held the thing out to her on the palm of his hand, as if it were some kind of specimen.

Elise took it from him. It took less than a second to identify it. Red plastic, shiny, it glittered back some of the moonlight that was just now appearing in the clearing sky.

A reflector. Like the kind that was on the rear fender of a bicycle.

Her mouth opened. No words came out, so she shut it again.

She looked at it again, more closely. The threaded holder on the back that had once enabled it to be screwed in place was cracked. Gallagher retrieved the thing from her.

Each looked the other carefully in the eye. Neither, they could see, was one to fool around with the truth. Elise wanted the truth, but it terrified her to hear it. When she saw that the dawning truth scared Gallagher as well, some of the coffee she'd just drunk started to rise back up her throat. She fought it back down just in time. They raced back to the Explorer.

Chapter Six

Elise didn't know where Gallagher was taking them in his big Explorer, but they were moving fast, spraying gray slush as they skidded out of the train station parking lot. Gallagher reached into a welter of wires and devices that were under his dashboard. He came out with a handheld mic whose curlicue connected to a CB radio. He twisted a dial on the equipment, then squeezed the mic, holding it to his mouth without slowing the vehicle which was now careening toward the center of town.

"TG here, looking for Deskman! TG to Desk! I've got a possible two-oh-seven. Repeat, possible two-oh-seven. Comeback!" He released the mic button in order to make a sharp maneuver around a slow moving minivan. When he pressed it again and repeated his plea, he noticed that his voice sounded different – he couldn't hear the electronic echo that should have been feeding back from the box. He looked at it, then he gawked at Elise. She was holding the other end of his mic cord in her hand. She'd unplugged it from the unit.

"Pull over," Elise said to him. It was hard for her, speaking to a man who was nearly three times her age, in this manner. But she had to do it. "We have to talk. There are some things I think you need to know."

* * *

Everybody knew Arthur Scanlon, or thought they did, and everybody thought the man they knew was the genuine article, but who could say if the Arthur they knew was the "real" one? Was it the smiling Grand Marshall of the Atlantis Day Parade that the voters knew? The 4-handicap bawdy jokester his golf buddies at Bamm Hollow Country Club in Lincroft knew? The humble, devout, highly-honored Lutheran philanthropist his fellow Monmouth County Republican dais-sitters knew? Was he really the brooding, distant, autocratic husband and father his wife and son knew, or the brutally urgent lover the rest of his women knew? Lou Rooney couldn't say, but no one knew the Arthur Scanlon that he knew.

As the Atlantis Mayor's Chief of Staff, it was Louis Rooney's dubious privilege and profound responsibility to know and serve that man, the one he, and perhaps only he, knew. For seven years now, Rooney had worked for Scanlon as the guy who took care of things. Prior to the Beamer (which, to be fair, was a job perc, not a gift), the only personal gift Lou

Rooney had ever received from Arthur Scanlon was a five-pound granite paperweight which sat on his desk. It was rough-hewn except for one highly polished flat surface in which was etched a verse from Luke: *Every valley shall be filled, and every mountain and hill shall be brought low; and the crooked shall be made straight, and the rough ways shall be made smooth.* He got Scanlon out of pinches, personal and political; he did what had to be done. As such, he saw the man at his worst and his best, at his weakest, his neediest, his most desperate, as well as at his most imperious. Lou Rooney was indispensable to Arthur Scanlon. It was the thing Scanlon hated most about him.

Lou Rooney sat in on meetings that the Mayor had with his department heads, his political advisors, even with the city's leading clergy representing the Atlantis Interreligious Fellowship for the Hungry and Homeless. He sometimes stood in for the man himself. One time, he consulted with the headmaster at Tolliver's to make certain that Joseph Scanlon's senior year went according to his father's plan. Last year, he'd traveled to Manhattan to consult with a very high-priced divorce attorney on his boss's behalf. Scanlon wasn't ready to get rid of Dorothy yet, but he did want to know what all the variables might be.

Lou sat in on meetings, sometimes as silent observer, other times as active participant. But no one sat in on his meetings with the Mayor. Yesterday they'd met, and the Mayor had stressed to his right hand man the priority level of concluding the indictment, and shortly thereafter, the conviction and sentencing, of the father-killer Jason Fender. It was not the first time

Scanlon had communicated this concept to Rooney, but it was the most emphatic. Something had apparently terrified the Mayor. Tonight, they were meeting privately, to follow up. The Mayor's office door was locked and the intercom turned off, even though it was eight o'clock and the whole fucking place was completely deserted.

"There's gonna be a dinner," Scanlon was saying. "Thursday night." They were sitting together on the couch in his office, no massive desk between them. Almost knee to knee. Coffee cups were cooling, forgotten on a table alongside them.

"I know. You told me three times already," is what Lou Rooney wanted to say. "It was practically my idea." He didn't though. He just nodded.

"Right."

"Monday morning..." Scanlon said.

"The grand jury," Rooney finished for him. No one knew that better than he did — he'd pulled the strings that had moved the date up. "No worries. They'll indict the kid. They got no reason not to."

"His lawyer..." Scanlon said.

"Has nothing," Rooney finished for him again. "And no one's helping her now."

"I don't know what you're talking about," the mayor said, raising his voice. "And let's keep it that way, okay?"

"Of course, no worries," Rooney reassured him.

An awkward silence followed. Rooney knew he was there to let the mayor know that he had done what needed to be done to make sure that nothing could happen that might enable Jason Fender to weasel out of Lemmy's murder, yet he had to do it in such a way that the mayor felt distant enough from any details. Scanlon wanted to know, but he didn't want to know.

Lou Rooney knew what it was all about. It had nothing to do with the murder, certainly nothing to do with seeing justice done. It had to do with what all that money he'd delivered was for: the mayor's political ambition. Rooney wasn't sure who specifically was being bribed, but he knew about the meet with Arturo Montalvo. He knew that the mayor's eye was on celestial goals, levels that were too high to even see Atlantis, New Jersey down below with the little people. What Lou knew was enough. It was enough to make sure that the mayor took him along. The tide of Scanlon's rising fortunes might not float all boats, but it would lift Lou Rooney's dinghy.

The mayor had shot his mouth off to the press about this kid more than he normally did, and Rooney knew why: Jason Fender was a white kid. The papers and protestors couldn't bust his balls for being racist this time. Which reminded him...

"Did you know she was a nigger?"

Scanlon looked at Rooney, confused. "She-who?"

"The kid's lawyer," Rooney said. "The one we're... not talking about. The court-appointed lawyer for the Fender kid. She's a young, good looking, smart mouthed black chick."

"How young?"

"Only a year or two out of law school," Rooney said.

Scanlon sighed. It was a big, full-body exhalation. Rooney had never seen him this edgy. This thing, this money, this dinner... it had to be very big.

Lou had suggested that Scanlon invite Montalvo and his wife to dinner in Lincroft when he phoned to thank him for the meet. To both his and Scanlon's amazement, although they didn't get Montalvo on the phone directly, Walter, his right hand guy, had called back the same day and accepted. Now it was a dinner party for twelve, with the new soon to be governor, a big shot in the Republican Party, and a couple of big money people. And all *their* wives.

"Do you need me to do anything else for Friday night?"

"I don't think so," Scanlon said. "Dorothy is organizing everything," he said.

At the mention of Mrs. Scanlon's name, Rooney felt a memory of pain in the back of his scrotum, and flashed on two visual images: a nearly perfect pair of breasts, and a distinct brown speck in a green iris.

"I want you to be around though," the mayor continued.

Not at the table, though, Rooney knew. That was all right. He didn't want to be rewarded with fancy trappings and invitations to gala events. He was happy to work behind the scenes, as long as the actual compensation was appropriately substantial.

"Dorothy's a nervous wreck, actually," the mayor said. "Maybe *you* could talk to her. Every time I do I wind up yelling at her."

Maybe I could lend her my recipe for crab dip, he

thought. He knew she'd have a house full of help and caterers. What did she have to worry about? Dorothy had done one thing: She called it a New Year's Eve *Eve* Party. Scanlon loved that for some reason. He was going to make it an annual event.

"Just so nothing goes wrong with the party, and the preparation for the grand jury," the mayor said.

"Nothing will," Rooney said. "I got this."
...And the crooked shall be made straight, and the rough ways shall be made smooth.

Lou Rooney drove straight to the Oceanfront Diner. He went right to the phone booth in the back. The waitress poured him a cup of black coffee and brought it to the table nearest the phone booth, but Rooney ignored her. He loathed the stupid rigmarole his idiot brother made him go through in order to call him, even if he sort of understood his paranoia. But Lester had always been that way, even when they were kids. One time when Lester was eight and Lou was ten, Lester had beaten the shit out of two boys in Lou's grade, just because somebody said that they had gone around calling him, Lester, "Loony Rooney." Both boys were bigger than Lester was, but Lester was crazy. After a while, no one called Lester much of anything. By the time they were both in high school, Louis was "Lou," and Lester was "Rooney." Hell, even their mother called her younger son "Rooney."

Scanlon had promised Lou that he'd fill him in on the big deal he was working on as soon as the dinner was over. With the new governor being involved, it must have something to do with an appointment to some important post in state government. He'd intimated that it was going to be a big deal for Lou as well as himself. Lou would believe that when he heard the full story.

Lou had promised Scanlon that the lawyer's process in trying to get Jason Fender off the hook would be interrupted, distracted by the sudden disappearance of that goddamned meddling school teacher – the kid's teacher, fucking do-gooder -- who was helping her. Lou also promised Scanlon that this time was not going to be anything like the Raumbaugh disaster. So now he was calling his crazy kid brother to make sure that what he had promised was in fact the truth.

* * *

Lester Rooney had parked around the corner from Ava's, so he told Daggett to drop him there. It was nine o'clock. He got out of Daggett's car – a Delta '88 he'd acquired since the last cock-up – and walked slowly around to the driver's side window. He felt good about things, so far at least, good enough to trust Daggett with the rest of it.

They kept their voices low. "You know where to take him, right?" Rooney asked Daggett, who sat fidgeting behind the wheel, looking forward through the windshield and occasionally sneaking looks at Rooney.

"No problem," Daggett said. He tapped a snappy cadence on the steering wheel with his palms to show how calm he was.

"Key?" Rooney asked him.

Daggett answered by leaning over and slapping his left buttock, indicating the pocket that held the key.

"Show me," Rooney ordered him.

Daggett dug in the hip pocket and pulled the key out. It had no ring. He held it up in front of Rooney's face, and then shoved it back down in the pocket.

"Be mellow, man," Daggett said. "I got this."

Rooney would, in his lifetime, be many things. Mellow would never be one of them. But he pulled his head out of the window, apparently ready, at last, to let Daggett finish the evening's business. "Call me from down there," he said, clearly wanting to walk away, but still looking back at Daggett, reluctant to stop giving orders. "I'll be home by one. There's a pay phone by the Seven-Eleven down the street from the place. I know the number. But I don't want to talk to you unless there's a problem. And I don't want there to be a problem. So, call, just let it ring once, hang up. That'll be the signal that all went well." He looked at the rear end of the Oldsmobile then, at the big lid of its ample trunk.

Rooney had one last instruction to impart. "Don't get creative, don't get funny. Keep it simple, and make sure he doesn't see your face." Then, finally, he turned away and walked to his car.

* * *

Daggett was supposed to pick up a couple of days' worth of supplies, then go directly to "the place," do not pass go, do not collect two hundred dollars. Once he got there, he was supposed to keep their

319

"guest" safe, secure and relatively comfortable. As long as he didn't see where he was or who had him, he could let him go, somewhere, Monday night.

He watched as Rooney got into his own car and drove off. When he was sure he was gone, he turned off the Olds' engine, got out, and locked the car. He walked around to the back, leaned over, put his ear near the trunk lid, and listened. When, after a moment, he heard what he'd been listening for, he crossed the street and went into Ava's.

He quickly scanned the crowded room. They were two deep at the bar, and most of the rest of the room was busy as well. Some band was setting up in the corner where a little foot-high platform made do for a stage. Stepping further in, he walked around to the left of the entryway, where they had two pinball machines. There she was.

One machine was out of order, the other was being played by a fat guy in a white baseball cap. Janice was standing very close to the fat guy, who was concentrating on his game, slamming the flipper buttons, cursing the silver ball. To a different observer, Janice, her hand holding a cigarette and resting lightly on his back, would have seemed to be deeply invested in the game and the man playing it. She wore a tight sweater and tighter jeans. Her boots made her seem tall. As she leaned in to follow the progress of the pinball player, her breasts gently grazed his arm.

She'd seen Daggett before he'd spotted her. She managed to catch his eye without losing touch with the big pinball player. Though they were twenty feet apart, a silent conversation passed between them, in the practiced language of their faces.

Daggett looked from her to the player and back to her. He raised his eyebrows and tilted his head. A question.

Janice looked wearily at the big fellow, who was bellowing in frustration at the loss of another ball, and who was paying no attention whatsoever to her. She looked back at Daggett. She gave the fat guy's arm a squeeze; he shrugged her off. She looked at Daggett again and rolled her eyes. She frowned, and gave an almost imperceptible shake of her head.

Daggett indicated the door with a tilt of his own head. He turned and left. Janice exhaled smoke upward, in the direction of her erstwhile companion's face, dropped her cigarette on the floor, stepped on it, and walked away without a word.

Daggett got into the Delta 88, started it up, and made a fast U-turn, bringing the passenger door near Ava's entrance just as Janice, her fake fur coat unbuttoned, emerged. She bent to look in the passenger side window. When she saw Daggett she got in, and they peeled out.

"Looks busy," Daggett said. "How'd you do?"

She handed him a small wad of bills, lit another cigarette.

Daggett looked at the money before stuffing it in his shirt pocket. "That's it?" he asked.

She gave him a sharp look.

"Seemed busy tonight," he said. "I'm just saying."

"No, I'm holding out on you," Janice said, looking away.

"Geez, no need to be sarcastic," Daggett said.

Janice was silent for a moment, then she exhaled a big cloud of smoke and allowed herself to relax into the seat. "You're right," she said. "Sorry. Lot of couples in there tonight."

"It's all right, baby," Daggett reassured her. "It's mellow, it's all mellow." As if to assert the truth of this last remark, he pulled a skinny joint from his shirt pocket. He lit it, took an enormous inhale, and passed it to her. Janice cracked her window. She tossed out her cigarette and took a puff of the joint. She passed it back to Daggett but he held his hand up.

"You hold it," he said, Mr. Magnanimous. "You need to relax."

"Thanks," she said. Janice kept the joint, taking repeated little puffs. Then she moistened her thumb and forefinger, pinched the lit end, extinguishing it, and dropped it into her cigarette pack.

"You getting tired of it?" he asked her, indicating with a motion of his head the place they'd just left and the work she'd been engaged in.

Janice leaned her head back, closed her eyes. "Maybe I am," she said. "Can't do it forever."

"Won't be too much longer, baby," he promised her.

"Why?" she asked. "You ready to replace me?"

"Oh, baby," he protested. "Nobody replaces you. I'm ready to marry you."

She snorted and he, despite himself, laughed too. "But I'm serious," he said. "It won't be much longer. Business is good."

"I see," she said, looking around at the car's interior. "Whose is this?"

"Mine."

"When'd'ja get it?"

"Today," he said, as he pulled up in front of their building. When Janice opened her door to get out, he took her arm and stopped her.

"I'm taking you on a little—a little vacation."

"When?"

"Now," he said. "Throw stuff in a bag. Three days worth."

She looked at him hard. "Are you serious? I'm fucking tired—"

Daggett changed his tone a little to show that he was, indeed, serious. "Three days' worth of undies and shit. We'll be back Monday night. But you gotta move now. You got five minutes."

Janice looked stunned, but she recognized that he wasn't kidding. "Now?"

"Right now. A little New Year's getaway," he smiled. Then he lost the smile, and repeated, "Five minutes."

"Oh…Kay. Should I bring some---"

"Nothin'," he said. "We'll be back Monday. Now move your pretty ass. Five minutes."

She was back in four. "Pop the trunk," she said.

"Forget the trunk," he said. "Throw it in the back seat."

She did. They took off.

* * *

The truth had a sour taste to it, like something that had turned. Tom Gallagher, Sr. wanted to spit.

He'd parked the car, turned the engine off, and listened intently to what this intense young woman had to say. Now they sat there in silence, Gallagher massaging his eyes and forehead as if he could rub order back into a chaotic world.

Now he had a much better idea what was wrong with his son. This girl wasn't lying to him. He could see that clearly. Gallagher had had his problems with Raumbaugh, but he'd been shocked to hear of his accident. Now it seemed as though it might not have been an accident at all. When he put together the puzzle pieces she'd provided -- Raumbaugh hiding his notes, suspecting he was being bugged, an accident that looked planned -- with the unseemly return of his prodigal son last night, and maybe now Mr. Bachman's disappearance, it was too terrifying to consider.

But he had to consider it, and consider it now. It appeared that someone within the police department -- until so recently, his police department -- was dirty. Someone had to have given out Raumbaugh's destination, and when he was going to be there. And Tommy Jr. must know who it is, which would explain why he was in his childhood room drunk as a lord instead of in his own place, or at his desk.

She was right. He wouldn't call the HQ. But what would he do?

He had no choice. Gallagher stopped rubbing. He turned the key in the ignition, signaled, and pulled slowly out of the parking space, turning right at the first corner and heading away from the middle of town at five miles per hour under the speed limit.

"Where are we going?" Elise Brantley asked him.

"Home," the ex-police chief said.

Chapter Seven

For all his "mellow" this and "mellow" that, tonight Daggett seemed anything but, Janice thought. He'd parked in a lot alongside a package store in Manasquan, telling her to "sit tight" while he ran in and got them a couple of things. This reminded Janice of her "working jeans" and her spiked pumps that she'd had on since she'd gone to Ava's. Right about then she felt like sitting loose, not tight. She turned in her seat and stretched her hand out to her overnight bag. She only had to unzip it a few inches to pull out her comfy sweat pants.

She undid her belt and the top button of her jeans, but realized then that changing would be easier, and less likely to entertain a random passerby, in the back seat. As she was already leaning over the seat, she just wriggled back there. She kicked off her shoes and emitted an involuntary sigh of relief. In a few seconds, after a bit more practiced wiggling, the jeans were off, the baggy sweats and sneakers were on, and she was starting to relax. She could even stretch out back there, if her overnight bag weren't in the way.

Before she rolled up her jeans and stuck them in the bag, she remembered the little tool she had been keeping in her right hip pocket for the last few weeks. It was so small, and flat, she sometimes forgot it was there. For now, she slid it out and tucked it between the bucket seats. *Doesn't matter*, she figured. *It's not even loaded*.

Janice could see Daggett through the window of the store, bullshitting with the clerk who was ringing up the cigarettes and liquor and putting them into a cardboard box. She hopped out. Opening the driver's side door, she leaned in and, feeling under the dash in the dark, taking care for her recently done fingernails, she found what she needed. She popped the trunk.

She pulled her bag from the back seat and walked to the rear of the car, wondering exactly what her erratic "boyfriend" was up to tonight. She swung the bag up to plop it into the roomy trunk, but she froze in mid-swing. There was a bicycle in there. What the-- ? Her first thought was that the trunk was roomy, sure, but a bicycle wouldn't-- Then she noticed that the bicycle was – not folded, exactly, but definitely crunched in there. Why would Daggett put a busted bike in the trunk of his brand new used car?

Janice leaned closer. It was dark. Maybe the little suitcase would fit if she --

She blinked, and stepped back.

She stepped forward, and looked in again. "Forget the trunk," Daggett had said. Yes, it was still there, under the busted up bike. She could not tell if the face she saw through the spokes of one of the wheels belonged to a dead or a live person. It certainly had enough blood on it.

Her eyes flashed to the store window, where Daggett was imposing his practiced sideways hand-shake on the clerk and hefting the box with his purchases. In that hot instant her mind made a remarkable number of difficult calculations. It reviewed her three-year history with Daggett. It measured the number of seconds it would take for him to stride from the store counter, out the door, and into the parking lot. It remembered the emergency twenties she kept folded in her wallet, estimated the cost of a taxi to Atlantis, and, most importantly, the likelihood of Daggett trying to catch up with her, what with him carrying a body in his car.

She took one more horrified peek at the cluster-fuck in the trunk, slipped the strap of the bag over her shoulder, turned on her heel and ran.

* * *

The first thing that registered for Daggett was not that Janice was gone, but that the trunk lid was gaping like a yawning hippopotamus on the nature show he'd been watching on TV when Rooney had called him five hours earlier – a lifetime ago. How? Who? And then, more significantly, *Oh, shit.*

The trunk, he was infinitely relieved to discover, still contained exactly what he and Rooney had loaded into it two hours earlier that evening. Now he saw that Janice, and her suitcase, were gone. He looked up and down the street. Nothing. He looked back at the store window. Jimmy, the clerk, was reading Amazing SpiderMan again, as he had been when Daggett had walked in.

Daggett slammed the trunk lid down, but instead of the reassuring click of its catch locking, he heard a small thud and pulled his chin back just in time to avoid being clipped by the lid bouncing back up. He was about to slam it again, harder, but then saw what the problem was. Somehow an end of the bicycle's handlebar was protruding. He opened the trunk lid again and leaned in to shove the bike back down. That was when a hand reached up through the frame of the bike, grabbed hold of his hair and yanked him down into the trunk.

* * *

Bachman knew that his legs, normally his strongest physical asset, were useless. They'd been scrunched under him in the horribly confining space for what may have been either a couple of hours or possibly an eternity. He had no idea how long he'd been out. He'd determined that it was a car trunk a few minutes after regaining consciousness. It was not so much the movement or the bouncing of the car or the muffled voices he occasionally heard, so much as the smell of old motor oil combined with cheap mildewed carpeting.

He'd been able to shift a little, enough to move his arms and head to at least keep them from becoming as cramped as his legs, though not enough to rub them together. He'd successfully removed the sack that blinded him or whatever was covering his face by scraping it against what turned out to be one of the pedals of his bike.

He was freezing. His teeth had been clicking and his arms had been shivering for some time, but now that the car had stopped his midsection was quaking with the cold as well. He'd never realized – he'd never needed to think about it before – that a car's heater didn't do much for the inside of the trunk.

He'd considered but then rejected screaming and banging. His skull was screaming in silent agony and the sticky stuff caking his left eyelid shut was undoubtedly his own blood. What would be the point of protesting from inside the trunk. Release? A far greater likelihood would be another crack to his head – or worse – and an even firmer shove back down into his painful confinement. No, he'd have to wait until an opportunity presented itself. If it did.

Then, one did.

He felt the car stop. He felt the left side, the driver's side, dip and then rise, then heard and felt the door slam. Whoever was driving had gotten out. Then the car jostled a bit more. A couple of more door slams rang through the vehicle and through Bachman's skeleton. He'd become so attuned to the subtleties of the shifting movements of the car that he could almost picture the invisible occupants – driver plus one passenger, possibly a girl, judging by the muffled timbre of their conversation – and he knew that the driver had not yet returned. He didn't know what the slight jostling signified, but then it stopped entirely and he was positive that for the first time since he'd regained consciousness he was the only living thing in the car. The biggest surprise of this already unpleasantly surprising evening occurred when he heard the release pop and the trunk flew open.

He didn't move. He couldn't, much. He couldn't see much either, though now it was because his one open eye was blinded by the painful intrusion of a streetlight after his long period of darkness. He squinted against it.

Even so, he saw at least a silhouette. Her form, dramatically backlit, was that of an angel, but was she a rescuing angel or the avenging kind? He couldn't see much, but when she leaned in he saw enough in her face to conclude that she was more surprised to see him than he was to see her. And then she was gone.

He was sure he didn't have much time, but he was just as sure that he was not able to toss the remains of his bike out, hop out after it and run away. He'd been wiggling his toes for the last few minutes, and feeling was just beginning to return to his knotty leg muscles. With his left hand he was able to massage his left leg, and he kept wiggling and trying to rotate his ankles. He heaved his shoulder against the bike frame and, with difficulty, got a little of it up off him. When he heard approaching footsteps he froze.

Through his slitted right eye he still couldn't see much, but his dilated pupils had contracted a bit. He clenched his jaw to silence the chatter of his teeth. The larger silhouette that stood over him now was not the woman. This was the man, the driver. He'd returned,

Bachman realized, and now it was his turn to be surprised.

The driver, his captor, slammed the lid down with ferocity. The feeling that coursed through Bachman when it didn't catch but instead flew back up was gratifying in an almost sensual way.

The man leaned in, and his long hair presented itself to Bachman, tickling the fingers of his right hand. Without thought, he opened and closed his fist, and he pulled the face down toward his own.

Now he could see the face, and it was more than surprised. It was agog. Shock turned to fury, with bared teeth, a scream, and a nauseating odor of whiskey, pot, and garlic. The man took a shot at him and, to Bachman's everlasting relief, hit the bike's derailleur instead. In the fleeting moment he felt like his beloved bike, though dead, was somehow defending him.

Bachman tightened his grip, grabbing more of the guy's hair and forcing his head sideways, then somehow reached his left arm around the bike's top tube to punch at his face. Now the man's full weight was on him, having lost balance and fallen face first into the trunk, feet up in the air. Their faces, in fact, were almost touching. The guy was screaming and cursing incomprehensibly; Bachman realized that he was screaming back. Spittle hit Bachman's face, his lips. His opponent now was reaching through the bike with one hand, trying to crush the hand that clutched his hair, clawing and punching sharply at his midsection with the other hand. Bachman knew that, though it kept that ugly, spitting, screaming mouth inches above his own, his only hope in this uneven fight was to never let go of that greasy hank of hair.

He had no sense of time, or of pain, only of persistence. He couldn't tell if his enemy or he was winning the fight. At some point Bachman, the bike, and his attacker had tumbled out of the trunk onto the street, but Bachman had not let go. When the cops came to pull them apart, he wouldn't release his fistful of hair. One shot from the cop's nightstick across his fingers did the trick though.

He could finally see. His own screaming had stopped; the other guy's hadn't. Now he sat on the sidewalk. His legs were still useless, but he felt the slush soaking through his pants, so he knew that sensation was beginning to return. His arms were pinioned behind him, his limp legs splayed out in front of him, his torso upright, his back against a streetlamp post.

There were at least three cop cars, lights flashing red-blue-yellow everywhere, and more cops than Bachman could see. One of the officers was talking to him, but his heart was pounding too loudly to make out what the man was asking him. Another cop was talking to the other guy, Bachman's maniacal attacker, who was cuffed to a rear bumper. He couldn't understand that conversation any better, but when that cop smacked the guy, his screaming finally stopped.

Bachman was under arrest. He smiled a smile of relief.

Chapter Eight

"OK girls. This is it. You chicks can split. I'll see you tomorrow night. Until then try to stay out of trouble, OK?" R2 sent Joni and Teena home, which was where he'd be heading in a few minutes, just as soon as he carried one more plastic barrel full of broken beer bottles out to the dumpster, turned everything off, and locked up.

It couldn't be more than ten degrees outside, and he'd left his jacket inside -- not to mention the fact that the sweat that covered his face and most everyplace else on him seemed to freeze up immediately upon contact with the frigid air. *Let's make this quick.*

The bottles slid and crashed into the recycle dumpster with a sound that seemed to be amplified by the stillness and the darkness and the cold. R2 turned to take the empty barrel back inside when he saw a figure standing between him and Ava's back door. His first thought was of the metal baseball bat behind the bar, uselessly out of reach right now. His second was that the intruder was about his height.

He took a step closer. It was a woman. With another step he could see the face. It was a girl. It was a woman. He knew her. His fight-or-flight response relaxed in his gut and his heartbeat slowed − not completely, about fifty percent.

The woman said his name: "Albert." Very few people even knew he had a name other than R2.

"Janice? What the fuck, Janice? I mighta killed ya." Janice had been in two different classes with him, in two different schools. They had both had home economics at Monmouth High when they were teens. And they'd shared a driving class that was thoughtfully provided by the State of New Jersey to people convicted of driving under the influence of a controlled substance. They were both pretty much clean and sober now, and you could make the argument that Janice, like R2, worked in a bar. Although Janice made her own hours.

When R2 got close enough to really see Janice's features he recognized in them a seriousness he'd never seen there before. He looked over his shoulder and peered into the darkness of the alley behind the bar, prompted by the fact that Janice looked as if somebody were after her. She sometimes plied her trade back here; it was one of the things R2 knew but didn't want to know. Was she being stalked by a crazed trick? With a sideways tilt of his head and a protective hand lightly touching her shoulder he directed her inside the empty bar.

The front entrance was already locked. He locked the back door behind them from the inside. From the multipurpose mixer nozzle he sprayed Pepsi into a couple of glasses and sat down with her at a table by the tiny stage.

Janice didn't hesitate. "I'm getting out of town," she said.

"When?" he asked.

"Now. Tonight."

"Where?"

"Don't know yet. Wouldn't tell you if I did," she added. "You don't want to know, because I was never here tonight."

He nodded as if he understood, which he did only partially. "Why? Or shouldn't I know that either?"

"I gotta – I just gotta leave. I gotta put some distance between Daggett and me."

She didn't seem to be talking about an ordinary spat, either a man-woman thing or a business associates' disagreement. There was real fear in her eyes. He knew Daggett a little. A skinny sleazoid, sure, usually wasted, always shifty. Daggett might steal the tip jar or deal weed in the men's room, but he wasn't somebody who intimidated people and Janice, he knew, was tougher to frighten than most. He looked closer at her face: no, nobody had socked her. Whatever it was that Daggett had done that had freaked Janice out so much that she had to split town, it must have been something else.

"I need traveling money, Albert," she said. Before he could react she added, "and the bitch of it is, I've got plenty of money. But it's hidden. Nobody can get at it, nobody'll every find it. Only-- only I can't go there now. The cops will be looking for Daggett. They probably are already, and this time it won't be for dealing."

She made him a proposition. She wanted $2500 "traveling money." She swore there was between $4500 and five grand in a metal box buried under a stone Madonna in the unused weed-choked patch behind the place she shared with Daggett. Daggett had no clue. Nobody ever went back there. When things cooled down, he could retrieve it. And keep it all.

She had to know that he, R2, was not somebody to be fucked with. Didn't she? Could he be sure? He looked at her again. She was obviously in trouble. Was it the kind of trouble that would make her do something foolish, like try to scam him?

Janice was looking down. R2 reached out with his thick left hand and lifted her face to examine it again. Janice, misinterpreting him, parted her lips.

"No, honey," he warned her, his thumb on her chin. "Look at me."

She did as he told her. He examined her carefully. She understood the difference between business and serious business. He decided to trust her.

Janice dug out a felt tip pen from the bottom of her bag. She looked at R2 and said, "Paper." He reached under the bar and handed her a clipboard with a stack of order forms for his beer distributor. Janice removed her fake fur and threw it off her shoulders so it draped over the chairback behind her. She went to work, spilling purple ink, writing, drawing... explaining.

R2 peered over her shoulder as she began what looked like a treasure map. He left her to finish what she was doing while he finished his closing procedures. Once he had decided to trust her, there was no point— he trusted her.

He had more than enough in the till, which he had planned to put into the safe. He wouldn't be making the bank deposit until tomorrow morning. He'd just transfer funds from his own account into the bar's to cover the dough.

When he came back with the cash – twenties, fifties, and a few hundreds – he stopped. She was still writing.

"How complicated is this treasure map?"

Without looking up or pausing in the writing she was now doing, she held up the map with instructions so he could see it. R2 took it, examined, and with an approving "Hmph," folded it and slipped it into his back pocket. It was another two minutes until she finished what she was writing on the second page.

Janice took the wads of bills and stuffed them deep down into her big bag without counting it. Trust. Then she folded the second page closed and hand it to him.

"This you don't need to look at until tomorrow at least. Okay?"

He took it, folded it once more, and stuffed it in the other back pocket, and nodded. She stood up from the table and hugged him very tightly, and he let her. He rested his chin on the top of her head for just a second. Then they let go. They walked to the back door and he unlocked it, but before he opened he had one last thing to tell her, and he turned her to face him.

Something was troubling R2... something about getting 5G's for $2500. "If there is as much there as you say, then next time I see you, we split the difference," he said.

"If there's a next time, it won't be for a long time, baby," she said. "We'll worry about it then. I'm not worried about it now."

He unlocked the back door and walked out to the end of the alley. There was nobody to be seen in any direction, and he waved Janice out. She came up the alley, disappeared through the empty lot, and into the night and the wider world.

*   *   *

Something about the Gallaghers' kitchen made Elise feel at home. It might have been the way that Mrs. Gallagher poured a few drops of spilled coffee from her saucer back into her cup, then put the saucer on top of the cup to keep the coffee warm while she went into her kitchen to get the cake for all of them to share. Whenever she entered a white person's home, Elise always wondered if she were the first black person ever to have crossed the threshold. She felt that that might indeed be the case in this house. Still, Mrs. Gallagher was clearly not a practiced phony, and she'd welcomed Elise when Mr. Gallagher – Tom Sr. – had brought her in, before she had any idea who she was or why she was there. Mrs. Gallagher was plump and short, sixties, a beaming source of warmth, as was her dining room where she, Elise, and both Toms now sat.

The warmth was a welcome relief from the slushy world outside, but that relief was short lived. Until Elise knew that Bachman was safe – until she could see him for herself, until she could touch him – there would be no relaxing for her.

Mrs. Gallagher's florid face was highlighted by the glow that came from the cut-glass light fixture that hung a little too low over the center of the dining room table; in that face Elise could see the younger Mrs. Gallagher of a decade ago. Elise could imagine her, squeezed uncomfortably into a school desk in Mr. Bachman's classroom. No physical discomfort could match the humiliation and despair that landed on her, drop by drop, with each teacher's remark about her misbehaving son. Mothers always worry; tonight, this gracious lady whom she had never met, this lady serving coffee and cake appeared to be worrying about her son in a way that Elise guessed she hadn't had to do since he was a teen.

Tom Gallagher Jr., she could see, was a mess.

When they got there, Tom Sr. had introduced Elise to his wife in the briefest way possible. Then he left the two women in the dining room, excused himself, and went to get his son. At least fifteen uncomfortable minutes passed before the Toms came back and joined them at the dining room table. These women sat together in an extremity of well-mannered awkwardness. Elise felt mortified imagining how mortified Mrs. Gallagher must feel sitting with her, a stranger to whom she had nothing to say. Elise worried what Mrs. Gallagher might think she, Elise, was there for, and what it had to do with her son, who Mr. Gallagher had said was in some kind of trouble. Elise worried that whatever Mrs. Gallagher thought, she, Elise, would disappoint her. Occasionally they heard the wordless sounds of father and son talking several rooms away. Neither could tell what was being said, although Mrs. Gallagher was probably better able to interpret the overtones of these particular sounds. The two women exchanged the smallest amount of polite small talk.

When father and son returned to the room, Mrs. Gallagher cleared a few things from the table and disappeared into her kitchen.

Tom Sr. introduced Elise to his son, the acting chief of police. She said hello. He acknowledged her with a slight upward jerk of his head. The elder Gallagher's face was ruddy; Tom Jr.'s was the color of tuna salad. His eyes were red, he had two days' worth of uneven stubble, his shirt was misbuttoned, his hair was uncombed, and he smelled a little like old cheese. She had seen this young man on several previous occasions, in city hall and in the police station. Had she gone to Atlantis High instead of St. Ignatius, they might have sat next to each other in class. But if she had seen him now, like this, outside of this house, she would not have known who he was. On the ride from the train station to the Gallagher residence Elise had learned that Tom Jr. had shown up at his parents' home, drunk, two nights earlier. He'd been distraught. His parents were finally able to determine that it was about Raumbaugh, who had been taken off life support earlier in the day. He'd called in sick the next morning, and today too.

Tom Sr. had been confused by his son's reaction to the tragedy. Yes, you feel for a comrade, even one who hates you because you got the job he'd wanted and expected for as long as everyone had been anticipating Big Tom's retirement. But you don't fall apart. You keep it together, especially if you're the chief. It didn't make sense.

It was starting to make more sense.

He'd asked Elise to start. She told them about the warning message that had been placed inside Bachman's car. She told them about Raumbaugh's alternate theories regarding Lemmy Fender's murder, and his reluctance to share them. She did not tell them how she knew about them, and she did not tell them about the detective's notebook. There would be time for that, if it ever became necessary.

"Mr. Bachman seems to be missing, Tommy," the older man said to his son. Tommy Jr., whose face was already downcast, appeared to wince as if from a blow at the sound of the schoolteacher's name. "Do you have any ideas? It's possible that somebody grabbed him, tonight, a couple of hours ago, at the train station."

For someone who appeared to be carrying the weight of the world on his shoulders, it was stunning to see him sink a little lower. But then he appeared, with some difficulty, to try to reinvigorate himself. He sat up straighter. He raked his fingers through his hair, and then repeated the gesture. He looked first at his father, then at Elise, and then at his father once more. But when he opened his mouth to say what he had to say, his mother interrupted.

Mrs. Gallagher bustled through the swinging door that separated the kitchen and the dining room in a hurry. "Do I understand correctly that you are looking for Mr. Bachman?" she asked the room.

They all looked at her and, as if they were a choral trio, they said "Yes" in unison, if not in harmony.

"Well, you might want to make a call, Tom," she said, addressing her husband. "Your police band radio is on in the kitchen. I heard chatter about two men arrested in Manasquan for fighting. One of the Manasquan policemen said something about how one of the men they'd arrested kept saying he was a teacher in Atlantis."

Elise stood, her hand to her mouth, knocking her chair over. By the time she'd finished picking it up and apologizing to Mrs. Gallagher, Tom Gallagher, Sr. was already on the kitchen phone with the desk sergeant in Manasquan. That conversation was brief, and then he placed another call and spoke in soft tones she could not hear. A moment later he was moving back through the swinging door, grabbing his coat and handing Elise hers.

"Come on," he told her. "It's him."

Then he looked at his son, who appeared to be in shock. "Stay here, Tommy," he said. He looked at his wife, and then back at his kid. "We'll have plenty of time to talk when I get back."

Mrs. Gallagher laid a hand on her son's shoulder. "Whatever's going on," she said to him, and also to them, "we'll figure it out." Then, to her husband only, she said, "Won't we?"

The old man's face seemed to soften, and then harden, and then soften again. He echoed his wife. "Whatever's going on, we *will* figure it out. Don't worry."

And then he and Elise were out the door.

* * *

A house with sixteen rooms is one in which the members of a large family could reside and only interact with one another when they truly needed to. There were only two Scanlons in residence at the rambling, three-story mansion adjacent to the water hazard on the par five fourteenth hole at Bamm Hollow, and they had nothing to say to one another.

Dorothy had never wanted the behemoth. She thought it was ugly and pretentious, two adjectives she often applied to her husband as well. She hated golf, and she loathed golfers. She'd have been glad to go on living in the condo in Atlantis, but she'd gone along when Arthur had insisted on buying the Lincroft house four years ago. That was before they decided that Joseph would be going away for prep school. One teenager, with his friends and his parties, could go a ways toward filling up a house.

But Joey had gone away, and often stayed away, even in summers, traveling with friends instead of spending a lot of time at home. He'd be a freshman at Princeton next year; though that was much closer geographically than the New Hampshire prep school, he'd probably visit even less frequently. When talking about it, he always referred to it as "your house," never "our house," never "home."

Hollow echoes of the life she'd imagined resounded in Dorothy's ears. Success, wealth, power... With the attainment of each of the grails of her dreams, she only found herself more isolated. She was a member, if not a committee chair, of the boards of four or five different charitable organizations, but she almost never went to meetings, although she did write big checks. Sometimes she became terrified when she couldn't even remember what she had once hoped her life would be like.

Arthur's massive physical presence, his overbearing need to be at the center of everything, to dominate everything, to control everything, might seem to be, if nothing else, a bulwark against the isolation. Not so. It turned out that being alone *with* someone, especially such a someone, was infinitely lonelier than being alone by herself. They still had sex from time to time, when Arthur wanted her. It was violent without being sadistic, and she never felt other than sadder and emptier when they finished. If she thought about it she wouldn't have been able to remember the last time they'd touched with kindness, or with any kind of feeling at all. So she didn't think about it.

She didn't even want to hit him anymore.

She used to.

She didn't even know if he was home at this particular moment. He probably wasn't, but he might be. It didn't matter.

Arthur had become addicted to the sycophancy that surrounded him. Dorothy had gone a different route. Funny how, for all their wealth and power and influence, they'd each simply embraced that which had made itself most readily available.

Tonight she moved in no apparent order through the chilly emptiness of the vast rooms in a state of distasteful anticipation. Tomorrow night she would play the role of hostess. She'd done it so many, too many times before, posing as queen to Arthur's king. Friday night's dinner party would be far from the largest she'd presided over, but it would be the weightiest. Picturing it now, anticipating the performance that she would deliver, made her realize that the depth of her revulsion for their pretense of loving one another was far greater than the depth of their actual mutual hatred.

Maybe this one would be the last one. The only thing she didn't understand was why she couldn't make that choice. But she couldn't. One day Arthur would end their vacuous simulation of the loving power couple, but it would undoubtedly be at his convenience. She could get ready psychologically, emotionally, even prepare legally. But she could not pull that trigger.

Until then, she'd play her part. She didn't know how not to. It had become her one and only occupation.

Of course, there was no actual work she had to do. It was more a matter of maintaining the correct facial expression. She would laugh and flirt lightly with the male guests, just enough to make them feel that they were important to her husband. She would be more beautiful than the women, but not so much more beautiful as to threaten them. So far as actual work, there was a small, powerful commando unit of caterers, cleaning women, decorators and others who had begun arriving days before, and who would disappear the day after the whole event, leaving not a trace that it or they had ever even existed.

Marcia, Arthur's secretary, had already written out the gracious thank-you-for-coming notes that Dorothy would sign the next day. Someone – maybe Louis Rooney, she thought with a laugh – would bring them by, wait while she signed them, then take them away and mail them.

Maybe one day Dorothy would just let Marcia sign them for her. They'd get into the mail faster, and that would be one less chore for the queen to actually do.

Why, then, could she not sit still? Considering how little she actually had to physically do, and how practiced she was at her role, why was Dorothy Scanlon as tightly twisted and as ready to explode as her husband, once upon a time, had often been. Her hair pained her scalp, and her lips kept sticking to her teeth. Her eyes could not rest on any single thing. Her hands couldn't leave each other alone. She turned on a television, then turned it off.

In the powder room at the rear of the first floor, the container of cotton swabs held, alas, only cotton swabs. She put it aside in disgust. In her vacant "upstairs parlor," the room with the amazing view of five different fairways, she almost spat her impatience when the magazine stand that should have had a little bundle stuffed in the middle of at least one of the publications had no bundle at all. Her medicine chest, she knew, held nothing worth considering. She reconsidered it anyway, as if she hadn't picked through the bottles there twice already today.

Nothing.

She went back downstairs, to the kitchen. Two Mexican women did their prep work, cutting vegetables, making some damned thing in a noisy blender, their eyes downcast, as silent and unobtrusive as humanly possible. They had undoubtedly been forewarned about their employer. Dorothy did not consider them at all as she snapped the phone from the wall and dialed the number that she had to dial. The Mexicans were nonentities. They may as well have been kitchen appliances as kitchen help. They didn't hear her say into the phone, "It's me," and then hang up. They cut their eyes at each other, but Dorothy did not look at them. Instead she kept the receiver in her hand, holding the phone's cradle down with one manicured finger. When, seconds later, the phone rang, she was able to answer it before the ring died.

The two invisible women preparing the hors d'oeuvres discreetly glanced at each other again. One, the older one, rolled her eyes. The other shook her head slightly. Dorothy saw neither expression.

The queen told the person on the phone what she wanted, listened for a couple of seconds and then hung up without another word and left the room.

Chapter Nine

They'd insisted on taking him to the emergency room. Bachman had wanted to go home and sleep (literally) with Elise in his own bed, which he had not seen in almost three days (but which seemed like three months), and which he'd despaired only a few hours earlier of ever seeing again. But neither Elise nor old Tom Gallagher would have any of that.

The bathroom they'd let him use in the Manasquan Police Station had no mirror, so he didn't have a good idea of what his face looked like until he saw Elise's horrified reaction. He and the maniac who had tried to kill him in the trunk had been taken in separate cars. Bachman had to be lifted off the slushy sidewalk by two cops, who put him in the back of a patrol car, and who ignored him the whole way to the station as he tried, each time a little more calmly than the time before, to get them to listen to his tale of assault at the train station and waking up in the trunk, a kidnap victim waiting to be a murder victim.

"I'm a teacher," he told them. Then he realized that he had no idea where he was. They weren't Atlantis cops; he would have recognized at least one or more of them. A nauseating wave of disorientation swept over him. How long had he been unconscious in that hellish darkness? He had no idea what town – hell, he had no idea what state – he was in. The nausea had abated somewhat when he got reoriented; there was a small plaque facing him, mounted on the grid that separated the front seat from the back. It said, "You are in the custody of the Manasquan Police Department." He didn't know if it was meant to be humorous or not, but he was relieved to know that he was only fifteen miles south of his own house.

"I'm a teacher," he'd repeated. "Atlantis High School." This might have been big news in Atlantis. Here—nothing. The two cops in the front seat never reacted to anything he said, and he spent the rest of the two-minute drive to the station house contemplating the lack of handles on the doors in the rear of the cop car.

Everything changed, though, within minutes of arriving at the station. He never saw his assailant again, which was just fine with him. His sense was that the man had been taken to a cell in the basement of the station house. But they never put Bachman in a cell. He would learn later that the dramatic shift in how he was being treated was the direct result of a phone call from Tom Gallagher to the home of Manasquan's

350

chief, who had in turn called the desk sergeant on duty. They'd gotten him a Styrofoam cup of coffee, shown him where he could clean up, given him a blanket to wrap around himself, and let him sit in an empty office. Then the cavalry had arrived.

Feeling had just begun to return to his legs when Elise walked into the office where he was sitting. He stood up when she came in, his blanket sliding to the floor, but the sight of her rendered his knees useless again, and he plopped back into the chair.

She didn't embrace him right away. He read the thoughts that flickered across her face as clearly as if they'd been printed on paper. First was shock; then she wasn't sure it was him; then she was. Her hand flew to her mouth, then both hands to the sides of her face, then her eyes widened and began to leak. Finally she stepped to him, quickly taking command of her emotions. She reached out to touch him, but she seemed to be afraid of damaging him.

"It looks worse than it is," he said, attempting to reassure her, but he couldn't know if that was true, since her reaction was the first reflection he'd seen of what must be his bloody appearance.

"Your – eye…" she said.

He'd rinsed his face in the men's room, dampening the coarse paper towels he found there and dabbing at it gingerly. That had hurt, but it had uncaked the blood around his right eye. It still didn't open all the way. He could tell from the way her eyes jumped from location to location on his face that the bruise that was throbbing around his right eye must be impressive to see.

They finally did put their arms around each other. She held him as tightly as she would a Faberge egg; he held her cautiously, afraid of bloodying her coat.

They left minutes later without even having to fill out any paperwork, thanks to Tom Gallagher's long-standing relationship with Manasquan's upper ranks. Bachman was surprised at first that they insisted on taking him to the emergency room at Jersey Shore Medical Center in Neptune City, not Monmouth in Atlantis. Later he understood. Later, when he learned all that Elise had to tell him, when he joined them in what might be called paranoia if it were not so well justified. Until all aspects of this mystery were brought to light, they would not trust Atlantis Police, the hospital in Atlantis, or anyone else they couldn't be absolutely sure of.

Mr. Gallagher left them at JSMC; Elise assured him that she would take Bachman home where her car was parked, by taxi, and that they would call when they got there, regardless of the hour. In the ER waiting room, Bachman told her everything he could about his nightmarish evening. It didn't take long. From when he got off the train and saw his mutilated bicycle until he regained consciousness inside the trunk, he knew nothing but darkness and ache. He learned that this had been a period of some two hours.

Someone – maybe Gallagher, maybe Elise – must have intervened on his behalf once again, because he was brought into an examination room in very short order. A doctor didn't come right away, but a nurse attended to his cuts and bruises, cleaning him up with cotton and disinfectant. Bachman kept talking to Elise, who had insisted on coming in with him. He wasn't one hundred percent sure that she was hearing him. She was listening intently, but he could see pain in her eyes when cuts on his scalp, above and below his right eye, along his jaw, and on the knuckles of both hands became visible as the nurse tended to them. He told her about Jason's mother, and Sonia, and their evening at The Pipes. He told her about Schmidt Happens, and the Dongan Stable fire. He told her that when Roberta Johansen pulled him close and peered into his eyes, he felt like she could see into his soul.

But he couldn't be sure she was actually taking any of it in, because he saw her wince every time the nurse lightly dabbed at each of his injuries. Her face was a mirror of his pain. She was feeling it for him; he doubted that such an act of empathy left much brain capacity for processing information aurally, especially information that added very little to the solution of the mystery – or mysteries – that remained before them.

Finally the doctor came. She put a couple of stitches through his right eyebrow, a couple on his badly swollen cheekbone, and a total of 30 on two places on his scalp, which required the shaving of the areas on his head. During these procedures, neither Elise nor Bachman spoke. When the doctor told them that she was almost finished, Elise slipped out into the waiting room to call for a cab.

Elise gave the driver the address. They sat silently for the whole ride. She held both of his hands in hers. He saw that her eyes and cheeks were dry now, and her breathing had gone back to normal.

The cab splashed to a stop at the front of Bachman's house. Elise paid the driver. Bachman took note of her car in his driveway as they walked gingerly up to his front steps and onto his porch. He tried a couple of times to reach into the right front pocket of his jeans, but his hands hurt too much to rub against the denim. Elise retrieved them for him and, despite everything, that touch excited him. Bachman didn't know if that was lust or love working, but whatever it was, it was strong, considering the circumstances. She unlocked the door and they went inside. She relocked it behind them and put on the chain.

She helped him up the stairs to his bedroom, then she went into his bathroom and turned the hot water on all the way in his big old clawfooted tub. While it ran, she came back into the bedroom and called Tom Gallagher. He heard her apologize for the lateness of the call. When she hung up she said to him, "Mrs. Gallagher sends her love."

Bachman's eyebrows tried to go up, and it hurt.

"The Chief isn't home yet," Elise said.

"I hope we don't have to go searching for him now."

"No, he called home. He's still in Manasquan. I think he's having a chat with your friend," she said.

"With friends like him, who needs murderers," Bachman said.

Home.

She helped him undress and get into the tub. When his clothes came off he heard her exhale with relief that only a few minor bruises were revealed. The

354

water was just this side of scalding hot, but she had added some kind of oil or something to it that gave off an aroma that he felt in his eyes as well as his nostrils. What it was or where she had gotten it he had no idea, but it seemed to have the added benefit of making the hot water tolerable, and he slid down into it.

Elise came into the bathroom, put the lid down on the toilet, and sat.

"Okay," she said. "I've got some news to report too."

"Good," he said, "because what little I learned isn't going to help us much. I feel like my trip was mostly a waste. And we only have — what, three-and-a-half, four weeks until the hearing?"

"Well, that's the first piece of news. The hearing has been moved up. It's 9:30 am, Tuesday. Three days from now."

Bachman's eyes popped, even the half closed one. When he saw that she was serious he began to slide down in the tub, but she reached over and grabbed his shoulder.

"Sit up, Billy. You can't get those wounds wet yet. And I've got more to tell you. A lot more."

* * *

Lester Rooney dropped the red telephone receiver gently in the red cradle which lay just inches beneath his pink scalp. He bared his ragged teeth in a lascivious grin of greedy anticipation. Then, looking up at his feet, gripped securely in his gravity boots, which were held in place near the ceiling, he did six more upside-down sit-ups, his arms crossed over his chest, before dismounting and standing upright. The inversion exercises were just one more way that he separated himself from the pack. Let all the other assholes get fat and slow and stupid. Rooney got harder and stronger, leaner and meaner every day. Not only that, but he also increased blood flow to his brain. This, he felt, made him wily. Rooney had a dictionary. He'd looked up wily. It was not just the name of a coyote.

He'd been doing his inverted sit-ups when she'd called him, but both phones were right at hand, so he'd called her back and made the appointment to meet her tomorrow evening, all the while dangling like a fruit bat at bedtime.

He wondered if his voice sounded upside down to Mrs. Scanlon.

He checked his watch. Only eleven. Daggett wouldn't be calling for a couple more hours. Maybe he'd take a quick nap. But first, he had two calls of his own to make. If he was going to fulfill Mrs. Scanlon's special delivery order tomorrow at 5:30, he would have to acquire some goods during the day. That meant zipping up the Parkway to his supplier in Newark. He made that call, and then he made the second one: to brother Louis. Lester needed cash flow, because he wouldn't be getting paid for his special delivery in cash. And Lou owed him big time.

* * *

At two thirty-five am, Bill Bachman sat up in bed before he realized that he was awake. Elise Brantley, who had only fallen asleep a few minutes earlier, sat up too. She touched his arm gently, and wondered for a moment if perhaps he should have spent the night in the hospital after all.

"What?" she asked him.

"Tomorrow," he said. He leaned forward and looked across her toward the clock glowing on the bed table. "Today," he said.

"What about today?" she asked.

"I've got to go to work in four hours."

"You can't," she said.

"What do you mean?"

"Here's what I mean." She took his hand and stood up, gently pulling him after her. She led him into the bathroom and switched on the light. She turned him to face the mirror.

They stood together, contemplating his re-remarkable, lop-sided visage, his purple cheek, his butchered hair, his Frankenstein embellishments.

"But I have to go to school," he said.

"You *would* have to call in sick," she said, "*if* school started tomorrow."

"How's that?" He was more disoriented now than he had been in the trunk. Elise smiled indulgently.

"It's still Friday, Billy. December 30. School starts Tuesday, the same day as Jason's hearing." They got back in bed and pulled up the covers.

"It's a good thing," he said.

"I know," she said. "You couldn't go to school looking like this."

"But I would have had to."

A bit of impatience crept into her voice. "That is what sick days are for, dummy. You are a mess. You are stoned off your butt on pain meds. You may have a concussion. Even if you don't, if you went to school looking like this, you wouldn't get anything done. All day long, everything in school would be all, 'Eek! Mr. Bachman! What happened? Did you see Mr. Bachman? Did you see Mr. Bachman?'"

He lay back on the pillow and closed his eyes. "I couldn't call in sick. I don't know how."

"What do you mean, you don't know how?"

"I've never done it before," he said.

"In eleven years you've never called in sick? Taken a personal day? Not once?"

"Nope," he said.

She sighed in amazement. She would have given him a little punch if he hadn't received so many real ones already, so she found an open spot on his cheek and kissed it instead.

"I'll bet your pal Bobby D knows how to call in sick," she said.

He nodded in agreement.

"You'll have to talk to him and have him teach you that trick, just in case you still can't go in on Tuesday.

He grumbled disagreeably, but said that he would.

"And don't worry," she said. "I've got work for you to do tomorrow."

* * *

Friday began, but there was no dawn. The sky above the ornate façade of Atlantis City Hall was slate when Louis Rooney pulled into his initialed spot near the building's rear door at 7:45. He took the stairs two at a time toward his second floor office, down the hall from Mayor Scanlon's. He gave Marcia a wave – what time did that woman get to work each day? – but when she waved to stop him to tell him something or other, he brushed her off, with a quick "Later, not now."

She probably wanted to warn him there was a newspaper reporter waiting for him on the couch down the hall, just outside his door. Not that it would have done him much good.

The girl – she looked like a kid to him, all wild curly hair and jangly bracelets – popped up from the couch when she saw him coming. "Good morning, Mr. Rooney! Alice Kimsbrough, *Atlantis Press*. I understand the mayor won't be in today, so if I could just have five minutes of your time I'll get right out of your hair."

"I really don't-- I really don't have time right now, Ms.... Ms..."

"Kimsbrough. Alice Kimsbrough. It's okay Mr. Rooney," she said. She started to rebutton her coat to leave. "I just wanted to get Mayor Scanlon's or your reaction to some stuff we're going with in tomorrow's paper about Mayor Scanlon. And his, you know, political future. You know, his plans."

She had his attention, but before he could take the hook, she threw out some more bait. "And the latest stuff on the Lemmy Fender case." Line, and sinker.

He unlocked his office door and showed her in, guiding her into a chair. He made as much as he could out of settling in, hanging up his coat, offering to take hers ("No, thanks. I'm fine."), opening his blinds, flipping through his phone messages, calling Marcia to bring him some coffee. He looked inquiringly at Alice

("No, thanks. Really, I'm fine.") and then, when he was out of stalling tactics and still could not figure out what to anticipate from this girl or how he would handle it, he finally settled in behind his desk.

He smiled at her. "Fire away," he said pleasantly.

"Thanks for your time, Mr. Rooney. I'll be out of your hair as quick as I can," Alice said again. "Mayor Scanlon has a year left on his term. Does he plan on serving out his term?"

What the fuck? Rooney thought. "What the— " He got control of himself. "Of course he plans to serve out his term."

"Will he run for reelection?"

"So far as I know he will," Rooney said. He was regaining his composure. This chick was just fishing. "I hope so. I'd like to keep my job." He flashed her the friendly smile again.

"Then, can I quote you that, so far as you know, Arthur Scanlon is not interested in becoming a United States Senator for New Jersey?"

What the FUCK!? "First of all, you may *not* quote me," he said. "In general. Ever. About anything. Are we clear on that?"

"Not a problem," the girl said.

"If I say 'Have a nice day,' you may not quote me."

"Okay, I understand."

"I don't ever want to see my name in your newspaper. Okay?"

"Loud and clear."

"And I don't ever want to see my words quoted in your newspaper. None of that 'anonymous source' crap. You follow me?"

"Absolutely."

"Good. And you still want to talk to me?"

"Oh, yes. Anything you can tell me just to help me understand things is of great use to me. And I won't quote you, or name you, or use anything that you, alone, tell me in print. If I were to do that after promising you that I wouldn't, I would lose my job. So, okay?"

"Okay, good. Thank you. Now, having said all that, I don't have any idea what you're talking about. New Jersey has two senators, and, if I'm not mistaken, neither of them is up for reelection for another four years."

"Of course. But is he thinking about it in the future? Or, let's say one of our senators were to, I don't know, resign or die or something. God forbid. The Governor would appoint someone to serve out the balance of the term. Would Mayor Scanlon have any interest in that? So far as you know? Off the record, of course? Just for my information."

He made his face a mask. He didn't know what to say. If he even acknowledged that such a scenario were possible, he would be violating everything he knew about loyalty to his boss. On the other hand, if he played stupid, wouldn't that make him... in the long run... seem, well, stupid? Once the very thing that this young reporter had obviously been tipped about began to unfold, which could happen within a matter of weeks if not days, how would it be if he had denied it?

This kid had him in a goddamned box. The backs of his ears were perspiring.

Keeping an eye on Alice Kimsbrough, he picked up his phone. "Marcia. Is the coffee ready yet? Because I could have grown the beans myself by now." He hung up without waiting for an answer.

He knew that playing dumb made you look dumb, but playing smart could get you hurt. He calmed himself before he spoke. "Ms. Kimsbrough," he said. "With all due respect, I have no idea what you are talking about." He stood.

Alice stood, and thanked him for his time. She walked toward the door, then turned when she got there. "Can you give me anything new on the Lemmy Fender murder case, Mr. Rooney?"

"Like what?" he said. "The grand jury is Tuesday morning. From what I've read in your paper, it seems as though the son will be indicted for murdering his father."

"Nothing on the coroner re-opening the inquest? Re-examining the victim's body, anything like that?"

Lou Rooney didn't answer her. He just stood where he was, keeping the same smile stationary on his face.

"Okay," Alice Kimsbrough said. "Thanks so much for your time."

He was still smiling at her back when she closed his door behind her.

As she walked up the hall, Alice exhaled for what felt like the first time in days. Marcia, the mayor's secretary, was walking toward her, carrying a cup of coffee for Mr. Rooney, the Mayor's chief of staff. When they passed each other, the older woman pressed a squarish, white, finely textured envelope into the younger woman's hand, without so much as making eye contact.

Chapter Ten

Bachman's alarm clock didn't go off, but he woke at his normal time. Elise watched him struggle to sit up, watched him as his consciousness picked up, one by one, the scattered facts of this morning's odd reality. She saw him touch his face.

It seemed like a year ago, but actually less than three weeks had gone by since she had watched him grind beans in his little antique device. She remembered it vividly, and was able to bring him hot coffee to ease his waking. He seemed surprised, then accepted the mug from her hand with silent gratitude. The fact that this man was unused to being served made it possible for her to serve him, she thought. It was a delicate dance she did with herself.

When he'd begged off breakfast except for the couple of prescription pain killers he washed down with the strong black coffee, she told him the plan, such as it was, she'd come up with for today. Bachman was to be her "legal assistant"; together they would interview Jason one more time prior to tomorrow's hearing. This would be the last chance. Any information they could glean might help sway the judge that there wasn't enough evidence to indict. If she could get Bachman in to meet Jason with her, maybe their combined presence could shake something loose. After all, she had finally gotten his attention, at their last meeting. Jason had seemed to be very interested in his teacher's excursion to find and speak with his mother. Maybe, maybe, maybe.

At the same time, she kept her fingers crossed that Dr. Patel would find something that would contradict his original findings, buried deep within the thick protoplasm of the weirdly preserved heart with which she had entrusted him. Fishermen had found the heart. The Maryland medical examiner had found the bullet inside, where it still remained. Now if Dr. Patel could find a clue that could connect the heart to its original owner. Maybe, maybe, maybe.

* * *

They got to the county lockup in Freehold a few minutes before nine. Elise had done what she could to make her "assistant's" face less shocking, rebandaging him as neatly as she could, then topped him off with a cap that covered the weirdest looking haircut in the world. When they approached the security office she looked at him and felt certain that it looked as though she were smuggling a criminal *into* jail; amazingly, the officer there checked them through with a minimum of scrutiny. She wondered if they'd get a second look when she escorted him out.

Fifteen minutes later they were in the little windowless conference room. When the young guard brought Jason in, his eyes were wary. A moment later the guard left, locking the three of them in, and Elise introduced Jason to her erstwhile helper. Jason did a double take. What he saw made no sense.

"What happened to you?" Jason said.

"Not important," Mr. Bachman said. "More important, what happened to you?"

"Nothin'," Jason said.

"Everyone was worried about you," his teacher said.

"When?"

"Nobody knew where you were. For two weeks."

"But—"

"But what?"

"Nobody ever knew where I was before, either. Nobody ever knows where I am."

He said that, and Bachman just looked at him. He put those words into the little room, and with three people and those few words, the little room became crowded. He said them without irony, without sarcasm, and without any kind of rancor. The only affect the boy evinced was a sense of purest wonder. No one ever considered where Jason was, with the exception of Lemmy Fender. Lemmy, who had laid his large hands on him. Lemmy, who had on occasion used him, for deliveries and pick-ups. Lemmy, who had taken him from one bedraggled apartment or threadbare house to another, criss-crossing the Jersey shore by way of its trashiest neighborhoods. Lemmy, who hadn't paid the electric or the heat. Jason's father, Lemmy.

Bachman was looking at the table top.

Mindful of the rapidly dwindling number of minutes between Jason and the judge, Elise broke the silence. "Mr. Bachman wanted to know where you were," she said. "When you were absent from school. On October 27th. And the days after that."

They both looked at her. Elise went on. She could not have stopped if she had wanted to.

"The day, the first day-- the first day you didn't come to school. Mr. Bachman was worried about you. He went to your house."

Jason looked at his teacher. Bachman looked at the mirror. Neither spoke.

"The lights were out, Jason. Mr. Bachman knocked. When nobody came to the door, he called. Then he went inside."

Jason was looking at him and listening to her. Intently. These were not the distant, detached, lost-soul eyes that had looked through her, past her, around her many times before. In these eyes she saw hunger. And questions. His lips made the shape of the beginning of *why?* or *what?* or *when?* but just stayed that way.

"He went inside, Jason. It was dark. He went into the kitchen-- "

"Elise." Bachman turned to her. Then he turned back to face Jason.

"Jason," Mr. Bachman said. "Do you know why you're here? In here, I mean?"

The boy eyed them, each in turn. Then he nodded.

"Can you tell us, Jason?" Bachman said. "Can you tell us about your father? About what happened?"

Jason looked at his teacher. Then he looked at his lawyer. He seemed anxious to speak, but something seemed to stop him. He looked at his teacher again. Mr. Bachman pulled back a bit. Then he stood.

"Elise. Ms. Brantley," the teacher said. "Is there – Is there some way I could speak to Jason alone? Just for a few minutes?"

Elise Brantley stood. This wasn't going to help.

"No," she said. "Absolutely not. I can't," she told him.

"Jason…" Mr. Bachman began. "I think Jason would just like to talk to me for a couple of minutes."

"It won't help," she said, and now she was speaking only to Bachman, speaking as an expert on the law. "Nothing Jason tells you is of any value in court. The grand jury won't care what you say Jason said. That's hearsay. Totally irrelevant from a legal standpoint."

"I understand that," Bachman said. He glanced at Jason, then he glanced back at her. "I think Jason does, too." He stepped closer to her. He lowered his voice, but not to a whisper, not to exclude the boy.

"I think Jason might like to talk to me a little. Then maybe, if he feels like it, he could tell you some of the things which might be helpful."

Elise spoke softly as well, but in a tone whose meaning was unmistakable.

"The grand jury convenes Tuesday," she said. "At 9:30 am." She looked at her watch. "We have forty-five minutes left for this meeting. Forty-five minutes with Jason. No more after today."

"Okay. I understand," Bachman said. "Give us ten minutes."

She pressed the button on the intercom alongside the locked door and called for the guard, who came right away. He looked not much older than Jason. He was confused by her request to exit the conference room temporarily and leave her "legal assistant" behind. He'd been told to let them in and let them out. Now he was being asked to do something different. He wanted to call the front.

Before he could take the phone off the wall, Elise fixed him with a look of cold command, and she played her card. "We have forty-five minutes to go with my client. I need to use the women's room. Now."

The young guard looked briefly at the prisoner and the lawyer's assistant. Stepping aside, he let Elise out and locked the door behind her. Then he escorted her to the public area where there were bathrooms for visitors.

Chapter Eleven

Lou Rooney had spent the first hour following his encounter with the reporter trying to figure out what had happened. He'd thought about everything he knew about Scanlon's plan – everything he'd not told that nosy chick. He'd called Arturo Montalvo's "assistant," Walter, on the pretense of checking what his boss' favorite booze was. Nothing in the man's demeanor indicated that anything was amiss.

He spent the next hour trying to figure out what the implications were for him personally. Finally he realized he could no longer delay calling his boss. Scanlon being Scanlon, you didn't want to be the bearer of bad news. On the other hand, you really didn't want to appear to have withheld something important.

It would be great if he could get Marcia to tell him – but no, that made no sense. If he had to be the bearer of bad, maybe devastating news, maybe he'd at least get some credit for alerting him – once he'd calmed him down. Probably not, though.

When he couldn't put it off another minute and there was nothing to do but make the call, he made the call.

Scanlon answered – but not Scanlon. The goddamned answering machine. Rooney was confused. Was this a reprieve – momentary at best, but a reprieve nonetheless? Or was it worse? Could he say what had to be said on tape? No way! But he had to say something.

"Mr. Mayor, it's Louis. Something has come up... regarding... the project we've been working on. Please call me when you get this message." He hung up.

He was considering his next move when the phone rang. It was so unexpected that he shoved his chair back from the desk. Had the boss heard the message and called him back immediately? There hadn't been enough time.

He picked it up. It was his brother.

* * *

The parking lot for St. Stephen's Roman Catholic Church in Freehold was vast and, at 4:30 on a Wednesday afternoon in the first week of January, completely deserted. It wrapped around the back and the side of the huge old church. On Sunday, most of its 420 parking spots would be filled. But not now. There was a light stanchion, but the corner where Lester Rooney's Olds waited was entirely concealed in gloom.

Rooney was waiting there to take care of two transactions in the same place: a delivery and a pick-up. The delivery was product, the pick-up was cash. Big brother owed him for the recent work. When Louis had whined that he wouldn't be able to get him the cash until late in the day, Rooney had snarled and complained; it wasn't that he needed the payment right away, but his brother didn't know that. Big brother would, as compensation for the inconvenience, come to him to drop off the money.

Dorothy would come and pick up. Rooney, who had already driven up to exit 15W and back to get the goods, had had enough driving for one wintry day, so he set up "shop" in a dark corner of the parking lot of the church. It was the same one where his mother had brought him and Louis every Friday evening and Sunday morning until she'd gotten tired of making excuses to Father Gonsalvo for her younger son's nasty style of fist-fighting. None of Father Gonsalvo's private "talks" had ever had their desired effect anyhow.

Mrs. Scanlon was scheduled to score from him around four. He left a little extra time for the transaction; he had a particular payment plan in mind for the mayor's wife tonight. Louis couldn't get there first, so he told him to come around five. Louis had as many memories of St. Stephen's and Father Gonsalvo as Lester did, so he knew just where to go.

Dorothy, on the other hand, had not had the benefit of a strict New Jersey Catholic upbringing. She'd gotten lost on the way, and had shown up a little later than expected. Nevertheless, Rooney stuck with

Payment Plan A. Mrs. Scanlon's money was no good tonight.

* * *

Lou knew right where to go. Lester was a royal pain in the ass, and an expensive one, too. But Lester had done what he'd been asked to do, and Lou had not had to think about how it had gotten done, and a deal was a deal. Keeping Lester calm and satisfied at moments like these was always the wisest move, no matter what else was going on. So he'd hopped in the Beamer with a brown envelope full of twenties and fifties and headed to church.

It was bitter cold. The darkness of the day had changed into the obscurity of the night without a discernible moment of transition. Lou sped into the potholed parking lot earlier than he'd planned and swung around the back of the church barely slowing down. There was Lester's shitbox Olds.

He parked a couple of spots behind it. The car was exhaling pollution from its tailpipe like a wheezing beast, and its windows were all fogged. The headlights and parking lots were off; an interior light was on.

Lou slipped the envelope inside his coat and stepped out into the cold. He was a little surprised that his brother, Mr. Paranoia, was sitting in a vehicle that did not allow him to see out. He walked to it and rapped once on the driver's window.

The window floated down, emitting a gust of humid air and the bell-like guitar chords of Dire Straits doing "Sultans of Swing," while revealing the ugly vision that was his younger brother's face in repose.

Lester was grinning at him, with the teeth that he'd never allowed a dentist or an orthodontist to come close to. Then motion caught Lou's eye and he saw why Lester was smiling.

A head of lustrous brown hair was rising and sinking, face down, in little brother's lap. The woman's blouse was unbuttoned and bunched around her neck. Her brassiere was unfastened in the back. The fact that the window had opened on such a cold night could not have been lost on the half-naked woman performing so earnestly, yet she did not miss a single stroke. Indeed, if it were possible to ascribe intention to a person's behavior without seeing her face, the fact that someone was observing her seemed only to intensify her efforts. Lester, stroking her hair without slowing her down, was clearly enjoying the discomfiture the situation inflicted on his brother at least as much as the blow job itself.

"Having fun?" Lou asked him, once he'd taken in the situation. The woman kept working.

"What's wrong, Louis?" Lester said. He widened his freakish grin, looking down and then back up at his big brother. The woman kept working, adding a little circular motion.

"Nothing, little brother," Lou said. "Do you want what I brought you now? Or are you too busy?"

His brother was about to answer him when both of them noticed that the head in Lester's lap had ceased its motion. No alteration in Lester's expression indicated that his physical state had changed any.

She held still for a moment. Then she turned her head to look up.

She gripped Lester's diminishing penis in her hand. She sat up.

"Louis Fucking Rooney?"

Somehow the girl blowing his brother had turned into the mayor's wife, Dorothy Scanlon. Louis opened his mouth, considered half a dozen different things he might say, rejected each, and closed his mouth again. *Lovely to see you again* didn't seem right at the moment.

Dorothy sat up straighter, Lester still firmly in hand. She looked at his face and said, "I thought your name was Rooney. Your first name."

Lester laughed. Dorothy looked incredulous. Louis opened his mouth again, and again nothing came out.

"He's your brother?" she asked Lester. "You're his brother?" she asked Louis.

"Who cares?" Lester laughed.

"No one, I guess," Dorothy said. Somehow they were in a conversation about the Rooney family. Louis thought he might have just become insane. He could see Mrs. Scanlon's breasts, as lovely as they had been when she'd come within an inch of shooting him in her condo. She turned now toward him.

"This is developing into a habit with you now, isn't it?" She gave Lester's now flaccid penis a little shake, and tucked it into his pants.

"What is?" Louis asked. It was the only thing he could think of to say. He hadn't glimpsed his brother's dick since they were kids, and he had hoped to keep it that way. Too late.

"Well, you-- you keep showing up at moments just – like – this," she said. There was a twinkle in her eye, and there was that glowing little island of brown in the green ocean of her iris.

Then he knew what was going on. What had been going on the day of his previous encounter with the First Lady of Atlantis.

"And you-- " she said to Lester. "I thought Rooney was your first name. Or your only name. I'll be damned. What is your first name?"

"What difference does it make?" Lester said.

"None, I guess. I just –" She turned. "And Louis Fucking Rooney," she said at him. As she rearranged herself back into her bra and her blouse, she laughed a little hysterically. From nowhere she produced a compact and demurely repaired her face. "Funny," she repeated. "How you keep showing up."

From the dashboard Dorothy took two quart-sized Zip-Loc bags stuffed full of blue and green capsules and slipped them into the Saks Fifth Avenue shopping bag she must have brought along for the purpose. Reaching into Lester's back seat she retrieved her black sable coat, and shrugged one arm into it. She patted Lester once more on the pants and, pulling the fur around her, opened the door of the Olds onto the inky Catholic darkness of the parking lot.

Lou, who didn't think there could be any more surprises for him in this day full of them, was nevertheless surprised again to find himself on the passenger's side of Lester's car, holding the door for Mrs. Scanlon. It was less chivalry than simple habit. He extended his hand to her and she took it. For a brief moment, as they stood illuminated by the interior light from the car, something passed between them: a warning? A pact? An understanding? Had either of them ever imagined what they would do, or what they would need so badly as to compel them to do it?

Lester's headlights switched on, revealing Mrs. Scanlon's car parked diagonally across the parking lot lines, twenty yards in front of the Oldsmobile. It was a twin of Louis' except that it was burgundy, not black. She walked through the beams, beeped her remote, opened the door, threw her shopping bag inside and drove away from the Rooney boys and their childhood church without a look back.

Louis, still at the open passenger door, pulled the envelope from inside his coat, tossed it inside, returned to his own BMW and drove away.

Lester remained in his car, with the engine still running and the headlights still on, savoring the moment. He glanced inside the envelope in an almost disinterested way, completely comfortable that his big brother would not be dumb enough to short him. What a fine night, he thought. They'd all come to him.

He zipped up his pants.

* * *

Neither of the BMW drivers, nor the driver of the Oldsmobile, ever became aware of the presence of a fourth car. It had been the last one to arrive to the early evening gathering, and it had entered the parking lot by the entrance on the opposite side of St. Stephens, although it had followed the third car there. It had pulled in with its lights off, and it had stayed as far away as was practicable. From the vantage point of this vehicle its occupant could, with the window down, observe just enough of what took place as was necessary. License plate lights helped with identification, and the moment when the man and the woman stood in the light from the car's open door was, with the aid of a very long telephoto lens, just what was needed. Maybe not a Pulitzer Prize-winner, but a storytelling shot if ever one were taken.

The driver of this fourth car, a gray 1978 Toyota Corolla, now drove away, in the opposite direction from which the others had gone. The man with her, the middle-aged photographer she'd persuaded to come along on this excursion, rolled his window up and pressed the rewind button on the bottom of his camera. The driver, in her mind's eye, could see the photo that would be made, could picture it emerging from the chemical bath. It reminded her of a picture that her English teacher had given her and told her to write a story about, way back in the eleventh grade. She twirled a fingerful of wild curly hair and drove slowly in the wrong direction until she felt safe enough to turn her headlights on, make a U-turn and double back to Atlantis.

Chapter Twelve

Ben Twoomey's darkroom and little adjoining office was a zone of visual chaos or delight, depending on your point of view. As the main (and sometimes only) photographer for the *Atlantis Press* for over seventeen years, he had seen a lot, and taken pictures of most of it. Black and white prints of all sizes, hundreds of them, were tacked and taped on every available inch of wall space. Head shots, two shots, formally staged pictures of politicians and business people at supermarket grand openings, grisly close-ups of accident victims, the pictures were a mosaic of decades worth of newsworthy events in an amazing disarray that didn't even accidentally correspond to any chronological order or, for the most part, any thematic scheme. There was Spiro Agnew happily kissing a squalling baby on the boardwalk alongside a shot of a woman looking out a broken window, with smoke all around her, at the fireman who was riding up to rescue her on a giant ladder.

The only organized group were the ones that completely obscured the office window. This was where he had collected certain photos which, although they would never be published, were among his personal favorites. Collecting them had become a hobby. They were of two kinds: men in suits in awkward positions – the eyes half open or crossed, or picking their noses, or adjusting their toupees – and women emerging from cars, with revealing glimpses of upper thigh and undies caught on film.

He was taping one of this last variety in place late Thursday night when Ira from circulation, Twoomey's drinking buddy, dropped in to bum a cigarette.

"Nice," was Ira's carefully considered evaluation of the photo in which could be seen garter clips and details of the underwear.

"I know, right?" Twoomey said.

"Got any more of her?"

"No more like this," Twoomey said. "But check these out." He laid out three 8x10 contact sheets, still damp, on his desk. Each showed five rows of six black and white shots.

"Look," Twoomey said, pointing at the first one, top left. "This looks like a guy sitting alone in his car, right?" He circled the shot with a yellow wax pencil. All the pictures in that row looked the same. Twoomey skipped down to the next row and circled another image.

"This guy here – I'm not sure who he is, but I've seen him somewhere – he comes up to the car here and talks to the driver. Some kind of meet-up, right?"

Ira nodded, then Twoomey slides his finger two shots to the right, and circles the third one in row 2. "But then *her* head pops up!"

Ira whooped and they both laughed and high fived. Twoomey's laugh evolved into a hacking cough. He waved at Ira.

"Wait, wait," he choked out. Then, when he'd regained breath control he asked his friend, "Do you know who this broad is?"

Ira's blank expression answered the question.

"It's Dorothy Scanlon."

Ira's expression didn't change.

"Mrs. *Arthur* Scanlon. The mayor's wife."

"No way."

"Way. Look at this one," the photographer said, pointing to a shot in the first row of the second contact sheet. In fact, there were about ten shots on the second sheet that looked almost exactly the same as this one. Twoomey circled a couple of these with the yellow wax pencil, apparently planning to decide later which one was the best. These had brighter light, and they clearly showed a man holding the door for the woman, both in full profile.

"How can you tell for sure who it is?" Ira asked. "They're so small." Indeed, each shot on the contact sheets was no more than an inch by an inch-and-a-quarter.

"Well, of course I couldn't be sure," Twoomey said, an unmistakable tone of professionalism and pride in his voice. Then, sounding like the magician revealing that the rabbit had been turned into three canaries, he said, "Which is why I made *this*." He turned to a worktable behind his desk and, with a pair of plastic tongs, lifted another 8x10 that was still damp and still had the acrid stink of silver iodide from the developer bath it'd come out of a few minutes earlier. This was a blow-up of the last little image which they'd been looking at.

Ira said, "Whoa. I— I mean, I don't know the lady, but the picture is clear enough that if it's her, she can't pretend it's not. The dude, too."

Twoomey smiled with satisfaction.

"You got a picture of the mayor's wife, doing some guy in a car?"

"Sure looked like it to me, though you can't *prove* anything from these shots."

"Is this the guy she was doing?" Ira asked.

"No. See, you can see the driver is still sitting inside. This guy helping her out... I'm not sure, but I think I seen him around city hall. Fact, he looks like that Rooney guy, the mayor's dude."

"Whoa," Ira said.

"I know, right?" Twoomey said.

"Whoa."

The two puffed their smokes quietly, admiring Twoomey's work.

"What's it for?" Ira finally asked.

"Whaddya mean?"

"The pictures. What didja take them for? Somebody doing an article on this?"

"Nah. These shots'll never run. You know that new kid, the writer with the crazy hair. Alice, I think her name is. She begs me to come with her. She's got a tip, she says. Something's up with the mayor, mayor's got some big deal party going on at his house, all hush hush, some big connected guys and political hotshots coming, some damn thing. I'm not paying that much attention, but she buys me two cartons of smokes, so I go, 'Ok, let's go.' Funny thing, she shows me this fancy card. It's, like, a thank you note for a party that hasn't happened yet... The whole thing is crazy. Funny though, the cards are dated for tomorrow night."

"Who's the note addressed to?" Ira asked.

"Mr. and Mrs. --- Somebody, some Italian name, I don't remember. Frankly, I don't wanna know, if you know what I'm sayin'. Anyhow, this Alice, she keeps telling me all this shit about the mayor and how he's gonna quit and run for Congress or some damn thing. But by this time I already agreed to go and shoot the pictures, so I don't pay that much attention."

"Damn," Ira said again.

"I know," Twoomey agreed. "Saddest part? This kid, Alice the reporter, she thinks she's got something she can use. She thinks she's gonna blow open some big corruption thing."

"She's not?"

"Course not," Twoomey said. "She's got nothing. Nothing but rumors, and some pictures that don't really prove a goddamn thing." He thought for a second, not ready to give up spotlight yet, or to denigrate his own work. "I mean, you could embarrass the shit outta somebody with these kinda shots. But the don't technically prove nothin'. Who knows, maybe she was helping this guy out by changing a fuse under his dashboard."

"'Changing a fuse,'" Ira repeated. "Good one."

"'Sides," Twoomey went on, exhaling a cloud toward the ceiling, "think about it. If the mayor's as connected as she thinks he is, then this fucking rag will never embarrass him – not with stuff like this, anyhow."

* * *

Tom Gallagher, Sr. didn't get home until almost dawn. He had hoped to spend the night at home with his wife of thirty-nine years, trying to figure out what exactly was wrong with their son. Instead, he'd spent the night with a lowlife drug dealer named Daggett in the basement of the Manasquan Police HQ. Along the way, he'd begun to get an inkling of what kind of trouble Tommy Jr. was in.

Tom Senior should have been exhausted, but he wasn't. In fact, he was almost ashamed of how exhilarated he felt. It had been six months since his retirement had begun and this morning, after having spent most of the wee hours questioning Daggett, was the most alive he'd felt in that entire time.

The role came back to him as if he had never left. All he needed was a few hours alone with the scumbag. He didn't need a "good cop" to play off his "bad cop." He was both, good cop *and* bad cop. And he didn't have to be all *that* bad. Fact was, other than helping this Daggett to his seat a couple of times, simple intimidation over the course of a couple of hours did the trick.

Daggett never veered from his story about the car and how Mr. Bachman had gotten into the trunk: he didn't know. A mystery. He'd gotten the car that afternoon off a guy who owed him some money, and he never looked into the trunk. This was obviously a lie, but Gallagher had conceded it – *gee, tough break, what a rotten thing for somebody to do to you* – and had focused instead on who he'd gotten the car from. Daggett was a decent guy -- who would have put him in such a compromising position? Daggett was having some difficulty focusing, he was so tired. He swore he didn't know it, and yet he was *trying* to remember the guy's name, he swore. After all, he *wanted* to help out. Gallagher could see that his memory was getting close. And then something funny had happened.

There was a knock on the door of the interrogation room. Daggett looked up, as if any change might mean something like salvation for him. Gallagher pointed to the chair, and Daggett slumped back.

"I gotta take a leak," he said, in the least aggressive tone he could. "I, like, get to use the bathroom, right?"

"Soon as I get back," Gallagher said, leaving the room and locking it behind him.

In two minutes the door opened again. Manasquan Officer William Keim came in, followed by Gallagher, who had two cold Dr. Peppers in his hands. "Officer," Gallagher said, "would you kindly show my friend Andrew here where the men's room is?"

"Um… the handcuffs, sir?" the cop asked. Gallagher had removed them hours ago, put them in his pocket. It wasn't fun if the guy had handcuffs on while you interrogated him. Unless you were interrogating Muhammad Ali.

"It's ok, Officer Keim," he said. "You'll be right back as soon as you've washed your hands, right Andrew?" And to the cop he said, "He's being very cooperative." Daggett nodded miserably.

When the detective delivered the unshackled prisoner back to the interrogation room, he looked a little better. Gallagher was drinking his Dr. Pepper and popped the other one for his guest. Daggett drew down several long, thirsty gulps, his adam's apple working. He burped.

Gallagher smiled.

"Ok. You've peed. You've washed up. And now you've had a nice cold drink. Right? So how is your memory doing now?"

Daggett put the can down, and spread his hands as if to say I would help you if only I could.

"I know you're trying, Andrew."

Daggett interrupted him, for the first time. "Nobody calls me that."

Gallagher looked shocked that he had made a *faux pas*. He checked the clipboard. "This says 'Andrew Jackson Daggett,' a fine patriotic name. If that's not what people call you, I apologize. What do your friends call you?"

"A.J."

"And you prefer that? A.J.?"

"Yes," he said. Then he added, "Sir."

"Well, I'm glad we've got that straightened out, A.J. So now, in the spirit of getting everything straightened out, I want you to identify one little thing for me." Gallagher's left hand had been behind his back since Daggett had returned. Now he brought it forth. He had his fist closed, like he was hiding a penny and Daggett had to guess which hand it was in. But it wasn't a penny. Gallagher opened his fist and there, resting on his palm, was a sandwich-size plastic evidence bag. Inside the bag was a small pistol. "This little thing yours, A.J.?"

Daggett's initial response, an almost imperceptible dilation and contraction of his pupils, would not have been noticed by an unpracticed observer. He denied ever having seen it, even after being told that it had been removed from between the front seats of his car. He'd shrugged this off, just another problem he'd inherited, apparently, when he'd gotten this vehicle.

But for all his bravado, this, Gallagher knew, was the moment that broke him. After yet another tedious forty-five minutes of probing, Daggett finally "remembered" a name – just a last name. Rooney.

It was kind of interesting how he'd said it. He'd whispered it, as if this Rooney were next door listening. As scared as Gallagher had made him, this Rooney was scarier to Daggett. Having given up the name, he kind of went all limp, like it was all over for him now. It was Rooney, he said, who must have hit this guy over the head. Rooney who must have put him in the trunk, bicycle and all, and then stuck him, Daggett, unbeknownst, with the car.

"Is that his last name?"

Daggett looked confused. "I guess. I don't—that's just his name. I don't know anything else."

"His first name isn't Louis, is it?"

Daggett snickered. "No, never heard him called that."

"He doesn't, like, work in the mayor's office, does he?" Gallagher was groping, but he had to be sure.

For the first time since the interrogation had begun, Daggett laughed. It was a sincere laugh, Gallagher could tell, as if the idea of this Rooney working in the municipal building were truly absurd.

And then, inspired, he'd asked him one more question.

"And it was Rooney, right, who hit that detective's car, knocked it into the lake last week?"

Daggett had looked up at him then, as if from the bottom of a deep hole. He couldn't say the name aloud again. He just nodded. After that, he wouldn't say another word.

That's when Tom Senior left. He had to go home now and have a conversation with his son.

* * *

Ira was hourly. Twoomey, technically also on the clock, had total freedom of movement at work because no one ever knew what assignment he was going on, or whether he had just assigned himself some barstool time. So Twoomey agreed to do some more darkroom work for another hour while Ira finished his shift on the loading dock. After that the two of them would take Ira's car to Bar B down in Belmar.

Ira was stilling looking at the black and white contact sheets and the 8x10 blow up when Twoomey went back into the darkroom. Since the pictures would never be used in the paper, Ira didn't think anyone would care if he just put them on the copier that was sitting right there, and make a copy of each one. On the way to the loading dock Ira saw Tatiana Rivera from accounting, the sexy Dominican he'd been trying to figure out how to approach for three months. He entertained her with the story of Dorothy Scanlon, the mayor's assistant, Rooney, and the dumb reporter who thought she could do an exposé on the mob in *The Press*. Tatiana loved the story, and she playfully slapped Ira as he juiced up the best parts. But she didn't believe who it was, she told him. Ira showed her the copies. Her jaw dropped – she recognized Mrs. Scanlon – and said something colorful in Spanish that Ira didn't understand. He was just happy to get a rise out of Tatiana. When she asked if she could copy those copies, he was reluctant. But she made this amazing little pouty face and said please so nice and promised not to show them around or say where she got them he said okay, and even got a little peck on the cheek for his efforts. Thus emboldened, Ira told the story even more colorfully to Elvis and Angel, his loading dock buddies. By the time the evening truck arrived, Angel had added whole new graphic dimensions and sound effects to it for the delight of the delivery guys who came for the early distribution pickup at 5:45. He was so unused to getting so much attention from his coworkers, Ira didn't even realize he'd left the copies on the loading dock when he went back to meet Twoomey. When he ran back there, no one was around, and the copies were gone. Must've gone in the trash, he figured, and thought no more about it.

It was neither ironic, nor was it coincidental in any sense of the word that the driver who had enjoyed Angel's version of Ira's story about the "autoerotic" incident involving the wife of the mayor of Atlantis was an employee of Montalvo Trucking; Mr. Montalvo had interests in many respectable businesses around the state, and specialized in short haul trucking, such as large bakeries, plumbing distributors and local newspapers required. He'd kept the picture copies on his clipboard, and at his next stop had faxed them to his dispatcher who loved a sleazy story and who, after enjoying them, sent them along to his boss, Walter Farrell, Mr. Montalvo's trusted advisor.

By 7:30pm, Arturo Montalvo received two important pieces of information from Walter, his loyal foot soldier who never failed to know what was going on where and when. Montalvo made two quick calls, while Walter called several other people, all of whom had been planning on attending an elegant and important late dinner at the posh golf course home of Mayor and Mrs. Scanlon that very evening. All of the invitees decided, under the circumstances, to stay at home and make no further mention of the affair.

Along with the first annual New Year's Eve *Eve* Party, Montalvo also eliminated the Mayor's broader political future. The Mayor apparently did not know yet, but Montalvo saw clearly that the next few months of Arthur Scanlon's public life would be associated not only with marital dispute, but also with the collapse of the murder case against the alleged father killer. The coroner had, magically, it seemed, found the victim's missing heart at last, and discovered the death to have been the result of a shooting at close range. Both events would clearly be tabloid fodder during the same time period that the new governor would be appointing a replacement senator.

* * *

At 8:00pm Arthur Scanlon steered his brand new red 560sl Mercedes up his driveway. It rode so smoothly over the polished, uniformly sized round pink stones that he felt as though he was floating on a cushion of air.

He had seen the vehicles of the caterers leaving as he arrived, pleased that everything must already be set according to plan. He opened his garage door with his remote, but changed his mind, deciding to leave the car outside where it could be seen. Nevertheless, he entered through the garage and walked through the kitchen, nodding to the Mexican women who sat together, waiting to begin their duties of the evening.

He scanned about for his wife. "Dorothy?" No response. Scanlon ascended the broad staircase to the second floor and entered his home office. There, his new answering machine seemed to be competing for his attention with his new fax machine. It occurred to him that it was odd that he hadn't seen Lou's BMW when he came in. Dorothy's was in its usual place in the garage though. Maybe there was a message from Lou on one or the other of these machines.

He looked at the fax first, tearing a page off the machine. He found the curly paper from fax machines annoying, but not as annoying as the sentence he now read. It only had two words, hand written in block capitals:

IT'S OVER.

What the hell could that mean?, he wondered. What was "over?" Some asshole must have gotten hold of his fax number or something. He placed it on the table by the machine and tried to dismiss it. It was *obnoxious* though. And so mysterious. "Fuck you," he said aloud to the offensive piece of paper.

He turned to the answering machine, pressed the button, and heard Lou's message from earlier, nearly twelve hours earlier: "Mr. Mayor, it's Louis. Something has come up... regarding... the project we've been working on. Please call me when you get this message."

What?! Could nothing go smoothly when he was busy with important city business of a delicate nature? The important, delicate city business that had occupied the bulk of his day and precluded his listening to phone messages was that he had been dining and having sex with an exquisite young woman of delicate taste in food and wine, indelicate taste in everything else, and an apparently limitless store of energy. He looked at the ceiling of his comfortable home office and asked aloud, "Can't I delegate responsibility to ---- " He was cut off, prevented from completing that question when the fax machine screeched to life right there. He had yet to be in a room when a fax machine was actually receiving a message, and it was kind of interesting, despite the obnoxious sounds that it emitted. This time the scroll of paper was longer. It had pictures on it, photos, arranged like a comic strip. There were three small ones, then a great big one. He tore the scroll off and looked at it from a couple of different angles, but it didn't make coherent sense until he turned on his bright desk lamp.

A guy in a car in the dark.

A second guy, outside the car.

Same guys, same car, and a girl who couldn't be seen before. He started to chuckle. The faces were tough to make out, but the guy standing looked a lot like...

Then he looked closely at the final picture, the large one. His dirty chuckle changed into a shocked intake of air. *How...? Who...? When...?*

The top edge of the page, he now noticed, had upside down printing that said, in small characters, Montalvo Trucking Inc. and a phone number.

He looked at the previous fax, the IT'S OVER one. Same identifying name and number.

He sat down at his desk chair for the first time, with the faxes. He picked up the phone on his desk. It was difficult to dial Lou Rooney's number, because his hand – actually both his hands were trembling too violently.

He would call his right hand man in a few minutes, he decided. It was time to go downstairs and find Dorothy.

* * *

Richard W. Goffman

In the formal dining room of the Scanlons' home, everything was set for the movers and the shakers and their well-coiffed wives and escorts. Everything that could be polished twinkled. Twinkling most of all was Dorothy Scanlon's sense of well being. Dorothy's body chemistry could not be better controlled than it had been since she'd scored what she'd needed earlier in the evening. She was stunning, she knew, in her tight black sheath dress with the spangles. She was flying. She was beaming.

She didn't know that Arthur was already upstairs. All the help had arrived on time, the house looked and smelled perfectly inviting, and the phalanx of workers stood ready to take coats, pass hors d'oeuvres, tend bar and otherwise make rich people feel comfortable.

Dorothy stood in the entry foyer of her elegant home, practicing her welcoming smile. Everything felt just fine.

Chapter Thirteen

TEEN FREED BY GRAND JURY
Insufficient evidence to charge son
in father's killing
Detective's death may not have been an accident
By ALICE KIMSBROUGH
ATLANTIS PRESS STAFF REPORTER

Freehold, January 2, 1984 – Monmouth County District Attorney David R. Glazer announced this morning that he had been informed by the Grand Jury that it had decided not to indict Jason Fender, 17, on homicide charges in relation to the death of Sylvester Fender, who was found killed on October 27th last year.

Richard W. Goffman

The teen had been apprehended in November after an extensive, multi-state manhunt and charged with manslaughter of his father. District Attorney Glazer had no further comment other than that the case remained "open," and that young man, while now free, remains a "person of interest" in the case.

The attorney for the accused, Elise R. Brantley, spoke briefly to reporters outside the County Courthouse. "There has never been a single piece of direct evidence to tie my client to the brutal killing of his father. Furthermore, substantial fresh evidence leading in another direction has emerged in the last 48 hours."

The 17-year-old had spent approximately seven weeks in police custody

Now free on bond, Jason Fender, an Atlantis High School junior, left the courtroom with his attorney and Mr. William Bachman, who had supported and counseled Fender during his incarceration. Bachman is a veteran Atlantis High School English teacher. Neither Fender nor Bachman spoke to reporters.

Brantley would not elaborate on what "fresh evidence" had come to light in the last two days in the two-month-old case, or whether or not there were any new suspects. However a well-placed source who asked not to be named told this reporter that the Fender case has now been linked to the death on December 20th of Atlantis Senior Detective Richard S. Raumbaugh. That death, previously ruled an auto accident, could be reinvestigated in the coming days. According to the source, capital murder charges could be filed in a matter of days if investigators can show that Raumbaugh's car, which was found upside down, smoldering, and partly submerged in Nessin Pond, had been intentionally forced off the road by another vehicle.

The most surprising revelation to come out of the Grand Jury proceedings was the supplemental autopsy report presented this morning by Atlantis Medical Examiner Dr. Ravesh Patel. According to this document, Sylvester Fender's death, which was previously said to be the result of multiple puncture wounds made by a knife or axe, was actually the result of a gunshot wound. According to the document, the knife wounds were made subsequent to the shooting. A .22 caliber bullet was recovered from the victim's heart. The coroner's original autopsy, which was completed on November 11 and which is a matter of public record, noted that the victim's heart was not present when the body was brought in. Citing the ongoing investigation, Dr. Patel declined to explain how, when, or where the heart of Sylvester Fender reappeared until after further determinations had been made.

The Grand Jury also took into account as evidence extensive notes which several police sources verified to be in the handwriting of Detective Raumbaugh, purported to have been made in the days leading up to his catastrophic auto accident on the night of December ninth. Copies of these notes have not been made public, nor have the contents of the notes, as they contain evidence in what is now an on-going and wider-ranging investigation. How these notes came to light weeks after Raumbaugh's death, and where they have been during that time, is not known.

The defense attorney, from the Atlantis firm Sostyoprak Wepner and Froelich L. P., pointed out that her client has been incarcerated, first in Monmouth Regional Medical Center, and subsequently in the Monmouth County Municipal Detention Center in Freehold, for more than six weeks, "despite the consistent and complete lack of any evidence, direct or indirect, linking him to this crime, the very act of which has rendered him an orphan." Asked if she were positioning her client for a wrongful arrest and detention lawsuit, Brantley declined to comment further.

District Attorney Glazer said that the state had been seeking to charge Jason Fender as an adult, due to the seriousness and the apparent violence of the crime. However, as a seventeen-year-old he remains a minor, and would now come under the jurisdiction of the Department of Youth and Family Services. At press time, the question of his custody upon his release remained unanswered.

HEARTLESS CRUELTY

* * *

GALLAGHER'S BACK
Semi-Retired Police Chief Re-Activated,
Acting Chief Takes Leave

ATLANTIS – Friends and co-workers who attended the retirement dinner for Atlantis' top cop Tom Gallagher, Sr. back in April could be lining up to get their gifts back.

"As of ten pm [Wednesday] night, I'm unretired," the 68-year-old former and now current Chief of Police for Atlantis told reporters in his office last night. "Don't ask me for how long, 'cause I'm not sure. Maybe ten years, maybe more."

Gallagher's successor as Chief was to have been Thomas Gallagher, Jr., the outgoing Chief's son. The younger Gallagher had been serving as Acting Chief since May 1. A clause in the senior Gallagher's contract made his retirement tentative, pending his replacement's full appointment. Tom Gallagher Jr. has been out sick from work for the last week and will, according to official police sources, be taking an extended medical leave. The younger Gallagher's exact medical condition has not been revealed.

Mayor Arthur Scanlon's office had no additional information on the reinstatement of Chief Gallagher who first came to work at the Atlantis Police Department in 1946, upon his return from active duty with the United States Army in the Philippines during World War II.

Gallagher was first appointed Chief of Police by Mayor Roland Hoover in 1967.

The recommended retirement age for Atlantis police officers at all ranks is sixty-five, however retirement is not legally mandatory at any specific age.

* * *

TRAFFIC STOP FOR TOP CITY AIDE LEADS TO ARREST
Mayor's Chief of Staff spends night behind bars

ATLANTIS – Mayor Arthur Scanlon has had several new reasons to give vent to his infamous temper in the last couple of days.

First, he had been known to be personally and vociferously espousing swift justice and a hefty prison term for alleged father-killer Jason Fender. The Grand Jury found insufficient evidence to indict Fender this morning and directed that he be released without prejudice.

Second, if the death of Police Senior Detective Richard Raumbaugh is ruled a homicide as now appears to be possible according to several sources, it will have been the third murder in Atlantis in 1983, increasing the previous year's total by 50%. Mayor Scanlon ran for office in 1980 on a law and order platform, and specifically pledged that if he were elected he would offer to step down if the murder rate did not fall each year during his administration. There were 13 murders in Atlantis in 1979, nine in 1980, eight in 1981, and only two in 1982. By contrast, the number of homicides in several surrounding municipalities, including Monmouth Beach, Asbury Park, and Neptune, have increased over the same period of time.

What may be the third straw came last night. Louis Rooney, Mayor Scanlon's chief of staff and longtime friend, was pulled over in Wilmington, Delaware, for allegedly traveling over one hundred miles an hour on Route 95 South. That stretch of Interstate 95 has a sixty-five mile per hour speed limit. According to a Delaware State Police spokesman, Rooney refused a Breathalyzer test and appeared highly agitated. When officers questioned him he attempted to drive away, and then allegedly resisted arrest. Six Delaware State troopers participated in subduing Rooney.

As of this time Rooney has been charged with speeding, reckless driving, refusing to heed various orders from officers, and resisting arrest. He may be released on his own recognizance, however at press time he was still in Delaware State Police custody.

The normally loquacious Mayor Scanlon has not commented on any of the incidents mentioned in this article, despite repeated phone calls to his office.

Chapter Fourteen

January 4, 1984 7:05am WRBachman
Now I get it.

I didn't have it all, even after Jason told me what he'd found. What he'd done. I found the missing piece this morning. It was then that I found the clue to the murder of Lemmy Fender, and began to put together this vision of the story.

The missing piece was waiting for me this morning in my mailbox. Sheri said it had been dropped off by a ninth grader. It was taped closed, and I could tell Sheri and Shari had been frustrated because it was too well sealed to peek into. She obviously hoped I'd open it there and tell her what it was. I have to admit I took some pleasure in denying her that. Opening it now, I found what I needed for the end of the story.

HEARTLESS CRUELTY

The last part came written on two pages that were some sort of wholesale beer order forms. When I saw them, I remembered that R2 told me he has a cousin here in AHS. I don't remember her name. I wonder what R2's real name is? But I digress.

Jason doesn't know the ending, but I think I may be able to explain it to him now. I have to figure out — well, hell, I still have to figure out a lot of things. Elise doesn't know all of it either, and she may be better off. Helen and Hilda need to know what happened to me and what my involvement in all this is about — but they sure don't have to know everything. I need to tell somebody, and Bobby D, I love you man, but you're a blabbermouth. Maybe Ellie. Or not. Knowing things can be a burden, especially things like this. Maybe there's nobody to tell it all to. Maybe that's why God invented journals. And drawers with locks to keep them in. So...

Jason got home from school a bit earlier than usual that day — the day his English teacher gave him a lift. He expected to find Daddy passed out drunk in the living room. Daddy usually woke up in the afternoon, drank beer and (before JCP&L turned off the power) watched cartoons, then napped until evening when he would go out. A good day for Jason was when he could find himself something to eat, make a sandwich for his father, and finish his homework before Daddy got up again. Daddy was at his meanest in the early evening, when he was fending off his second hangover of the day — his "hair of the dog" hangover -- and would often take a swing at him for obscure reasons. Two nights earlier he'd choked him so hard Jason had actually blacked out

403

for a couple of seconds. When he'd awakened, his father was gone.

This night would be different.

Lemmy had been awakened by a visitor that afternoon. J (I'm not being cute here. I don't know her name, and I don't want to. She signed herself "J", so J she is here.) was an old girlfriend – she had lived with Lemmy, briefly, in the early seventies, in a low rent dump in Asbury Park. Maybe Lemmy pimped for her – it's hard to say for sure.

Apparently J had quickly tired of her three-part role in Lemmy Fender's life: cash machine, baby sitter, and punching bag. She determined to split, much like Jason's mother, Roberta, had done four years earlier. Only this time, Lemmy had recognized the signs and beaten her to it. J came home from a night out with girl-friends determined to leave and move in with one of them the next morning, only to find the shithole apartment empty of Lemmy, Jason and just about everything of any value. Her ceramic Felix the Cat lay in pieces on the bedroom floor, with, of course, no sign of the meager stash of twenties she had kept balled up inside it. Making matters worse, they had made their departure in J's green 1960 Ford Galaxy.

All that was ten years ago. J didn't run into Lemmy again for two years, and when she did he blew her off, saying the car had died a week after they had "broken up," professing ignorance (a specialty) about owing her anything else and, finally, threatening her with violence if she didn't fuck off.

Funny thing about J, though. She couldn't let it go. She should have. Many people advised her to let it go. Lemmy wasn't swift, but he was known to be dangerous. What could she do? She couldn't complain to the cops, obviously. Most people steered clear of Lemmy Fender, either because they had good taste or common sense. J moved on, of course. But she filed it away. And for reasons of her own, she apparently felt, on a chilly recent autumn night ten years after the fact, that the time had come to get back her own.

She'd kept Lemmy in her sights as best she could all those years, and she knew where he was living now. If he could afford to rent a house in Atlantis, even a crappy one on Taylor Street, then he could afford to make her whole. She would explain it to him nicely. And if nice didn't work, she would try something else.

She figured the kid was gone by now or, if he was still around, would still be in school at two in the afternoon. And so she confronted Lemmy, the bear, in his cave.

Lemmy was a sight to behold. He was snoring on the ratty couch in the living room of the little Taylor Street house which was lit only from the windows, as the electricity had apparently been turned off. Standing over him she couldn't for the life of her remember what could ever have possessed her to put any trust or anything else into the hands of this lummox. He had on nothing but a dingy pair of tighty whities which had long ago ceased to be either white or tight. A pink pair of women's fuzzy slippers were on the floor next to the couch.

If revenge were what she had been looking for, J could have exacted it easily right then and there. Not a soul on earth would have blamed her, nor would anyone have cared about the loss. She dismissed the idea.

"*Lemmy,*" *she said.* "*Lemmy, wake up you fat fuck.*"

No response. Looking around, J determined that there was little here to take that would recompense her for what he'd taken from her, and he didn't appear to have a car outside, so she called his name again. Still nothing.

Taking only a small amount of pleasure from it, she kicked him, hard, with the pointy toe of her boot, in the soft spot just below his kneecap. The snoring became snorting and gasping, the eyes opened.

Lemmy's first glimpse of J was upside down, but even after he reoriented himself, it still took him a few seconds to figure out who she was. The list of people who were pissed off at him badly enough to kick him in his sleep was lengthy. But then he got it.

Lemmy sat up on the couch. "*Fuck, J. That hurt.*"

"*Sorry,*" *she said.* "*Had to get your attention.*"

"*Whaddaya want? You ain't still after me about that shitbox car, are you? I told you——*"

"*You told me a bunch of bullshit, Lemmy. I'm done with the bullshit. Here's the deal. I want five hundred bucks. Between the car and everything else you stole from me, I think that's more than fair.*"

"*Fair?*" *he protested.* "*I——*"

She pointed the long nail of her left index finger at him and cut him off. "*Stop now. This is not a negotiation. And this is not like before. I want five hundred bucks, or——*"

Now Lemmy stood. Eighteen inches taller than J, and two-and-a-half times her weight, he loomed over her. *Despite her bravado, she took a step backward, toward the kitchen. As she did so, she reached into her coat pocket with her right hand and showed him why she felt she had the wherewithal to make a non-negotiable demand.*

Lemmy had seen guns before. He'd had them aimed at him before, many of them far bigger than the petite twenty-two short that J was pointing at him now. For reasons that neither he nor anyone else understood, no one had ever actually shot him. Yet.

Lemmy wasn't brave, but he was stupid, which sometimes looks the same. He walked toward J.

"You gonna shoot me over a car that didn't run? You gonna shoot me for five hundred bucks?"

She took another step backward, putting her in the middle of his kitchen. "I'd just as soon not, Lemmy," she said, pointing the gun at a spot midway between his sagging tits. "But I will if you make me."

"J--- "

"You know me, Lemmy. You know I won't quit about this. I'm done waiting."

Lemmy licked his lips. "Yeah, I know you, J. I know what you like." He looked down at himself as if he had just realized that he was nearly naked. "I know what you like," he said again, and he put a hand in his underwear.

"I swear to Jesus God I'll shoot that fucking thing right off," J said, adjusting her aim. "With pleasure I will."

"Three hundred," Lemmy said, ignoring her threat.

"I told you, I'm not ne--- "

"*You do me right now, you get three hundred, and we're done with it.*"

What? She'd come to get her dough and go. The thought of giving Lemmy anything at all made her crazy. The thought of him touching her made her sick to her stomach. How could she have ever done it, even a decade ago? She knew she must have, but she had effectively purged the memory over the years.

He smelled awful, she realized, like onion farts. But she was thinking too much, and this encouraged him. With his right hand he reached out and grabbed her left, the empty one.

J screamed "*No!*" as he drew her to him, but still she didn't pull the trigger. He brought his other hand around to hug her. J stepped down on Lemmy's bare foot with the heel of her boot and twisted it. This sent a shock of lightning through him and loosened his grip a little. If their height differential were less she'd have simply kneed him in the balls. Instead she took a little step back and kicked. The sharp leather toe found its mark, driving into the big man's scrotum.

Lemmy roared his outrage. Despite the pain he leaned into her, bear-hugging her to his chest. Together they toppled to the floor in a bellowing mass, a thundering avalanche that buried her. Plates and silverware on the kitchen table jumped and a glass with two inches of milk fell off the counter and broke in a hundred pieces. The sound of their impact with the kitchen floor and the sounds of his grunting and her screaming almost entirely masked the sound of the gun's explosion.

Then all was still. There was no echo.

It was still for a minute – an eternity, almost.

Lemmy moved, but not on his own. With a strength she never suspected she possessed, J shoved upward. She was driven by a remarkable stubbornness that refused to accept a fate that included asphyxiation under nearly three hundred deadweight pounds of flesh. She half crawled, half rolled out from beneath him, and she got to her feet as quickly as she could.

J caught her breath. When she was breathing normally again she took a towel she found on a kitchen stool, and cleaned a little spot of blood from her jacket. Her right hand was bruised from being squashed between them, and burned from the gunshot. Examining it, shaking it, and then bringing it to her lips, she looked about for a moment, but quickly realized that now there would be no searching for Lemmy's cash.

It wasn't revenge. And it wasn't five hundred bucks. But now, at least it was over.

J solved this equation quickly. She had made a contingency plan just in case the evening had wound up this way, even though she somehow never thought that it would. She left Lemmy's house no richer than she'd entered it, yet somehow feeling even, and headed out of town, to a friend's place in the country, to just chill for a week or so. Under the circumstances, things might have gone worse. She got to her car and left without encountering or even seeing a neighbor, comfortable in the knowledge that at least nobody knew.

But somebody saw.

Jason came home from school, a little perplexed from having gotten a ride home from his teacher, something that he'd never experienced before. Figuring he'd be less likely to wake Daddy if he were sleeping on the couch, he went around to the back door. *Before he could put his key in the lock, however, he looked through into the kitchen. And he saw.*

He saw Her. He saw her back, her jacket, her hair. Her hair was brown and poofy.

Mother was facing Daddy.

Jason watched it all, stunned, dazzled. It seemed like a movie playing out before him, broadcast through the medium of the back door window.

It was Her. She had finally come back, and she had faced up to Daddy.

Then she was gone.

Jason waited several long minutes after she left, after he heard her car pull away, before he put his key in the lock and opened the back door. In the twilit gloom he walked to the kitchen drawer next to the sink and took out the flashlight he kept there. Then he went back over to where Daddy lay, half on his side.

Daddy hadn't moved since She had squirmed out from under him. Jason stood over his father, looking down at the side of his face which was distorted from leaning into the linoleum. With difficulty he rolled him onto his back.

Jason saw the neat little red hole in the middle of Daddy's chest. It looked just like a pencil eraser, but blood had already begun to mat the hair there. He squatted on his heels and studied the hole closely. Then he looked at Daddy's face.

Daddy was looking at the ceiling, but he wasn't seeing it.

HEARTLESS CRUELTY

Jason caressed his father's throat, gently feeling for a pulse. There was none. He checked the other side. Nothing.

Two of his teeth and his nose were broken. The lips were parted and torn, and the middle of the face was blackened. The smashing-in of his face alone might have killed him, but Jason knew that that was not it. He looked again at the red spot that was now the size of a soda bottle cap.

Jason got up and sat on the living room couch in the near dark. He reached into the pocket of his black raincoat and took out his cigarettes. There were only two left. He smoked one. When he'd smoked it down to the filter, he lit the other one from the first one, and smoked it too. When that was done, he stood up, ready to do what he had to do.

The hole in Daddy's chest had been made by a bullet. The bullet had entered Daddy's chest, right over the heart. There was no exit wound on his back or anywhere else. The bullet had come from a gun. Her gun. When the police eventually came, they would find the bullet. The bullet would lead them to the gun, and the gun would lead them to Her. That's just the way things worked.

No way he would let that happen.

She'd left when he was so young, a baby really. He didn't know if his memory of her was from seeing her, or from staring at the photograph she'd sent him the Christmas after she left. Jason always knew his mother was out there. She had finally come back and confronted Daddy. He had tried to hurt her again, only this time she hadn't let him do it.

411

She had done it for Jason. Now he would do this for her.

He removed his raincoat and draped it over the back of the couch. He unbuttoned his shirt, took it off, folded it once and lay it across the raincoat. He started to take off his undershirt, but then decided to leave it on.

Jason followed his flashlight's beam back into the kitchen and opened the drawer again. He removed from it what he needed: a big carving knife with a serrated edge; a claw hammer; and a long, flathead screwdriver with a yellow handle. With these tools he went to work.

The work was hard. There was a lot of cutting to do — fat, muscle, connective tissue and other stuff -- until he got down to bone. Daddy's sternum was hard as stone and two inches thick. Even on a little fetal pig it took some effort to cut it. Instead, he broke some of the ribs by prying with the screwdriver, and made a space using by spreading the rib cage with the screwdriver and the hammer.

Then there was more cutting to do.

Remove the pig's heart...

There it was. A fat, greasy thing, not so red as he'd thought, streaked with yellow and white lumps... And, in the lower right corner, a hole that looked like a nailhead.

It did indeed contain a tiny metal slug.

When he was done, and Daddy's ripped up heart, and the incriminating bullet, were inside the Ziploc bag, Jason lay back on the linoleum. He was drenched in sweat and as covered with gore as the corpse alongside him. If anyone — say, a nosy English teacher, for example – had poked his head into the kitchen at that particular moment, he would surely have thought there were two dead bodies lying mutilated on the floor.

Jason may have fallen asleep there for a few minutes or hours, but when he woke up in the pitch dark he knew exactly where he was and exactly what had happened. And he knew exactly what he had to do next.

He had to take a shower. Then he had to take what he had removed, he had to leave what remained, and he had to disappear.

And he did.

Chapter Fifteen

His face had begun to stop hurting; that is, when he smiled, the wrinkling at the corner of his right eye didn't elicit tears. This was fortunate in that he couldn't stop smiling after he and Elise made love.

She sat now leaning back against his chest, his arms wrapped around her from behind, his legs outside hers, his nose buried in her hair, her breasts resting lightly in his hands. It was the first time in ten days that she felt neither the crushing weight of the grand jury deadline nor the desolate fear for Bachman's whereabouts or his condition. The resulting relief seemed to have rendered her both buoyant and serene. It was an ideal condition in which to make love, and in which to bask wordlessly afterward.

The mirror on his dresser showed them, their contrasting skin tones in a rhythmic woven pattern of comfort and contentment. Every instinct told her not to speak, that this was one of those moments that come rarely in life and should not be spoiled with words. Or questions. But Elise had not become who she was by relying on her instincts.

"You know, don't you," Elise said.

"That you love me?" he asked, though he knew that wasn't what she wanted to talk about.

"You know who killed Lemmy."

"I know who didn't kill him," he said. He waited to see if she would ask another question. When she didn't, he added, "Your client did not kill him."

"Will you help the police catch the killer?"

"Why are you asking me this?" he said into her ear and squeezed her back against him tighter.

"'Why?' What do you mean 'Why'?" she said, without moving her ear away from his tongue. "Are we going to start keeping secrets from each other already?"

"Aren't you, as an attorney, an 'officer of the court' or something?" The palms of his hands slid across her nipples in the most distracting way. "I mean, aren't there things you're, well, better off not knowing?"

Elise Brantley, Esquire, sat very still for a few seconds. Then she took William Bachman's hands and placed them down beside them on the bed. She rolled away from him, then came back and faced him, sitting cross-legged and hugging a pillow to her chest.

"Okay, that's true," she said. "So just tell me this: Is someone going to get away with murder?"

"I don't know."

"What do you think?"

He didn't answer right away. Instead, he looked at a point in space over her head, as if envisioning something. Then he looked her in the eyes. Beautiful eyes.

He took a deep breath. "I don't know who shot Lemmy, though I think I know the first letter of her name. Literally. That's it." Elise's left eyebrow went up at the use of the feminine possessive pronoun. He ignored it. "I think, I mean I assume that she's gone into hiding, left the state, maybe the country. That's purely a guess on my part. I don't know anything else about her, and I have never set eyes on her." His eyes flicked away from Elise's for a moment, and they both realized that this wasn't entirely true.

"I know *almost* nothing about her," Bachman corrected himself. "Name, face, whereabouts… nothing."

Elise struggled to read between the lines of what he was saying and what he was not saying. "So… if you don't know who she is, then—"

Bachman interrupted her, although he didn't like doing it. "I know who she is not, and that's enough." He looked deeply into those eyes to see if being enough for him was going to be enough, under the circumstances, for Attorney Brantley.

"Here's what I think," he went on, in a tone that he hoped conveyed how emotionally exhausting he was finding this conversation. "And I didn't know that I thought this until I thought it, just now, so I hope it comes out right. I realize that there is justice and then there is Justice. There's the truth and then there's the Truth. I think Lemmy Fender abused his son. Badly. I think he abused other people during his life, and I think one of them killed him. I don't think she planned on doing it. And I don't think it would be Justice if she were caught or prosecuted."

*   *   *

Although the house at 370 Taylor Street remained a crime scene in the ongoing police investigation, Elise was allowed to bring Jason there, accompanied by two Atlantis cops and a detective from the New Jersey state police, to enter the house on Saturday morning to get a few things. All he removed were some schoolbooks and a framed picture of his mother, a beautiful, petite young woman with dark windblown hair seen laughing at the camera in black and white. There was nothing else.

Jason was not completely out of the woods legally, she knew. If the state wanted to, it could charge him with withholding, removing, or destroying evidence in a murder case, very serious crimes. Under the circumstances however, she believed that these possibilities would be considered sometime much farther down the line; and considering what Jason had been through, punishment, even prosecution, seemed highly unlikely. There was almost no one who didn't think he'd been punished enough already.

Her firm had given her a little petty cash for case-related expenses, which she had given to Bachman, asking him to buy Jason some clothes. They often invested a few bucks to purchase a conservative suit so that a scruffy client could look the part of an upright citizen. Bachman bought underwear and socks, jeans

417

and sneakers, a sweater, gloves, a scarf and a winter coat. Elise and Jason swung back to Bachman's place and picked him up, and then she drove to the Atlantis train station and dropped them off.

The sky was winter grey in Atlantis when they left, as it was after they changed trains in Penn Station and emerged from underground in upper Manhattan, but it began changing to snow shortly thereafter. The further north they traveled, the snowier it became.

"It's up to you, Jason," his teacher said to him as they sat side by side, both looking out the window at the whitening countryside zipping past.

"I understand," Jason said.

"She's not well."

"I know. You told me that already."

"She uses a wheelchair."

"I know. You said," Jason said, his voice even.

"I think she's very nervous about this. But she wants very much to see you."

"Why is *she* nervous?"

"Aren't you nervous?" Mr. Bachman said.

"No," Jason said. Then, "Yeah. I guess so."

"Okay. I guess she feels about the same."

They didn't speak for a minute or two. Then Mr. Bachman took his eyes from the window and turned to look at the young man riding alongside him on the 4:50 Amtrak to Albany and Saratoga Springs, New York. "You don't have to--- "

Jason interrupted him. "I know. You told me already. I don't have to do anything I don't want to do. I don't have to stay there if I don't want to. I can stay for a little while, or I can come back with you tomorrow, or I can..." Jason turned and returned his teacher's gaze. "I know all that stuff. Do you know— Do you know what she wants?"

"No. I have no idea. I just know that she thought what she did – when she left, I mean, when you were little – she thought it was better for you. And she still thinks about you and cares about you."

It was such a preposterous idea, and one so fraught with different possible meanings that Bachman felt a little ashamed. He taught his students to avoid ambiguity – or at least to know it when they read it. But who was he to say who felt what? He had no secret means of seeing into someone else's heart. All he ever really did was to hope for the best.

Jason and Bachman looked away from each other. Bachman settled back in his seat, while Jason took off the new puffy green parka Bachman had bought him at J.C. Penney with the money from Elise's firm and tossed it on the empty seat across from them. They both looked at it. Jason didn't ask any more questions, and Bachman didn't offer any more reassurances, or warnings, or suggestions.

The train roared and rattled north, and neither the man nor the boy knew what to expect at the end of the line.

Made in the USA
Charleston, SC
02 September 2012